THE ANTONIDES LEGACY III

THE ANTONIDES LEGACY III

Charlotte Murphy

Copyright © 2020 by Charlotte Murphy.
All rights reserved.
First Printing: 2018
ISBN 979-866-505-0003

DEDICATION

For Zeus. Thank you for believing in me, listening to me and thnking that everything I write is amazing.

Contents

Mortania & the Known World x
Prologue 1
Unlikely Alliance 9
Dangerous Liaisons 12
Assassin Awaits 18
Another Lifetime 22
Keep Your Friends Close 30
Honour Among Thieves 38
My Brother's Keeper 51
Civil War 62
Loyalty 74
Connect The Dots 82
Denial 100
A Price on A Head 108
No Samai Allowed 118
Among Friends 129
Defiance 136
A Clear Conscience 142
A Mother's Love 150
Fealty 157
Achilles Heel 166
A Father's Daughter 175
Moving Forward 192
Days of Futures Past 201

Friend or Foe	208
Old Friends & New	215
Revelations	224
Vengeance & Redemption	231
Preparation	244
Espionage	257
Salvation	269
The Queen	276
The Resistance	289
The Legend of Mortan	296
What Lies Beneath	311
What the Heart Wants	323
Clarity	335
The Front Line	345
The War	354
Transformation	366
Rebirth	384
The Maker	395
Family, Friends & Fate	410
Among Gods	423
Victory	431
The Choice	444
Intended	459
The Price of Happiness	469
A New Era	479
The Antonides Legacy	492
Epilogue	512

Pronunciation Guide 518
Acknowledgements 519

x

MORTANIA & THE KNOWN WORLD

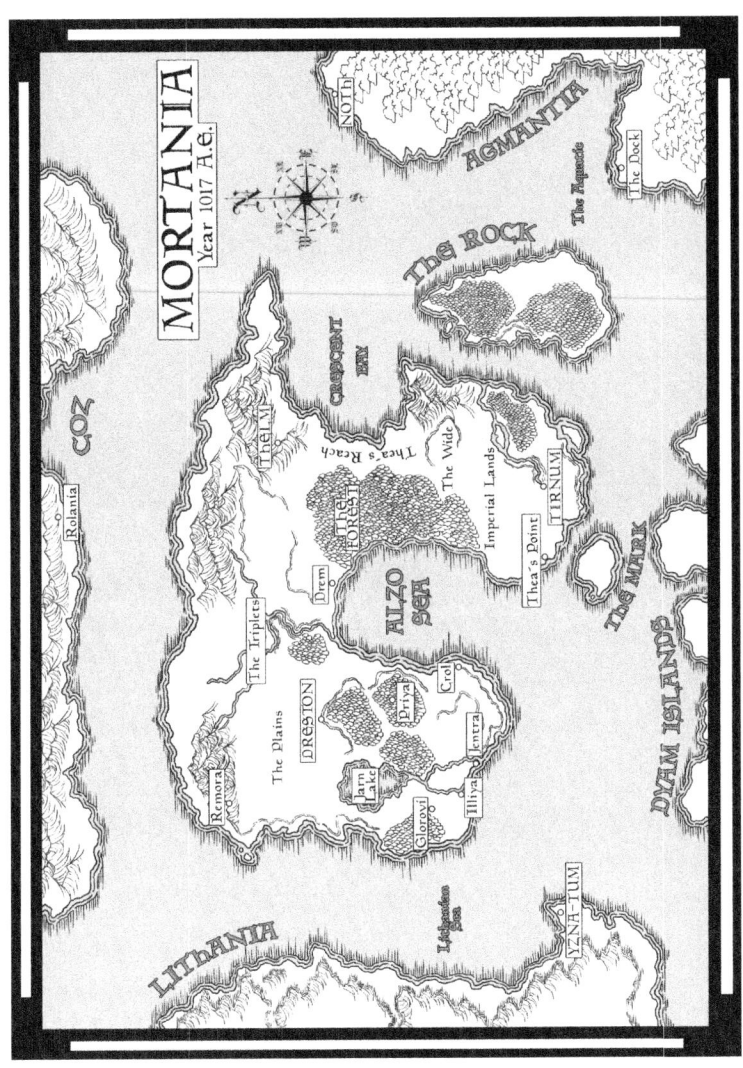

PROLOGUE

VOLTAIRE PALACE, AGMANTIA
993 A.E.

King Alexander XII of Mortania and his young queen, Rowan Illiya-Antonides, walked the breathtakingly beautiful grounds of the Voltaire Palace in Agmantia.

They were accompanied by their hosts, the Crown Princess Nucea Voltaire and her father, King Juba XIV. The royal couple were on a long-discussed trip to discuss various trading options between the two nations, but what had started out as an official engagement, had turned into somewhat of a vacation.

Since their first meeting almost five years ago, Nucea and Rowan had got on like a house on fire and now, their schedules had given them cause to physically meet again. The young women had kept in contact over the years through extensive letters, so when the time had come for Alexander to make the trip to Agmantia, Rowan had leapt at the chance to accompany him and visit her dearest friend.

Agmantia was a paradise to all who visited and when one first arrived, the majestic beauty of it was overwhelming. From the exotic birds that flew above them, making their various calls, to the succulent though unfamiliar fruits that could be found growing in the trees, Agmantia was utopia.

They walked now through the gardens of the gargantuan palace nestled within the jungles of northern Agmantia.

The palace had been built miles from the capital city of Noth, which was just a few hours ride west. It was hidden among trees that had been planted specifically to hide it and did so now, after centuries of moulding to the way of the planters. The trees and growth all around the tropical atmosphere, surrounded the striking white marble of the palace, that shone when the sun hit it just right.

There were no sunrises or sunsets more beautiful than the ones from the view of the Voltaire Palace and the inhabitants counted themselves lucky every day that they got to experience such a wonder.

The palace, though a building to be held in admiration was at the heart of it; a home. Nucea and her younger brothers had grown in the palace along with countless generations before them. Political events all took place in a much smaller palace in Noth, where travellers and dignitaries and royals from other lands could attend. Only true friends of the Agmantian royal family could stay at the Voltaire palace.

In the comfort of the large though private escape, Alexander walked and talked comfortably with Nucea's aging father while behind them at a steady pace; Rowan and Nucea kept a good distant to speak of other things.

"Another one?" Nucea's voice was gentle as she rested her delicate hand on her friend's arm.

She was a beautiful woman, with warm brown skin and large light brown eyes to match. Her auburn coloured hair was twisted into tight, neat locks that were always arranged artistically down her back or piled high atop her head. As custom, she wore headdresses that identified her as both royalty and the heir to the Agmantian throne.

Rowan nodded and stopped walking, still staring off at her husband. He looked magnificent even from behind, his lean frame and broad shoulders that held the weight of a kingdom. Still, her heart ached and even the cascading waterfalls, lush growth and image of her beautiful husband couldn't deter her from her pain.

"I am so sorry Rowan…truly I am." Rowan shrugged as though it didn't matter but they both knew it did. It mattered a great deal.

"I know he hates me," she said quietly, devastated to have voiced her fear aloud. Surely, that only made it more true.

Nucea turned to Rowan and placed the woman's hands into her own, shaking her head as she did so,

"No Rowan, don't ever think that way. Alexander could never hate you, especially for something you have no control over!"

Rowan continued to stare at Alexander as a solitary tear escaped her eye and fell down her tanned cheek,

"All he wants is the one thing I can't give him," she replied softly, painfully.

She turned to her friend, her green eyes blazing as they stared back into Nucea's brown ones. "What if I can never have children Nucea?"

"Rowan don't think that way!"

Rowan tried to stop herself from crying, but the tears came out like a flood gate and Nucea quickly took her hand to lead her off their path into a secluded alcove.

Water rushed around them, bizarre and colourful birds filled the warm air surrounding them but Rowan saw none of it as she folded into her friend's arms and sobbed uncontrollably.

"Why won't the Gods grant us a child Nucea? I've done everything I've been asked, I'm his Intended, everything is the way it should be but this!"

Nucea hated that she didn't have the answers, that she couldn't make her friend feel better,

"Maybe things are the way they should be," Rowan looked at her friend incredulously, her eyes immediately filled with anger.

"I should be this unhappy? Alex shouldn't have an heir after six years of marriage?" Rowan protested angrily. "I hear what they say about me, Rowan Illiya, the Barren Queen."

Nucea couldn't hide her shock as she placed her jewelled fingers over her mouth. Her thick braid of tightly woven locks hung over her shoulder while her other shoulder remained bare from the style of Agmantian dress she wore.

"Maybe your Gods are preparing you for something, something better?" Agmantia was a monotheist nation and so her faith in the Gods of Mortania was limited. Where they too believed in the Everlasting power, they worshipped the power as an entity onto itself and not the people they saw as being given the gift to harness its power.

"Anything is better than this! I can't go through another miscarriage Nucea, I just can't!"

"Rowan!" the women jumped at the sound of Alexander's voice. "Where are you my love?"

Quickly, Rowan waved her hand across her face and there was suddenly no evidence of her previous tears; her make up as perfect as it was before. Nucea sighed, hurt that her friend felt she must hide her pain from the one person who could understand and help her through it,

"I'm over here Alex!" she called back and quickly made her way back to him.

Alexander rounded the corner of a gleaming white column just as she stepped from beyond and when he saw Rowan, his relief was obvious. His emerald green eyes lit up as he saw her and his steps quickened to get to her,

"I looked back and you were both gone, I thought something might have happened to you."

"What could possibly befall her here Alexander?" Nucea shot them a cheeky grin that made him laugh,

"My apologies Princess, I should know that we are in no safer place than this palace. Your Assassins are but a stone's throw away are they not?"

Nucea smiled that cheeky grin again and shook her head,

"You know as well as I that the location of the Agmantian Assassins is a well-guarded secret. Not even you great prince, can know how near or far they are." Nucea raised her right hand and with a quick gesture of her fingers, an arrow with white tipped feathers landed directly in the space between Alexander and the two women.

Rowan and Alexander gasped before they looked around in amazement, making Nucea laugh.

"Although, they are much nearer than you would think."

The trio laughed together, and Rowan's face lit up, a far cry from the sorrow that had been there only moments earlier,

"Where is my father?"

"His majesty grew tired and his attendant took him in. We'll discuss the trade alliance tomorrow when he's feeling better." Nucea nodded with a sombre smile.

"I shall speak with him before he retires, excuse me. I'll see you both tonight."

Nucea kissed Rowan's two cheeks and Alexander in turn kissed Nucea's before she left them and headed into the palace.

Alexander turned to Rowan when the princess had left them, and his smile was immediately gone. Rowan was worried as she held her hand to Alexander's cheek,

"Is everything okay?" Alexander removed her hand,

"No Rowan, it's not. Why are you hiding from me?"

"Hiding?"

"Don't play coy with me."

It was clear he was not in the mood for games, but she didn't know what could have possibly upset him. He was dressed in loose, cropped navy-blue pants with a white tunic and matching silk slippers as was the custom in Agmantia. His long black hair was loose, the only thing identifying him as the king he was, was the large sapphire broach that had his sigil pinned to his chest. Even without the finery, no one could deny he was royalty; he was a prince to his core.

Suddenly his eyes softened as he said quietly,

"When are we going to talk about the baby we lost?"

Rowan was choked up and immediately turned away from him, saying nothing. She didn't know what to say to him after yet another loss, a loss that was obviously her fault. They had no trouble getting pregnant, *she* had trouble holding the babies.

"You're not the only one hurting Rowan…why won't you talk to me?"

Suddenly she was infuriated and turned back to him with fire in her eyes. This wasn't about him; it was about her failure as a wife and a queen.

"What am I meant to say Alex? That I feel like a failure because I can't do the one thing required of me?"

Alex was silenced but looked at her in disbelief, sadness and oddly; disappointment.

"Is that what you think? Rowan…I love you, whether we have children or not. We have our entire lives to try if we have to!"

"Maybe I don't want to try anymore!"

There it was.

The truth she hadn't been able to admit since they lost their fifth child three weeks ago.

Alexander looked down at her in her navy-blue maxi dress that left her shoulders and arms bare and was held up by a thick gold hoop that circled around her neck. Her long curly hair was currently piled up into a high ponytail and she had never looked lovelier. Despite her pain, Rowan was the most beautiful thing that Alexander had ever seen.

"I don't want to hurt like that again," she confessed. "Not ever!"

Rowan turned from him then, ready to shield her tears but Alex reached out and pulled her back into his arms to kiss her.

Rowan let go of her anger and shame to melt into him as she always did, wrapping her arms around him until he finally stopped kissing her and looked down into her eyes.

"Then we won't."

"What?"

"We'll speak to your sister, ask Rayne how we can continue to be together and not get pregnant." What he was saying was madness,

"Alex, I have to get pregnant. You need a child, the Everlasting needs another Keeper, and Mortania needs an heir!" Alexander shook his head.

"I need you...just you. Everything else can wait," Alex kissed her again.

"Alex," she whined, knowing he was just trying to make her feel better but what he was saying was unthinkable. That the monarch would not have an heir would be going against everything they knew; everything they had been raised to become.

"Rowan, I love you and that's that. If we have a child of our own, that would be wonderful but if we don't, that's fine too; Brennan will be my heir."

"I'm sure he'd love that," Rowan smiled at the thought of her brother-in-law who loved living without the responsibility of being king.

"He'll learn to, if that's what it takes to keep you happy. Nothing is more important to me than you."

Rowan teared up for a completely different reason and leaned into her husband to kiss him softly. She should have trusted him before; she should have known he wouldn't abandon her.

They returned home days later and in the years, that followed, Rowan and Alexander stopped trying for a child. Rowan was happy to avoid the pain of losing a baby but the want for one, still yearned within her no matter how she tried to deny it.

One night; when Rayne came to administer the tonic, Rowan had been using to avoid getting pregnant; Rowan told her she no longer wanted it.

"Are you sure?" Rayne asked her little sister gently as they sat in the Queen's Rooms of Tirnum Castle.

"One more try" Rowan said quietly, too scared to hope even in this early stage. "…just one."

UNLIKELY ALLIANCE

"Kill…your daughter?"

The words were laughable, but Baron Lyon Dreston was positive this was not a joke.

The look on King Curian Greybold's face was one of unshakeable sincerity.

The king took a single step toward Lyon before taking a seat in a nearby chair. It was a simple wooden thing, no embellishments of any kind making it completely unfit for the man who occupied it.

"Yes," Curian leant back in his chair and steepled his fingers under his chin. "Briseis has become…problematic and she must be dealt with accordingly."

"Your majesty," Lyon couldn't quite comprehend what he was hearing, "She is your daughter!"

"I am aware of her relationship to me and I am also aware of her hold on this country!" Curian rose from his seat, angered, before looking down on the Baron.

"You have spent time with her yes, seen her Six?"

"Yes, your Majesty bu—"

"I wish you to remain in her confidence so I can know if she is aware of my plans for her."

Lyon looked up at the king in confusion and dread.

What he was asking was barbaric simply because Briseis *was* his daughter. The fact that Lyon also wanted her dead was of no consequence, he was no relation to her.

"What plans?" Lyon asked fearfully.

"Until I know I can trust you, I will keep my plans to myself. What I need from you, is to be in her confidence. I need to know her movements so I know she isn't watching mine."

"What will you achieve by taking her life?"

"What do you care when you wish the same!" Curian bellowed at him and Lyon was silenced. Curian eyeballed him contemptuously,

"I'm aware that you covet power and status. The money you have, so you don't bother yourself with making more, but I know what's in your heart Lyon…what you yearn for." Lyon looked at him defiantly although there was something that still betrayed his fear.

"I've read your correspondence that border on impertinence but for the aid you bring to the kingdom, I chose to ignore it."

"So, you admit it," Lyon was suddenly bold in his response as he squared his shoulders and looked over at Curian. "You admit you do not raise me higher on purpose."

"How much higher do you wish to be?" Curian snapped looking around. "You are the last hereditary Baron in all Mortania. You have gold, lands and vast armies at your beck and call and yet you want more. No man that ungrateful should ever be rewarded."

"Giving me my entitlement is not a reward, it's my right!" Lyon barked at him; all protocol forgotten.

"The fact that you believe so is where you falter Baron, and yet…" Curian went silent for a moment and Lyon was hung on his every word.

Curian stepped closer to Lyon once again and glared at him,

"Despite your contemptuous nature, you can, for once in your life do something for the greater good and get the rewards you speak of." Lyon scoffed,

"What greater good?"

"The greater good of Mortania Baron! Briseis must die for our country to survive!"

Lyon looked at him in astonishment. The king truly wished to see his daughter dead. What, aside from the obvious could she have done to warrant this response? Unless, the king hoped to replace her with someone better?

"The Samaian legends are true…there is one, one that will save the land?" Curian faltered for a moment, uncertain and he seemed to shrink into himself.

"I don't know," he admitted. "But I know it isn't Briseis."

"Then who is it?" Curian shook his head, that was the ultimate question.

"We don't know but Briseis can find out. Find out everything about her military operations and the Redeemer and I will reward you." Lyon scoffed,

"Old promises. Why should I believe you now?"

Curian shrugged,

"You have no reason to, only that you know by now, that you can't possibly get rid of Briseis by yourself. With my help, you might have a chance."

"Might?"

Curian stepped away from him back to the door of Lyon's chambers,

"What happens when she's gone?" Lyon demanded before he added. "You will still be in my way."

The admittance was so bold it was terrifying, but he couldn't take it back now. If the king thought he could recruit him to help kill the princess, then he had his own cards to hold. Curian smiled sadly at him over his shoulder,

"I will not stand in your way Baron Dreston," he murmured. "Get the information and the path to the throne is yours."

Curian turned to leave and with a swipe of his hand, all the lights in the chamber snuffed out.

DANGEROUS LIAISONS

General Gardan Beardmore widened his eyes when he received the news from one of his messengers at Sentry's Keep.

"You are sure?" he pushed while the young man nodded with fear at the implications of what he had just delivered.

"Get yourself something to eat and some rest," he patted the young man on the back who bowed before exiting and closed the door behind him.

Gardan slumped back into the chair behind his desk, the tip of his sheathed sword hitting the ground as he did so. The desk was scattered with paperwork regarding the armies and the city guards, all who were under his jurisdiction. He was constantly on the clock, even now when he had planned to go back to his small home on the outskirts of the city and get some much-needed rest…before this had been brought to his attention.

While this news was unwelcomed at any time, Gardan was aware that things had changed significantly now that his relationship with the princess had taken a more intimate turn.

He'd returned to Sentry's Keep after leaving the princess's rooms…after leaving her bed. He'd returned to for some papers he would need to go over, but the messenger had been waiting as all knew not to disturb him when he had an audience with the princess.

Gardan ran his hands through his hair and took the biggest sigh as it finally settled within him what he had done.

He had slept with Princess Briseis.

He had taken her virginity no less, if what he felt was confirmation enough. Now, he had to tell her that her father wanted her dead.

The messenger revealed that a response to Queen Nucea's message had been found and all explanations pointed to it being an assassination request.

Everyone knew the Agmantian Assassins were the most dangerous sell swords in the Known World. No one with a target on their head from the Assassins ever made it out alive. Whether the person died in a second or a day, the Assassins always met their mark. For Curian to have put this price on Briseis' head, said a lot about his fear of her.

Gardan knew she was no saint, but did she really deserve to be murdered by her own father? She was only a child in many ways.

A child you bedded.

Gardan cursed violently at the truth of it. At twenty-seven years old, he was ten years older than her. He knew of course that there were brides younger than her, mothers even with husbands twice their age, but she was his princess, she was *the* Princess.

A princess you find attractive

Briseis was beautiful, everyone within a thousand feet of her knew it but he had never allowed her beauty to cloud his judgement. Now that he had bedded her, been inside her…everything was different. In the short hours since he'd been with her, he no longer saw her as some rigid no feeling thing, that barked orders at him. She was a luscious, supple female who made the most beautiful sounds when he was buried deep inside her.

With a heavy conscience, Gardan rose from his chair and stepped into the dimly lit spiral staircase, that led from his office to the courtyard below. He entered the dead of night and made his way cautiously back towards the castle.

He mounted his waiting horse and swiftly rode the short distance to the castle doors. He dismounted and was permitted of course without question, until he was finally outside the princess' chambers once again. The guards raised their eyebrows at him as he spoke,

"Please tell her Highness that I'm here to speak with her."

It might have been paranoia, but he saw the look that passed between the two guards posted outside of her door; the same guards that were here when he left earlier this evening.

One guard entered and when he returned, Briseis' handmaiden Endora was with him.

"Please come in General, her Highness has just finished bathing and will be with you in a moment."

The pretty Samaian girl stepped aside for him to enter and Gardan waited patiently as she disappeared into Briseis' bed chamber.

Gardan had been in the princess' room many times before but he had never really looked at what was in there. He saw now that there were no pictures, no sentimental things of any kind but rather sculptures and paintings of scenes that all looked…powerful.

There were paintings of lightning striking at night or bonfires rising into darkened skies, the embers billowing with life off the canvas. Everything screamed destruction and he knew now it was at odds with the young woman he now knew so intimately.

He lost himself in the treasures of her rooms when suddenly, the hairs on the back of his neck stood up and he knew she was in the room. He turned and sure enough, she was in the doorway of her bed chamber, but it was like seeing her for the very first time.

She was in a long silk robe as white as her hair, tied snugly around her small waist. Her hair was loose, still wavy from the braids she'd had earlier and not yet brushed out. Her face was bare of paint and dare he think it, she looked virginal. She looked younger than he had ever seen her, and it clawed at his chest. He had taken advantage; he had been weak for the want to be close to someone and used her in the process.

Never in his eleven years at the palace had she been this…exposed to him and he couldn't immediately tell if it was intentional or not.

"What are you doing here?" she demanded icily, her grey eyes boring into him with such fury he almost looked away. Gardan bowed hastily,

"Forgive me your Highness but I—"

"Do you think because of this evening you can take liberties?" her eyes narrowed but as usual, he ignored her anger and his fear of it and answered simply.

"No, your Highness, I have news…about your father. I didn't think it should wait."

For the first time, since he'd known her Briseis looked surprised and dare he say, relieved. He watched as she stood a little straighter and walked towards him. He couldn't help but notice that despite the warmth of her meeting chamber, her nipples were erect beneath her robe. Those same nipples that had been between his lips only an hour or so before. She took a seat on the soft couch in front of him, crossing her legs, making the silk robe part revealing her smooth creamy legs. She had dainty silk slippers on her feet, one of which bounced impatiently.

"Go on,"

Gardan cleared his throat,

"A messenger was waiting for me at Sentry's Keep. They've informed me that his majesty the king has sent a request to Queen Nucea, to have you killed by their assassins."

For the second time, Briseis looked surprised but this time it was followed by amusement. She chuckled,

"I never thought he would have it in him I must say." Briseis thoughtfully tapped her bottom lip.

Gardan licked his lips as he watched her worry her lip with her finger and remembered how it had felt to kiss her. Her moans had turned him on simply because he'd never imagined she could make such sounds. She was always his princess, not a woman. That however, had all changed and he wasn't sure whether he liked it or not.

"What would you like me to do your Highness?"

Briseis sat there for a long while, unmoving; her foot had even stopped bouncing as she contemplated her next move. She looked beautiful even as she plotted revenge and Gardan found himself looking away because the thought was becoming too intrusive.

"Have my father watched daily and let me know his dealings," she finally said. "I'll think about what to do with him later. I'd rather focus my attentions on our lovely guests, the Barons."

"Yes Princess," he bowed as she stood from her chair then turned to head back into her rooms. He watched her walk away and for some reason, she stopped and turned her head to him,

"Was there something else General?"

In a moment of lustful insanity, Gardan marched across the room to Briseis, spun her around to pull her into his arms and kissed her. He pressed her delicate frame into his own and felt himself harden against her lithe body. It felt amazing to have her in his arms again, like he'd been starved of oxygen and was finally able to breathe. His kiss was deep and for a moment he forgot who he was, who she was and kissed her as though his life depended on it.

When he had kissed his fill, Gardan lifted his head and looked down into her stormy grey eyes, suddenly terrified at what he had done. She would kill him for this surely, but somewhere in the back of his mind; he thought it was worth it.

"Only within these walls," her voice was unnervingly calm. "Will you be permitted to touch me in this way; do you understand?"

"Perfectly your Highness," the smile that spread across his face was infectious as he nodded before lifting the princess into his arms and carrying her into her bed chamber.

When the door closed gently behind him, Endora looked on from the audience chamber. With a mischievous smile and click of her fingers, the candles in the room, snuffed out and she exited the room towards her own.

ASSASSIN AWAITS

Saicha Voltaire and her younger brother Aslan, watched the Agmantian coastline slowly disappear from view. The rolling mountains and jungle terrain of their homeland, moved farther and farther away, as the ship they sailed, took across the Aquatic to Mortania. The glittering lights of Noth Bay got smaller and dimmer as they sailed until there was nothing but darkness and the memory of the light that had once been.

After their mother's revelation that they were to help the Mortanian royal family - if by help one meant assassinate one or the other - Saicha and Aslan had been instructed to leave the following day. They didn't have time to waste, their mother had said, as they packed lightly for a trip with no obvious end. They would come back to Agmantia of course, but when; who could tell?

For Aslan, it was his first time to the other continent while Saicha had sailed all over the Known World on her missions as an assassin. Aslan, as the youngest royal sibling was tasked with more homely duties, such as inland trade and diplomacy that only usually took him from one side of Agmantia to the other, and all the places in between. Rian, as heir was tasked with the more heavy-duty negotiations with foreign lands because he would one day be king.

The younger siblings had set sail with a handful of armed men but none of which could be identified as royal soldiers. They were disguised as traders, making it easier to get through Mortanian customs. They would be on hand if any danger came to the prince or princess although they could protect themselves.

Saicha was of course an assassin and Aslan could use a sword expertly but regardless of their own skills, they were royalty and would be protected as such. They had no real idea of the situation in Mortania and whether they would be met with immediate hostility or whether it would be concealed.

Saicha stood contemplating all of this when her brother turned to her,

"How does it feel leaving home again?" Aslan watched as his sister looked out onto the dark open water; the stars lighting the way for miles at a time.

"The palace is not my home Aslan," Saicha leant up from the side of the ship, turning her back on Agmantia.

"No, then where is home?"

Saicha turned her hazel eyes onto her younger brother then turned away without answering,

"What is your problem? Do you want to go back to the Guild, is that it?" Saicha started to walk away but Aslan reached out to grab her shoulder.

Before he touched her, Saicha twisted and grabbed his wrist in a secure hold that had him cry out sharply before she let go. Aslan shook his wrist out,

"Okay, okay I get it, you're a deadly assassin and can kill me in three moves," he hissed rolling his eyes. Saicha glowered at him,

"You're wrong Aslan," she snarled, her teeth glaring at him. "It would only take one."

Saicha turned away again, heading toward her cabin when Aslan called out,

"You're still my sister!"

She couldn't help but smile as she disappeared inside. When Saicha finally reached her cabin, she fell onto her spacious bunk and let out a pent-up breath. She was glad to be travelling again as she was starting to feel boxed in at the palace. She had meant what she said to Aslan, the Voltaire Palace wasn't her home; the Guild was.

The Assassin's Guild, nestled within the Ecacia Mountains was where she had grown and trained and bled to be the woman she'd become. While she would never regret her time with her assassin family, spending most of her life with them had distanced her from her blood family and she was feeling it the more time she spent with them.

She knew her mother had suffered while she was gone and missed her terribly; as she had missed Nucea, but now she was a fully qualified assassin; feelings seemed redundant. Saicha didn't have time for them when she missed the thrill of the hunt, the rush of the kill. This mission to Mortania, though seemingly mundane, offered an opportunity to expand her skills and see what she was capable of.

In addition to that, she didn't feel she belonged to the palace anymore and rather resented her place as the Agmantian princess. She had been teased mercilessly for it by the other novices in her early days at the Guild and so she always felt she had something to prove.

She'd only been a princess for nine years of her life and even then, she'd asked to go the Guild; knowing she could be more there, then she could ever be as a princess.

Her mother knew and respected that she had a special set of skills and that she would not hesitate to use them if necessary. Nucea knew that Saicha would kill Briseis or Curian or both if she gave the word. Saicha had no feelings towards it whatsoever, a mission was a mission and if she was called to assassinate a princess or a king, she would.

Saicha rose from her bed to take off her weapons but before she had the chance to untie her sword belt, she heard a distinct cry from outside her cabin door. A smile spread instantly across her face, and she rushed out of the cabin and onto the open deck, just in time to see a large falcon land on the edge of the ship, right beside Aslan.

Her brother jumped back, making her laugh as she stepped forward and the bird glided perfectly to land on her outstretched forearm.

"There you are pretty girl," she cooed at the bird.

"You brought the bird!" Aslan said exasperatedly but Saicha just shot him a hateful look,

"Her name is Aurora and yes I brought her. How else are we meant to let mother and father know what's going on in Mortania?"

"Send ravens like normal people," he said rolling his eyes as he stepped closer to her.

"You know full well that Aurora is faster than any regular bird." Saicha stroked the falcon's head with the back of her index finger. "We'll need mother to know anything important as quickly as possible."

Aslan shrugged and turned away from her, seemingly back to the other men who had congregated on the relatively small deck of their ship.

"Whatever just keep her away from my food. She's always stealing meat off my plate."

"That's because she knows you don't like her," Saicha teased,

"I don't like her because she steals my food. It's a vicious cycle what can I say."

Aurora cried out causing Aslan to jump and cover his ears before huffing and storming further away from them. Saicha laughed and stroked her bird again,

"Good girl," she said as she disappeared back to her cabin.

ANOTHER LIFETIME

Trista stood frozen to the spot, staring into the familiar face of Thorn Remora.

She hadn't seen those blue eyes for almost two months and now, having him in front of her, she felt relief beyond words. Belatedly, she threw herself into his arms, grateful that he was alive and well. Thorn hugged her back, tightly,

"I never thought I'd see you again," his breath was warm against her hair and beyond her control, a single tear escaped. She had missed him, despite her confusion about her dimming feelings, she had missed him terribly. She knew she had a lot of explaining to do, so much to apologise for but that could wait for the moment.

"What are you doing here?" the questions all seemed to appear at once in her mind. "How did you even find me?"

"Yes, how did you find us here?"

Oren!

She'd forgotten all about him, the immovable force that he was and the moment they'd only recently shared. Slowly, Trista turned to look at him and Oren's face was like stone. What was she supposed to say? What did one do when confronted with their fiancé and the new man they were insanely attracted to?

"My mother confessed that Trista was on her way to Thelm." Something about what he said didn't sit well with Trista, but she didn't know what it was. "I didn't know if I should try to find you all the way across the country but I'm glad I did!"

It was a mighty coincidence that Thorn had found them, but there was something else worrying her that she couldn't quite put her finger on.

Trista smiled sweetly but asked again,

"That's amazing Thorn, really but...how did you find me *here*, in this inn, in Drem?"

Even if Oren wasn't standing behind her like scepticism personified, he had a point. Of all the inns in Drem; how had Thorn found her in this one?

"I'd stopped to water my horse and get some more supplies when I saw Dana in the bar. I couldn't believe it either!" Trista turned her eyes to Dana who just shrugged, completely bewildered. Thorn saw the exchange and stopped smiling,

"Is something wrong...do you not want me here?"

"Uh no, of course not!" she said too cheerily but Thorn laughed nervously,

"Why do I get the feeling I've walked in on something I shouldn't have?"

"Because you have," Oren's deep voice rumbled behind her.

"Oren!" Trista hissed.

"And who are you?"

Thorn's whole demeanour changed as he looked passed Trista at Oren with contempt. Trista realised absentmindedly that Thorn had never had to deal with another man asserting his authority around him because everyone in Remora had been beneath him. Whether Thorn could hold his own or not, Oren was significantly bigger than him and she didn't want Thorn to get hurt. She had seen what Oren could do to someone he didn't take a liking too.

Oren uncrossed his arms and stepped closer to Thorn but in doing so, brought himself closer to Trista's back. She could feel the hard plain of his chest through her clothes and she almost blushed,

"A friend, and who are you?"

"Trista's fiancé," Thorn replied matter of factually, emphasising the last word.

Please Thea, take me now.

At that moment, Trista felt Oren go very still and not just physically. She couldn't explain it but one moment, he was a physical presence behind her, his warmth radiating onto her and next… there was nothing.

"I see, I'll leave you two to…catch up."

She didn't bother to turn around and looked at him, the coward that she was.

She watched Oren open the door, the sounds of the bar outside flooding through and then shutting out as he left. Trista closed her eyes before taking a deep breath,

"Trista who is that?"

Thorn looked at her as though he couldn't quite believe Oren's impertinence.

"Thorn…we need to talk."

"I agree, let's get something to eat and…"

"No, we don't have time for all that. I…we; Dana, Lamya, Oren and me, we have something very important to do. We were getting ready to leave tonight and now you're here…" it was clear he was confused.

"I can come with you; I was coming to find you…to be with you."

Trista looked to Dana and Lamya for help but Lamya shrugged apologetically and Dana smiled encouragingly.

"Ladies, could you please excuse us for a minute?"

"Of course," Lamya replied before ushering Dana out of the room and leaving them alone.

When the door closed, Thorn was immediately on her,

"I thought we'd never be alone!" he picked her up into his arms and swung her around before holding her in a tight embrace. He breathed her in but despite how familiar he felt, she didn't do the same. She didn't find comfort in his touch the way she once had and didn't know what to do with his onslaught of affection. Even after their engagement they hadn't been that affectionate, this was new territory.

"I missed you so much Trista," he mused before letting her go and looking down into her eyes. "Why did you leave like that...what happened?"

The guilt that never seemed to leave her, reared its ugly head. She knew he would have so many questions, but she wasn't sure if he was ready for the answers.

"That's what we have to talk about Thorn. Things are different now...I'm different."

"What does that mean?"

And so, Trista began her story.

She told Thorn about her birth parents, her true heritage and what that now required her to do. She told him about her time in Dreston, training with Rayne and how she had been captured by the Dreston City Guards. She told him how Rayne could have possibly died in order to get her to Priya and how she and Dana had been injured in the process.

She told him about Priya, the twins, the family she now felt connected to and the fact that Gorn was now dead because of her.

"Gorn, Oren's father died to protect me Thorn, to make sure that I survived to fulfil my destiny."

"What is your destiny?" Trista got frustrated. She already felt like she was wasting too much time explaining this to him and this was only making things worse. Why was he being so obtuse?

"Haven't you been listening?"

"Of course I've been listening Trista but what I think you're saying, is that you're going to kill the princess!"

He stood up from where he had taken a seat on her temporary bed, angry but she wasn't entirely sure why.

Trista stood up to face him, looking him dead in the eye when she said,

"That's exactly what I'm going to do."

Thorn looked at her as though he'd never seen her before and in many ways, he hadn't. She was a completely different person to the one he had known. Getting married to Thorn, being happy about taking her place in Remoran society, felt like a different world now, another lifetime. He looked thoughtful as he said,

"You're not the Trista I remember."

"I hope not," and she meant it. "We're leaving tonight for Thelm…what you do is up to you."

Trista turned to leave, ready to walk away from his judgement and him. That seemed to answer the question she'd been afraid to ask herself for a long time. Thorn reached out and caught her arm,

"Wait, where are you going? Don't I get a say in this?"

"A say in what?"

"Your life Trista," he urged as though it were obvious. "You're my fiancé, what you do affects me too."

She knew it was a mistake not to have corrected him right then and there.

"Thorn, I don't know how else I can explain this to you. I am the rightful heir to the Mortanian throne and I am going to reclaim it…by any means necessary." Trista made sure she was looking directly at him when she said,

"Whether you're a part of that journey or not…is entirely up to you."

Thorn looked at her surprised,

"You're serious?" Trista said nothing, "Then I'm coming with you."

It wasn't the answer she wanted, and, in some ways, she was ashamed of that. She wanted to frighten this small-town boy into running back to said small town. This was bigger than Thorn or their old life together and she wanted him out of it. She protested but he held up his hand to silence her before pulling her into his arms again,

"Trista, I love you. I left my family and my home to find you and now that I have, I'm not leaving."

"It's dangerous; we don't know what's out there!"

"Whatever it is, we'll face it together."

What could she really say to that?

"I'm going to need some time to get my head around you being a princess and having powers," he said it with a laugh which said a lot for his belief in them. "Even so, we're going to get married and I have to be by your side."

Thorn lowered his head then to kiss her and just in time, Trista tilted her face, so he caught the corner of her mouth instead. She squeezed him into a hug, trying to pretend she thought that was his intention and hated herself for it.

She didn't know where to begin explaining that she no longer loved him, she most definitely didn't want to marry him and the only person she wanted to kiss, was Oren.

When they finally left the comfort of their room into the open area of the bar; Oren wasn't there. Dana and Lamya approached them, Dana with enquiring eyes but Trista was scanning the room for Oren.

"He said he'd be back in a moment," Dana offered. "I think he's checking on Titan."

Trista was thankful for Dana's tact, momentarily setting her mind at ease. She might have caught him with a whore, and he might have someone special back home, but she felt she needed to explain her relationship with Thorn, at least to get his reaction to it.

"Thorn's coming with us,"

"Where?" Trista tried not to laugh but Dana's outburst was exactly what she was thinking.

"You didn't think I would leave my fiancé behind do you, not after coming all this way!"

He was too cheery, and it was beginning to get on Trista's nerves. He was so content to fall back into the way things were and even that wasn't like him. The Thorn she knew had been reserved and kind and patient; this Thorn was abrupt, offensive and just plain annoying.

"Thorn, take it easy okay. A lot has been going on before you arrived, and things are going to take a little adjusting."

"Like what, your little friend from earlier?"

All three of the women looked at him, confused by his hostility towards Oren, someone he didn't even know.

"I told you who Oren is to me, to all of us; a friend and he was a part of this group long before you and you're going to have to respect that!"

Trista knew she shouldn't have been so mad, but she was agitated, and Thorn was seriously beginning to get on her nerves. More than anything, she wanted to speak to Oren, so she knew if their friendship, considering how fragile it was; was okay. She'd practically begged him to kiss her earlier after screaming at him in the middle of the street, she had to make sure things were back to normal.

Thorn threw his hands up in mock surrender, his eyes twinkling with mockery and mirth,

"Okay I'm sorry!" he chuckled to himself before turning to Lamya, completely disregarding that Trista was so obviously mad at him. "So, who might you be?"

Lamya was just as perplexed by his behaviour but manners stopped her from being impolite.

"My name is Lamya Rubio, it's a pleasure to meet you; Thorn, was it?" he nodded as they shook hands.

"The pleasure is mine," he turned back to Trista and clapped his hands together. "So, when do we get this show on the road?"

"Right now," the three of them turned to the sound of Oren's voice who they hadn't seen approach them. "Get your horse fiancé, I'm ready to go."

KEEP YOUR FRIENDS CLOSE

Fires were constantly lit throughout the rooms of Tirnum Castle, but the cold would not shift. Those who lived in the capital were accustomed to it, but Lyon was not. His wife and father-in-law, familiar with the colder regions of the north handled it better, but Lyon was not adaptable. He was born and raised in the desert city of Dreston and so was naturally warm blooded and tan. The constant chill was debilitating to say the least.

He sat now, in the meeting chamber of his rooms within with Erik and Geneiva, having a light breakfast. He was dressed in relatively simple clothing, a white shirt and black leather pants with his black embroidered waistcoat open at the front. Erik was in much the same attire although everything was buttoned, pressed and just so, just like the man who wore them. It was stifling to watch; the man did not know how to be loose and just let go.

They sat discussing trivial things when Geneiva, reaching for a slice of toasted bread, unexpectedly knocked her teacup, spilling some on the white linen tablecloth. The waiting maid quickly jumped in to clear the mess,

"Are you alright my dear?" Erik asked with concern as he reached out to her but Geneiva nodded, swatting his hand away affectionately just as the maid replaced the teacup and returned to her place beside the door.

"Yes father, I'm just a little under the weather…my time has arrived." She added the last part quietly and Erik's eyes widened in alarm although he smiled with obvious relief.

"Well thank heavens for that!" he exclaimed and both Geneiva and Lyon looked at him questioningly.

"You do not wish Geneiva to be pregnant?"

Erik's eyes turned sharply toward Lyon before looking away and quickly reaching for his own teacup. The older man took a small sip before answering,

"Well no...not during a war, naturally."

"What does the war have to do with anything?" Lyon questioned, irked by Erik's excitement at the prospect of Geneiva's empty womb.

"W-well during these uncertain times, I would not wish Geneiva any undue stress or us any added problems. A baby on the way would create a whole new dynamic while there are more pressing things to contend with."

Erik took another sip from his cup and made a point to then bite into some toasted bread and butter.

"I see." Lyon replied although he didn't see at all. Why Erik was opposed to Geneiva getting pregnant was something he would think on later. In the meantime, he would make it his priority to make sure she was with child...and soon. Lyon cut into the bacon on his plate before saying,

"His majesty came to visit me last night." Erik raised a concerned eyebrow,

"What did he want?" Geneiva asked quietly as she sipped some water.

"Just that he requires my assistance once again during the war; that he valued my contributions during his rebellion and hopes I will continue to support the crown."

Erik scoffed, unimpressed,

"We know he appreciates your resources Lyon, but will he compensate you for them?"

"Considerably so, if his words are anything to go by."

"I hope they are worth more than they were during the last war," Erik was flippant with his comment but when he looked over at Lyon, he realised the other man wasn't amused with his comment. Erik cleared his throat,

"Just make sure he is serious this time. We can't afford to risk everything on broken promises."

"What exactly have you risked Erik?" Lyon narrowed his eyes, challenging the older man who was beginning to get on his very last nerve. While there had always been tension between them because of Erik's jumpy disposition, he had never had real cause to dislike the other man but that was changing rapidly.

Surprisingly, Erik narrowed his eyes right back as he said,

"You forget I have now publicly entered into a marriage alliance with you that was not overseen by the crown. I have risked my title and privilege by aligning myself with you!"

As the words left his lips, Erik seemed to realise they were not alone and looked around at the silent maid and the one guard who always remained with them. The man said little but was a constant presence for their protection against the unknown dangers of the capital. Erik rose from his seat, throwing his napkin on the table in front of him,

"Come Geneiva, we should be going." Geneiva followed obediently, turning to bow to Lyon.

"Good day husband," she kissed him lightly on the cheek and exited the room with her father.

With angry eyes, Lyon watched them depart and knew emphatically that Erik was hiding something from him.

***

Briseis stood in front of her bedroom mirror smoothing out the material on her dress. It was black, a colour she favoured for how it contrasted against her hair and made of velvet from

Cotai. It had a fitted bodice as was the standard but low cut, her breasts separated by a deep boning cut down the middle. The bell sleeves extended over her hands and the skirts billowed around her now bare feet. Despite the cold of the castle, with the use of her powers she was able to maintain a comfortable level of heat in her chamber rooms when she was in attendance.

As she stood admiring herself, Endora exited her wardrobe with a pair of matching heeled slippers and lowered to place them on her feet,

"Has the General left any messages for me yet this morning?"

"No, your Highness," came Endora's small voice from the floor. "Just the usual correspondence."

"Good,"

Briseis had the most curious sensation, realising she was both happy that Gardan had not contacted her and disappointed at the same time.

On the one hand, if he had become too close to her after their intimacy she would have been annoyed by his change in character. It was precisely his indifference to her that she had found attractive. On the other hand, she wanted him to contact her for those same intimacies.

Had he enjoyed it as much as she had?

Briseis laughed to herself at how much of an actual teenager she was acting.

After sleeping with Gardan the first time, she hadn't thought much about what happened. It had been painful at first, but the more she had let go and allowed him to do what seemed to come so naturally to him; it had felt incredible. He'd left that evening awkwardly, no longer sure where his place was with her and she hadn't known either. When they had finished, he had immediately got out of her bed, dressed and with a polished bow; left her rooms.

Briseis had laid there for a while, unsure of how to feel until she'd called for Endora and had a long and soothing bath. Her body felt tender in the places he had invaded so expertly; as far as she knew, and she found herself feeling vulnerable in ways she didn't understand.

Hating the feeling, she'd washed and dressed for bed but then the door had knocked, and he was there once again. Even though so much had changed between them, he had been the same; professional and straightforward and even more gorgeous. She knew that now, she found him ridiculously attractive, especially now that she had seen him naked and the magnificence that was his body.

Briseis felt the heat rise in her neck at the thought of his body and member and so, embarrassed she turned to focus on her dress. She smoothed her hands over the bodice, just as Gardan had done to her bare stomach when the door to her chambers knocked. Briseis jumped out of her thoughts as Endora, finished with her shoes got up to get the door.

The young girl returned moments later,

"General Beardmore is here to see you, your Highness."

It took everything inside Briseis not to smile and because of that, she hated it. She set her face into its usual nonchalance before replying,

"Send him in,"

"To your bedchamber?" Endora exclaimed, momentarily forgetting herself. Briseis shot her a look and Endora cowered into a curtsey.

"Right away your Highness," she scurried out of the room and moments later, Gardan replaced her.

He was dressed as he always was, in his black uniform; his blonde hair and moustache, shaved but which added a rugged look about him. She wondered how she hadn't noticed how handsome he was before. His lips were full, and she now knew could do the most wonderful things to her body when placed in just the right places.

Briseis straightened as he bowed,

"What is it?"

He held up a roll of paper he held in his hands,

"Strategies, you asked to see the strategies used in the most recent Mortanian wars." Her heart was beating too fast,

"So I did," Briseis reached out and took the papers from him to place them on one of her side tables. Gardan continued to speak behind her,

"The men you asked to be sent to Thelm departed this morning. All who remain are ready to leave for The Wide when you give the word; many are eager to start the war." Briseis nodded both her approval and understanding. She was more than ready to get started with this war and have her place as the only heir to the throne solidified.

"So am I Gardan because as confident as I am in our ability to win; it worries me not knowing exactly what we're up against."

"Have you…felt anything else from them Princess?" Briseis shook her head, going over the small lettering on a map that was included with the battle strategies that Gardan had brought. There were details about the land that ran beneath them and what was better for fighting or using against your enemies in battle.

"Nothing tangible and so I must be prepared for any eventuality."

She finally turned back to him and she watched as Gardan nodded his head in agreement. She watched as he flexed his fingers around the hilt of his sword, strapped to his side; fidgety. He shifted his weight to another foot before saying,

"Captain Janssen is now head of the Royal Sentry and will man them from Sentry's Keep. I've left him a thousand men to man the city."

"Will that be enough?"

"Not nearly enough, but we need all available hands ready and waiting on The Wide. The Kings Guard will also remain in the city for the king's protection of course until he joins the army himself."

Briseis had almost forgotten about Curian Greybold and his correspondence with the Queen of Agmantia.

"Oh yes, my father. How is that deviant little traitor?"

"There has been no more communication with Agmantia your Highness, but he continues to be monitored."

"Good, keep on him. I don't want any more surprises. We'll leave for camp in two weeks. I want everything ready by then as I will not be returning to the capital until the war is won."

"Yes Princess."

"Was there anything else?"

"No, your Highness, that is all."

"Good, now close that door."

Briseis watched as Gardan's eyes widened a fraction before he turned to do her bidding. Once the door was closed, he returned to his original position and looked over at her.

Briseis' heart thundered in her chest as she looked over at him, looking back at her; his gaze entirely different to how it had been only moments before.

"If I were just a woman and not your princess…what would you do right now?" She watched Gardan lick his lips and wondered at how that registered deep within her,

"With your permission?" he asked quietly, and she nodded once.

Gardan began to unbuckle his sword belt and let it fall unceremoniously to the floor before unbuttoning the four large buttons down the front of his leather sleeved fitted shirt. She watched as with one hand he began to untie his trousers and walked toward her.

Briseis tilted her head to look up into his face and sucked in a breath as Gardan lifted her into his arms and placed her on a small table at the back of her bedroom. Still looking into her eyes, he lowered his hands and lifted her skirts until they were bunched around her waist and her small clothes exposed. He made quick work of disposing them and when they were discarded on the floor, he stepped into her and pulled her towards him.

Briseis was practically breathless with anticipation and excitement while her heart pounded in her chest.

Was this how all lowborn women were handled?

Briseis couldn't take her eyes off him as he fumbled around between them and with a firm thrust; he was once again deep inside her.

Briseis cried out at the sharp pain, still so new to the sensation but leant back against the stone wall as Gardan held her waist to thrust into her again.

Briseis gripped the edges of the wooden table as she lost herself in the throes of passion and forgot everything about the coming war.

HONOUR AMONG THIEVES

The Voltaire siblings sparred with each other on the deck of their ship while their loyal crew worked around them. They'd had a good wind this morning and were making good time to Mortania, but until they arrived, they had nothing but time on their hands.

Saicha stood with her bare feet braced, in a white linen bralette and long harem trousers, fitted at the ankles with gold cuffs and a pair of *sai* in her hands. Her younger brother Aslan stood across from her in the same trousers, black with a gold fabric belt and topless, with a *katana* as his weapon.

Saicha struck first and Aslan dodged expertly, before they morphed into a blur of skilled moves. They fought each other with incredible speed, the crew keeping out of their way as much as possible to avoid getting hurt, but it didn't stop them crashing into crates and then using them as missiles to distract the other.

"Faster Aslan!" Saicha snapped at her brother as she swiped at him and he dodged the tip of her *sai* by mere inches.

"How much faster do you want me to be!" he cursed as he spun and landed a strike above his sister's head. Saicha raised her arms and caught his blade within the prongs of the *sai* before twisting it and disarming him. One *sai* was back at her brother's throat and the other above her head,

"That fast."

She stepped out of her stance and returned her *sai* to the holders at her sides. Aslan dropped his katana to the floor, catching his breath as he stood up straight.

"Do you ever get tired of being right all the time?"

"Don't you ever get tired of being lazy and disgusting?" Aslan fanned her off, no interest in the fight she was trying to pick with him. "Pick up your weapon Aslan, that's priceless premium Agmantian steel."

"I know what it is Saicha," he replied mimicking her, his brown eyes twinkling with mischief.

"Then have respect for it! Your weapon is pa—"

"Part of you, respect it as you would your own body!" Saicha went silent. "God, anyone would think I trained at the Guild." Aslan rolled his eyes and turned toward a water bucket that was laid out for them.

"There's nothing wrong with having rules Aslan," his sister said quietly, suddenly very pensive. Aslan scooped out some water with the ladle and poured it over his head, wetting the deck in the process. He did it again, the water cascading down the varying lines of his taut, sculpted stomach; before taking a long drink and turned to his sister.

"There's nothing wrong with breaking them either, when the need calls for it." Saicha rolled her eyes but didn't say anything,

"No," her brother urged, a challenging look suddenly on his face. "Say what you were going to say." Saicha took the ladle from him and took a more elegant sip before saying

"Why, it's not like you'll listen."

"If it's another one of your lectures, no, I won't. Stop judging me for the choices I didn't make. You chose to leave home and train to be the world's greatest fighter, not me!"

"Assassin!"

"Killer!" Aslan snapped back and Saicha went silent again. Despite his earlier anger, Aslan seemed to think better of it and sighed,

"I respect your skills Saicha, but I don't have to live my life the way you do. Why can't you accept that?"

"I accept it," she was immediately defensive.

"Fine, but you don't like it and that's fine too, but it doesn't give you the right to try and change me." Saicha took another drink,

"I'm not trying to change you,"

"Then what do you call criticising everything I do? Just because you found your calling doesn't mean the rest of us have or even got the chance!"

The crew that worked around them continued to do so but there was something in the air that said they were all straining to hear what would happen next. Aslan went to walk away but Saicha reached out and stopped him,

"Wait, what are you talking about?" Aslan spun around, almost making her lose her balance, shocked by his outburst.

"Rian didn't ask to be heir, the same way I didn't ask to be the spare because you ran off!" Saicha was taken back,

"I didn't—"

"No, you didn't think because you didn't think of anybody but yourself! You wanted to be an assassin, so you left without even talking to us about it."

"I was nine years old Aslan; I didn't think you would even care." Aslan looked at her like she was crazy then even more damning, as though he pitied her for it.

"We're your brothers Saicha, of course we'd care," Saicha didn't know what to say. Her brothers had always just been her brothers, playing with each other and being each other's best friend while she was left alone.

"You didn't think about that did you," Aslan continued. "The same way you didn't think about what your leaving would do to Rian and me."

Saicha hated feeling guilty and now, it was the most potent she had ever felt it. She didn't think a lot about the family she had left behind when she went to the Guild and it was clear that they had thought a lot about her. When had she become so selfish? She went to say something, but it seemed her brother wasn't finished,

"How do you think it felt watching mother pine for you as though we didn't even exist, at eleven and eight?" She didn't know how that felt, she just needed to be away, she knew that even then.

"We don't blame you for being her favourite Saicha, but we do blame you for leaving us to deal with that alone." Aslan turned to walk away again but suddenly Saicha found the words she hadn't been able to say, to herself; much less anyone else. She rushed to stand in his way, pushing her palm against his chest to stop him walking away from her,

"How do you think it felt *being* that favourite and having pressure put on you to the be just like her?" It was clear from the look on his face that the thought hadn't occurred to Aslan.

"I'm the only daughter of a benevolent and practically perfect queen; someone I could never live up to…I had to get away Aslan. I knew that even then." Almost instantly her brother looked apologetic and she almost hated him for it. She didn't want his pity, just his understanding about the reasons she had left.

"I didn't realise. I guess we've all had our problems with mother, in our own way." Saicha shrugged,

"She means well," Aslan nodded and the two of them stood looking at one another, their faces so alike. Where Saicha was all elegance and angles in her cheekbones and sparkling hazel eyes, Aslan was all lean jaw and chiselled features. His hair was shaved to the skin around the sides but grown into a neatly trimmed high top of tight black curls. Saicha's hair was braided away from her face with the cultural beads of Agmantia added to the ends.

Embarrassed, Aslan stepped back from his sister and began to stretch,

"Well, enough of that mushy stuff, I'm hungry!" Saicha smiled to herself,

"All you do is eat!"

"Oh contraire big sister, I also indulge in the delights of beautiful women and as there are none here, I must behave until we reach Mortania." Aslan sauntered off as Saicha continued to laugh at him,

"They should lock you up, you need to be tamed!" Aslan spun around into an elaborate bow, a mischievous grin on his face,

"Special is the maid who can tame my lust. Rare indeed is the maid who can tame my heart!"

Saicha laughed dismissively as her brother disappeared below deck.

***

The night ride from Drem was an awkward one.

Despite their reluctance to speak to him, Thorn didn't seem to understand the precariousness of their situation and so continued to speak from his position at the back, the entire way.

Seemingly oblivious to Trista's sharp responses, Lamya's polite explanations; Dana's deferring answers and Oren's complete and utter silence, Thorn went on about his journey before finding them. Trista tried to drown him out, annoyed with him for even being there but he kept riding alongside her, trying to ask about what she had been up to since leaving Remora.

They were normal enough questions; she had left him without an explanation, but he didn't seem to accept that she didn't necessarily have all the answers. She had told him as much as she knew before leaving Drem, the rest was a new adventure waiting to happen.

"How are my parents?" she asked, trying to get him to stop asking her questions. When had he got so insensitive?

"Your parents are fine; your mother spends much of her time alone any way and once you left; the other woman had next to nothing to say to her."

She had known her mother was ostracised as much as she was in Remora, but this revelation angered Trista more than she cared to admit. Her mother didn't have an unkind word to say about anyone, she didn't deserve to be isolated the way she was. She wished then that she had said goodbye to her mother, she deserved more than that; she hadn't even left her a note.

"Do you know if my parents are okay?" Dana asked and Trista was grateful for the distraction. The hopeful smile on Dana's face was so pure, it made her happy that Dana had always had a relatively happy life.

Trista looked to Thorn who was riding between she and Dana and watched his face go deathly pale.

"Thorn…what is it?"

Thorn looked over at Dana riding to his right and regrettably said,

"I'm so sorry Dana,"

"Sorry for what?"

Trista reigned her horse to a stop and everyone else followed, even Oren at the head of the troop stopped beside Dana to witness the response.

"Your mother, she…she died."

There was a silence so thick, it felt suffocating before there was a choke of disbelief from Dana, who fainted. Her hands loosened from the reins of her horse and she fell.

Instantly, Oren reached out and caught her with his powers, stopping her from hitting the ground.

"Dana!" Trista called out as she jumped from her horse and rushed to where Oren gently lay her on the ground. Lamya, Trista and Oren crouched by Dana's side as Oren, slightly tapped her cheeks to get her conscious.

She came around almost instantly but when she finally opened her eyes and looked up at them looking down at her, she burst into tears,

"No!" she cried before curling into Oren's arms and bawling. Oren held her as all at once, he, Trista and Lamya looked up at Thorn who was still sat on his horse.

"How could you?" Trista barked at him, her eyes shooting venom in his direction.

"I didn't…it just…slipped my mind."

Trista felt the heat rise in her hand as she clenched it into a fist and before she did something a lot more regrettable, she swiped her hand at him and knocked him clean off his horse.

Thorn fell to the ground, hitting it hard and cried out as the ground connected with his head.

"Trista!" Lamya called out in surprise but she didn't care as she got up from where Oren held her best friend and marched over to Thorn on the ground, groaning in pain.

"How could you!" she screamed at him now. "Her mother is dead, and you didn't think to tell her that immediately!"

Thorn struggled to get to his feet, but when he did, he held his hand to where he'd hit his head.

"How did you do that?"

Trista was about to lose it,

"Are you serious?" she tilted her head to the side, trying to get a better look at the person in front of her because it wasn't the Thorn she remembered, or had loved. He looked at her finally and seemed to remember something,

"I'm sorry I just…I'm sorry Trista!"

"It's not me you should be apologising to!" she screamed again, above the sound of Dana's wailing. Trista turned to look at her friend, hurting and weeping in Oren's arms and knew this wasn't the time. Still furious with him, she turned her attention back to Thorn and with a heavy heart asked him quietly,

"How did she die?"

Thorn looked over to where Dana was crying and without taking his eyes off her he said,

"When Dana didn't come home, she went crazy trying to find her. She asked my mother for help, the town, everyone but when we couldn't find her…she just gave up. She stopped eating and sleeping, waiting for Dana at the front door."

Trista's heart cracked in her chest at the realisation of what had happened, but she had to know,

"How did Mrs Black die Thorn?"

"Her heart gave out,"

Dana's mother had died from a broken heart and she had caused it. If Dana hadn't followed her to Dreston, her mother would still be alive.

"We'll camp here for the rest of the night," Oren suddenly called out and everyone silently agreed. "Unless there's anything else you'd like to share tonight?"

Oren's distaste for Thorn was clear in his voice and Trista didn't even care to scold him for it, Thorn had messed up.

Trista watched as Oren stood with Dana in his arms and carried her further away from the road to sit her down on a grassier patch of dirt. The moon over head gave them the light they needed but a few feet from her, Oren ignited a small fire.

Lamya tended to the horses, tying them to a small root that was protruding from the ground, and helped Oren as he took a blanket from Dana's horse and wrapped it around her shoulders as she cried.

Trista had never seen Oren so affectionate before and she hated that she was jealous. Dana had just lost her mother and she couldn't help but be resentful that Oren's arms were around Dana and not her.

Finished with the emotions of the day, Trista left Thorn as he rubbed at his possibly bruised back and went to unpack her bed roll. They got ready to settle in for the night in silence and when she was finished with her own roll beside Dana's she crawled beside her friend and wrapped her arm around her in a tight hug,

"I'm so sorry Dana…truly I am," Dana said nothing but squeezed her friends arms tighter around her and continued to cry into the night.

Oren was up before everyone else going through his training exercises. He let the rest sleep, conscious that they weren't as fit as he was and of course because Dana would need some time before they got back on the road. He kept a sound bubble around himself as he moved smoothly through the sparse blades of grass beneath his feet. Where they had camped so suddenly by the side of the road, was dusty more than grassy but it had been enough to sleep on.

He had only been training for a few minutes or so when he saw Trista wake up and follow his movements with her eyes. He didn't say anything, not caring whether she watched him if she learned something but before he'd finished thinking it, she slowly got out of her bed rolls and walked over to join him.

She hadn't bothered to put on shoes and tiptoed over to where she watched him for a moment before beginning to mimic his moves. In a few tries she finally had it and they moved together in unison. He extended his bubble and he saw her relax as the heat from within warmed her.

They performed their stretches in silence, concentrating on focusing their magic, making it become part of them. Trista couldn't manifest her magic as Oren was, but the determination was there, the awareness of the power that dwelled constantly inside of them.

As they neared the end of the stretches, Trista said quietly, "Oren...about Thorn," Oren stopped for a second before sighing, finishing up his stretches then turning to her. His eyes were void of any emotion and she didn't know what to make of it.

"What about him?" Trista shrugged as she turned to face him, she didn't have to feel afraid; she hadn't done anything wrong.

"I know he complicates things now,"

"For who?" the question surprised her,

"Well...for all of us." Although now she wasn't so sure,

"Not me," he shrugged as he said it, the teal of his eyes almost dull as he stared back at her unblinking. "Why would he?"

Trista smiled as bravely as she could and nodded with a small smile,

"No reason,"

"Good, are we done?" she nodded. "You have company."

She felt someone's hand on her shoulder and knew exactly who it was.

"What are you two doing ou—" he seemed to lose his train of thought. "Why's my hand warm just here?"

Oren lowered the bubble and walked past Trista and Thorn before she had the chance to reply. Trista turned causing

Thorn's hand to drop from her shoulder and she told herself it wasn't the reason she'd stepped away,

"What is that guys' problem?"

"What's your problem?" Trista hissed at him. It was too early in the morning and Dana was still asleep. Lamya had begun to stir she now saw, Oren handing her a mug as he lit a fire to make breakfast. Thorn threw up his hands in mock surrender,

"Hey, what's wrong with you?"

"Don't you have any shame? We're still mad at you!"

"And that changes things how?"

Trista couldn't understand who this person was. This was not the Thorn she could have possibly thought she loved, when did he become so unkind? She stepped up to him, so her face was inches from his own and looked up into his eyes,

"One more wrong word from you and I will leave you by the side of the road, do you understand me?"

"Tris—"

"Do you understand me?" Thorn looked at her as though a realisation had come to him and as it did, he simply smiled.

"Perfectly,"

"Oren has done an amazing job getting us this far, have some respect."

"Oh yes, Oren," Thorn shifted his weight to his other foot, thinking suddenly. "His father was Gorn you said, the one who died trying to save you." She didn't understand what that had to do with anything,

"Gorn Antos was the General of my father's armies, he deserves your respect too. Don't you ever forget that!"

On the word *ever*, she shoved his shoulder with her own and marched over to her friends, leaving Thorn to watch her walk away.

Thankfully, Dana began to stir and so Trista went to kneel by her friend and gently stroked her hair,

"Hey…how are you?" Dana looked as though she might cry again and so Trista cupped her face as she lay looking up at her,

"You don't have to do this,"

"What?" Dana's voice was gravelly from sleep and the crying she'd done before, but her eyes were alert.

"Dana, it's my fault you left home. If you want to go home, be with your father and sister…I won't stop you."

Dana shook her head just once,

"There's nothing for me in Remora now. I'll see my family when all of this is over…my place is with you."

Trista hated that she felt relieved, but she couldn't deny she was elated that Dana chose to stay with her. She lay down with her and pulled her into a hug, the two girls holding each other for different kinds of support.

"Are you sure?" Trista asked, just to be sure and Dana mumbled into her shoulder,

"My place is with you."

After a quick breakfast of oats and bread, they were all packed, wrapped up and getting ready to head towards to Thelm when Lamya approached Trista,

"Your Highness?" Trista raised her eyebrow as she wagged her finger at Lamya and the older woman laughed,

"Trista, could I speak with you?" Trista nodded and took her hand so they could walk away from the others.

"What is it Lamya?"

Lamya looked uneasy for a moment before attempting a reassuring smile,

"How well do you know Thorn?" Trista laughed,

"I've known Thorn my whole life, we grew up together…" her thoughts left her as she looked over to the boy, she thought she had grown up with. "Before getting close to Dana…he was my only friend."

"I see," the uncertainty didn't go unnoticed.

"What's wrong?" Lamya sighed as she looked over at Oren helping Dana into her saddle and Thorn tightening the bridle on his horse.

"It's probably nothing,"

"Tell me," Trista insisted and Lamya reluctantly gave in,

"I can't read him Trista, it's like there's a block there."

"What kind of block?"

"It's difficult to explain but where I can usually feel someone's intentions or fears or happiness for example, with Thorn…I feel nothing."

Trista turned to look at Thorn who had now mounted his horse, waiting patiently for them to be ready. He stared straight ahead, out onto the open road, now slowly lighting up with the rising of the sun on.

Trista didn't like the way Thorn had been acting since meeting him in Drem and if Lamya had this feeling, then perhaps there was something wrong with him.

Trista continued to look over at Thorn before he caught her looking at him and smiled, so she smiled back.

Why hadn't he told them about Dana's mother sooner, he'd had many opportunities and something like that wouldn't slip your mind considering he'd met Dana before anyone else.

"Keep an eye on him for me Lamya," Trista responded quietly and made her way back to the others.

"Of course, Princess," Lamya nodded obediently.

MY BROTHER'S KEEPER

Curian sat with General Ignatius Rarno in the main tent of his war camp drinking strong wine imported from Cotai. He had only began drinking it in the years he'd become king as his new-found wealth had allowed him to even sample it. Growing up, working the grounds of the Illiyan estate, the finer things in life had not come easily, if at all.

It amused Curian through the years, how easy he had been able to adapt to expensive tastes. The best silks for his clothes and the best wines and meats for his palette had all been so easy to enjoy. Now, food and wine tasted like ash in his mouth and until the threat of his daughter and the impending war were dealt with, nothing would ever taste good again.

The two men had departed from the capital shortly after Curian's discussion with Baron Dreston, but the king had declined to discuss it until they were completely out of the city. Now, in the desolate and cold expanse of The Wide; Curian divulged his plans with his closest friend and ally.

"I have had no real assurances from Nucea and so I must take matters into my own hands," he said regrettably. Rarno, lounged in a high-backed chair, looked over at his king. He had tremendous respect for his friend but there were times, such as this that he had to question his judgement and even his sanity.

"What have you done?"

"I had a talk with our friend the Baron,"

"Friend?" Curian chuckled before taking another sip from his goblet and leaning back in his own chair. The two men were wrapped in thick furs against the vicious cold that roared outside.

"I'm sure he can become quite friendly in these circumstances." Curian replied with a smirk.

"Stop with the riddles Cur, what does Baron Thelm have to do with anything?"

"Thelm? No dear Rarno, it's Baron Dreston I'm talking about." Rarno looked confused but his interest was piqued.

"What could you possibly want from that jumped-up charlatan?"

Curian turned sombre for a moment as he looked down into his glass.

"A great many things now…" Rarno looked over at his best friend with concern.

"Curian what's wrong?" Curian took a deep breath,

"I've asked him to assist us in killing my daughter." Curian said simply but Rarno was instantly enraged.

"How could you do something so stupid? The less people who know about this the better!"

Rarno jumped from his seat and looked out of the tent like a mad man before drawing the opening shut and marching back to Curian.

"Calm down Ignatius,"

"Don't tell me to calm down when *she*," Ignatius pointed toward the tent opening, his eyes wide with fear. "Is out there!" Curian's own eyes widened before they narrowed into slits and he stared his friend straight in the eye.

"Do not forget yourself Rarno."

"As long as *you* don't forget! Briseis is *dangerous* Curian; a better swordsman than you or me, not to mention her power! She will destroy us if she finds out what we're up to!"

"It won't come to that," Curian sipped at his wine.

"It will if you continue to be reckless with the information!" Rarno snapped but Curian still said nothing. He was confident that Baron Dreston would be so caught up in trying to get his own rewards from the situation, that he wouldn't contemplate telling Briseis.

"He will do what needs to be done,"

"Will you?" The challenge was there and Curian rose it,

"You doubt me?" Rarno looked at him, shaking his head,

"She's your daughter Cur, what's to stop you from changing your mind when the time comes?"

Curian fell silent as he peered into his wine goblet and sighed heavily,

"My conscience," he said eventually, quietly. "My conscience stops me changing my mind about killing her."

Rarno said nothing for the moment as he looked over at his friend. All the fire from his original rage had disappeared and he saw nothing but a broken man where a king should be.

"What are you saying Curian?"

"I'm saying what I've been saying Ignatius…I don't deserve to be king." Rarno's fire returned as he growled his disapproval. He gripped the back of the chair he stood behind; his knuckles white.

"Not this again!"

"YES, THIS AGAIN!" Curian bellowed as he stood from his own chair, knocking it to the ground behind him. He slammed his goblet onto the table top, sending dark red wine all over it and finally soaking into the furs that lined the floor.

"It will always be this until I have paid for my sins Rarno, all of them!"

"What sins Curian? You took the throne from a man who abused its power; abused his people!"

"You don't honestly believe that, do you?" Curian was amazed as he looked his friend in the eye.

"I believe in you Curian, in your determination to rid Man of that Samaian tyrant!"

Curian outright laughed and Rarno was taken back,

"You find our suffering amusing?" Rarno accused but Curian continued to laugh as he walked to a side table where the wine was kept and poured himself another drink.

"I find your ignorance amusing," Curian replied as he drank heavily from the new goblet before placing it back on the table to pour himself another. "Baron Dreston will get us information on Briseis' war effort which we can use against her."

"You're making a terrible mistake Cur,"

"Cur?"

Rarno stepped back, swallowing before he took a humbled bow, realising that the time for informalities was over.

"Your Majesty,"

"Leave me," there was nothing further to add and so Rarno left the tent and when he did, Curian slumped back into his chair. He hated speaking to Rarno in such a way, but it was not to be helped. He needed intel to destroy Briseis because he knew his armies and even his power would never be enough. His daughter was smart but he had to be smarter. Having an inside man was the first step into learning how far she had come in her efforts to defeat the Redeemer; and take over his kingdom.

***

Lyon Dreston entered the Great Hall of Tirnum Castle and made his way to the long table at the front, just below the dais. When they were in attendance, Lyon could sit with either the king or the princess as their valued guest. When they were not in the Great Hall; however, he was permitted to sit as close as was allowed to the throne. He positioned himself comfortably there and servants immediately appeared to attend him.

Despite the prestige of his position, it was clear the other nobles had no interest in being around him. It didn't bother Lyon personally, but he realised the complications this would undoubtedly bring if he didn't have the other nobles on his side. Given the chance, any one of the Mortanian aristocracy would try to dethrone him if it were in their interests to do so.

He had Erik and therefor Thelm in his pocket but there was something off about the way the older man had been behaving. Erik's behaviour during their breakfast this morning had piqued his suspicions and he didn't know if he could truly trust his father in law. Thelm was of course the only other barony in the realm and so commanded the most forces, but those forces still took commands from Erik. If Erik wasn't truly on his side, then his armies wouldn't be either.

As servers, brought out various delicacies, Aml approached him and leant down to his ear.

"My Lord, Lord Weilyn has just entered the hall. Do you wish to speak with him?" Lyon piped up immediately,

"Yes, bring him over." Aml nodded and headed to the end of the hall where Lord Norto Weilyn had entered with his eldest son, a skinny young man named Puca. Lyon watched when Weilyn looked up, once Aml approached him and acknowledged him with a nod before heading in his direction. It took him an age to get there as he stopped and spoke with other men who seemingly took his interest. Lord Weilyn laughed and joked and flashed his fingers full of gold rings until his parade finally reached Lyon at the front of the hall.

Lyon was irritated, he hated to be made to wait and the way Norto smiled at him, he knew this man had done it on purpose.

While in Dreston, Lord Weilyn had been more accommodating; humbler but now he was confident. It seemed being in the capital, closer to his own province, gave Weilyn a protection he lacked while across country.

Lyon stood from his seat and greeted Norto as was customary, when ordinarily he would have remained seated. In this new game, he wished to play, the rules would have to change and so he chose to play nice to achieve his own aims.

Norto Weilyn took the seat beside Lyon while his son took the seat beside his father. Norto's dark brown skin and perfectly shaped beard was marred by a large scar slashed directly across his face. While the colouring had begun to fade, it was a declaration of what he had gone through during the Samaian War. He wore his scar with pride as evidence of what he had sacrificed for Mortania.

Aside from his scar, everything else about Lord Weilyn was in prestige condition, from his crimson doublet and matching trousers with a stark white shirt. Strong leather boots were on his feet along with large jewels on the knuckles of all his fingers.

Weilyn was of Agmantian heritage and so was accustomed to wearing expensive and dazzling jewellery. They were a nation known to exhibit their wealth in the most elaborate of ways. He was a tall man and draped himself in the most exquisitely tailored and decorated cloth.

"Welcome Lord Weilyn, how has the capital been treating you?" Lyon asked as Weilyn took a sip from a goblet that servants had filled with wine. It seemed it was never too early to drink in Tirnum.

"Tirnum is a most wonderful and bountiful place, it always treats me well. I see the same can be said for you?" Lord Weilyn gestured to their seat at the bottom of the dais and Lyon smiled what he hoped was modestly.

"It is true, I've been elevated in his majesty's eyes but not unjustly," Weilyn nodded, agreeable.

"That much is clear Dreston; we all know what you contributed to the war effort." Lyon nodded appreciatively. "How is your new wife? I was deeply hurt to not have been invited to the wedding."

Lyon smiled as he took a sip of water and looked at Norto over the rim of the glass,

"You have my apologies Norto, it was a last-minute decision."

"So last minute that you discussed it with Erik after we left you in your rooms in Dreston many weeks ago?"

There were a few ways in which Lyon could play this but only one would bring Lord Weilyn into his confidence.

"We did not wish for any of our noble brothers to be incriminated in what the crown might see as a slight against them." Norto nodded his head as though he completely understood. He continued to sip his wine before saying,

"And now?"

"Now, his majesty and the princess have taken no offence and I wish to bring all my friends into the confidences I have with them."

"Is that so?" Weilyn was intrigued. "What are you proposing Baron? It seems there is always something up your sleeve."

Lyon shrugged, unseemly but there wasn't much else he could say,

"You understand my position and my feelings towards the crown. I merely wish for all of us to get what we want."

"And what is it that we want Baron, you seem to be quite sure on this." Puca finally spoke up and Lyon found he didn't like it. Who was this skinny little weed who thought he could question him? Still, the game must be played,

"Titles, riches, power, I assume we all want these things."

"We already have these things Baron; the crown gives them to us."

"And how soon before the crown takes it away?" Lyon fired back although not loudly. "The princess herself as asked for a tithe that we have both provided but who is to say she won't use our own forces against us?"

"My men are loyal to me," Norto replied confidently but Puca seemed angry,

"I won't stay and listen to these traitorous words, and you shouldn't either Father!" Norto turned to look at his son, eyes as firm as steel and just as deadly.

"Do not presume to tell me what to do boy," Puca looked to Lyon embarrassed then back to his father. "Return to our table and sit with your mother."

Without another word and clearly embarrassed, Puca quickly departed from the table and marched to the other end of the hall.

"It pains me that he is my heir, the boy is reckless and weak…a deadly combination."

Lyon didn't reply, happy to let Norto supply his own negative opinions of the boy.

"Puca doesn't realise that just because someone wears a crown, it doesn't make them infallible."

"Not at all," Norto sighed deeply before taking another large gulp of wine and then looking straight into Lyon's eyes.

"I have title and wealth as you say but I do not have power as Puca seems to believe. I am but miles away from the capital and so I am bound by my distance to remain loyal in case I am invaded."

"What cause do you have to be disloyal?" Lyon asked, genuinely confused as to what issues Lord Weilyn may have. He had gone over the pros and cons of getting the other nobles on his side and Weilyn had more reason than most to stay loyal to the crown.

"The taxes are extortionate and continually rising. Even with the help I receive from Noth Bay, from my mother's people located there; I am still struggling Lyon."

Lyon never would have known, he'd always assumed being lord of the main port of entry to the country, that Norto was insanely wealthy.

"While her father was in power, there were issues but since he hides his head in the sand and allows Briseis to do as she pleases, it has only gotten worse."

"What do you propose to do about this Norto? If the taxing and fear of invasion are as imminent as you claim, then surely you wish to make a change."

Norto shook his head and held up his hands in surrender,

"Oh no, this is not my fight." He explained. "I heard your complaints at your home and while I understand them, I do not have the power or the wealth as you, to do anything about them." He sounded regrettable and Lyon saw the pain in his face.

"No matter my interests, you play a dangerous game Dreston." Norto murmured quietly,

"Our interests are one and the same," Lyon replied just as quietly and to his credit, Lord Weilyn didn't look away, confident in his own approach to what was a sensitive subject for all.

"A ruler who would secure the advancement of man is all I have ever wanted, and I will do what is necessary to attain that." Lyon raised an eyebrow. "Additional forces during these tumultuous times that I could count on for aid would be most beneficial…preferably from the south."

Lord Weilyn raised his own eyebrows and smiled before reaching out for his goblet again,

"It seems I am in aid of forces in the North considering the tithe and arms I have given our royal hosts."

"As I said, our interests are the same Lord Weilyn," Lyon's eyes darted momentarily to the end of the hall where people were fussing as someone else entered the room. He saw quickly that it was Erik and Geneiva and turned his attention back to Lord Weilyn.

"Here comes Erik now, perhaps the two of you can have a more productive conversation?" Norto Weilyn nodded his head as Lyon rose from his seat and met his wife and father-in-law before they got to the table.

Taking Erik's hand in greeting, he pulled into his ear and said,

"Weilyn can be swayed. Do what you must."

Without waiting for a reply, Lyon exited the Great Hall and made his way to his rooms.

When he arrived into his bedchamber moments later, a young woman was standing at the foot of his bed. She was dressed in the sheet gossamer material he favoured when entertaining, but he had not requested her presence.

"Who are you and what are you doing here?"

She bowed her head,

"Senior Aml said to be here for you, that you would be in need of me." Lyon raised an inquisitive eyebrow,

"Where is Alaina?" the girl looked away, almost ashamed,

"Recovering," was her simple reply. Lyon was confused and then annoyed at his initial response to her answer. Guilt was not something he was familiar with, but then again, neither was being afraid of a teenager who could rip his flesh from his bones.

"I see…your name?"

"Pia,"

"Good…take off your clothes."

Pia did as she was commanded and within minutes, he buried his guilt inside her.

CIVIL WAR

Another day and night passed as the ship carrying the Agmantian royals pierced through The Aquatic on its final stretch towards Thea's Point.

The siblings had continued their sparring on the deck of the speedy vessel and now, as the sun of the third day shone bright in the sky; they continued their training.

Aurora flew overhead, returning to the ship occasionally to peer almost questioningly at her mistress for a while before taking off into the skies once again. Saicha had been gifted the bird her fist day at the Guild, as did all novices to the order and the connection they shared was deep. Not just a bird, but a faithful companion, Saicha loved Aurora more than most people. She confided in the bird when she was at her loneliest and found there was no one who really understood the royal who had no real place in the world. She was an assassin, but so were thousands of others before her and would be after. Saicha wished to find something to fulfil her, where the Guild and her royal birth had not.

Saicha trained that glorious morning with her brother for a long while before trying her hand with two of the other crew members who travelled with them. She took it easy on them initially, her assassin training surpassing their own but when she truly began to sweat, she picked up the pace. She was once again in her training pants and bralette, while the men were topless in the heat, but almost as though they had stepped through a doorway into a snowstorm, the temperature dropped.

"What in the world…?" Aslan looked up into the sky at the sun that was still shining but the air had turned harsh, the wind caressing their skin like fingers of ice.

"What's going on?" Saicha asked as she straightened out of a front roll and returned her *sai* into their holders. She wrapped her arms around herself as she too looked into the sky.

"Captain?" Aslan turned to the captain of their ship, Atla who watched them occasionally from the side lines. He was an old man, a seaman who had seen many years on the open water and when he sighed, they knew a tale would follow.

"No matter the season anywhere else, once we cross over into Mortanian waters, the air grows cold." Captain Atla looked out toward the Mortanian coastline way out in front of him as he spoke.

"And Mortania, is it just as cold?"

"We only spend our time in Thea's Point and of course the capital but yes, in the south it remains bitterly cold your Highness."

"The *south* of the country remains cold; how can that be?" Saicha asked as she reached for a discarded blanket on one of the daybeds that were left for she and her brother's use; and wrapped it around her shoulders. Atla sighed again before turning to his princess and explaining,

"We Agmantians do not bother ourselves with the trials of other nations but a few have heard of the Mortanian Prophecy."

"Prophecy?" the siblings said together. Aslan having retrieved his own blanket as the rest of the men busied themselves with readying the ship and sails for the changed climate. Ropes were untied and retied where appropriate to accommodate the change in wind and for the sails they would need.

Atla nodded before turning to look out again onto the water where the thinnest line marked the Mortanian coastline. The large, middle aged captain folded his bulky arms across his chest before speaking,

"Mortania has been ruled for over a thousand years by the Samai, but the throne was taken from the last Samaian King, Alexander by Curian Greybold."

"We know the story old man, what does that have to do with prophecies?" Saicha nudged Aslan in his ribs with her elbow as he stood beside her. He hissed as it connected and rubbed at his side in pain,

"It has been said," Atla continued as though Aslan hadn't spoken. "That in order to restore balance and magic to the world, the Samaian heir, will rise up and reclaim the throne." Aslan rolled his eyes, clearly not impressed with tales of lost heirs and weather anomalies.

"But what does that have to do with the extreme weather conditions?" Atla turned to them again, his face sorrowful.

"Until the heir takes their place, the land will perish as it has been doing for the last eighteen years. Destruction like that can only go so long without destroying everything around it."

"Even the weather?"

"Even the weather," Aslan laughed, clearly not buying into the story but it was obvious that Saicha wasn't as dismissive.

"The elders," she said gently. "The elders told us about an assassin named Lebai who was hired to kill a man who had taken the throne from one of our ancestors Aslan."

"So, what does that have to do with heirs that control the weather?" Aslan laughed again but Saicha just rolled her eyes, annoyed with his attitude and his behaviour.

"Lebai killed him before anything serious happened but we were always taught that if he hadn't, there would have been dire consequences…maybe this is what they were talking about?"

Aslan looked on thoughtfully toward Mortania but seemingly deciding that there was nothing to really consider, he once again laughed and turned away,

"We have never had powers; you can barely cook!" Aslan was in hysterics but Saicha was deadly serious,

"Maybe because our ancestor didn't kill their usurper…the assassin did."

Aslan was silent, still sceptical but stubborn enough not to admit that he was intrigued. In Agmantia, magic of any kind was reserved for learned men and Shaman who trained about the laws beyond human reach. Sure, some could cure illnesses and make barren woman grow ripe with seed but nothing like changing the course of nature.

"It's nonsense," he finally said, "climates change all the time."

"In their natural order…not like this." Saicha's hazel eyes looked worried for a reason neither of them yet understood. "Something is going on here Aslan, something we don't really understand."

"Do we have to understand it?"

"Yes, especially if people are going to die for it!" she snapped at him and for once, he didn't retort with some idiotic and sarcastic reply. Aslan understood, as they all did, that war meant killing; killing people you'd never met just because you'd been ordered to. While one could come to terms with their duties, it didn't make it any less wrong.

"Mother said we didn't know the Age of Antonides, maybe that has something to do with it?"

"Maybe, but Rian is the eldest, he would have known the Samaian king."

"He would have been five years old, barely old enough to know anything." Saicha was thoughtful as she walked over to the side of the ship, the blanket still wrapped around herself. "There's more going on here Aslan and I want to find out what it is."

"Why, Mother told us to find out if the Greybolds are worth allying with. That's all we need to do."

"Why are you so happy to do the bare minimum all the time?" Saicha snapped at him, annoyed but Aslan just dismissed her with a wave of his hand,

"Why are you always on hand to do too much? Not everything is a test or a competition; there's no one to outdo here Saicha!" Saicha turned to him, her eyes narrowed accusingly.

"What's that supposed to mean?"

"Forget it," Aslan turned to walk away but Saicha stayed him with her words,

"No, say your piece or hold your tongue."

Aslan stopped his walk away from his sister and turned to her with emotionless eyes.

"Don't threaten me." Saicha stepped toward him,

"Or what?"

"Threaten me again…and find out."

They stood staring at one another, goading the other to make the first move but for what felt like forever, neither of them moved. The atmosphere was tight with their anger as Saicha stared down her younger brother before scoffing and turning away,

"Don't turn away from me!" Aslan snapped and reached out to grab her. Saicha spun out of his near grip and within seconds the siblings were fighting.

All weapons forgotten, the prince and princess were fist brawling on the deck of their ship, their crew looking on in astonishment. No one intervened as the brother and sister rolled around the deck punching and kicking at each other in a dance of deadly manoeuvres.

No sooner had it started then Saicha had her brother in a chokehold, Aslan clawing at his neck to get her to let go. Just as his eyes began to roll back into his head, Saicha finally let go and dropped him to the floor.

"Don't ever test me Aslan," Saicha struggled to get her breath back and the words across. "You won't be so lucky next time."

Aslan choked out on the floor, fighting to breathe as a crewman approached him with water that he slapped out of their hands in anger,

"You. Will. Never." Aslan choked out as Saicha went to walk away from him again but stopped in her stride. Aslan finally made it to his feet, and staggered towards his sister to look directly into her face. Even with her now busted lip and slightly bruising eye, she was as beautiful as their mother,

"You will *never* change who you are," he said between harsh breaths. "You can run to the Ecacia Mountains, you can become an elite and deadly assassin Saicha but you will never *not* be a princess of Agmantia...try as you might to deny it."

"I deny nothing," there was hardly any conviction in her words, making Aslan chuckle.

"You can kill every mark, win every battle, you can even beat your little brother to a pulp but it will never change the fact that you will never be the best at being what you were born into, and you hate that."

"You're not making any sense!"

"You will never replace Rian as heir and that kills you more than anything because you think you're better than him...you think you're better than us."

Saicha didn't say anything and in Aslan's eyes, that damned her. She didn't even bother to try and correct him; she saw what he thought was the truth in his eyes.

"You know nothing Aslan," her voice broke on her brother's name and when she saw that he noticed, she stormed away from him, embarrassed.

Aslan didn't bother to consider the guilt that took over him and stormed to his own rooms instead.

Another day rolled by before they approached the Mortanian coastline and could finally make out other ships on the water.

Within a few hours they were preparing to sail into Thea's Point and Aslan and Saicha were amazed at the busyness of it all.

Their Agmantian counterpart was a port named Noth Bay in their capital city of Noth. While it had constant trade from outside the kingdom, there was an order to things that was seemingly missing from here. In Noth, ships could only enter at certain times and exit at certain times and had to sail into perfectly aligned bays that were regimented by strict guards and overseers. Their ship in comparison had seemingly sailed into the nearest available dock.

Saicha had dressed in her usual robes that when appropriate could be readjusted to conceal her identity and always, concealed her weapons. She was armed to the teeth, which to enter Mortania was not a crime but if she looked imposing in any way, could cause problems in other establishments.

She had her hood down, her long brown hair still braided. No jewels or adornments identified them as anything but well to do seamen, alighting with their crew and that was how it would remain.

Aslan was dressed in a similar fashion with layers of comfortable robes that cuffed at the ankles, wrists and around his waist in navy blue with the remaining robes in white and grey. Their attire protected them against the harsh wind of the port, despite the abundance of people around them.

A few people looked their way as they disembarked, as they did with most newcomers to the Point. Eyes lingered on them because despite their simple attire, their thread looked considerably more expensive than those around them.

The poverty of the country was immediately apparent from the beggars on the sea front, to the urchin children actively stealing from those who were less aware. They darted in and out of the crowd, pickpocketing where they could and being dragged to small cages along the side of the street, when they were caught by guards.

The cages it seemed were the lesser of two evils as Saicha watched a young boy try to slit his own throat when a city guard tried to put him in chains.

Disturbed, Saicha turned away from the commotion and continued with her brother into the city by the sea. A medley of smells, voices and colours smacked them immediately along with the distinct intensity of the atmosphere,

"Do you feel that?" Saicha asked as they finally stepped onto the main street of Thea's Point and Aslan nodded,

"Yes…fear," he replied quietly.

The siblings made their way towards the first tavern they saw, but before they had the chance to enter, a tumble of arms and legs smashed out of the doorway and into the trampled and muddy street.

The two men fighting were tearing the skin from one another as the siblings and other citizens and patrons looked on in bewilderment. Some urged the fighting on while others screamed for it to stop.

"BREAK IT UP!"

The crowd turned in unison to the sound of a large man who came barrelling out of the tavern with an axe in his hand. He swung at the two fighters who quickly sprung apart to avoid decapitation. The three men were panting and heaving violently as adrenaline coursed through their veins.

"You stay clear of my establishment Crane, you hear me?" the tavern man barked at one of the men,

"Keep serving filthy Samaian dogs like him and you're going to see me every day of your life Eli!"

Aslan and Saicha looked sideways at one another as the man still on the ground, the Samaian, stood up, dusting himself off before spitting blood onto the ground,

"I'll defend what is right for me and mines!" he spat at Crane who made to lunge for him again but Eli intervened, placing the large axe between them,

"Leave Crane, NOW!"

The crowd held their breath, waiting to see what Crane would do but seemingly thinking better of it, he cursed and barged through the crowd into the street.

Saicha and Aslan watched as Eli helped the Samaian man up from the floor,

"Any who have a problem with the Samai, have a problem with me!" Eli called out and helped the other man back into the tavern. The crowd dispersed, the theatrics over and took their gossip with them.

The siblings turned to one another before Aslan made his way into the inn and Saicha followed Crane into the crowd.

***

Briseis stood outside on the surrounding grounds of Tirnum Castle, practicing her archery. There were targets at different points on the flat grassed area where she trained, and she tried to hit them now in the dimming evening sun. She nocked another arrow while Gardan stood a good distance away from her and other guards were dotted around her.

She released the arrow, hitting the target dead on as two figures approached from inside the castle.

Gardan placed his hand on the hilt of his sword until he recognised the thin figure of Baron Thelm and his serving man. The Baron inclined his head to the General who did the same before turning back to the princess. He watched as she took a shot and it landed closer to the target but not quite making it as the one before. He approached her cautiously,

"Your Highness, Baron Thelm is here to see you."

Briseis turned her cold eyes to Gardan before lowering her bow and arrow and turning to hand them both to the valet waiting beside her.

The Baron bowed, as did his serving man as Briseis held out her hand and another servant handed her a goblet of water.

"What brings you here Baron?"

"I have news your Highness…about Baron Dreston."

Briseis drank her beverage and stared at him over the rim of the goblet. By the time she had finished, and he still hadn't spoken, she said,

"I'm waiting."

Flustered, Erik straightened up as he said,

"He was speaking with Lord Weilyn and when he left, he asked me to align myself with Norto to get more information out of him."

"How does this help me?" Briseis said, clearly bored as she turned away from them and retrieved her bow and arrow from the valet and arranged herself to take another shot.

"Norto, has informed me his honour that he and Lyon plan to align with each other against you. With Lyon's troops already placed here in the capital and Weilyn's in the South, they look to form a formidable host."

"And what part do you supposedly play in this Erik?" Erik cleared his throat,

"I am to provide more aid from the North, to cut off the pastures into the city and so restrict any deserters or men who wish to rally against us in your name."

Briseis nodded as she took another shot but missed by a hair's breadth.

She nocked another arrow almost immediately and aimed, arms straight and in perfect form.

"Good," she said and let the arrow loose hitting the target dead on. "You may go."

Her tone was final and Baron Thelm scampered away with his attendant. Once again, the princess raised her bow and arrow, form flawless as she aimed at the target.

Gardan took a hesitant step toward Briseis and said,

"Princess…what would you like to do about Baron Dreston?"

Briseis let the arrow loose and it hit the target directly in the centre.

"Kill him."

When the princess had finished her archery, and dismissed him for the evening, General Beardmore made his way to his home situated off the castle grounds.

It had been a very long day, coordinating Briseis' various machinations and he had a lot to think about before a new day began, namely the price that Briseis had put on Baron Dreston's head.

While he realised that anyone could be killed for less, Briseis' bloodlust was beginning to worry him. She had always been ruthless but now that he was sleeping with her, her behaviour seemed less explainable. He knew the woman she was, and it was difficult to exact that from the killer she so clearly loved to be.

Gardan knew he couldn't stop Briseis killing Dreston, once she had her mind made up about something, there was no going back but it didn't sit well with him that he knew she was going to torture him.

Why that bothered him now, he didn't really know, but as he got himself ready to turn in for the evening and let go of the stresses of the day, Gardan wondered where his new-found care for the princess would eventually lead him, as he fell asleep to the memory of her face.

LOYALTY

The road to Thelm was long for more reasons than one. With Dana, distraught over her mother's death, Oren only speaking when absolutely necessary and Lamya trying to find common ground with everyone to keep the delicate peace; Trista was exhausted.

She wasn't speaking to Thorn, she had no idea what she would say to Oren if she tired, and she felt responsible for Dana's mother's passing. She avoided speaking to Dana because of it and every time she looked at her friend, the guilt threatened to swallow her whole.

As well, as her guilt over Mrs Black's death, Trista was also dealing with her feelings towards Thorn and Oren. She wanted more from her friendship with Oren, that much was abundantly clear, but her new annoyance with Thorn was something else entirely. He was a different person she was slowly realising, but it didn't stop her knowing and thinking about the boy she had grown up with. The boy who had put wildflowers in her hair on the way to some fete or other. The boy who had sat and spoken with her when no one else wanted to.

She had to tell him that she didn't feel the same way about him, but she didn't know where to begin. He was going to be heartbroken if his travelling to find her across the country was anything to go by. He had travelled hundreds of miles to find his fiancé who had unceremoniously left him without an explanation, how could she repay with disloyalty?

She had made a tremendous mistake not making it clear that she didn't have the same feelings for him; but she was too afraid. She knew that if she told Thorn she didn't want to marry him; he would ask her what had changed her mind and her feelings for Oren would undoubtedly come to light. He wouldn't let it go otherwise because nothing else had changed.

You're royalty now.

True, she had discovered she was a lost princess that could wield incredible power but, did it make her royalty? Whether she felt royal or not, it was an alternative explanation for Thorn; they were just too different now. She couldn't concentrate on this war and finally ruling a country if he was a constant distraction. Still, she had to be brave and tell him that things were different.

Also, she couldn't shake the feeling that she was ultimately dismissing Thorn for someone who had absolutely no interest in her.

Despite continuing their training where they could, she knew Oren was different with her now and she hated it. He might never have been a talkative person, but there was something in his previous interaction with her that she found she missed. She'd thought they were getting closer, building a real friendship after saving her from the attacker outside the God's House in Crol and his apology for being with that street walker but that seemed to have died away.

"Is everything okay?"

They had stopped to water the horses before they begun to last stretch to Thelm and Trista approached Oren cautiously. He turned to her briefly before looking away again as he brushed down Titan.

"Everything's fine. We should be in Thelm soon, from there, we head to the Council."

"I meant…with us."

He stopped brushing for a split second before continuing, "What do you mean?"

Trista sighed, knowing that she had to be clear if she was ever going to get anything out of him.

"Our training has been different and after Drem, I thought that we were friends."

"We are friends,"

"Then why aren't you looking at me!" she snapped.

She immediately regretted it because it showed how worked up she was getting and he didn't seem to understand or even care why. Oren stopped brushing Titan and turned to her fully, his large arms crossed over his chest and looked down at her,

"I apologised in Drem for the way I'd been treating you. I guess it's going to take a while for me to get out of my old habits."

"That's not what I mean Oren," she rolled her eyes but he challenged her,

"Then what do you mean Trista?"

Trista looked into his gorgeous eyes and knew she couldn't tell him, at least not here. It was too exposing to say the least and if he really didn't have any inclination what she was talking about; maybe it was best she kept her feelings to herself.

"Forget it," she turned back to her own horse when he said,

"How's your fiancé?"

Wide eyed Trista turned to him and threw her arms up in the air,

"See, that's what I'm talking about. Why would you say that?"

"Say what?"

"Why would you ask me about Thorn, you see him just as much as I do!"

"I'm not the one marrying him."

"Neither am I!" she hissed viciously "I don't ca—"

"Is everything okay?"

Trista felt a pair of arms wrap around her waist and her body shuddered at the incredibly wrong timing for Thorn to approach; not to mention, her complete lack of desire for him to be there.

"Everything is *fine* Thorn, what is it?" she pushed his arms from around her waist, stepping away from him. Oren chuckled to himself and led Titan away from the stream he was drinking from.

Trista watched Oren walk away and the rage inside her bubbled over at his dismissal,

"Are you sure you're alright?" Thorn asked her softly. "You seem a little flustered?"

"I'm fine Thorn," Oren was now stood with Dana and Lamya. He wrapped his arm around Dana, probably making sure she was okay, but Trista was furious. Why didn't he hold her like that, why didn't he care about her in that way?

"Good, can we talk then…before we set off again."

Trista turned from looking at her friends to look instead at Thorn who seemed to have no inclination that she was angry. Frustrated and anxious, Trista ran her hands through her long hair, pushing it to one side of her head.

"What do you want to talk about Thorn?"

"Isn't it obvious? You've been avoiding me since I got here." Trista felt uncomfortable.

"No, I haven't,"

"Yes, you have," Thorn chuckled as he reached out to pull her into his arms. Trista looked into his face but looked away again out of guilt,

"Talk to me Trista…what's going on?"

"Nothing's going on, I just…I just don't have time for all this right now!"

She pushed out of his grip and she saw the hurt on his face,

"All this…you mean us?"

"Yes, I mean us!" she snapped, stepping further away from him so she could be in her own space.

"Thorn, I am on my way to fight a war without an army! I don't have time to deal with anything else!"

"Trista, you're my fiancé; is it wrong that I want to spend time with you. I haven't seen you in weeks!" Trista narrowed her eyes at him,

"Did you not hear what I just said?" her eyes blazed. "People are going to die if I don't get to Thelm in time to complete my training so I can kill Briseis. Where in that time do you think, I have time to just sit and do nothing with you!"

Thorn was taken back, his head recoiling in surprise as he looked down at her.

"I see," Trista didn't give him the chance to say anything else as she turned and marched determinedly away from him; bravery could come another time.

A few hours later, the quintet stopped for a short break to relieve themselves. The girls dispersed in one direction and the boys in another. Once he was done, Oren stepped from behind the tree he had used and headed back to their horses on the side of the road, before he got there however, he caught a glimpse of Thorn behind another tree.

Thankfully, he had already pulled up his trousers but before he had the chance to look away, Oren noticed something odd.

He stopped, looking intently at Thorn now and realised that he was in fact staring at the tree; not moving or even blinking. Adding to the oddity of the situation, Oren saw distinct black smoke circling around Thorn's head. It was nothing like any power he had ever seen but he continued to watch as Thorn muttered some words he couldn't quite make out. Unsure what to make of it, Oren continued to watch him until the smoke slowly dissipated, Thorn blinked and turned away from the tree.

Oren turned back towards the horses, before Thorn noticed him and waited for the girls to return.

Thorn walked back to him just as the girls appeared from behind their own trees and roadside shrubs. Oren made his way over to Trista once Dana and Lamya were out of earshot,

"I need to speak to you, now."

Taken back by his abruptness, Trista didn't say anything but walked a short way with Oren and turned to face him,

"What's wrong?"

"How well do you know Thorn?" Trista rolled her eyes,

"Why does everyone keep asking me that? I've known him my whole life, why?" Oren turned his eyes to the remaining trio behind them and slowly put a sound bubble around them before saying,

"I saw him using power just now."

"What?" Trista was clearly stunned. "What kind of power are you sure?"

"Of course, I'm sure. It wasn't like ours but it was power…power I couldn't even feel." Trista was thoughtful for the moment. Lamya had expressed her concerns about Thorn and now Oren had a problem with him too but this was a little extreme.

"Well…his mother is Samaian, maybe he inherited something from her." Oren looked at her with scepticism,

"He's half Samai?" Trista nodded,

"His mother is Lady Avriel, the one who…"

"Was meant to teach you growing up, I heard." Oren went silent again for the moment, clearly thinking things through before he said,

"I don't trust him."

"What's new there, you haven't liked Thorn from the very beginning."

"I said I didn't trust him, that has nothing to do with whether or not I like the little weasel." Trista rolled her eyes,

"It has everything to do with it. You want some reason, any reason to hate him!"

"That's not true. I saw him using powers Trista, powers he neglected to tell us he has!" Stubborn now and just to try and hurt him she fired back.

"It's none of our business, least of all yours, he doesn't have to tell us everything."

Oren looked at her once again in disbelief before folding his arms across his chest in that way that told her he was extremely annoyed.

"Why are you so quick to defend him?"

"Why are you so quick to condemn him?" she replied defiantly but Oren merely laughed at her.

"You trust him, fine. Just don't expect me to."

"I don't!" Oren shook his head at her and returned to the others before remounting Titan.

"We have a lot of ground to cover before we get to Thelm, make sure to keep up!" he called out and everyone nodded their agreement. He turned Titan toward the main road and trotted off in the direction of Thelm. Everyone else mounted their own horses and followed until it was only Dana left behind and she sat waiting for Trista to get on her own horse.

"Trista, you okay?"

Trista watched Oren and Thorn ride away and hated that she knew Oren was right; something was going on with Thorn and she had to figure out what it was. It couldn't be a coincidence that Lamya had her reservations about him and now, possible powers?

"I'm coming," she called out trotting over to Dana and mounting her horse.

She would find out what Thorn was up to sooner rather than later.

CONNECT THE DOTS

Curian sat in his tent on the ever-increasing war camp going through finances and inventory for the war.

Being king was not all riches and power, there was hard work to be done; something he had learned in his early days on the throne.

He was no stranger to hard labour of course, having grown up working the grounds of the Illiya estate with his father, but he had always been responsible only for himself. Once he'd married, he'd been responsible for his wife, but she had died before he'd become king and so had no one to share his kingly burdens.

While Rarno was his most trusted friend, there were things Curian felt he could not confide to him.

Ignatius Rarno was high-born; the son of a wealthy military man and so there were elements of hardship that he could never understand. He had never gone days without food; never had to sleep outside in the dead of night in the most bitter of winters. He had never wanted for anything and for that, Curian could never truly relate to him. They were friends through their love of Man and its restoration to the Mortanian throne. They had a common enemy and that drove their loyalty to one another, loyalty as brothers in arms.

Still, Ignatius had never known what it was like to be looked down upon by others; to want what they had and think it so far out of reach. Curian, in many ways, was still driven by his want so many years later; and the need to be accepted by people who had looked down on him and his kind.

Ignatius had befriended a man who he'd seen raise an army in the name of Man and chose to align with him in his quest. He did not however, truly understand how deep his craving went. It was more than power or status or even to cement his place in history; it was the want for a woman.

Even now, as the effects of the Everlasting circulated around him in the form of harsh winter winds and decaying lands; all Curian could think about was Rowan Illiya; the woman who had stolen his heart; the woman he could never have.

Curian ran his hands threw his thick beard as he contemplated whether or not she could still be alive. He knew how powerful she was meant to be, but was she really able to hide from him for eighteen years?

He had questioned the other surrounding nations, the Coznian Empress Ailonwy to the North and of course Queen Nucea in the East. He had gone has far to attempt to question the Phyn but their King, Venelaus had rejected any line of communication. The Cotain emperor, Bragoa had given him access to his country in the early years and while they had found many Samai who had fled Mortania's persecutions, they had not found Rowan and her child.

He had started a war to win the woman he had been in love with since he was a child and still, he did not have her. To all others, Curian was a conqueror but deep inside, he was a failure. Rowan was the prize; Rowan would have been the victory and without her, this was all for nothing.

For that reason, he knew he couldn't allow Briseis to destroy Mortania. He hadn't known what his killing Alexander would do to the country and now that he did, he had to fix it. If killing Briseis was the answer, then so be it. Losing his daughter was far better than losing a country he hadn't meant to destroy in the hope of catching a woman, he had already lost.

As he lost himself in his thoughts, a guard entered the tent and bowed.

"There is a message for you Sire."

Curian motioned for it to be brought in and moments later, a young messenger entered and handed him a small scroll.

Curian shooed him away and as the messenger departed, he broke the waxed seal and opened the scroll to find a letter from Baron Dreston:

Your Dearest Majesty,

I write to inform you that Baron Thelm and I have allied ourselves with Lord Weilyn of Thea's Point against the efforts of Princess Briseis.

While the former will provide aid in the north for any attacks that may befall us there from the Samaian army, Weilyn's men will be on hand to defend against Briseis' men and reclaim the throne for you once she has been defeated.

As you may know, the princess as a group of young people named the Six who are trained in the ways of Samaian magic. It is in our best interests to destroy these individuals so she may not use them against us.

BLD

Curian held the scroll over the open candle flame on his desk, allowed it to catch fire before dropping it in an empty goblet and letting the flames die.

While Thelm's displeasure with him was obvious due to his unsanctioned marriage deal with Dreston, it was a surprise that Lord Weilyn was in Dreston's pocket against him. The man had always done well for himself manning Thea's Point and Curian had thought him content in his station.

Curian sighed before reaching out for a sheet of paper and began to pen his own message back to Dreston.

Baron,

Your information is appreciated and so your duties remain the same. Keep Briseis and any others close to her in your confidence and report all to me. I will need something tangible in order to determine a way to dispose of her.

Curian, the Conqueror.

***

Saicha Voltaire followed the man named Crane into the crowd of Main Street until he arrived at a small establishment that on a good day, might have been a home. The street, though packed with people was a far cry from some of the dives she'd encountered in her travels as an assassin for the Guild.

Cobbled streets filled with horse droppings and whatever people brought on their feet from ships and the surrounding lands, Thea's Point was a cauldron of activity, bubbling with adventure.

The side street that Crane turned down and the house he stumbled into, had fading paint on the outside wood and the framing practically falling off. There was no light behind one cracked window at the front of the house, while the other was boarded up completely.

As the disgruntled man disappeared into the building, Saicha leapt into action, sneaking her way to the small opening between Crane's house and another. She walked silently along the outside walls until she came to a small opening. It clearly had no other purpose but for ventilation as it faced a brick wall and was barely big enough to fit through.

Barely.

Saicha spied through the opening at Crane who, after haphazardly lighting a candle, had taken a seat at a table that looked to be on its last legs. He drank directly from a bottle of ale before smashing the now empty bottle against the wall across from him. He got up from the seat again, seemingly in search of another bottle which, soon enough, he found before slumping on the floor and drinking from it.

Saicha rolled her eyes and quietly, climbed through the opening, approaching Crane silently from behind. She stood there for a good two minutes before he noticed her. Even then, it was her shadow he noticed and spun around, wide eyed. He dropped the bottle, the brown contents spilling out onto the dirty wooden floor

"W-who are you? W-what do you want?"

"Answers," she replied. "And you're going to give them to me."

Saicha reached down and dragged Crane to his feet by the scruff of his shirt. He tried to fight her but one punch to his nose had him reeling in shock and pain.

"You bitch!" he growled at her and tried to go for her again, blood trickling down his nose. Easily, Saicha dodged his attacked and turned to kick him in the back sending him crashing onto the floor.

She marched over to him, entertained suddenly at his attempt to get away from her and spun him over so he was on his back. She punched him once more in the face, making him cry out again as he brought his hands up to cover his face.

"You broke my nose!" Saicha stepped away from him to pick up a wooden chair she'd seen.

"Most likely," she picked up the chair and walked back to Crane, slamming the two back legs either side of his head, locking his hands against his face. The front legs wouldn't go around his body of course, so she leant forward on the back of the chair to choke it into his arms. Crane cried out as his own hands pressed into his smashed nose,

"No, where were we?"

"W-who are you?" his replies were muffled but understandable. Saicha smiled behind her hood and mask.

"I'm your murderer if you don't tell me what I want to know." Crane's eyes widened.

"I don't have the money, tell Davy to give me a little more time."

"I don't know who Davy is, but I'm sure he'll find you soon enough." Crane whined out his pain as Saicha pressed the chair into him again, her arms rested on the back of the chair.

"Tell me about your fight just now,"

"What?"

"Your fight, with the Samaian man. Why did you want to hurt him?" Crane managed to lower his hands, so they were resting uncomfortably just below his chin.

"You fight for them?" Saicha didn't say anything. A look of hatred crossed Crane's face as he spat the blood that had pooled into his mouth into her face.

Luckily, her face was covered by her mask, but it stained her clothes and sprayed against her hood.

"Now…that wasn't nice, was it?"

Saicha raised herself up from the chair, before slamming it back down onto his chest immediately, splintering the wood against his chest.

Crane cried out in shock as Saicha grabbed one of the broken chair legs, snapped it in half against her raised knee and crouched down so the jagged end was at his throat.

"Now, tell me what I want to know, and I might not kill you; deal?"

Crane nodded furiously; his eyes wide with fear as Saicha pressed the stake further into his neck.

Saicha returned to the inn where she and Aslan had found Crane but when she arrived, Aurora landed on her shoulder.

She stroked the bird lovingly before retrieving the message attached to her leg and read that her brother and their entourage had found alternative accommodation. Aslan had arranged a horse to be ready for her and within minutes, she had mounted and made her way to the edge of the small city.

Saicha arrived at the seemingly abandoned outhouse where she was met by the crew that had arrived with them on the ship. She handed one of them her horse and marched straight into the house to find her brother embraced with a scantily clad young woman.

"It's the middle of the afternoon for God's sake."

Aslan looked up from where he was nuzzling his face between the girl's breasts and grinned wolfishly.

"I've been on a boat for countless days' sister; be grateful this is all you've walked in on." Saicha lowered her hood and mask,

"You're disgusting."

"Thank you," he said winking at her before turning to the young woman. "Make yourself comfortable upstairs, I need to talk with my sister."

The woman took her leave without question and jiggled herself up the stairs.

Saicha stepped into the open plan kitchen and living room area to where her brother was sat at a small breakfast table. She took off her outer robes completely, they were stained with blood after all and dropped her larger weapons on the table before taking a seat opposite her brother.

"Did you tell her who you are?"

"Of course not, I'm not a fool."

"Debatable, so…who goes first?"

Saicha was surprised to see a map of Mortania laid out on the table top. Bowls of fruit held the corners down and little markers had been placed on the map showing the locations of Aslan and herself and the king and princess.

"What's this?" she asked pointing to a marker placed further north in Thelm.

"The Lithanian Council apparently; Mother said they may be useful."

Saicha nodded,

"Thelm seems to be a significant player in all this."

"Go on," Aslan urged, leaning back in his chair to listen.

"I followed Crane to some hole in the wall he called a home and watched him attempt to drink himself into an early grave. Once I beat the shit out of him, he started to talk about the war and the Samai."

"What did he say?"

"Mostly that he hates them and that he's not the only one."

"Misery does love company,"

"It looks that way. The crown has declared war against the Samai and called all able-bodied men to arms. There are those that side with the king and others that don't, that's part of the fight we saw earlier."

Aslan nodded,

"I spoke with the innkeeper and he said there have been attacks just like it not just in the city but on-board trade ships." Saicha raised her eyebrow at that curiosity.

"Pirates attacking ships in the name of the crown, stealing cargo and killing people on board, Samaian or otherwise."

"What about counter attacks? So far, all I've heard is that people are attacking the Samai; what are they doing in retaliation." Aslan shrugged,

"Damned if I know but it must be something if the crown has declared war against them."

"Why would the crown declare war against Samaians but that same crown asks us to kill their princess?"

The siblings sat for a moment in silence, thinking things over before Saicha decided quietly,

"I need to hear it from them."

"Them who?" Aslan was confused,

"The king and princess; we need to know what they think of this situation."

"Situation? Saicha, they started it."

"And yet one wants us to kill the other, why? Who and what is this princess and why would her father want her killed? Don't you want to know?" Aslan shrugged,

"Not really,"

"Well brother, since I'm the one who will probably have to take her life; I do!" Aslan smiled cheekily but nodded his understanding.

"So, what will you do?"

"Get the information I need." Saicha stood from her chair before leaning over the table and moving the 'Saicha' marker to Tirnum Castle. She winked at Aslan before heading upstairs,

"Try and keep it clean!" Aslan called over his shoulder, "The maids hate cleaning blood out of your clothes!"

Later that evening, Saicha was washed, dressed and looked every inch an assassin. Her Guild uniform was essentially the same as her usual robes but entirely in black and with more than a few hidden compartments for various weapons and gadgetry. Tonight, however, she wasn't on the hunt, at least not for a kill and so a lot of her weapons were left behind at the cabin with Aslan and their men. She looked at herself in the bedroom she had been assigned and smiled at finally getting to use her skills.

She had been stifled at the palace for the last few years and revelled in the opportunity to spread her wings.

Her mother had questioned why she'd left the Guild if she was so unhappy at home. She hadn't been able to explain to Nucea that she had felt the same dissatisfaction at the Guild and had run home to escape it. She was happy to be using her skills again but when it had been all she was, she found she was missing something…she just didn't know what it was.

Pushing her personal feelings to the side, Saicha lifted her mask around her mouth and lifted her hood over her head so only her eyes were visible and left her room. She'd left her brother between the thighs of the working girl he had brought back and with a roll of her eyes at her pleasured screams, Saicha set off back into the city.

If possible; Thea's Point was livelier at night and it was a struggle to get through the packed streets; particularly on horseback. The small city was heaving with people buying from late night markets; bartering, whoring and drinking both on and off the street. The cacophony of sounds was almost welcoming as it reminded her of the Guild.

Hundreds of people from all over the world lived there; trained there and brought their cultures and traditions with them. A variety of foods cooked in the kitchens with chefs from Coz and Cotai and a collection of flowers and herbs grew in the gardens; having been donated by novices upon entry.

The Guild was a world away from this place, but she liked to be reminded of her home in the little things she encountered. She missed her home and her friends at the Guild, but she knew; *felt* that there was a reason she had left more than her dissatisfaction with her vocation.

Saicha continued determinedly through the city towards Tirnum. Once she exited the tight crowds of the Point, she set her horse off at tremendous speed onto Thea's Road. The ride from the cabin to the Point was a short one, but the ride from the city to Tirnum was considerably longer. Even when she pushed her horse to its limits, it still took her a long while to reach the small town that surrounded the immediate city walls.

It was here, she dismounted and set her horse in the stall of a small barn. She approached the old man that sat on a short wooden stool beside it and dropped a silver coin into his hand,

"When I return, my horse should still be here; understand?" the old man looked up at her and blinked once very slowly,

"Of course, assassin," Saicha didn't respond and took her leave to continue on foot towards the castle. She avoided the castle gates completely and instead kept to the shadows, between the houses and small market stalls that had been erected against the city walls.

Guards patrolled the battlements along it, never far from the outhouse where she assumed, they were stationed. When she was clear to do so, Saicha leapt onto the wall and began to climb. She thanked the Gods for her Phyn leather gloves as she dug her fingers into the rock and ascended toward the night sky. Once at the top, Saicha checked for the nearest guard and when their backs were turned from her, she climbed over the battlement across to the other side and descended the other side of the wall. Agile and silent, Saicha climbed down until she reached the inner city. Still keeping to the shadows, using the night as her ally; she headed onto the brick lined streets of the inner city and ran towards the castle at the centre.

It took her a while, navigating through the darkened streets and having to redirect herself when she came across a dead end. Decidedly she leapt up onto the roofs of the brick horses and ran light footed and unseen towards Tirnum Castle.

Once close enough, she headed straight for the castle walls and after another strenuous climb and descent on the other side; still undetected made her way into the belly of the castle.

***

Lyon sat on a lounger in Princess Briseis' audience chamber waiting for her to come out and receive him.

Briseis had invited him to a small gathering in her private quarters and while he had been delighted to attend, he had been hesitant to accept. Briseis told him that they would be joined by the Six and he hated admitting to himself that he was terrified of them and their power.

Still, it was his only way to get as close to the princess as Curian wanted, even though being the sole focus of her attention was unnerving.

A young Samaian girl had admitted him entry and while the Samai didn't usually take his fancy; was very appealing. She darted in and out of the room now, asking him if he wanted anything to eat or drink but what he found he wanted was her. Since Alaina had betrayed him; he'd not seen her, and he needed someone regular before he got back to his girls in Dreston. Maybe this young Samaian could fill the position.

She put some small delicacies on the table in front of him and he reached out and grabbed her arm,

"Why don't you come and sit with me."

"Lord, I have work to be getting on with," she pulled her arm away, but he held firm,

"It wasn't a question." Dreston pulled her towards him so she fell into his lap. The girl was stuck between not disobeying her superior and wanting to get away from him. It didn't matter, he liked them better when they were afraid.

"What's your name little Samai?"

"E-ndora," she was scared but defiant; he heard it in her voice. Dreston pushed some stray hairs from her face as he went to kiss her face, he felt a sharp pain in his stomach and instinctively pushed her away from him. As soon as she was off his body, the pain went away. Dreston looked up at her,

"Did you do that?" Endora lay against the lounge chair where he had pushed her, her eyes wide.

"Lord I…"

"You little bitch!" Dreston lunged for her but as he did so, the door to the chamber opened,

"Baron?" Dreston looked to the door where the princess, General Beardmore and the Six stood in the doorway. "What on earth are you doing?"

He didn't answer immediately but Briseis took one look at Endora and suddenly, the Baron was pulled away from the lounge chair and went crashing to the floor. The food that Endora had place earlier, went flying across the table. Briseis took one further step into the room and looked down at Dreston sprawled on the floor,

"Never in your life will you attempt to defile someone who is in my service do you understand me Baron!"

The room shook with her force of her words that while everyone else was silent, Lyon shook his head obediently.

"Yes Princess, of course Princess!" he couldn't not apologise quicker as Endora scrambled to her feet and bowed her head politely.

"Are you alright Endora?"

The Six, General Beardmore, Lyon and Endora alike looked at the princess in utter confusion. Briseis didn't acknowledge them until Endora answered,

"Yes Princess,"

"Good, you are excused for the evening. The baron and I have much to discuss."

"Yes Princess…thank you Princess." Endora exited quickly before Briseis could change her mind and closed the door firmly behind her.

"Get up!" Briseis snapped as she walked into the room and her entourage followed her. Lyon got to his feet and stepped back from the eight pairs of eyes staring back at him.

"Try anything like that again Lyon and I will kill you, do you understand me?" Lyon nodded,

"Answer me when I'm speaking to you!" Briseis shouted again,

"Yes, Princess. You have my most sincere apologies!"

"I don't want your apologies; I want your cooperation."

General Beardmore reached out and took the princess' overcoat and placed it on the chair the baron and Endora had vacated. The Six took various seats around the room while the general took a stand beside the door."

It was obvious this man never left her side so how could he get close to her with Gardan constantly in the way.

Briseis tapped the space on the lounge chair beside her and sceptically, Lyon joined her, straightening his clothes as he did so.

"So, tell me Lyon…how do you like the capital?" he was taken back. The princess had been threatening him only moments before, what game was she playing with him?

"It is most accommodating your Highness."

"As am I," she said leaning towards him but instinctively he leant back, rejecting her.

"You're afraid of me," Briseis chuckled to herself. "Understandable but I promise you, you have nothing to be afraid of as long as you cooperate." Lyon was wary but managed to maintain his composure,

"I try to do all I can for you princess," Briseis fanned him off.

"Enough with the prostrating Baron, I know you adore me as do my Six," she gestured to the teenagers around them who all nodded.

"I've brought you all here to tell you that you eight, the General included are my most trusted. There is nothing I will not and cannot share with you."

"Is there something you wish to share with us now your Highness?"

"As a matter of fact, there is," she turned to look at the baron again, giving him a look, he wasn't able to ignore."

"I want you to forgive me for my outburst just now Baron but I didn't like the idea of you with my maid as I had a much more royal partner in mind for you."

General Beardmore cleared his throat behind them and the Six went silent. Lyon instinctively raised his hands so his intentions could not be misconstrued.

"Your Highness…are you well? You do not seem yourself." Briseis only laughed again.

"Come on Baron…I see the way you look at me."

"I have done not—" Briseis pressed herself into his body suddenly, ignoring his words as Lyon's eyes darted across the room to where General Beardmore stood; ever watchful. The younger man, although not looking in their direction had a whole new stance about him; rigid…angry even.

"Tell me you haven't thought of this," Briseis was saying and Gods help him, the way she purred was his undoing. He turned his head to look back at her and their lips were inches apart. Briseis leaned forward and pressed her mouth gently against his for a few precious moments before pulling away,

"The things we could achieve…you and I." she trailed her delicate fingers up his chest before stopping them on his lips.

"Your armies; your gold…my power…all of it could be ours. She leaned into his ear and whispered.

"Why be a Baron…when you can be a King."

Lyon licked his lips that had turned incredibly dry and swallowed loudly.

"If this is your wish your Highness then I can only obey," he replied, still so very unsure whether this was a game.

"From this moment on, my Six and my general will be on hand to protect you against any who might harm you. If they find out about our intent to align, it may anger them." Dreston nodded his head,

"So," Briseis leant over to kiss him gently. "Just between us…yes?"

"Yes, your Highness…thank you your Highness."

Briseis sat up,

"Well, if you'll all excuse us; General Beardmore and I need to discuss some further things for the war effort."

"Yes, of course."

Lyon got up frantically from his seat on the chair and bowed before scurrying out of the room. As he did so, the smile on Briseis' face dropped, and she turned to look at her Six.

"Keep an eye on him."

Six pairs of eyes looked at her and nodded before exiting the room themselves and closing the door behind them.

Gardan remained by the door as Briseis stood up from the lounge chair and walked graciously into her bedroom. Her bathing chamber was the room beyond and with the use of her power, water began to flow from the large metal tap. She warmed it as she went to stand behind the screen she used for undressing and began to unbutton her dress.

He followed her without question and stopped on the other side of the bathing pool while she undressed on the other.

Moments later, the princess stepped from behind the screen naked and stepped leisurely into the waiting warm water.

Gardan watched her as she lowered herself into the water and raising out of it again, like an ethereal water nymph. Her personal bathing chamber was smaller than that of others in the castle but still had two large holes cut into the stone floor. Two other rooms on either side of the holes were where the maids kept her fragrances, oils and robes that she required before dressing.

"Come here Gardan,"

"Princess?"

"Don't make me repeat myself."

Gardan swallowed away his apprehension and slowly stepped forward to where Briseis sat in her stone bath. She was high enough above the water that her supple rounded breasts were on display to him.

Unable to look away, Gardan looked his fill before clearing his throat and steeling his impression.

"You are angry with me?"

"It is not my place to be angry with you, your Highness."

"It might not be your place but that doesn't change that you are in fact…angry."

Gardan said nothing. Briseis smiled and stood up so that he could see her in her entirety,

"Look at me."

Gardan turned his eyes to hers and locked them there,

"Look. At. Me." She repeated and this time; he lowered his eyes until he'd seen all of her that could be seen.

"Speak," she said.

"I was angry that you kissed him…that he touched you…that you touched him." Briseis smirked as she nodded.

"Baron Dreston is a vile human who would have forced himself on my maid if I hadn't come in at the right moment. He believes himself a seducer and I am using that to get him to trust me. I scared him when we were in the Imperial Lands and on second thought, I realise that that was counterproductive. Until I learn what he is up to with various members of my court; I must have him on side. He can die once I get what I want."

"Yes, Princess."

"That is the first and last time I will explain myself to you Gardan, do you understand me?"

"Yes, your Highness."

"Good…now undress; and join me."

As Gardan began to unbuckle his sword belt, he stopped and looked sharply towards the small open window across the room. Briseis lowered herself into the water,

"What's wrong?"

Gardan didn't reply and ran over to the window, peering out as far as his head could allow and looked around. There was nothing but darkened sky with stars dotted intermittently. The wind was still, chilly on his cheeks but essentially, nothing.

"I thought I saw something," he said quietly before stepping back inside and closing the small wooden pane that acted as a covering. He turned back to the princess and continued undressing before joining her in the tub and losing himself in her kisses.

On the other side of the window, resting on a small ledge cut into the slate, Saicha shook her head with an amused smile before making her descent back into the castle below.

DENIAL

It was the dead of night and Trista and her companions had gone to sleep by the side of the road. Thelm was a number of hours away but they had exhausted themselves enough to warrant some rest before the last stretch to the northern city.

Despite their small delay, they did know that the soon they got to Thelm the sooner they could be free of one another. They needed some distraction, something to get them out of their various issues. Lamya was the shining light among them, but even she didn't have enough emotional strength to make everyone happy.

So much had happened to them all since leaving their perspective homes; the use of powers; training, losing loved ones and everything else in between and everyone was travelling with the weight of their own thoughts.

It was these thoughts that ran through Oren's mind as he tried and failed to get some sleep. He lay on his back, resting his hands behind his head as he looked up at the stars. They had decided against a fire in case anyone saw from the road and instead Oren had used his powers to create a warm bubble of air to keep everyone warm.

The wind hit gently against the outside of the bubble; tiny bits of debris hitting the invisible shield as Oren lay staring into the sky. He took a deep breath as he thought about his father as he did most nights. Despite going to a Gods House to pay his respects; he had not truly mourned Gorn and couldn't until he had an official goodbye. There would be rights and military honours that should be bestowed upon his father and he would make sure he made it out of this war alive in order to give that to him.

As well as thoughts of this father, Oren thought about Iona and whether she was okay. He had told her to go back to the house after hiding out for a while but, whether she was safe, he couldn't know. Would she stay in the house she had shared with them for so many years, without them actually in it? He thought of her now, making bread in the mornings and yelling at him to keep his room clean. He missed her terribly and hoped with all his heart that he would see her again.

As he lay thinking, something caught Oren's attention. He turned his eyes to find Thorn climbing out of his bedroll and step out of the protective bubble. Though the bubble was invisible, he knew Thorn had stepped out because he wrapped his arms around himself and shuddered before heading off into the trees.

Thinking he was just going to relieve himself; Oren went to turn away but not before a flash of light caught his eye and he raised himself onto his elbows to look in its direction, Thorn's direction.

Once again, Oren saw the smoke like power circulating around Thorn's head until slowly, it faded then was gone completely.

He knew he should wake Trista but what would he say?

Thorn was walked back to the camp, making Oren lower himself onto his back once more.

He'd talk to Trista in the morning and make her deal with it. At least then, she couldn't blame him for being biased towards her special little friend.

When day broke, the group got ready to continue their journey. They got ready in silence, the five of them with pressing thoughts of their own when Oren slowly approached Trista by her horse.

"Trista…can I talk to you for a second?"

Trista looked up at Oren from where she was strapping her pack to her horse and simply nodded before stepping away from the others and turning to face him with her arms folded across her chest.

It was a beautiful dawn with a mixture of colours melted into the sky, but her mood didn't reflect that. Trista missed the days when she would wake up early just to watch the sunrise and revel in the beauty of the sky. Now, everything was plagued with uncertainty and upset from herself and the people around her. She was in no mood for Oren right now and not just because she was frustrated about her feelings for him. They stood facing each other when suddenly the air went still and she realised he had put a barrier around them,

"What's going on?"

"It happened again, last night while everyone was asleep; Thorn went into the trees and used some kind of power."

"Not this again," Trista rolled her eyes at which Oren was taken back.

"Excuse me?"

"Oren, I'm not in the mood for your dislike of Thorn this morning okay."

"Trista, I'm trying to protect you."

"This is protecting me?"

"I don't trust that guy and I'm telling you so you can do something about it; of course, that's protecting you!"

"What do you want me to do about it Oren? Confront him; call him out on it, throw him on the side of the road somewhere?" This time Oren rolled his eyes,

"Stop being so childish and listen to what I'm saying and not what you *think* you heard. I think he is dangerous!"

"And I *don't*, he's my friend!" Oren looked at her intently, curiously before he crossed his own large arms across his chest and replied.

"He's a little bit more than that though…isn't he?"

Trista scowled at him; literally scowled at him as she stepped a little closer to him,

"Whatever Thorn is to me, is my business, not yours!" Oren didn't miss a beat,

"No, it's not, but your safety is and I need to know what's going on with him!"

"If you care so much Oren, why didn't you call him out on it last night?"

"Maybe I thought bringing you the information so you could question your *friend*, was better than me beating the truth out of him!" Oren shouted at her. "It seems I was wrong to put such maturity in your hands."

"Don't make this about me, when you're the one who can't see past your jealousy to think better of Thorn!" Oren laughed at her, venom in his eyes and the words that came from his mouth.

"Don't flatter yourself Trista," he looked her up and down. "There is nothing he has for me to be jealous of." Trista swallowed down her shame. Oren shook his head as though he had just realised something, that he was stupid not to have known before.

"You're so blinded by your love for him that everything is clouded with you, isn't it?"

"What?" her disbelief was clear,

"You're so in love with him you can't see what's right in front of you. Sort that out princess before you get us all killed!" Oren turned to walk away from her, but she grabbed his arm and he turned back round with a contemptuous look on his face.

"How dare you speak to me like that!"

"Oh, I dare, why wouldn't I?"

"Because I am your Princess and soon to be your Queen, so you watch how you speak to me."

Oren almost looked impressed before a smirk emerged on his face and he folded his arms across his chest again

"So, the royal bitch has finally come out to play, I wondered how long it would take you to pull rank."

"How dare you," she looked at him hurtfully. "How *dare* you." Trista struggled not to burst into tears so instead, she fuelled her embarrassment and her rage and marched away from Oren, out of their sound bubble. She walked determinedly over to where Thorn was stroking his horse's mane and pulled his arm, so he was facing her,

"Do you have powers?"

"What?"

"Do not play with me Thorn, I am *not* in the mood! Do you have powers or not?"

"Trista what's going on?"

"Answer me!" she yelled at him, her heart beating too fast with rage. Lamya and Dana were now looking at them, waiting for the answer as well. Oren had come to stand by Titan and looked on expectantly.

Thorn looked at her in his smart clothes and smart hair that she used to find attractive and with an arrogance that she had never seen from him, he said,

"No."

"Then why does Oren think you do?"

"How should I know!" Thorn protested, shock and confusion on his face. "I don't know what he's said to you, but I don't have powers!" He said it like the word was dirty, like it wasn't something he could ever be a part of.

"Thorn...please don't lie to me."

"I'm not lying, I... hey...hey what are you doing!"

Trista didn't realise Oren had come up behind her and without warning he grabbed Thorn by the throat and held him up in the air, inches off the ground.

"Oren!"

"Show her!"

"Yo...cho-king...me!" Thorn clawed at Oren's hand wrapped tightly around his neck as he kicked his legs, dangling in the air.

"Oren let him go!"

"Show her your powers!" Thorn continued to choke as Lamya, and Dana looked on and Trista urged for Oren to let go.

"Oren stop, you're killing him!" Trista pushed at Oren with her powers but met a solid resistance she had never felt before. She had been training with Oren for weeks and had come up against his blocks, but this was something different. He was too strong, and she couldn't stop him.

Trista concentrated on Oren and willed him to move but apart from a slight shift in the dirt, he just wouldn't budge.

"Oren *please* don't kill him!"

Suddenly, Oren let go and Thorn fell to the floor in a choking heap of clothes and limbs. Trista rushed over to him,

"How could you!" Trista screamed up at him as Oren looked down at them without remorse. Trista cradled Thorn into her arms as he struggled to catch his breath,

"If he had powers don't you think he would have used them against *you*!"

Still Oren said nothing until Lamya stepped forward and placed a delicate hand on his forearm.

"Let's go Lord Antos," he didn't respond but he turned with her and got onto Titan.

Oren waited there while Trista helped Thorn to his feet and Lamya and Dana got their things together.

"Are you okay to ride?" Trista asked Thorn.

"Just keep that *savage* away from me!" Thorn yelled out as best he could, his voice hoarse. "I'll be fine."

When they were all finally on their horses, the atmosphere among them was worse than ever and they set off for Thelm in silence. Thorn was beside her, Dana and Lamya in front and Oren at the head of their procession.

"Thorn…he was just trying to protect me." Trista found herself saying, not sure if Oren could hear her from his position at the front but knowing it was true.

"From who, me? Would I ever hurt you?"

"No, of course not but he…he doesn't know you and he was really sure about what he saw."

"Trista, I don't know what he saw but we have known each other our entire lives. Are you really going to believe that barbarian over me?"

"Don't call him that," Trista snapped. Despite his terrible behaviour, Thorn had no right to speak about Oren this way. "Oren is a warrior…and my friend."

"You sure he's not more than that?"

"What?"

"I see the way you look at him Trista…the way I hoped you would one day look at me."

"Thorn I…"

"Is something going on with you two?"

"No! Of course, not!"

"Do you want there to be because you haven't so much as slept near me since I found you." Trista looked away from him embarrassed and cornered.

"I'm not talking about this, not now. Oren is a friend, a teacher; an amazing fighter and one day he will lead my armies against my enemies; can you say the same?"

"No, I'll be the one by your side; watching that army fight in your name and him possibly dying for you."

Where was, this coming from? This wasn't the Thorn she remembered at all,

"Speak of him in that way again and I promise you when we get to Thelm; I won't stop him from hurting you." She was serious and somehow, he knew it.

"Trist—"

"We are *not* going to discuss my friendship with Oren ever again."

Without giving him the chance to reply; Trista steered her horse away from him to take her place next to Dana and continued her journey in silence.

A PRICE ON A HEAD

Saicha was back at the hideaway in record time, having pushed her horse as far as it could go. She'd barely brought the horse to a stop before handing the reins to one of their aids and heading into the house.

"Aslan!" she yelled into the open space as she removed her outer robes and took a bottle of wine from the kitchen table. She'd drank a whole mugful before calling out again,

"Aslan, get your behind down here!" Saicha poured herself another full mug and one for Aslan as her little brother came stumbling down the stairs half dressed; rubbing sleep out of his eyes.

"Stop yelling…immediately," he said, his voice hoarse but Saicha just rolled her eyes.

"What on earth were you doing?" Aslan looked at her as though she were asking a ridiculous question.

"You left me for hours with a whore and wine; what do you think I was doing."

Saicha looked at him with complete disgust before taking a seat and putting her feet up on the table, crossing them at the ankle. Saicha looked at her brother over the rim of her mug as she took another sip;

"There's more to life than whoring and drinking Aslan."

"I'm sure there is dear sister but," he leaned forward and snatched her mug out of her hand to take a large gulp. Saicha cursed under her breath before leaning up to take the cup she had originally poured for him and sat down again. "Until I discover what that is; I'll be content drinking and whoring."

Aslan took another drink before finally taking a seat in the chair opposite his sister.

"So, find anything good?"

Saicha went on to tell Aslan about what she had heard at the castle between Baron Dreston, the princess and her General.

"One thing that is clear," they both continued sipping at their mugs of wine. "The princess is the major player here; nothing happens without her say so."

"Okay, so what should we tell Mother?" Saicha chewed on her bottom lip, contemplating her response.

"I'm not sure there's anything to tell her just yet. We need to hear the king's side of the argument."

"We've heard his side; he wants his daughter dead and you've just said she's out for blood. Let's just kill her and go home."

"Let's?" Aslan fanned her off,

"Particulars, all I'm saying is that you've said she's dangerous; so why not just get it done?"

"Mother asked us to question why anyone would warrant death. I won't kill her just on her father's say so *or* what I heard; there's no honour in that." Aslan almost choked on his wine as he let out a harsh laugh,

"You're an assassin Saicha, what do you know about honour?"

Saicha narrowed her eyes at him,

"If you knew anything about our teachings; you would know that to be an Agmantian Assassin is not about killing for sport or pleasure. We don't take any mission that would question our integrity or moral standing so there is indeed honour in what we do. There is a code Aslan." Aslan waved her off again,

"Code shmode, what do you suggest we do then?"

For the millionth time since they'd left Agmantia; Saicha rolled her eyes at her infuriating little brother. When was he going to understand that this was a truly intricate mission and they had to make sure they made the right choices?

"We find out what the king is actually up to, then we decide. In the meantime, I'll send Mother a message with Aurora that we need a little more time."

Aslan nodded and stood up from his seat,

"Good, so we set out tomorrow?" Saicha nodded,

"Yes, we need to find out where he is; should be easy enough in the city."

Aslan turned and headed back toward the stairs.

"Keep it down please, some of us need to sleep."

"Some of us," Aslan said pointing to his sister and mouthing the word 'you'; "need to get bedded."

Saicha picked up her now empty mug and launched it at him. Aslan simple laughed as the mug hit the wall and fell unceremoniously to the floor, before making his way back upstairs to bed.

***

The following morning, Briseis was training once again with the Six. They were in the enclosed training yard of Tirnum Castle, just below Thea's Tower, the largest tower of the castle; surrounded by palace guards and other officials, dignitaries and castle staff going about their everyday life. Unless specifically instructed, training sessions were never hidden away from onlookers as Briseis quite liked the idea that her prowess was witnessed by others who would spread the word throughout the kingdom.

It was a cold morning, as most mornings were now, and so they were all dressed in their fighting leathers trimmed in thick furs trying to keep the cold out. They went through their drills in order to work as one with both their magic and their weapons. Gardan was there for the latter while Briseis joined them now for the former.

They were getting progressively better at their techniques and while she might not have told them directly, Briseis was very proud of them. Not only for their progress but for how much closer it brought her to victory.

She had not felt much from the Redeemer recently, and she knew they were heading North although she had heard nothing from Thelm.

The men she had stationed there had sent no word of anything out of the ordinary.

Everything seemed to be the same, but she ordered her men to remain there in case something changed.

Aside from Thelm, Briseis was receiving daily news regarding riots in the city streets as well as the rest of Mortania. Men, Samai, Agmantians, Coznians, everyone was fighting amongst themselves and she loved it. As long as there was discord among the Mortanians; they wouldn't think to rally against the crown in the hope of something better. She knew the Samai gained strength in numbers, so the more that were wiped out by the fighting, the better. Their power, if potent enough would generate and she couldn't allow their Redeemer to gain any more strength from them.

She continued to run through the drills with the Six members until she took one of them aside, a young man by the name of Duncan. He was the eldest of the group and seemingly the most powerful.

"Walk with me." Duncan followed obediently, steadying his breathing as he powered down and his flames disappeared.

"Any news on the Baron?"

"Nothing substantial Princess. He spent the evening with a servant girl, against her will might I add but no communication with anyone other than his man Aml."

"I see, I want you all to keep a close watch on him. I have plans for our friend Baron Dreston and I don't want anything getting in the way of that."

"Yes Princess."

"I want him dead as soon as its possible and you will help me do it." Briseis turned her attention to Gardan who stood across from them now watching the training. She was more than a little disturbed by the fact that she was hiding her intentions from him but she knew it was for the best.

"My general has reservations about how he should be handled so I cannot include him in this mission, do you understand?"

"I will tell no one," Briseis nodded, a sign that he was dismissed and Duncan ran back to his training.

Briseis watched them all for the moment and once again thought on her decision not to include Gardan in her plans. What he thought of her had become something she considered recently, and she wasn't sure how she felt about that. She knew if he found out about killing the baron, he would be angry with her and she didn't want that. The fact that she cared, made her angry. For too long Baron Dreston had gotten away with being the richest man in the kingdom and therefore thinking he was owed something. That would end as soon as she got what she needed from him: his lands, his gold; everything would be stripped from him before she took his life for even thinking that he could outsmart her.

Seeing she was unoccupied, General Beardmore walked over and stood by her side,

"Is everything okay Princess?"

Briseis looked up at him and sighed before looking back at the Six,

"Yes, everything is fine."

***

Curian sat with Lyon and Rarno that same morning in the war tent at basecamp.

He had chosen to remain there, preferring the outdoors and the sight of his growing forces rather than the confinements of Tirnum Castle. The place that had once been so coveted with its gargantuan scale and endless riches both literal and figurative, had once been all he could think about. Living there with Rowan and finally being worthy of having her but it was not to be.

Now, he hated the very stone that was meant to keep him safe.

The three men were systematically going through the list of conscriptions who had arrived only moments before. While there were, some who had been dragged into camp kicking and screaming, there were many who had arrived of their own volition.

The youngest Curian had seen, was a boy of maybe fourteen who didn't look as though he could hold a broom much less a sword. He had chosen not to dwell on the image of the scrawny boy with eyes too big for his face. He chose not to admit that that little boy looked a lot like him at one point, desperate and starving.

"With the addition of Dreston's men stationed here in The Wide, that would bring our total to thirteen thousand fighting men."

"My remaining three thousand are stationed in Thea's Point as back up and Baron Thelm has assured me that his three will be stationed in Thelm as reinforcement should we need them." Dreston finished and he and Rarno turned to look at their king.

Curian was sat in silence, staring out into nothing wrapped in layers of dark fur. The cold of the days and nights were getting vicious and the three men wrapped themselves in layers of leathers and furs to try and deter the icy winds and increasingly steady snow.

"Men or boys?"

The two men looked at him, clearly confused as he focused his attention on them completely. Lyon thankfully said nothing but Rarno just looked tired as he said,

"Arms to win your war Curian, that's all that matters."

"*My* war?" Rarno was smart enough not to answer that. "My war indeed." Curian mumbled to himself as he reached out to take the latest conscription list into his hands and went through the names.

"Twelve?"

"Your Majesty?" Lyon asked.

"There is a twelve-year-old on this list!"

"We need hands to cook meals, fetch bedding and food and the like." Curian breathed a sigh of relief as he looked at the description and saw that the boy was to be used as a kitchen aid.

"No children are to fight in this war, do both of you understand me?"

"We would never…" Curian shot Dreston a look of contempt that shut the man down immediately. "Yes, your Majesty."

Curian let out another pent-up breath before Rarno begun to speak,

"We've received a message from Agmantia your Majesty, from Queen Nucea."

Curian's interest was piqued as he looked up from the conscription list still in his hand

"Good news I hope?"

"Not bad news. She says one of her most trusted is looking into your request and you will have your answer soon."

"Diplomatic as ever I see," Curian was deflated.

Agmantia were meant to be the salvation he needed to defeat Briseis. If the Agmantian Assassins could get rid of her, then there would be no reason for Briseis' war.

Despite his position, he was powerless to stop her going ahead with it and he knew many of the nobleman were on her side, for what they saw as his lack of action against the Samai.

He didn't know what more they wanted. He had rid them of Alexander's reign eighteen years ago and despite the deterioration of the land that was completely out of his control; what else was he expected to do?

Everything would be righted, Curian mused to himself; all would be well once the Agmantians got involved.

He turned to Lyon, not particularly interested in speaking with the man but needing to hear it anyway. He was dressed as ever too loudly, and it irked him.

"Do you have anything better to report?" Dreston nodded,

"I believe so your majesty, I was invited to speak with the princess last night and it was interesting to say the least."

"Oh?" Rarno asked,

"Yes, while with the princess she expressed that I was now included in her inner circle and there was nothing she wouldn't share with me."

"Well that's fantastic," Curian piped up. "What have you learned?"

"I've learned that she wishes to ally herself with me and make me king."

"King!" both Rarno and Curian bellowed in astonishment.

"Upon marrying her of course. She was quite obvious in that being the requirement."

Rarno and Curian looked at each other then back at the baron, unable to process what he had just declared.

"Where is Briseis now, she did not return to camp with you?"

"The men tell me that she will return shortly; she spends most of her time training or in war meetings with her General." Rarno spat the word and all heard the distain in it.

"Why have you not brought him into your plans Dreston; he seems to be the closest to her?"

"Too close one would say," Rarno said venomously but Curian shot him down with a look before turning to Lyon.

"Though General Rarno may be correct in his assumption that is exactly the reason we can't get General Beardmore involved. He is the closest to Briseis and as such would never betray her. I have seen him take down a man for simply speaking to her incorrectly before she could."

"Perhaps he did so as mercy," the king said and the two other men nodded in agreement and a silence fell over them as they contemplated the implications of Lyon words. Rarno was the first to speak,

"It seems Baron Dreston may be the key after all. If we can get you to bed Briseis and get her secrets, then all is not lost! She won't know anything about our possible alliance with the Agmantians"

"Rarno you forget yourself; she is my daughter."

"The daughter you wish to kill, and you're worried about a man bedding her?"

"I wish her evils to cease; that doesn't require defilement in the process!" Curian bellowed and Rarno smartly said nothing. Curian narrowed his eyes angrily at his best friend and said,

"I do this thing for reasons beyond your comprehension but do not ever think, that I am comfortable with taking the life of my only child!"

Curian rose from his seat at the head of the table and turned to Baron Dreston,

"Do what you must but find me a way to lessen her power."

"Yes, your Majesty," Curian left them and marched directly out of the tent.

NO SAMAI ALLOWED

Trista and her friends had been travelling for hours, but on their final stretch to Thelm, they came to a stop.

Ahead of them lay a strip of buildings that looked to be the remnants of a very small town. This close to the city, towns and villages lessened, as to the north were the notorious mountain tribes and further south was The Forest and the sea.

As they got closer, they saw that it was more a large market than a town, with a number of stalls lined up but ransacked and broken.

It was clear from the tendrils of smoke rising from the rooftops and the steadily rising groans of the people coming into focus; that something terrible had happened.

"What the hell happened?" Dana asked in horror as she rode in beside Oren. Lamya, Trista and Thorn pulled up the rear and the five of them looked down at the three, injured people on the floor in front of them and the broken market beyond. Dana jumped down and rushed to the person, a man closest to her and saw instantly that he was dead. Knowing there was nothing she could do for him she hurried to the woman closest to him and saw that she was unconscious from a deep cut to her head.

The other four dismounted and entered the battered town, surveying the devastation around them. While Dana worked on the woman on the ground, the rest of them uncovered a heap of corpses and stalls still burning with small fires.

"What in the world happened here?" Lamya asked as she turned her face away from a dead child in the middle of the road. "I can't see through all this pain."

"Bandits," Oren supplied the answer as he came up behind her. Trista looked over at him from where she extinguished a small fire, annoyed with his very presence but saying nothing. Oren crouched and placed his hand to the ground. It was freshly trampled, and the air was thick with an intensity that was hard to describe.

"We should leave…they could be back any minute."

"We have to help these people Oren," Dana looked up from where she had cleaned and attempted to patch up the woman's wound. "We can't leave them here."

"We didn't put them here," Oren said simply.

"What do you suggest we do, leave them here to die?" Dana stood up to challenge him and the others looked on. She looked up at him, her hands on her hips in defiance, showing no fear of the menacing warrior in front of her.

"Do you suggest we take them with us?"

"I don't care what we do as long as it's not leaving them in the middle of the street like roadkill!"

"We need to leave before whoever did this comes back to finish the job."

"I didn't think the great Oren Antos would be scared of a fight." Oren scoffed, looking down at the small girl.

"I'm not scared of anything, but this isn't our fight."

"Oh no?"

Everyone turned to face where Trista was facing a barely upright wall. Oren, never one to be shocked actually looked disturbed. "Then what do you call that?"

"Oh Gods," Lamya covered her mouth with one hand and her heart with another.

"What does that mean?" Thorn asked innocently and without looking back at him but walking towards it, Oren replied,

"This is the symbol for the Everlasting," he reached out towards the faded orb with lines coming out of it and traced his fingers over the crudely painted thick red 'X' across it. "It means no Samai allowed."

"Damn right it does," the five of them turned towards the voice that had spoken and were met by a large group of armed men; bandits as Oren had guessed.

There were probably fifteen or so of them, thinly armoured but heavily armed and instinctively, Oren and Trista stepped forward while Dana stepped back, edging closer to her horse where her staff was strapped. She unhooked it and held it gently by her side.

Lamya and Thorn remained by each other's side, the former reaching into her robes for the dagger she always kept with her.

"Where are you headed?"

"None of your business," Trista replied. "Now get out of the way. We don't want to hurt you." The leader, they assumed he was the leader from the way he carried himself at the front, burst into disparaging laughter. His companions followed suit,

"You think you can hurt us?" the leader said, baring a full mouth of crooked and dirty teeth. "We're going to be the ones doing the hurting sweetheart."

Trista drew her sword, but the men just laughed even further,

"Tough one I see," the leader stepped forward with his men following suit. "Let's see how tough you are when me and all my friends here, take you in the dirt like the Samaian filth you are."

Oren stepped forward drawing both his swords, the steel slicing against their holders making a screeching noise that sent shivers down everyone's spines. The laughter immediately ceased,

"Give me a reason to use these," Oren warned through gritted teeth. The bandit leader looked from Oren to Trista, then back again.

"Oh, is this your whore?" Trista hated that she felt uncomfortable, and it wasn't anything to do with the bandit calling her a whore, but the implication that she belonged to Oren.

"We'll save you for last," the leader looked Oren dead in the face. "So, you can watch us tear…her…in…two." The man licked his broken chapped lips and Trista felt like she'd be sick.

In an instant, the bandit leader rushed forward, drawing his sword as he did so and going straight for Trista. Trista was ready for his attack, to defend herself but quicker than she could register, Oren was in front of her, blocking the bandit leaders overhead strike. The man was momentarily shocked by the resistance he faced but rose to the challenge soon enough. He and Oren engaged in suddenly fierce combat, as the rest of his men moved in.

Trista quickly moved from behind Oren and made her way toward the men, Dana now at her side and Lamya just a little way behind. The men thought their job would be easy, but Trista reached out her hand and pushed them back with her powers. The force was powerful, knocking the fourteen remaining men in a wide radius, slamming against the walls of the broken buildings around them.

The women used the bandit's disorientation to their advantage, and Trista barrelled towards two of the men closest to her. She stabbed one through the gut and after pulling her sword from inside him, she sliced open the belly of the other. She moved onto to their comrades, to kill or dismember, she didn't care. Dana and Lamya each attacked a man of their own, using their size to get away and under their vicious attacks until they had an opening to kill.

She turned briefly to where Oren, having cut the lead bandits arm off, held him against the wall with his power while he fought with another two bandits. Knowing he would be okay, but not sure why Oren had chosen to have the man hanging there, Trista turned her attention to where Dana smashed her thick staff across the back of another man, knocking him into the ground.

During their travels, Trista was not the only one who had trained with Oren. Dana had continued the training she had started with Nyron and Naima but since then, they'd encountered no one to try it on. When Trista watched Dana, ram the end of her staff into the back of the man's head, knocking him completely unconscious, she knew her best friend could handle herself.

Her observations took only a few seconds, but in that time, another bandit almost caught her off guard, but Trista elbowed him in the face. The man screamed out in pain as his nose shattered. Trista kicked him in the groin as he stumbled backwards, then fell to the floor in excruciating pain. She didn't bother to attack him again, running over to where another bandit suddenly grabbed Lamya from behind. She was in the middle of stabbing a man through the throat, when his comrade came up behind her. He dragged her back by her hair, turning her neck at an awkward angle but Trista ran up and severed his hand from his arm.

Shocked, the man stumbled back clutching his bleeding arm to his chest. Lamya turned, in her own amazement and smiled thankfully. The girls didn't waste time with talking as they both turned onto another foe. Dana and Oren were still engaged in their own battles, Dana now sweeping a man's legs from under him before ramming the end of her staff into his throat, breaking his windpipe. The two men that Oren had been fighting lay broken on the floor beside him while another two approached him; desperate to be the one to take him down.

Trista stopped briefly, catching her breath when all of a sudden,

"Trista behind you!" The final bandit, one they'd obviously lost count of, barrelled towards her and hit her with a solid punch to the face. Trista stumbled before collapsing onto her back, her vision dazed by the punch.

Her attacker stood over to crouch, ready to pummel into her but Trista pushed at him blindly with her power sending him flying clear across the street and into the wall of the building behind him.

With the lack of control and concentration, the wall cracked around him from the force at which she'd thrown him, knocking him unconscious. Dazed, Trista tried to get to her feet, looking for her sword before she felt someone grab hold of her hair and drag her to her feet.

"Aaargh!" Trista screamed, her head still ringing from the punch.

The man who had grabbed her held her hair to bend her neck back as he put a knife to her throat.

"Let him go!" he screamed near her face, his breath rancid and spit flying everywhere. "Let them go or I'll kill her!"

Her neck was bent so far; she could see nothing but sky and inches of a scruffy beard. With her face burning with an impending bruise and her vision blurred, Trista closed her eyes and *repelled* at the body behind her, sending herself darting forward and back into the dirt, face first.

The man's knife had been so close to her neck, it sliced deep into her neck as she fell forward. Blood oozed out of her neck as she pressed her hand to it, trying to keep it in.

She staggered toward her sword she finally saw discarded on the ground before she almost fell onto it, but someone caught her at the last moment.

"I've got you."

Lamya's red hair was all Trista could see clearly as she began to get faint from her loss of blood. Lamya placed a cloth against Trista's neck,

"Press down as hard as you can."

Lamya walked her back to the horses, Trista's sword now in one hand.

As they walked quickly back to their steeds, Trista eyed Dana rushing over to them, a bloody staff in her hand.

"Where's…Oren?" she said faintly,

"I'm right here," came Oren's voice as he ran up to them. Even in her dazed state, she saw fists were covered in blood.

Oren took her from Lamya without saying a word and lifted his bloodied hand to her wound. His hand began to glow, and Trista shrieked out in pain, before her head lolled in exhaustion.

"What did you do?" Lamya demanded, Dana now by her side.

"Sealed the wound," he said moving his hand away so Lamya could see that he had indeed closed Trista's flesh around the wound. It looked angry, like a welt that could easily be ripped open "It will hold until we get to Thelm, but it won't last forever and hurts like hell."

Oren leant Trista against Lamya again before quickly leaving to mount Titan. When he returned, he lifted Trista with his magic onto the horse with him.

"I can…ride," she said faintly as her head lolled backwards against his arm. Oren didn't reply,

"Yah!" he said as he took off into the town, leaping Titan over the discarded bodies, that he, Dana, Lamya and Trista had left behind.

Lamya quickly rushed over to Trista's horse, taking its reins to have it run alongside her own. Dana was already mounted and took off after Trista and Oren but Lamya turned and didn't immediately see Thorn.

In all the commotion, she hadn't seen him once…

"Thorn…Thorn!" she called out, worried before she saw him step out from behind a half-broken door, eyes wide with shock and shaking. Lamya rolled her eyes and yelled down to him,

"Keep up!" Lamya mounted her horse and took off after the others. As she left, she didn't notice Thorn straightened and walked casually over to his own steed, mount and trot after them with absolutely no urgency.

When they finally arrived in Thelm, Trista was incredibly weak having lost so much blood. Thankfully, there was no resistance or delay getting through the city gates but when they stopped at the mouth of the city, Oren called out,

"We have to get her cleaned up quickly," Oren held Trista close to him with one hand while the other held Titan's reins.

"We should head straight to the Council, there's no point in getting her settled just to move her again."

"She needs help now Dana!"

"We all need help!" Dana snapped back at him, taking the others by surprise. "We get her to the Council where she needs to be any way and we can all get the help we need."

"Dana's right Oren," Lamya came up quietly beside him in the busy street. "The Council would be better equipped to help us and Trista."

"Or-en," Trista breathed out against his chest. Oren looked down at her,

"What are you up to?"

A city guard called out to them and Oren looked down at him, not in the mood for his attitude,

"We need The Academy; can you tell us where it is?" Lamya said sweetly.

Many years ago, the Lithanian Council became known to the wider world as The Academy in order to protect their location and true purpose. The gargantuan building was indeed a place of learning for all who wished to use the information that was housed there, but their affiliation to the ruling families of various nations was kept secret. People from all over the world travelled there to learn in medicine and sciences and the arts; the same way that others went to Agmantia to train as assassins and Gifted.

It was a way for the Lithanians to hold onto their history as they tried to create the haven and knowledge hub that once was Yzna-Tum. Lamya knew exactly where The Academy was located but it quelled the guard's questioning. The guard, smitten by her beauty, pointed down the main street.

"End of the road, turn left and follow the long road up the hill, you'll find it."

"Thank you, sir," Lamya said sweetly once again and when the guard caught himself smiling, he quickly cleared his throat.

"Now get out of here!"

Oren didn't need to be told twice and motioned Titan into a gallop to get Trista the help she needed.

***

"We go to Thelm," Saicha Voltaire declared as she descended the stairs of their hideaway to the open kitchen where Aslan sat eating breakfast. He had just spooned what looked like porridge into his mouth but it wasn't clear where exactly he would have got it from. As far as Saicha knew, her brother couldn't cook.

"We do?"

Saicha held up the small note she had in her hand and threw it on the table in front of her. She took a seat at the table and poured herself some water before taking a large gulp. Aslan read over the note before putting it back on the table.

"When did you get this?"

"Aurora was at my window this morning." Aslan rolled his eyes at the pride in his sister's words. He couldn't fathom how in love she was with her bird,

"Okay, so we find this," Aslan looked at his mother's words again. "Redeemer and then what? What does that even mean?"

"It's like Atla said and the legend of Assassin Lebai, this Redeemer is meant to claim the Samaian throne."

"And mother wants us to find them?" Saicha raised her eyebrow as if to say, 'it looks that way.'

"If mother wants us to find the Redeemer than she must have already picked a side. If that's the case, then I say we get rid of the princess; daddy's happy and I can go home to a bed and a woman who doesn't smell like horse shit."

Saicha chuckled to herself,

"As colourful as that description is little brother, I will not kill the princess just yet. We stick to the plan: find the king and hear his side before we make any bold decisions."

"And the Redeemer?"

"You read Mother's words, we have to find out if this person even exists and what they plan to do about taking the throne. With any luck, I won't have to kill her."

"Scared?" Aslan teased as they both stood up from the table and he placed his bowl in the sink then made his way over to the staircase.

"Hardly," Aslan poked his tongue out at her making her laugh. "Aslan?"

Her brother stopped to look at her,

"Where did you get the porridge from?"

"One of the guards picked it up for me in town."

"I bet he did," Saicha laughed at her brother's resourcefulness. "Get the men ready, we leave in twenty minutes."

AMONG FRIENDS

The Academy was located at the end of a very long road surrounded by a multitude of trees, shrubbery and flowers. It meandered up into the hills of Thelm so the large building that housed the Council, was hidden almost entirely by the nature around it.

As Oren, Lamya, Dana and Thorn rode their horses towards the main gate, sweating profusely from their ride as well as the heat, it was difficult to believe that directly to the south it was the bitterest of winters. Thelm it seemed, was as yet untouched; if only just this part of it. That the northern most city in the kingdom was as warm as it was, was an issue in itself. Traditions and trade here were entities all on their own and it seemed the weather was no different

The road leading to the large entrance was well travelled and just to the right of the arched entryway was a Guard's House. From here, the roof of a large greenhouse could be seen along with the wooden frames that meant a vegetable garden. There were tall towers that belonged to a building that was still yet to be seen.

Trista had fallen unconscious by the time they approached the guards that were stationed there and was barely breathing. The five horses and riders came to an abrupt stop and Lamya called down to the guard that approached them authoritatively.

"I am Justice Lamya Rubio, here to see my grandmother Chief Justice Yeng. My friend needs help immediately!" Lamya gestured to Trista unconscious in Oren's arms and the guard nodded quickly,

"Yes Justice, go right through to the main building. The Infirmary is the last building to the right, but attendants can direct you further."

"You have my thanks."

Without further delay they set off into the compound and towards the main building. When they finally emerged from beyond the trees and gravelled walkway, the entrance to The Academy was a monster of a thing. A large wooden door, under a stone covering was open and two attendants stood outside waiting for them in black pants and boots and red doublets. They looked pleasant enough but when Oren demanded to be shown to the Infirmary, their displeasure was apparent.

There was an opening between the main building and another and he was directed through it as Lamya and the others dismounted. Stable hands came and took the reins of the horses as they slowly approached the front door.

Lamya, used to the grandeur went straight to the attendants but Dana and Thorn looked around in obvious amazement at the stone structure before them and the nature that shielded them from the outside world.

"My apologies for my friend, our other friend is in a lot of pain, I am Justice Rubio."

The attendant smiled now, pleased with the apology.

"I am Jed, Chief Justice Yeng is expecting you. She did not know when you would arrive, but she told us to be ready. I will take you to her once you are washed and rested, she is currently with the Council." Lamya nodded her thanks and turned to where Dana and Thorn had stepped up by her side.

"These two and the others who went to the Infirmary are my honoured and special guests, you must treat them with the respect you would any other Justice." Jed bowed,

"All was explained by Chief Justice; I will show you to your accommodations while you are with us."

The other attendant remained by the door while Jed led them through the door.

The foyer of The Academy was an incredible thing on first sight. High ceilings and light streaming through the tall glass windows was wonderful and one could truly understand the majesty of the place. There were endless corridors and doors leading to various places of learning and entertainment.

Along with the largest library on the continent, The Academy housed five thousand full time students; half of which lived on the compound. There was an Infirmary, stables, baths and gymnasium along with various other buildings for meditation and other forms of training including military and equestrian.

It took a few moments but when they arrived in the dormitory halls, Jed led Thorn to his room first.

"You will be housed here with the other males,"

"Males and females are housed separately?" Dana asked.

"Unless you are a couple, same sex or not, we are housed separately for use of the washrooms and the like; couples have en-suites."

"What's an en-suite?" Jed looked confused but Lamya smiled,

"It is a bathroom that is connected to the room itself Dana." Embarrassed, Dana said nothing, but Jed only turned to show Thorn into a small though comfortable looking room. There was a single bed in the corner with a small desk and chair and a wardrobe for his clothes.

"The washrooms are three doors down on your left," Jed offered. "Should you need anything else, please ring this bell." He gestured to a long rope hanging beside the door.

"Lunch will be served at midday in the dining hall."

Thorn didn't say anything but nodded his thanks and stepped into the room, closing the door without any word to

Dana or Lamya. The women looked at one another, confused but said nothing as Jed led them to the female dorms.

"Our other friend, Oren, where will he sleep?"

"We will find a room for him."

They took a small flight of stairs to another level and after Jed showed Dana where she would be sleeping and the female washrooms, they led Lamya to another much larger room at the end of the corridor.

"Justice Rubio, your room is your old one, but we have since cleaned it for you in preparation for your arrival." Lamya nodded her thanks with an added smile.

"If you need anything, please ring the bell and lunch is again, at midday."

"Thank you, Jed, but, when can I see my friend? She was taken to the Infirmary."

"You can visit whenever you wish; the physicians will determine who can receive visitors." Dana nodded her thanks with a smile.

Jed turned from them then and disappeared down the large corridor. Lamya stepped into her old room and Dana followed, stopping in the doorway. Lamya scanned the room she hadn't been in for nearly twenty years and felt at peace.

"I won't stay long," Dana said. "But I just wanted to say thank you,"

"Thank you, what on earth for?"

"For being here, for getting us in here so quickly. Just…everything."

Lamya smiled and walked up to Dana to pull her into her arms for a tight hug,

"We're halfway there," she said into the young girl's ear. "Now that we are at the Council, my grandmother and the other Justices will do all in our power to get everyone ready for the battle to come. Everything will be fine Dana."

"I hope so," Lamya pulled away from her and the two women smiled at each other reassuringly before Dana's smile faded slightly.

"What is it?"

"I killed a man today."

"What?"

"Today, one of the bandits…I killed him."

"They were going to kill us Dana,"

"Oh, I know, I'm not sorry he's dead. I'm amazed that I did it…I killed a man."

"I see," Lamya pushed a strand of Dana's now very long brown hair away from her face that was smeared with dirt, blood and sweat.

"You are capable of many things Dana, even killing and before this journey is over you may very well have to kill a lot of people. Are you ready for that?"

"I think I am…that's what worries me." Lamya smiled, "The short time I spent with Nyron, I always wanted to learn to protect myself and Trista if necessary but now I know what I'm capable of…it feels like so much more."

"It's a great responsibility to go into battle knowing yourself or others may not return, but if you know you are doing so to do what's right, then you have to hold onto that."

Dana nodded,

"I will," Dana pulled Lamya back into a hug. "Thank you again."

They agreed to meet back at Lamya's room in an hour then make their way to the Infirmary. The girls went to Thorn's room but he wasn't there and thinking he would be visiting Trista, they made their way to the Infirmary instead.

Oren sat beside Trista's bed watching her sleep once she'd been admitted.

She had lost a lot of blood that while the physicians had replaced with the use of skill and a little magic; from where he didn't know, she was still very weak.

She was out of the woods for now, but he hated that she had been hurt in the first place. He should have protected her better, kept her out of harm's way and this wouldn't have happened.

One of the assistants had told him there would be a room available for him in the dorms but he'd refused to leave until he knew she was doing okay.

Once they had patched her up and she was resting comfortably; he'd made his way to the dorms to wash and change then returned immediately.

When he got back, the girls were outside arguing to one of the attendants,

"What's going on?"

"They won't let us see Trista, they said only one visitor at a time."

"Who's in there with her?" Oren asked, on edge. Everyone who cared enough about her was standing right in front of him.

"They won't say," Dana huffed.

Oren looked at the puny little man and pushed past him into the room where Trista slept,

"Sir, you can't go in there! Sir!" the man tried to shout but was restricted because of the other patients. He grabbed after Oren's arm but one look from the mighty warrior and he shrunk back.

Oren continued his march to Trista's bed side and was surprised to see a woman sitting on the chair beside her bed.

The woman didn't look up at him or acknowledge his presence in any way.

"Who are you? Get away from her!" Oren snapped, all etiquette and protocol out of the window as he placed his hand on the hilt of his sword.

"She's beautiful."

It was all she said before the woman stood from the chair and turned to face Oren.

The early afternoon sun streamed through the window lighting up her face and in an instant; Oren dropped to one knee in submission,

"My humblest apologies your Majesty."

Oren atoned as he came face to face, with Queen Rowan Antonides of Mortania.

DEFIANCE

Briseis lay asleep in bed with Gardan after an intense lovemaking session when she was jolted awake by a sensation so intense, she knew exactly what it meant. She couldn't put her feelings into words, but with a certainty she couldn't explain, Briseis knew that the warrior she had been looking for had well and truly awakened. The feeling pulsed within her like a heartbeat, an essence of pure energy that literally took her breath away. Briseis sat up, holding her hand to her chest as she tried to regulate her breathing.

"Briseis what's wrong?"

Her name sounded odd coming from his lips as he had always referred to her as *Princess* or your Highness. She found she enjoyed when he called out her name when they made love and now, when he was trying comfort her.

Gardan was sat up now beside her, his arms around her shoulders as she took deep breaths in and out.

"Water," she breathed out and he quickly jumped from the bed to fetch her a goblet of water from her dresser.

She registered briefly his tight naked buttocks before he turned back to her and held the cup to her lips, holding her while she did so. She took a few sips until she felt well enough to speak and Gardan sat on the edge of the bed beside her.

"Are you okay?"

"We must leave today."

"Leave for where?"

"The Wide," she drank some water again as she still felt incredibly weak.

This was different to all the other times she had felt the Redeemer; it was as though there was an added presence of some kind. The energy she felt now was extremely powerful and in the recesses of her mind, Briseis knew it would only get stronger.

"They are on their way to us; I can feel it Gardan."

"What are you going to do?" he asked quietly, unsure of how he could help her when everything to do with her powers, was so far out of his control.

"I will kill her," she said it with such finality it made his blood run cold. "I will kill their precious Redeemer, then Rowan when I find her and anyone she cares about. I'll destroy the entire Samaian race if I have to before I let them beat me."

Briseis turned to look at Gardan but he had nothing left to say, this was all beyond him.

"My father remains at The Wide yes?" Gardan nodded, "Tell him to send additional men to assist Baron Thelm's men. Anything that comes out of Thelm and I mean anything, I want them slaughtered do you hear me?"

"Yes Princess."

Gardan watched Briseis as she turned over in her bed and lay there, unmoving until she went back to sleep. Gardan took a deep and laboured breath and prayed Briseis would find the outcome she was looking for because if she didn't, Gods help them all.

***

Lyon sat with Aml in his rooms going over the last few items on their inventory. They had been instructed by General Beardmore that they would be heading out to The Wide with the might of the crown in a matter of hours and he had to make sure his household was in order.

Geneiva would play her part by way of handling the domestic capacity, but he; through Aml would handle the finances and everything else that entailed.

He had been travelling to and from the Imperial Lands for the past few days to speak with the king but living at a war camp for an unknown amount of time took a lot more preparation.

"Where is Alaina?"

"Lord?" Aml looked up from the inventory book he was populating, confused. Lyon didn't bother to register it and spoke again,

"Alaina, you took her from me when she betrayed my trust, but I wish her to accompany me to The Wide. Where is she?"

Aml cleared his throat,

"She went to perform the task you set her and succumbed to an infection?"

"Succumbed?" Lyon was confused as Aml nodded his head and finally the penny dropped.

"I see," Lyon turned away from Aml and looked out of the window that overlooked the sea.

He'd always loved the sea even though living in Dreston didn't give him much ways to indulge in it. He spent time in his summer homes in the south near the water, but admittedly it was never enough.

"Find me a replacement immediately."

"Yes lord," Aml said quietly. "If that is all, I will make arrangements for our departure."

"Yes, make sure Erik and Geneiva are ready also"

"Yes lord," he heard Aml depart and exhaled.

Lyon couldn't put his finger on it, but something was going on. The princess' sudden departure to The Wide, despite it always their destination was unexpected. What had changed for her that she now wanted to head out to war so quickly?

He would have more time to spend with her once they got to camp he knew, but considering her affiliation with General Beardmore, he was no longer entirely sure where he stood with her.

He was running out of time to get the all his players on the chessboard and indebted to him before Briseis discovered what he was up to and had him killed.

Baron Lyon Dreston was particularly fond of his life and planned to do anything necessary to keep it.

***

Curian was walking through camp that afternoon, speaking with his most senior officers about the current situation.

"The men are getting restless your majesty," one of them said. "The weather is unforgiving, and they are not being used."

The questions were there:

Why were they just waiting around?

Why were they not fighting or even marching to fight?

"The men are worried your majesty,"

"Worried about what?" Curian said with Rarno by his side although he knew what was coming. The officer swallowed before answering,

"They wish to fight and are worried, as ever respectfully; that there is in fact no war."

Curian was silent for a moment, steadying his anger that he knew didn't need to be directed at the officer.

The atmosphere was tense, everyone waiting for his response as they continued to walk through the bitter winds of the camp.

"His Majesty wil—"

"MESSENGER!" the deep voice of a soldier calling out the arrival of a messenger distracted them all and they turned to see the rider approach.

The green clothed rider dismounted and bowed respectfully, out of breath before approaching Curian with an outstretched note. He took it, nodding his thanks before ripping Briseis' seal from the top.

After reading, he re folded the paper and turned to the officer,

"It seems your men have their wish."

"What is it Curian?" Rarno asked,

"Have a party of men from each unit set out for Thelm, the Redeemer has arrived there, and we must see the might of their army. If there is any opportunity to dispose of the threat before they arrive at The Wide, then I want your men to take it."

The officer was delighted and bowed his thanks before marching away to issue his orders.

"What's going on?" Curian turned to Rarno and said,

"Briseis has informed me that the Redeemer is in Thelm; she felt their power apparently."

"Apparently?" Rarno was sceptically. "We're sending able bodied men out into the country on a whim?"

"It is not a whim!" Curian snapped. "Despite my plans for her, Briseis has learned to use the Everlasting much better than I ever did and I believe what she says." Rarno nodded. Even he understood the Briseis was powerful in the way of the Samaian power.

"Get your men ready to leave at a moment's notice, this war is going to begin sooner than any of us expected."

A CLEAR CONSCIENCE

The day was drawing to a close by the time Saicha, Aslan and two of their men arrived in the Imperial Lands.

The sibling team had stopped in Thea's Point to restock for the journey including furs and of course food and Saicha bought a few beauty products she'd failed to bring from home.

"No one cares what you look like big sister, I promise you!" Aslan teased as they arranged travel for the rest of their party back to Agmantia.

They wouldn't need as many men and if Rian was asked to send an army to Mortania, then those men would be better used as a part of it from the very beginning.

"I care," came Saicha's blunt reply as she placed the lipstick, eye powder and a few scented oils for her hair into her bag.

"Why, is there someone you want to impress?" Saicha ignored him, "Someone special back at the Guild you want to run his fingers in those scented tresses!"

Aslan began to laugh himself hoarse but Saicha simply ignored him until he said,

"Are you a virgin?"

"*Excuse me*, that's *none* of your business!" Aslan huffed,

"That means yes,"

"No, it doesn't, it means what it means!"

"If you weren't, you'd just say," Aslan shrugged as he paid for the extended dock space and turned to head back to their horses and remaining men. The Point was cramped as always but it was with an air of excitement today that hadn't been there when they arrived.

"You shouldn't be asking me that, I'm your sister!"

"If we were Coznian royalty, we could be married so what's the difference?" Aslan laughed teasingly.

"The difference is we're *not* Coznian; we're Agmantian and in light of that, we will not continue this ridiculous conversation!"

Saicha stood staring at her brother after her rant and Aslan raised his index finger to his lip; his chin resting on his thumb and said,

"So, what you're saying is, you're a virgin *and* you've never been kissed."

"Argh!" Saicha huffed her annoyance and walked away with Aslan's laughter following behind her.

They'd sent a message back to Nucea and Rian with Aurora before heading off towards the now desolate area where Briseis and Curian held their army.

They dressed warmly, not used to the cold anyway as Agmantia was almost always hot. It had its wet months, that fed the precipitous rainforest regions of the country but was constantly warm. During the hottest summer periods, richer families would head out of the cities to the coast. There were steps carved into the marble that lined the cliffs and one could walk all the way down, directly into the sea.

Before she'd left for the Guild; Saicha had enjoyed spending time with her mother and father at their palace home in Awnelle, in the province of Aulandri to the south of the continent. It was during those times that she really got to spend time with her mother without her being interrupted with matters of state.

"How do you think Rian is doing?" Saicha asked as they rode steadily through the broken trees and snow-covered ground a while later.

It had amazed them that snow was so thick only an hour or so from the city and Thea's Point.

"I think Rian is doing perfectly as he always does." Saicha looked at her brother,

"Why'd you say it like that?"

"Like what?"

"Like you're resentful," she said but Aslan didn't reply and for some reason she knew not to push it,

"Do you know he wants to marry?"

"To whom?" Saicha was shocked, Rian hadn't mentioned anything about marriage or even that he was seeing someone. She knew she and her brother weren't best friends, but she had been home for two years, she thought she would have heard something about his betrothal

"Luna."

"Oh," was all Saicha could think to say.

Luna Boltese was the daughter of a High Lord in Agmantia and as such had grown up among the royal children as well as people of her own station.

She was also, the love of Aslan's life.

She was in fact Rian's age but Aslan had loved her near his entire life, but this seemingly wasn't reciprocated. Saicha and played with the girl before she had left for the Guild and even then, she had known Aslan's love for her.

"Does she want to marry him?" Saicha finally asked and Aslan sneered,

"The Crown Prince who will one day be king or the spare political failure three years her junior…who would you pick?" Saicha rolled her eyes but was serious when she replied,

"If a woman is swayed by titles and grandeur, why would you want her?"

Aslan didn't reply but when she turned her eyes to him, her brother smiled appreciatively and took off into the snow.

It was a long while before they came upon anyone, but when they did, the siblings were astounded at what they found.

"There they are...we'll have to go around."

"Why?" asked Aslan.

"I don't wish to explain to the Mortanian army why Agmantian royalty, one of whom not to mention is an assassin, are travelling through their forces on their way to Thelm."

"I see your point," Aslan said with a cheeky smile. "So, what's the plan?"

Saicha surveyed the numbers before her and after a moment or two she said to the whole team,

"We wait for nightfall, then Aslan and I will go and speak to the king."

"How are we meant to do that?" Aslan asked but Saicha just winked at him,

"We'll rest here until then," the men agreed without question and lay in wait for night to come.

Aslan had to admit that he was impressed with his sister's agility and how she was able to manoeuvre them into the king's tent without making a sound later that night.

She had told him to follow her exact steps so he wouldn't make any noise and by following her footprints in the thick snow; he was able to comply.

There were guards stationed around the tent as was to be expected, but brother and sister took care of them easily. Not wanting or needing to kill anyone just yet, Saicha had brought with her a sedative powder that when inhaled, knocked a person unconscious.

She crept up to the first guard and gently blew the powder in his direction. He sneezed before swiping at his nose and falling to the floor with a thud. She dragged him back into the trees to sleep it off, while Aslan did the same to the other guard.

Saicha motioned for Aslan to follow and within moments, they both stood hooded in the King of Mortania's war tent.

Saicha stepped forward, her face covered as she loomed over the kings sleeping body.

As though he could sense her presence, Curian opened his eyes and wearily said,

"Alexander?"

"No," she and Aslan stepped forward. The king went to yell but Saicha shook her head,

"No guards…no noise. If I wanted to kill you, I could have."

"W-who are you, w-what do you want?" Curian stuttered as he tried to sit upright.

"You asked Agmantia for aid and we have answered."

"You have come for Briseis?" he said hopefully,

"That all depends on you."

"What must I do, I'll do anything!"

"To get rid of your daughter; why?" Aslan asked this time.

Curian got out of his bed to face them on his feet. He was a large man and so wrapped in his furs, he looked like a bear. His hair dishevelled and eyes wide; he looked at them and said,

"She has become a danger to herself and Mortania. I didn't know what I created but she must be stopped. The only way to do that, is to kill her."

"Why can't you do it? Why involve Agmantia at all?"

"She is smart, cunning…evil. Any attempts I would try on her life; she would see coming. I hoped someone of your talents could rid us of her without the war; the bloodshed."

"And what happens to Mortania once Briseis is killed?" Saicha asked. "What will you do once your only child and heir is no longer of this place?"

Curian took a moment to answer before looking away, "I will find a way to atone for my wrongdoings…I will find a way to make amends."

"Amends for what?" Aslan again.

Curian said nothing for a very long time but the siblings didn't push him; realising that this man was dealing with something they had yet to fully understand.

"Have you ever…hurt someone and realised it much too late?" the question was rhetorical and so they didn't answer. "I hurt many people…too many and now I need to fix it. Can you help me or not?"

"Why should we?" Saicha asked simply.

"If you were not going to help, then why have you come!" Curian snapped and stepped forward but Saicha drew a dagger and Aslan reached to the hilt of his sword, both shaking their heads under their hooded robes.

"We do not take death lightly old man, and neither should you. This is a thing that can never be undone. For this act, we must ask why, and you will tell us."

The tip of Saicha's dagger was inches from his face and Curian stared at it, eyes wide as he swallowed and slowly stepped back,

"Tell us old king," Aslan murmured. "Tell us why we should help you clear your conscience."

This time there was no hesitation as Curian opened his mouth and replied defeated,

"Because I am too weak to do it alone."

Saicha felt Aslan turn his head briefly to look at her but she said nothing as she lowered her dagger and replaced it within her robes.

"You called us Alexander when you awoke...who is he?" Curian looked down, ashamed and Saicha waited patiently to hear his response,

"He is the person I hurt...the man I wronged."

Saicha and Aslan were silent for a while as they pondered the old king before them. Aslan said nothing, knowing his sister was the one running the show and sighed inwardly as she finally said,

"We will do this thing," Curian looked up at them instantly, eyes wide with joy that tears rimmed the edges. "Tell no one of this meeting, not even those who might have known you called for us."

Curian nodded,

"Resume preparations for your war as normal..."

"With Briseis dead, there need be no war!"

"Resume preparations as normal," Saicha repeated herself sternly "Briseis will die as you've asked."

Curian said nothing to Saicha's knife sharp response. Without another word, Saicha turned and exited the tent with Aslan close behind.

They didn't speak until they were back in the relative safety of their own camp,

"When will you do it?" Aslan asked as he dismounted but Saicha shook her head,

"Not me,"

"Who then?"

"The Redeemer." Aslan was confused but as she dismounted her own horse and removed her hood and mask, Saicha explained,

"Curian feels regret for killing the Samaian King and if legend and Mother are to be believed; that king was the Redeemer's father. This kill isn't ours to make Aslan, but the princess must die; that much is clear."

"Curian asked for Agmantia's help, not some person we don't even know exists or who might not be up to the task!"

"I realise that Aslan and we will help, I just won't make the kill myself…it's not my place."

Aslan shook his head but shrugged as he began to undo his robes,

"I hope Mother agrees with you."

"She will. She asked us to determine whose side we should be on and we have. We will side with the Redeemer and help defeat Briseis' army."

A MOTHER'S LOVE

Rowan Illiya-Antonides stepped graciously from around her daughter's bed in a long black gown beautifully embroidered with silver thread along the bodice and sleeves. Her hair was piled on top of her head in an abundance of curls that was slowly greying at the front and back.

Her eyes looked tortured, sad as she approached Oren to place her delicate hand on his shoulder, indicating that he should rise. He did so immediately and looked down into her eyes, his face a picture of adulation.

"At ease," she said, acknowledging his military stance and Oren complied. "To whom do I owe the safety of my daughter?"

"Oren Antos your Majesty," he said quietly, looking straight at her and just as Rowan's head tilted questioningly, her eyes lit up with sheer joy. Rowan reached her arms out to pull Oren into a hug.

Oren hugged her back, tightly and they stood that way for a moment before Rowan pulled away to hold him at arm's length. She looked up at him with a beaming smile before reaching up to cup his cheek,

"You've grown so much I didn't recognise you…but I see him now. Where is your father?" Oren's eyes turned away and Rowan caught her breath as she pulled Oren into a hug again.

"We've all lost so much," she whispered into his chest as they held one another. "I'm so sorry Oren."

"Thank you, Aunt Rowan. Naima and Nyron will bring him soon to perform the rituals…will you, do it?" Rowan looked up at him,

"The twins are here too?" she asked excitedly, and Oren nodded with a smile,

"They will be."

"Of course, I will perform the rituals for Gorn...he was one of the best men I ever knew, along with your Uncle Theon."

Rowan pulled away again but this time, she took his hand and they walked back to the other side of Trista's bed.

Rowan looked down at her sleeping daughter, Oren's large hand between hers and sighed.

"I want her to wake up as much as I don't."

"Why?" Rowan took a moment before she said,

"I don't want her to hate me when she does."

Oren said nothing, it wasn't his place but even he knew that Trista had some underlying issues with her mother that would have to be addressed.

"She's so beautiful," Rowan said softly, and Oren nodded, "Yes...she is."

Rowan looked up at him, once again with a questioning look.

"Does she know?"

"No,"

"I see...I have a lot of explaining to do."

"Yes, but not that...not yet."

"Very well."

The two of them stood watching her for a moment longer before Oren turned to her,

"We've travelled with some companions; one of whom would like to see her desperately and were denied entry."

"That's my fault entirely, please, tell your friends to come in." Oren nodded and left her side to let Dana and Lamya know they could enter. Oren didn't dwell on the fact that Thorn was still nowhere to be seen.

"Your Majesty," Lamya said instantly as she dropped into a curtsy and Dana followed although she didn't look happy about it. Rowan made her way to them and smiled at Lamya,

"You must be Lamya, your Grandmother has spoken highly of you. Thank you, for all that you have done for my daughter."

"It has been my utmost pleasure your Majesty." Lamya said.

When Rowan turned to Dana however, she visibly straightened and asked,

"And what is your name?"

"Dana, Dana Black. I'm Trista's best friend…where have you been all this time?"

"Dana!" Oren snapped at her, a huge scowl on his face but Rowan lifted her arm gently, silencing him. She lowered it again and placed it demurely in front of her as she replied,

"A perfectly valid question and one that I will answer in due course. Thank you for caring so much about my daughter Dana, but I think my explanations should go to her first."

"Then start talking."

Everyone's head turned to Trista's bed where she was now wide awake and looking directly at them.

She was still laying down of course but she was looking over at them with determination and clear resentment; to who, they weren't sure just yet, but it wasn't hard to figure out.

"Trista!" Dana rushed over to her and collapsed onto her friend in a loving embrace. Trista closed her eyes as she held Dana closely,

"Are you okay?" Dana asked softly as Trista hugged her back as best, she could.

"I've been better," she joked. Dana got up from their hug and stood beside the bed with Trista's hand in hers. Oren and Lamya approached the end of the bed, looking down at her and she smiled her thanks.

Rowan stayed back, looking over at the quartet.

"Thank you," Trista said looking at Oren. "I remember being on your horse…thank you." Oren simply nodded.

Everyone was quiet, not sure of how to approach the situation,

"Could you help me?" Trista said carefully, her neck sore from her cut and bandages. Dana helped her to sit upright, fluffing the pillows behind her so she could rest comfortably. Once she was done, Trista smiled at her friends,

"Could you leave us for a moment please?"

"Of course, we'll be outside if you need anything." Lamya said quietly. With a kiss from the girls and an unexpected bow from Oren, Trista's three friends left the room; leaving her with the mother she had never really met.

Rowan and Trista stood for a long time looking at one another, not saying a word. There was a clear energy pulsating between them but neither of them addressed it.

"They were right," Trista piped up almost angrily. "I do look like you."

"No, Rowan replied softly. "You look like your father."

Trista looked away, her heart beating a little faster at the compliment but not wanting to dwell on it too heavily. She would never know or meet Alexander; Rowan was standing right here, finally.

Rowan was everything and nothing she had ever imagined. She was petite but her aura made her seem twelve feet tall. She had an air about her that was so positively regal it was hard not to feel intimidated. The gown she wore was immaculately tailored, clinching in her small waist and she even wore jewels. For some reason this angered Trista and out of nowhere she flared up at her,

"Where *have* you been?"

Finally, Rowan stepped forward and once again went to the other side of the bed. She took a seat in the vacant chair and held out her hands to take Trista's but, the young woman pulled her hands away. Hurt, Rowan retreated her own hands and folded them neatly into her lap.

"The night your father was killed," Rowan choked on the word and Trista hated that she felt sorry for her. It was spiteful but she didn't care.

"I escaped with you and my Lady in Waiting and Queen's Guard Captain Lenya." Rowan continued. "My sister Rayne had already evacuated the city along with many others loyal to us and I had no way of contacting them until I got to safety. Once, we were free of the castle, we travelled the distance to Thelm, relying on royalists to get us safely out of the capital and into the North."

Rowan took a moment, the memories so obviously painful,

"I was trying to return home, to Illiya where I thought I could find a way to protect us. I knew those walls like no other and I thought I could keep us safe there." Tears pooled in the pits of Rowan's eyes as the memories and pain of her ordeal came flooding back.

"I was so wrong Trista," her voice faltered slightly as she looked up at her daughter, eyes brimming with tears. "We were together only a year before I couldn't stop our power from radiating…you were just too strong. I knew I couldn't risk leading Curian's men right to us and so…I decided to let you go."

Rowan reached out then and although Trista tried to snatch her hands away, Rowan didn't let her and gripped her child's hands like a vice,

"It was the hardest thing I have ever had to do Trista; you have to know that! I had just lost your father and our entire family was lost to the cause; all I had left was you!"

"I had to send you away to protect you, to protect *us*; surely you understand that?" Trista tore her hands away again.

"I might understand Rowan; I just don't agree with it!"

"What should I have done?" Rowan asked simply, although tears had now escaped and dripped down her face. "What should I have done in your mind?" Trista was angry.

She didn't have the answers, that was Rowan's job. This woman was meant to provide answers to the questions that had been brewing inside her from before she could remember.

"I don't know!" Trista screamed at her and instantly regretted her. Her throat was still very sore from her wound. "I just know that I would *never* have left my baby all alone!"

Her head collapsed onto the pillows from anger and exhaustion. Trista turned her face away from Rowan while her own tears threatened to fall.

"Trista…please…I never meant to hurt you."

"But you did!" Trista snapped again, turning back to Rowan this time; tears making her eyes shimmer. "You hurt me without even knowing it! Every day I knew something was missing; that I was different, that I didn't belong and *you* did that to me. My entire miserable life is *all* your fault!"

It felt good to say it out loud and so Trista continued,

"Everyone tells me how powerful you are, all the gifts you have and you couldn't use any one of them to keep me?" Rowan looked horrified, tears falling freely now as she truly saw the depth of Trista's pain.

"Trista, I had used most of my power to get us out of Tirnum alive. After a year of the Everlasting being under Curian's control, there was barely anything left to protect us." Trista rolled her eyes and something in Rowan changed.

Gone was the repentant and softly spoken woman begging for forgiveness and in her place, was a queen who was not about to be spoken to disrespectfully.

"Trista no matter how you feel right now, you will not dismiss me like this. I am your *mother.*" Trista looked her up and down and sneered,

"Some mother, I haven't seen you my entire life!" Trista yelled again, this time not caring about the pain it was causing her as the tears flowed freely down her cheeks. "Where were you when the other girls hit me and called me names and always left me out? Where were you when I *needed* you Rowan?" Rowan didn't say anything.

"You were hiding. Here, wherever but hiding like a coward in your fancy clothes and lavish jewels while I was *alone;* alone without you or Papa or anyone! At least dying was the reason he left me…maybe you should have done the same."

Trista didn't hear or see Rowan's pain more than she *felt* it. It sent a sharp pain through her chest that she fought to ignore; just like the intense guilt at the words she didn't even mean. She couldn't take them back now…she didn't know how.

Rowan said nothing.

She rose quietly from her chair beside the bed and left the Infirmary, stopping once to wipe her face, but never turning to look back.

FEALTY

The Infirmary attendants helped Trista out of bed a few hours later and helped her wash and dress for what was now dinner. Despite not wanting to see anyone since her fight with Rowan, she was ravenous and getting a little cabin fever.

Her wound, though not deep enough to cause any long-term damage, had caused her to lose a lot of blood and so she felt incredibly weak. Even with the transfusion, it would be a day or two before she felt truly herself again.

Dana had returned earlier in the day and explained that she and Oren had met Lamya's Grandmother, the leader of the Council. She explained that they hadn't discussed much, waiting of course for Trista to arrive before they went into any details. Trista thanked her before the attendants came in to administer some more medicine and asked Dana to return later.

Later arrived and Trista had been put in a simple but elegant dark green dress that while brought out her eyes; more importantly had a high neck to cover the bandage around her neck. It had long sleeves with black lace embroidered on the cuffs and hem and clung to her figure. The dress was the most elegant thing she had ever worn, and she shied away from it, not sure how to act in it. The attendants told her not to worry and when they applied some light make up and her curls bounced in all their wonder behind her, she didn't feel so self-conscious about her appearance. Dana arrived some time later and they made their way to the dining hall.

Dana was similarly clothed in a dress of the deepest blue with silver lace but it only had one sleeve. It was nothing like the fashions they had seen in Remora or even Dreston but things were clearly done differently here in Thelm. Dana's hair had been washed and brushed until it shone and with some added make up, she looked wonderful.

"This makes a change doesn't it," Dana smiled as she took Trista's hand.

They walked out of the Infirmary toward the Main Hall, directed by an attendant who walked quietly in front of them.

"A welcome change, that bath was wonderful!" the girls giggled. "How is everyone?"

"We're okay, a little worried I guess but…okay."

"Worried about what?"

"The war of course," Dana looked at her quizzically.

It was interesting, Trista noted that Dana was much more prepared for this battle than she was. Perhaps not physically but more so mentally where Trista still hadn't quite got her head around the fact that she would be expected to fight and kill people or that other people would be doing so in her name.

"Yes…that."

"Yes, the thing we've been travelling weeks to do." Trista nudged Dana playfully,

"I know, I just…it's so real now." Dana silently agreed. "What about Thorn?" Dana looked immediately apologetic as she shrugged.

"I don't know, no one's seen him since we got here."

"What do you mean, didn't he come to visit me?" Dana shook her head.

Trista was saved having to respond as the servant in front of them stopped and gestured to the doors of the Main Hall.

It was a set of large double doors at the back of the large entrance hall. The entrance to The Academy was a short distance behind them, and people milled about going in various directions and talking amongst themselves.

"Please enter when you are ready."

Another servant pushed open the large doors allowing them to enter and Trista and Dana immerged into a sea of chairs and elaborately decorated tables filled with food and people. Enquiring eyes watched their entrance but Trista tried her best not to be intimidated and look straight ahead. The eyes she did catch looking at her were friendly and it slowly eased her fear.

At the far end of the hall she saw one distinctly large table that ran horizontal to the room as opposed to vertically like all the others. Here sat five robed figures with Rowan sat on the left and Lamya on the right of an older woman directly in the middle. It wasn't hard to work out that that must be Lamya's grandmother and so the rest; the remaining members of the Lithanian Council.

Just below them on another table, with two empty seats that Dana and Trista would seemingly take; sat Thorn, Oren and to her surprise, Nyron and Naima.

The girl's faces lit up as they laid eyes on them and not caring who was around them, ran down the aisle towards the twins who stood from their seats to greet them. Trista crashed into Nyron's arms as he came out from behind the table and squeezed her tightly in a loving hug.

"You made it," she whispered into his chest as tears filled her eyes. "I thought I'd never see you again."

"Come on Tris," Nyron said pulling away to look down at her lovingly. "You can't get rid of me that easily."

He wiped an escaped tear from her cheek as she giggled before hugging him again. She left him to swap positions with Dana who pulled away from her hug with Naima.

"I'm so glad you're both okay,"

"Me too." Naima replied squeezing her lovingly.

It wasn't until the old woman rose from her seat, that Trista acknowledged anyone else. She had red hair like her granddaughter but the colour had dimmed with age. There were grey streaks throughout that added to her distinguished demeanour, along with the tailored robes and dazzling gold broach. Her eyes were kind and her smile genuine.

"Welcome Princess, to Thelm and the home of the Lithanian Council." Her voice soothing yet authoritative at the same time. "I am Chief Justice Yeng and these are my fellow Justices Lorien, Lobos and Antyen."

She motioned to an Agmantian man, a Mortanian man and a Coznian woman respectively. Justice Lorien had disapproving eyes, Trista thought; as though he were constantly judging everyone around him. Justice Lobos seemed nice enough, with his greying hair and deeply set blue eyes that pierced your soul with one glance. Lastly, Justice Antyen was a beautiful petite woman, as was natural of her race with thick black hair currently tied in a long braid that hung over her shoulder against porcelain white skin and almond shaped eyes. She smiled at Trista where the others had not and so she smiled back.

"Please, take a seat, eat and we will discuss all after dinner."

"Thank you for your hospitality," Trista said carefully and took the vacant seat in the middle of the table between Dana and Naima. Oren and Nyron sat on one end and Thorn was at the other beside Dana.

Trista looked down the table and smiled briefly at him, and while he smiled back there was something missing from it that she couldn't quite place.

"Is he okay?" Trista whispered to Dana who shrugged as a servant came by offering them food. Not thinking too much of it, she turned to the other end of the table where Oren was looking her way. She smiled tentatively at him and he nodded his head before turning back to his meal.

Dinner proceeded with laughter and conversation between all in attendance and for the first time in a long time, Trista felt safe. She was washed and fed and all the people she cared about were safe in the room with her. She felt a little weary because of the medication they had given her but nothing too strenuous and now, more than anything she was restless. She wanted to get started with these preparations and find out more from Rowan.

She knew she had been cruel to her mother but the anger that had bubbled inside of her at what she saw as a selfish move on Rowan's part couldn't be hidden any longer. It had come out harsher than she had intended but it didn't stop it being true.

She was hurt and Rowan had a lot to prove for her to begin to trust her. Until then, they had a lot of plans and decisions to make, about Briseis and the war that would change all of their lives.

The last of the students and faculty exited the Main Hall and Chief Justice Yeng rose from her seat,

"Come, we shall all meet in the Council Chambers."

Everyone proceeded to follow her through a small door just off the side of the head table. It led up a few flights of winding stairs directly into a large circular room with a sizeable round table in the centre.

It was clear that chairs had been added as the positions were cramped but it would hold the twelve of them just the same.

Chief Justice Yeng sat at what could be described as the head of the table due to the decorative chair that was placed there, and starting from her right everyone else took their seats. Trista ended up between Thorn and Dana and had a clear view of Rowan and Oren opposite her who were speaking in hushed tones.

This irritated her.

What did Oren have to say to her mother that no one else could hear?

The room nodded their agreement and Trista's face heated up.

"We all know why we are here," Yeng continued once everyone was seated and glasses and jugs of water had been laid out on the table. "Her majesty Queen Rowan who has been with us for some time now, has finally been reunited with her only child and heir to the Mortanian throne, Crown Princess Trista Antonides."

"Firstly, I must say welcome once again to the princess." Trista nodded, shy and unwilling for the focus to be on her just yet. "We have anticipated this day for many years and are happy that you have made it to us safely."

Hearing her full, true name from someone else's lips was still intimidating.

"The princess has travelled many days to find us and now that she has, we must put into action what we have been preparing for, for the last sixteen years."

Trista's eyes shot up at that and looked at Yeng questioningly,

"Sixteen…years?" Yeng smiled at her,

"Of course, how do you expect to go to war with no army? We had to get you one. High Lord Antos, if you would please."

Yeng sat down and to Trista's surprise, Oren stood up. He looked amazing, she thought with his hair tied back in a tight ponytail and all in his usual black. A fitted shirt that displayed his muscles and black leather pants; separated from his shirt by what appeared to be a silver belt. He had left his swords at the door but they were never far away.

"Thank you, Chief Justice." His commanding voice boomed through the room. "I had hoped that my father would be here to discuss these plans but as he is not, it seems the task has been left to me."

Trista's blood boiled as Rowan reached out and stroked Oren's forearm comfortingly and nodded her understanding; as did everyone else.

"My cousins, Lord and Lady Antos have been irreplaceable in the management of distant soldiers who are set to join us in a matter of days."

"The summons has been distributed across Mortania, Coz and also to the distant Cotai. Once our assigned eight thousand arrive in Thelm, we will make our way through Thea's Reach to The Wide where we will engage in war with the Greybold army."

Oren turned to Nyron as he reclaimed his seat and Nyron stood to speak. He was dressed similarly but had an open doublet over his shirt with multiple chains hung loosely around his neck. The hairs on his chest pushed through the top of his shirt.

"We have the significant advantage of higher ground and as such, my sister will be able to lead a company of archers to take out the first line of defence. We have four thousand reinforcements from Cotai who will be managed by Captain Justin Theronos."

"Where is the Captain now?" Rowan asked and as Trista turned her eyes back to the twins for the answer, she caught the distinct clench of Naima's teeth.

"He will be joining us momentarily," Naima offered the response. "He has been living in Cotai for many years and has only now decided to make the journey back." Dana nudged Trista under the table and without looking at her, she nodded. There was something going on there.

"With your permission your Highness," Nyron was now saying. "We will officially appoint the heads of units and get each ready for our imminent departure from Thelm."

The table went silent and it took a moment for Trista to realise that everyone was looking at her! Trista felt Dana take her hand under the table and thankfully, she squeezed it before rising from her seat.

"Thank you Lord Antos for your thoughts but I'm afraid I'd need to discuss these options further…" Trista swallowed down her nerves but still felt her palms get clammy as she turned her eyes to Yeng.

"Thank you for waiting for me to discuss these plans but I feel I need to better understand things before I risk lives."

A good-natured chuckle echoed around the room and nervously she said,

"I'd like to speak with H-high Lord Antos for a moment as he will lead the army into battle."

Trista hated that she saw Rowan's nod of approval as she turned her eyes to Oren who was looking directly into her eyes. Her stomach did backflips just as Rowan said,

"Is this an official and formal appointment for High Lord Antos to become Captain of the Guard and therefore General of the Antonides Army?"

Trista didn't lower her eyes as she continued to stare into the man she had grown to care so much about. He would never feel the same way for her she knew, but he would be around to protect her always and she would trust no one else with this but him.

"Yes…if he accepts?"

Oren rose from his seat and made his way to where he had left his sword and brought it around the table to stand by her chair.

Instinctively, Trista stepped out from behind the chair to stand in front of him where Oren proceeded to fall to one knee, resting on his blade and said,

"I pledge my sword and the fealty of my House; Antos to yours; Antonides. I will honour and protect you, kill any who would oppose or harm you and die for you if necessary. From this day to my last day, my sword, my shield, my life and my heart…is yours."

Oren rose from the floor and looked down at her. The room seemed to bubble with the energy that cackled between them. They had created something, a bond and Trista felt it deep within her. The words she must say seemed to float into her mind and she repeated them,

"I, Princess Trista of House Antonides accepts the fealty of Oren of House Antos…thank you General."

There was a thick silence around the room as they stared at one another until Yeng spoke,

"My private chambers are through there, take as long as you wish."

Trista turned to nod her thanks and when she walked to enter the room; Oren was close behind.

As Trista and Oren disappeared behind the door, Nyron leant into his sister and whispered,

"You heard that he changed the words too?"

"Yep," Naima said smiling at the now closed chamber door.

ACHILLES HEEL

The air was chilled with the onslaught of the magically assisted winter that approached them from all angles.

Everything surrounding them looked bleak and on the brink of death and as they watched the Greybold Army gather in the Imperial Lands, stretching further out into The Wide; Aslan and Saicha knew that death for this land was not far away.

The numbers were vast and as they watched wagons and carriages of weapons and supplies enter through the recently fortified main gates; they finally knew what they would be up against.

"How many do you make?" Saicha asked quietly as they sat atop their horses amongst some trees lining the army camp.

"I'd say, twelve maybe thirteen thousand, so twelve actual foot soldiers to do real battle." Saicha nodded her agreement as she continued to scan the army below them.

"Rian will be able to get another five thousand here in good time. The Samaians need at least eight thousand to make it an even playing field, anything more is a bonus."

"We can only hope," Aslan said disbelievingly.

"What?"

"I just don't think we should hold our breaths, for all we know this Redeemer," he said the word cynically, "could be nothing but a child wanting to play war with no army to back it up."

"True, but their cause is the right one and Agmantia will support that."

"Oh, you speak for Agmantia now?" Saicha said nothing.

No, she didn't speak for Agmantia, but their mother had asked them to determine who was worthy of Agmantia's aid and she believed the Samaians were.

"Let's go."

The siblings continued their path around the Greybold army, wrapped in their furs against the icy winds and snow. The camp was wide and heaving with activity even as they made their way closer to the opening of Thea's Reach.

The large opening that led north all the way to Thelm was the quickest though much more treacherous way to travel. For four people on horseback, the dangers would be minimal, but the cliff face was steep on one side and The Forest rose up high on the other. Trees as tall as mountains loomed over Thea's Reach, leaving little room for manoeuvring. There was one way in and one way out and currently, the siblings had to get in without being seen.

Given their small number, it was easy enough but still foreboding that any little sound could alert scouts of their presence. Saicha, Aslan and their aids walked as slowly as they could through the shrubbery and forage until they suddenly came upon an opening.

There in the centre, they saw six teenagers who looked to be sparring. As they watched intently, one of them held out his hand and a sword from the floor flew into his hand. Aslan gasped but Saicha continued to watch, fascinated as the young man advanced on one of the others. The one he approached did the same thing and suddenly had a broadsword in his hands.

What continued in front of them was a blurred melee of skill, sword and sorcery of the likes neither Agmantian had ever seen; even Saicha. She had grown with ruthless assassins but they used weapons and poisons and other things of this world;

this was something else. As they fought with such speed and agility, there was a black mist around each of them that shot out in varying intervals.

This mist knocked opponents over where swords could not reach or morphed into solid walls that their opponents would slam into and be unable to get around. One of them jumped, unnaturally high into the sky before landed a hairs breadth away from the boy he had just knocked to the ground; splintering the ground beneath him as he did so.

"What *is* this?"

"This…is magic," Saicha said quietly. "This is real magic, not like the Shaman at home with their spells and potions…this, this is true power."

As she said it, Saicha began to walk herself and her horse along, keeping her eye on the teenagers in the opening.

"Saicha," Aslan hissed. "Where are you going?"

"I'm getting out of here before they finish training," she hissed back and their accompanying aids, nodded their approval.

"We keep to the left we'll eventually get to The Forest," she said before her brows knotted together. "I've heard stories about that place but we will follow it none the less…at least until we pass their camp." Everyone nodded and followed her in silence, unsure of how to take in what they had witnessed.

It was dark by the time Aslan and Saicha crossed the last of The Wide and arrived at the mouth of Thea's Reach. Here, they could smell the ocean although they couldn't see it as it was hundreds of feet below. They heard the crashing of waves against the sharp, jagged rocks and the roar of the heavy tide.

On one side was the ominous forest that no one dare venture into and on the other was a precipice from which to fall; no one could survive. The ground between the two elements was weak and crumbled irrationally through lack of care once the Samaians were no longer in power. They had fortified the ground with magic but when that ceased, it crumbled away year by year.

At the opening of Thea's Reach stood a large looming gate. What had once been an official entrance between the north and south of the kingdom, had now fallen into a bandit's favourite hideaway.

Those brave enough to make the journey through the Imperial Lands and across The Wide would have to deal with opportunists trying to make some coin.

The old guard post had long been abandoned once the Imperial Lands were no longer inhabitable and so, any criminals had free reign to intimidate who they wished.

It was these types of men who Saicha and Aslan encountered as they attempted to ride through the partially closed gate that towered over them.

"Man or Samai?"

"Agmantian." Came Aslan's short reply.

"Get down off that horse Agmantian and state your loyalties."

Saicha rolled her eyes, she had somewhere to be.

"Let us pass and no harm will come to you," Aslan said simply as he looked down at the three men stood in front of them in tattered clothes and crude armour; completely out of place in this bitter cold as well as for their clear intentions.

"I like them furs," the one closest to Saicha commented, stepping forward and grabbing the slack reins of her horse. "Give 'em to me."

"Let go of my horse." Saicha said as Aslan and their two aids dismounted.

"I've never been with an Agmantian girl before," he said licking his chapped lips and Saicha felt physically sick.

"And you never will. Aslan, handle this before I have to."

Aslan drew his sword, as did their two aids and strode up to the bandits and proceeded to cut them down.

Saicha was impressed with her brother's skill as he played with his opponent for a few moments before running him right through the stomach. Their aids were less extravagant with their attack and simply parried until an appropriate opening presented itself and one hacked at his attacker's shoulder, severing his head while the other sliced straight through his skull.

"Happy big sister?"

"Ecstatic," Saicha said with a smile as the bodies were discarded and her brother remounted so they could make their way into the Thea's Reach.

***

Barons Dreston and Thelm arrived at the Greybold camp and settled into their perspective war tents. They were sat in a meeting with Lord Weilyn going over their plans to take over control from the princess.

The king and princess, who had now arrived to The Wide, were situated a little further from the camp due to their status and so Briseis could be closer to her Six.

"I have the forces in the south, Thelm in the North and Dreston in the West. While Lyon of course has the most coin, our combined gold will be able to fund our stay in the field for weeks at least."

Weilyn seemed overly confident but for once, Dreston was not offended or annoyed by this. It was this confidence that while would help them win the war and also deflect Briseis' attention from him.

If Briseis saw one of the Barons acting out more so than the other, she may be inclined to have them killed rather than him.

Despite what she said, he knew that the princess was not his biggest fan. If he could at least wear down her forces before she did anything about that then he would be safe. It was simply a matter of biding his time until Briseis was weak enough to be taken out; either by their gathered forces or the king himself.

"Everything is falling into place," Erik acknowledged. Lyon looked over at him questioningly. The man had been considerably quiet the last few days, Lyon had observed but he couldn't work out the reason behind it. He kept mainly to himself and when in the attendance of others, he said little. His behaviour worried him but with so much else to contend with, he had to put it off until later.

In any case, Geneiva would soon be with child and then any questions of Erik's loyalty would be solidified.

"Once we have news of the Samaian forces from Thelm, we can better understand what we are up against. We don't want to be outnumbered when we take out the princess."

"When will we know for sure?" Lyon asked

"Briseis and her father sent men to Thelm fairly recently, but it should only be a few days before we get a raven." Erik confirmed and all the men nodded.

"When we get the numbers, we organise our own men and take off the weakest sections. We'll have men in Thea's Point, The Wide and Thelm to cover all bases." Lyon nodded,

"I will inform my advisors at home that trouble is to be expected and to assist the crown in their efforts."

Baron Thelm stepped from behind the table and nodded to the other two men,

"If you would excuse me gentleman, I must prepare."

"Of course," Weilyn said as the other two men stood to shake his hand before he left the tent completely.

Lyon didn't take his eyes off Thelm the entire time

***

After feeling the surge of power from the Everlasting, Briseis settled in the Imperial Lands with the Greybold army.

She lay now with Gardan in the bedroom of her tent going over the expedition sent out to Thelm when one of her guards called out to her. She permitted them entry as she sat up in bed with the bed clothes covering her modesty,

"Baron Thelm is here to see you your Highness, he says he has news."

"He may enter, I'll be out in a moment."

Gardan sat up and kissed her bare shoulder before she got out of the bed,

"What do you think he wants?"

"Other than to annoy me, who knows."

Briseis put on a nearby robe and slippers before stepping out of her bedroom and into her audience room where Baron Thelm was waiting. He stood immediately and bowed low. The tent was warm despite the frost outside, braziers and fur rugs all around to create a comfortable space for the princess. Everything was there for her comfort as if she were still at the castle.

"My sincerest apologies for interrupting your evening princess but I thought this could not wait."

"I'll be the judge of that," she said drily as she poured herself some coffee from a small ceramic teapot on a nearby table.

Erik cleared his throat,

"I have just left a meeting with Baron Dreston and Lord Weilyn who have revealed their plans to take the crown with distribution of their forces throughout the kingdom." Briseis stopped pouring momentarily as she looked over at him,

"Continue," Thelm nodded and went into what Weilyn and Dreston had just revealed to him.

"You have done well Erik and you will be rewarded for your efforts; on that you have my word."

"Thank you, Princess,"

"Continue to hide your true intentions from them but we still have a way to go in this war. You must be ready when I call."

"Yes your Highness," Briseis nodded his dismissal and Erik left hurriedly.

"It seems I'm the only one completely on your side."

Gardan stepped slowly out of her bedroom, shirtless and came to wrap his arms around her before kissing the inside of her neck. Briseis sighed as she leant her head back onto his shoulder and revelled at how good it felt to do so. Who would have thought that having someone to talk to would be so…refreshing?

"So, it seems…they must all die."

Gardan took a deep breath and cleared his throat. Briseis turned around to face him, looking intently into his eyes.

"You disagree?"

"Does it matter what I think?"

Briseis stopped for a second when she realised that it did.

"What would you have me do?" Gardan studied her for the moment before he replied,

"Apprehend them, question them; find out who else may be behind these machinations and ruin them."

"Why waste time with all of that when I could kill them and take their lands anyway?"

"Because when you become queen Briseis, you still need people to run the provinces for you. No matter how powerful you are, you can't be everywhere at once."

He had a point but she didn't want to need the noblemen, the very idea angered her. Gardan pulled her into his arms and kissed the top of her head and not for the first time, she hated that she liked it. Despite her power, Gardan made her feel safe when she was surrounded by enemies.

"I will do whatever you command but please think about what they can do for you in the long term, rather than act on you short term anger."

Briseis said nothing before lifting her head and tilting her head to kiss him. What Gardan didn't know wouldn't hurt him or her relationship with him. Baron Dreston was as good as dead.

A FATHER'S DAUGHTER

Oren closed the chamber door behind them and when Trista finally turned to him, there was pure terror on her face. In that moment, she didn't care that she was attracted to him or that he intimidated her, right now Trista just needed someone to know that she was terrified and that she had no idea what to do.

"I can't do this Oren," she admitted but he smiled reassuringly.

"Calm down Trista okay, you're doing fine."

"I don't think I am!"

"You're just worried," he said quietly walking over to a small table in the middle of the room with four chairs around it. He rested his hands on the back of the chair closest to him and flexed his fingers as he gripped it. "You're worried that you might be doing something wrong."

Trista walked to slump into the chair opposite him in her wonderful green gown and held her head in her hands,

"I can't do this...I just can't."

"We both know that's not true, just take it one step at a time." Trista raised her eyes to his and shrugged,

"But what's the *first* step?"

Suddenly his expression turned serious and Oren cleared his throat to look at her,

"Well, you took the first step by appointing me as your General. Now, we come up with a plan of action; of attack and we take it from there."

"Yes, but how do I do that Oren?" she said desperately. "I'm so grateful that you know what to do but people are going to ask *me*; turn to me and I won't have the answers."

"Do you think every monarch does at first or if ever?"

"I wasn't born t—"

"You *were* born to be this Trista, that's what you keep forgetting. This is your place, this title; this honour…it's all yours. You can only learn how to do it if you embrace it properly."

"I know bu—"

"But what? Naima, Nyron and I will be here with you; you'll never be alone and plus…you have your mother."

Trista shook her head defiantly, standing up from the chair she had collapsed into,

"No, I don't want anything to do with her!"

"Trista you can't shut her out," he said quietly.

"Why not, she did it to me. She shut me out of my life by taking my memories away and now she wants to act like nothing happened! Why doesn't she get to suffer!"

"Is that what you really want?" he asked standing and walking over to her, his arms folded across his chest. "Do you really want to spend the time you have fighting with her when you could be learning, growing and understanding everything else about your family?" Trista hated that he was right and it only made her want to cry. Instead she said,

"Why are you on her side, why are you defending her?"

"I'm not defending her; I'm protecting your interests."

It was so logical, it made her face heat with shame. As she was about to find some way to defy him and Rowan's involvement, Oren unexpectedly reached out and took her hands into his. He uncurled her fists that she hadn't even realised she'd clenched and smoothed his thumb over the tops of her knuckles.

"She's your mother Trista and despite what's happened… she loves you." Trista looked up at him, angry that he was being so reasonable about this when she just wanted to scream and hide from everything. "Deal with your issues later but if you want to be a good ruler and learn what you need to win this war, then maybe she can help you."

Defeated, Trista nodded her head and Oren squeezed her hands comfortingly before turning to exit the room. When he returned, Rowan was with him.

"You wished to speak to me?" she asked quietly, and Trista nodded.

"General Antos believes you would be of use during the planning stages of this war and I am inclined to agree. Will you help me?"

"Of course I will."

Trista gestured to the table between them and they all took a seat, Oren taking the seat closest to her and not Rowan. Oren cleared his throat,

"As Nyron mentioned, we have the advantage of higher ground and I see no sense in changing any of his plans regarding the regiments, other than that I will lead the ground troops and not Captain Theronos."

"Who is Captain Theronos?" Trista questioned.

"An army brat like me," Oren replied with an amused smiled. "He and the twins grew up together, but after the war; much to Naima's dismay he left to live in Cotai." Trista's face looked at Oren questioningly, but he squinted his eyes at her as if to say, 'later'.

"If you lead the ground troops, what will he do?" Rowan asked.

"He'd manage his own men as reinforcements, the last line of defence as it were."

"I don't think he'll be happy about that, not seeing any of the action." Rowan countered,

"I respect he may want to be front line, but I feel it would be best for the leader of the army to in fact lead it."

"I disagree," Oren turned to Trista.

"What would you suggest your Highness?"

"I would suggest that you don't leave my side. As my right hand and leader of my army, I can't very well have you on the front line…I'll need you."

She didn't want to hope, but Trista watched as Oren's eyes softened,

"You are right now the most powerful warrior I know. At the very least, I would like to reserve your power until the end where it may be needed most." Rowan nodded her agreement,

"Trista is right Oren; you must be by her side as long as possible before engaging in open war." Oren looked at her intently before replying,

"I will do as you wish."

Trista knew he wasn't completely happy about this but his honour wouldn't allow him to voice it.

"Nyron however will lead the front," Trista added, turning her eyes away from him so not to feel guilty for taking the front line from him for her own selfish reasons. "I appreciate all you say he has done for us these past years, but I do not know Captain Theronos. I'd prefer someone known and trusted at the front."

"I agree, Nyron to man the Calvary and front line; second to Naima's trebuchets and archers." Rowan added

"Captain Theronos will man and distribute the rest of the army as needed…I do not think it wise to send all of our forces out at once." Trista looked to Oren for confirmation and he nodded,

"No, section by section," he laid his palm on the table top one in front of the other. "A wave of soldiers to take out anything that comes our way."

"What will be coming our way?" Trista asked looking between her mother and Oren. "Do we know what kind of numbers we are up against and how we fare in comparison?"

Oren looked somewhat pressured but said,

"As we know from Lamya, Baron Dreston has a formidable force, by now already stationed among the Greybold army. That could be anywhere between ten to twelve thousand men. Our own forces combined with that of the four thousand from Cotai will bring our total to twelve thousand." Trista nodded although she didn't feel very confident,

"You forget Trista," her mother said reassuringly. "Where we may lack in numbers we make up for in high ground, resources and of course magic. The sooner we all come together, the more power will generate giving us a much better advantage."

Trista nodded again, this time more confidently. She looked into her mother's eyes and before she lost her nerve she said,

"What would my father have done?"

The room went quieter than it had ever been, and Rowan sighed before looking down into her hands then back up at her daughter,

"I don't know what he would do in this situation Trista, but I know what he did do." Trista sat still, anxious to hear the next words from Rowan's lips

"Both before and during the war, your father went to see Curian to negotiate peace. I advised him against it, sure that Curian would kill him on sight but he did it anyway. While we know that his mission was futile, it was always your father's way to exhaust all none violent avenues before resorting to fighting."

Trista knew she wanted to be like her father and if his method could bring peace without fighting, then why not try to do the same?

"When I was with Rayne, I asked her about something called Mind Messaging. I read about it in a book she gave me, can you, do it?"

Rowan turned to look at Oren, then back at Trista before realisation hit her.

"You wish to speak with Briseis."

Trista nodded as she worried her lip,

"I was connected to her once before; I don't know how but I heard her. Maybe I could do so again willingly and talk of peace."

"She won't give it," Oren said; Trista turned to him,

"I have to try, don't I? Try to end this before thousands of people have to die."

Rowan leant forward, worry on her face,

"Trista, I know what I said about your father, but what he did, got him killed. His compassion got him killed; please don't make the same mistake."

"It's not a mistake to do what's right Rowan, and I think this is the right thing."

"Trista, you can't win this trying to be Alexander," Oren said sharply and instantly regretted it as Trista shot him a look of pure venom.

"I'm not trying to be my father General; I'm trying to be a good queen!"

"A good queen wouldn't put her life in unnecessary danger!"

"A good General would follow orders!" Oren banged his fist on the table,

"I'm not just your General!"

Trista went silent although she remained defiant. Rowan didn't move as Trista and Oren stared each other out before he finally turned away,

"I'm not just your General Trista, I'm your cousin and your friend and I don't think this is the right idea for our people. You could get hurt somehow or expose your location or…"

"Thank you for your input General but my mind is made up." She hated to speak to him this way but it was the only way she knew he wouldn't question her. Trista turned to Rowan, dismissing Oren completely. "I will need your help in connecting with Briseis, can you help me or not?"

"Yes," came Rowan's reluctant and quiet reply

"Good, I'll speak with you after the meeting."

Oren didn't comment as he shook his head in obvious disapproval.

The three of them returned to the audience chamber, where the others stood to welcome the royals back into the room. Trista inclined her head before walking back to her seat but not actually taking it.

All the eyes in the room looked at her expectantly and with a deep breath and a clear voice she said,

"I have spoken with General Antos and Queen Rowan and we have established an initial plan of action. While I deal with this, with the queen's help, I would ask for the continued hospitality of the Council for myself and my friends."

"You need not ask this of us your Highness, but it is granted none the less." Chief Justice said sweetly,

"Lord and Lady Antos will continue their communications with our able-bodied fighters. When the time comes, Lord Antos will lead the front lines and cavalry while Lady Antos will administer construction of the trebuchets and our archers.

Captain Theronos, it has been decided will orchestrate the backup troops upon his arrival to the Council."

Everyone nodded in agreement and absentmindedly, Trista turned to look at Thorn who was completely expressionless. He sat still, not looking at anyone in particular.

"On that note, I think we should all get some rest and once our additional forces arrive we can arrange our departure to The Wide. Thank you all…so much for your help in my journey so far."

Trista turned to look at them all individually and her heart was warm at how far she had come with at least one of them by her side. Everyone began to file out of the room,

"Rowan…if would remain behind with me please."

Rowan nodded and when all the others had left, she stood from her chair and gazed over at Trista.

"You did wonderfully," her voice was quiet, tentative as she walked over to hr daughter. Trista wasn't in the mood for sentimentality right then and so she said,

"Thank you…when can we begin the Mind Messaging?"

Rowan paused ever so slightly, making Trista tilt her head questioningly at the guilt that spread across the other woman's face.

The longer she spent with the woman, the more she realised she did look like her mother and she didn't want that to be true.

"Rowan?" Once again, Rowan hesitated to respond, "Rowan what is it?"

"I can't perform the Mind Message Trista."

Trista's face transformed from confusion into a hideous scowl,

"You lied to me…*again*!" Trista spat at her before slamming the chair she had been stood behind into the table and turning to exit the room. She pulled open the door and stormed down the spiral stair case.

"Trista wait!" Rowan called after her as she rushed to follow her down the stairs but Trista ignored her. She marched determinedly down the stairs until she arrived in the Main Hall.

The others had already dispersed within the building to who knew where and so there were only a small number of diners and students remaining in the hall. They bowed as she went past but she didn't bother to acknowledge them; furious with Rowan's betrayal.

On and on she marched, barging past people with Rowan calling her name until she was finally out of the Main Hall and in the large open foyer that led off into the rest of the building.

"Trista please wait!"

"Go away Rowan!" Trista finally called after her just as she had to stop in the middle of the foyer because she didn't know where she was going.

"Trista please!" Trista spun around to face her mother, almost bumping into her,

"Don't Trista please me! What could you possibly have to say?"

"If you'd just let me explain!"

"Explain why you lied to me again. Please I'm all ears!"

Trista was screaming now and more than a few people had stopped to watch the spectacle. Rowan's eyes darted around them, frantic as she caught sight of the people looking on. Her eyes filled with tears as she looked at the beautiful young woman who had nothing but hatred for her,

"I'm waiting!"

"Excuse me, is everything okay?"

A young female attendant approached them with a cautious smile and Trista turned to her, raged beyond all control,

"Can you show me where the dormitories are?"

"Of course, your Highness, this way." The woman replied with a polite smile and Trista turned to follow her immediately. Her blood boiled when she saw that Rowan was still following her,

"Go away Rowan!" Trista yelled again, following the attendant, desperate to find the way quicker.

"Why won't you let me explain, why won't you listen to anything I have to say?" Trista stopped dead in her tracks and spun around to face her mother,

"I don't want to listen to you because I *hate* you!" The shock was registered on Rowan's face a she stared back at her daughter. "I hate you and your lies and how you walk around here like everyone owes you something!"

"I don't want to listen to anything you have to say Rowan because you're a *liar*. You're a liar and a cheat and a Gods damn hypocrite, so stay the hell away from me!"

As the venomous words left her lips, Trista felt the most tremendous slap connect with her face. Her head spun, her vision momentarily blurred as her head rocked and she instinctively placed her palm against her face before turning to glare back at Rowan. Rowan stood there breathing heavily as tears streamed down her face and her eyes radiated with hurt. Trista's heart constricted, and she felt exactly as she had done when she told Rowan, wrongly that she wished she was dead.

"Everything," Rowan began with her teeth clenched with rage. "*Everything* I have done to survive for the last sixteen *years*, has been to protect you; to keep you safe and alive and *this* is how you treat me." Her voice cracked with emotion but she continued anyway.

"I'm sorry I wasn't there for you Trista. I know nothing can replace the years you grew up without me, but you can't continue to blame me for things I can't change!"

Rowan stood there crying and Trista continued to hold her now burning cheek before looking away from her mother, ashamed.

"Every day I wanted to be with you. Every day I wanted to go to Remora and take you, Gods and prophecies and destinies be damned, but I couldn't! I couldn't put you in danger, don't you understand that!"

"Even now, I won't perform the Mind Message because Oren is right, anything could happen to you during that connection. Anything could happen to me after not having the power for so long, I might not even be able to control it as I once could. I gave up that control Trista, I gave up that life for you; to protect you as best I could!"

Trista's own eyes began to fill with tears, but she refused to look at Rowan; she didn't want to feel guilty from the pain she saw there.

"I'm sorry I lied to you about being able to do the Mind Message but it's just too risky. I didn't want to ridicule the first real decision you'd made about this war. I didn't want to embarrass you in front of Oren, I…I just wanted to help."

Trista finally looked up at her and replied angrily,

"How did you think lying was going to help me? You would have had to tell me eventually!"

"I know that Trista but I wasn't thinking about that. I was thinking about the gratitude in your eyes instead of hatred!"

"And you thought that would change with more lies!"

"I thought, it would give us some time to actually talk to one another, for you to get to know me; for me to get to know you!" Rowan snapped at her, clearly hurt. "You act as though you were the only one torn from someone!" she raged on, this time clearly not worried about what Trista thought anymore.

She had some things to get off her chest and it seemed the time was now.

"You're angry at me for not being around, for not having the family you were born to, I get that; but the reality Trista, is that Curian took our family from you *and* me!"

"You didn't even meet a portion of the people I lost in that war, including your father! You haven't lost your sisters, your husband, your cousins and uncles and aunts and generations of people who relied on you to protect them!"

Rowan didn't bother to wipe the tears from her eyes or unattractive bubbles from the tips of her nose as her pain poured out and eventually Trista's did too. Watching this woman who she had heard and viewed as so undeniably strong break down this way was heart-breaking…and she had caused it.

"I'm sorry you hate me, I am, because I love you more than anything in this entire world, but don't for one second, think that you are the only one in pain. Don't you dare think that you're the only one hurting or lost or alone!"

Rowan turned from her then and marched down the hallway in the direction the now silent attendant had been leading them. Trista stood, watching after her mother for a long time, her own tears glistening on her cheeks when the attendant finally touched her arm,

"Are you okay your Highness?"

"I can find my own way from here." Trista said quietly, too ashamed to look the attendant in the eye.

"Are you sure?" Trista nodded and turned from the attendant and walked off into the Academy.

For hours, Trista walked the grounds of the Academy, listening and watching the people that lived and worked there.

She watched them going about their lives and marvelled at how happy they were with such a horrible person in their midst.

She had said terrible things to Rowan and deserved everything her mother had said to her in return.

Trista was selfish, she saw that now; selfish and cruel and Rowan didn't deserve half the abuse she was throwing at her. She had never thought about what Rowan had lost during the war, everything had been about her and it wasn't the first time that someone had called her out on it.

When had she become that person who only saw the small picture and didn't give a damn about other people's feelings?

Trista was ashamed, and it was this guilt that had her knock quietly on Rowan's door later that night.

It was late, but she knew this had to be done now or risk losing what little relationship she did have with Rowan.

Her mother opened the door dressed in a delicate nightdress and shawl, her long black hair loose, all finery and jewels gone and she looked…small.

Gone was the air of superiority and in its place, was an aging woman in a great deal of pain. She was still beautiful, that could never be denied but Trista could see now where she had been so wrong. Everything she had seen of Rowan up until his very moment was a front, a mask to protect herself against…*out there*.

This woman stood in front of her, was her mother, not the queen who had lost everything.

"I'm so sorry Mama," Trista whimpered and when Rowan held out her arms with a warm smile, Trista folded into the hug and wept.

They stayed up talking for hours

Trista explained about her life in Remora, growing up with Gwendolyn and Matthias Freitz and her relationship with

Thorn Remora. She confessed that they had intended to marry but didn't go into any further details. Rowan questioned her about Avriel's treatment of her and Trista had to confess that she'd never had much contact with Avriel until she'd Ascended.

This troubled Rowan but instead of dwelling on it, they went on to discuss Rowan's life growing up in Illiya, as a highborn lady. Rowan talked about her parents, Josef and Mysten Illiya and her older sisters Rayne and Renya and of course; about Trista's father, Alexander.

"He was a wonderful man," Rowan said softly as they lay on her bed side by side looking at one another. Rowan had given Trista one of her nightgowns and so the two women lay in bed, snug under the covers learning about the other.

"He was so handsome and sweet and loving; there was nothing he wouldn't do for me or his people."

"Lamya says some people thought him arrogant," Rowan smiled knowingly, looking off in a way as though she were thinking some distant memory.

"Your father could be, difficult, yes. It is the Antonides way after all."

Rowan winked at her and despite the teasing quip, Trista blushed because she knew what she was referring to.

"There was something about him, something charismatic and mysterious that I loved him almost instantly. Even if we hadn't been Intended, I think my heart would have belonged to him anyway."

"Intended?"

Rowan's eyes widened slightly and she looked away,

"What is it?"

"I forgot there is so much you don't know,"

"Then tell me...please."

Rowan sighed but nodded just the same,

"Royal custom is that members of the royal family have, arranged marriages of sorts. There are laws and spells that determine who will marry into the royal line and provide the new heir and so forth. I was chosen for your father."

"Chosen?"

"Yes, it was found that I was to be the next queen and I did my duty." Trista looked mortified.

"What if you didn't like him?" Rowan laughed,

"Then it would be a very unhappy marriage, as many can be but fortunately, I was lucky enough to love your father very much…and he loved me."

Trista was astounded as she mulled over the idea of being forced to marry someone you didn't like or even know. Suddenly, a thought occurred to her,

"Will I…?" Rowan looked at her and nodded slowly. "Who?"

"…it hasn't been determined yet."

Trista's mind raced; there was someone out there she was destined to marry! As she thought it over, the obvious conclusion came riding along with it; that that someone wouldn't be Oren. This hurt her more than she would ever like to admit,

"When you are crowned," Rowan was saying. "We can perform the rituals to find out."

"Mama, what if I don't like the person who's chosen for me. What if I want someone else?"

"Like who?" the question was simple enough but Trista couldn't bring herself to answer it. She didn't want anyone knowing her feelings for Oren when she knew they weren't reciprocated.

"No one in particular," she mumbled. "It just seems unfair that I'll have to marry someone before I've ever even been in love."

"You didn't love Thorn?" that question was easier,

"No…I didn't."

Rowan smiled reassuringly,

"We have a long time before you have to worry about your Intended Trista. I was thirteen when I spent my year with Alexander, getting to know him and adjust to life at court, but then I didn't have a war to think about."

Rowan went onto to explain the kaleidoscope of fun, frolicking and extravagance that Trista could never have imagined. The parties and galas and balls as well as political dinners and engagements that Rowan had been expected to sit in on as Alexander's betrothed were mind blowing to comprehend.

"I wasn't there of course for his Ascension but I was there for your father's Coronation and he permitted me to be present during Thea's Appearance."

"What does that mean?" Rowan smiled over at her and reached out suddenly to delicately stroke her daughter's face. Trista closed her eyes briefly, revelling in her mother's touch and how content she felt that she was finally with her.

"It means that at some point after receiving the Everlasting, usually your Coronation Day; Thea will appear to you and offer you a gift."

"What kind of gift?" Trista was almost afraid to ask,

"It varies but your fathers was a choice."

"What kind of choice Mama?"

Rowan sighed and the most tremendous pain but also admiration was in her eyes,

"Thea asked your father to choose between me and a long reign…he chose me."

"I don't understand…" Rowan's eyes began to well up again but she quickly wiped them away,

"Thea knew that I would have trouble conceiving, even before we understood what that would mean and she told Alex that he could choose to have another wife; another more fertile wife and live to a ripe old age or…stay with me and die young."

Trista was astounded as she looked over at her mother. Knowing now, that Rowan had trouble to even conceive her, made her feel guiltier than ever before. What else had this woman gone through in order to be here with her right now? Trista's own eyes welled up as she felt so incredibly sad for Rowan and all she had lost.

"He loved you,"

"Too much it seems but, enough about me," Rowan sat up to fluff the covers around her daughter. "The sun is almost up, get some sleep; you have a long day tomorrow."

Trista nodded with a sweet smile and adjusted herself in the warm cosy bed, finally with her mother wondering what kind of choice Thea would have for her.

MOVING FORWARD

Baron Lyon Dreston lay sleeping in his war tent that nights in the Imperial Lands with the servant girl Pia laying naked beside him. Their nude bodies were covered with furs as they lay on his featherbed, braziers burning out around them, having warmed the space for their earlier actions.

The baron breathed in deeply, content in his sleep when he was unceremoniously dragged from his bed. His eyes shot up, fear immediately taking over him as he called out for help.

"What is the meaning of this!" he demanded as hooded armed men dragged him to the ground, his nakedness on show for all. "How dare you, do you know who I am?" he screeched as the four large men looked down at him in a heap on the floor.

Pia huddled on the large bed above him, cowering away from the men who at this moment had no interest in her but she didn't know when that might change.

"We know exactly who you are," one of the men spat at him and proceeded to grab a hold of the Baron's long hair, while another took hold of one of his arms and dragged him out of the tent into the bitter cold.

Sparsely littered soldiers around the camp at the late hour watched in amazement and confusion as the naked baron was hauled through the snow past their camp fires and scattered weapons. He was dragged through piles of dirt and horse droppings, even slammed into the legs of the horses themselves.

"Unhand me! Aml! Guards! GUARDS!" he screamed but no one heard him, or at least, no one was listening.

The Baron continued to yell as he was drawn through the snow, his body lugged until it was battered with the scrapes and cuts from overturned roots and sharps rocks. Lyon fought as best he could with his hair being pulled and soldiers armed to the teeth all around him. He screamed, yelled and bucked all the way until he was suddenly kicked violently in the stomach.

He had never felt pain like it.

Debilitating, crippling pain like one could never imagine.

"Shut up!" the guard snapped who had kicked him and Lyon spluttered out a mouthful of blood before gargling down his cries.

They continued to drag him through the snow and dirt until he was suddenly descending into a dark, cold and wet place he couldn't begin to locate. Panic took him over and he screamed out, forgetting the warning he'd just received.

"AML! AML HELP ME!"

"Speak again and I will gut you and feed your insides back to you."

The guard threatened him so easily, Lyon knew he was not to be played with and silenced his cries instantly.

The guard who had a hold of his hair, yanked him sharply, ripping hair from his scalp. Lyon yelped in alarm before his now freed head smacked onto the cold, stone floor.

Where am I?

He wasn't able to dwell on his surroundings for too long as he tried to adjust his eyes to the darkness that surrounded him.

The floor was firm icy stone and with the descent into this darkness he had to be underground but...where?

Shuffles from around him told him his captors were moving but it wasn't until a light descended into their midst, that he truly saw any of their faces.

The Six.

It wasn't all of them, but he recognised a few of their faces.

He didn't know where the light was coming from but he could tell now that it was coming from where they had dragged him down into this place. It descended the steps that seemed to be cut into the very rock that surrounded them and behind it, came a member of The Six named Duncan. Accompanying him was one of the other Six members, a girl and who came to stand in front of him, beside Duncan.

Duncan approached him with a pleased look on his face and Lyon shuffled back, knowing what this young man was capable of. He had seen him in training and he was considerably more ruthless than the other members.

Duncan looked down at him, in his fine fighting leathers and with a wave of his hand, Lyon was drawn up from the floor and was floating in the air for all to see. He tried to over his modesty, but his arms were stuck, stretched out like a sacrifice.

Duncan swiped his hand again and Lyon was slammed against a wall he hadn't even seen and ropes gathered around his wrists and ankles.

"Please! Why are you doing this!" he screamed out, tears having begun to fall sooner than he would have liked to admit. Duncan merely laughed as he finished his magic, tying Lyon to the wall in an X shape.

"Illegal marriage, conspiring against the Crown Princess, uniting your armies with other territories to gain power…need I go on." Lyon immediately denied it.

"It was not me, it was Thelm's doing, it was all Erik!"

Duncan laughed again before his face turned sour and he reached out and slapped Lyon…with magic.

Once. Twice. Three times, Duncan made the slapping motion that sent Lyon's head rocking from side to side so hard, that teeth fell from his mouth.

Lyon bled from the mouth,

"IT WAS ERIK!" he screamed again, sagging against his restraints before his eyes widened in pure fear.

"Let's see what truth we can get out of you shall we?" Duncan sneered as with his index finger, he made a slow slicing motion and Baron Dreston's flesh began to split.

***

The night was long, cold and dark and even when they woke from dreamless sleeps, the air was still grey and dark with despair. The winter was more bitter here it seemed, on Thea's Reach and on the second day of their travel towards Thelm, Saicha, Aslan and their companions fought to keep warm.

Wind, snow and ice beat against them, rising from the crashing waves that thundered somewhere far beneath them. They rode steadily along the precarious ground, desperate not to put too much unnecessary strain on it. How an army was meant to get across it without casualties was beyond them; but it was the only way. Whatever army was on the other end of this path could only get to Tirnum through here, or risk losing days and advantages by going around.

Saicha was confident that the Samaian army would have thought of this, but if not, they would definitely need Agmantia's help.

"We'll rest here," Saicha called out later that evening as she spied an abandoned ruin among the overgrowth, leading to The Forest. At one time, it may have been an outpost or even a residence but now it simply served as shelter from the bitter winds.

The group steered off to the left and settled their horses comfortably, before getting a fire started and making something to eat. Their attendants saw to most things as Saicha turned from them and began to sharpen her weapons. Within a few moments, her brother joined her,

"Should we not gain as much ground as we can while there's light?"

"We've travelled a night and half a day, aren't you tired?"

"Of course, but I'd much rather not be in this narrow ravine," Aslan said looking around at the looming trees on one side and the open precipice on the other. Saicha rolled her eyes but not unkindly as she giggled at her brother's worry.

"This is the furthest point along The Path before there's no turning back Aslan. It's best we spend the night here, so we can ride straight towards Thelm." He nodded although it was evident he wasn't convinced. Saicha patted him on the shoulder,

"Lighten up little brother, you'll be fine."

"I better or you'll have to explain to mother what happened to me." Saicha laughed again,

"It's you, I'm sure she'd believe anything could have befallen you!" Aslan fanned his sister off as she continued to get ready to turn in for the night.

As they lay in their bed rolls, there was a familiar cry in the air and Aurora appeared in the darkening sky before landing comfortably beside Saicha.

"Good girl!" Saicha congratulated her as she found a treat for her feathery friend. Aslan rolled his eyes and turned over,

"What does Mother say?"

"It's not from Mother, not directly anyway." Saicha scanned the small note in her fingers once she'd got it free from around Aurora's leg. The bird was chilly to the touch as was to be expected in this weather but she soon warmed up by the fire they'd flared up.

"It's from Rian, he asks how many men to bring to Thelm." Aslan thought for the moment before saying,

"No…not to Thelm,"

"What do you mean?"

Aslan smiled at her and proceeded to tell Saicha his idea.

The following morning, the siblings rose early to begin the hours long journey to the northern city. The stretch of land connecting the north of Mortania to the south was large but they needed to get to relative safety.

As they packed up their things, Saicha attached she and Aslan's message to Aurora's leg and with a loving stroke on the intelligent bird, she let her free once more.

She had to admit that Aslan's idea was a sound one and she was sure her mother would be proud of it, as well as Aslan's diplomatic development. She wasn't that much older than Aslan but he was a hot head at times that had gotten him into trouble more than once.

"Let's go," she called out and within moments, they had headed off.

They reached Thelm in a matter of hours, having pushed their horses to the brink of exhaustion. Cautious to the terrain, they had moved as swiftly as they could. How the land on Thea's Reach had become so volatile, she hadn't fully understood, but in her years at the Guild it was widely discussed and known to be dangerous.

They passed through the colossal statues of some old king or warrior, a name she had never known; it's arms outstretched seemingly welcoming travellers into the city. The quartet rode on for a few more minutes before the entrance to Thelm loomed ahead and once they approached the gates; armed guards were there to meet them. Four of them stood on top of two makeshift guard posts, as temporary as their positions there, most likely. They looked completely disinterested in the people who approached them but questioned them none the less.

"Who goes there?"

"Traders, from Agmantia." One of their aids called out,

"What are you trading; I see now wares!"

"No wares, we come to purchase dyes!"

He held up a pouch of coin and the guard nodded approvingly,

"Open up!"

Seemingly by magic, as no mechanism could be seen, the gates to the city began to open and the four of them rode in.

Thelm was a large city, the third largest in Mortania and so had the population to suit. Backed by towering mountains in the north but lush and fertile lands further inland and to the west, Thelm was the beating heart of the north. People from all over travelled here to settle where the atmosphere of the southern capital was a bit too much to bare. Here, one could find suburbs and good schooling and universities. Tirnum was where you went to compete through life once all your lessons were learned.

They continued to walk through the tightly packed streets, marvelling at the sounds and smells of all around them. The cold weather had not reached this far north just yet and so the ground was not hard with frost and snow. There was still a chill in the air that could not be ignored, but it was nothing like what they had just left.

"I need to rid myself of these furs, I'm going to burn up."

"Soon brother," Saicha laughed. "We need to find the princess."

"And how do you suppose we do that?"

"We head to the Lithanian Council, Mother said they would be helpful remember." Aslan nodded and followed his sister as she dismounted and walked her horse through the tight streets.

As the roads became more congested, their aids relieved them of their horses and walked them to a nearby inn; saying they would meet them there later in the day. The royals nodded their thanks and headed further into the city.

There was an obvious military presence in the city, but whether they were there to deter or defend was unclear. Saicha, ever observant saw that while most bore the colours and arms of House Thelm, there were others baring the Greybold sigil and others still with a sigil she was unfamiliar with. A gold fire breathing dragon on a black field jumped out at her occasionally, but she couldn't place the name.

Navigating their way through the twisted streets and dark alleys with screaming children and bellowing vendors, soon became too much and Aslan approached a city watchmen,

"Excuse me good man, could you direct us to The Academy."

Nucea had confirmed in her letter to refer to the Lithanian stronghold as such,

"Straight on, turn right at the end of the street and straight up the hill."

"You have my thanks," he and Saicha made their way to the Academy.

Upon arrival, another guard post awaited them and this time, Saicha approached,

"Good morning gentleman, perhaps you would grant us admittance. We need to see the Chief Justice."

"Are you expected?"

"No,"

"Then get gone!"

Saicha raised a perfectly arched eyebrow and smirked at him,

"Do you know to whom you speak?"

"I know to whom I speak lady, a stranger armed to the teeth asking to speak to the leader of this establishment. I will not let you enter."

Saicha went to step forward but Aslan stayed her,

"Sister, calm. He is merely doing his job."

"Who are you?" the guard demanded but Aslan looked him from head to toe and said,

"You will know soon enough...come sister."

The siblings left, unable to let anyone know that Agmantian royals had come to the Academy. Anyone could determine anything from that information, and for now; they wanted it kept quiet.

"I could have ended him easily," Saicha said annoyed as they walked back down the hill. Aslan laughed,

"I am aware of your skills Saicha but no one need die just because we can't tell them who we are."

Saicha shrugged making Aslan laugh even harder,

"Who thought I would be the voice of reason?" Saicha smirked as she continued down the hill,

"I go back tonight. I will find this Chief Justice and they can lead me to the princess."

DAYS OF FUTURES PAST

The day after talking with her mother, Trista was having lunch with her friends and new-found alliances.

It was an informal affair, with everyone in attire; except Rowan of course who always dressed like she was going to a banquet.

Trista was reeling from the night spent with her and all she had learned about her family and their history. There was still so much she was going to discover about the Antonides dynasty and she couldn't wait to do so.

Though unfortunately, there was the problem of a war to get through first.

It didn't seem real, with her mother and friends around her eating a hearty meal, that there were in fact people rallying to fight for her.

The Council had explained that riots had already begun in various towns and cities across the country, of people both for and against her uprising. Lamya had also explained what she'd learned on her travels and a lot of it wasn't good. There were sympathisers of Curian's cause and a lot of those people were willing to take up arms for him. She just had to make sure she had enough arms to fight back.

The first of those soldiers had already begun appearing at the gates of the Council, and with them came the impending reality that this was all real.

Nyron, Naima and Oren took charge of the new recruits, housing and feeding those that were in need and arranging them in their various sections. Archers, foot soldiers, cavalry could all be found training in the Council grounds as they arrived throughout the day.

Trista was overcome by the power she felt in watching their numbers grow, growing in her honour and name. Countless Samaian males and females arrived and reported to either of the Antos', and it was on that note that Naima cleared her throat and turned to Trista,

"Trista, we need to tell you something"

Trista turned with an expectant smile and reluctantly Naima said,

"We don't think there is enough space to house the growing recruits. With the numbers, we expect and those who have already arrived, we won't be able to keep everyone here much longer."

"When did you realise this?"

"We've always known, or at least anticipated it." Naima admitted guiltily. Trista was confused,

"We all agreed that we would wait for more to arrive before arranging our own departure to The Wide. Why wasn't the severity of this situation expressed then?"

No one said anything but from the corner of her eye, Trista saw Oren nod his approval and her heart flipped in her chest.

"How long before we can't house everyone?"

"At the rate of the arrivals so far, we would need to be out of here within a few days, a week at the most."

"A week!" Trista gasped.

Not only did that mean they would have formidable numbers in a week, it meant they would be ready to go to war in a week.

A war she was completely not ready for, no matter how much training she'd been doing. She'd run through her usual drills with Oren earlier that day, but she knew nothing could prepare her for what lay ahead.

"How many men do you have now?" Thorn asked, and everyone turned their eyes to him.

Thorn had been practically mute since their arrival and in their discussions and meals, he had provided no further insight to what was going on with him.

While this was unlike him, Trista was so relieved she didn't have to speak about her lack of feelings for him that she had let it continue. She looked at him now, staring oddly into the room at seemingly no one in particular even though he'd spoken.

"Right now, we have eight thousand with another four on their way here from Cotai." Nyron offered to which Thorn simply nodded,

"And you expect these men to arrive within the week?"

There was something odd about his speech that she couldn't quite place but watched him intently as Oren offered the reply this time,

"Yes, at which point, if her Highness permits, we intend to move out the first line of defence and get stationed in The Wide."

"Hey sis, you might not have to be here when Justin arrives!"

Nyron slapped his sister on the back and with a distinct growl, she pushed her chair back and marched away from the table and out of the Main Hall.

Trista looked at Nyron who smirked, while Oren shook his head disappointedly,

"What?" Nyron laughed, although he seemed to know exactly what as he shovelled some food into his mouth.

"We'll move out as soon as Captain Theronos' men get here." Trista said firmly, "Oren, we'll discuss this later?" she said looking over at him and he simply nodded.

"Excuse me,"

Trista got up from her chair and left the room to find Naima.

Trista found her some time later, unsure of where she'd disappeared to, on the Archery lawn, just as she released an arrow that landed directly on target.

Naima turned to the young men and women who were looking on, her hair tied back in a sleek ponytail, face fresh of makeup and the fitted fighting leathers she so rarely wore.

Naima was a lady through and through, but it didn't stop her being an incredible fighter.

"Training with a static target will always be easy, I expect no failures here because there is no test. The true test comes, when your target is one hundred metres away on horseback and only getting further."

Trista watched her cousin with fascination as she paced up and down past the newest recruits.

"Be aware of your body, the air, the movement around you in order to determine what will be a true shot or a wasted one. Vigilance is what will allow any arrow to meet any target. Try again."

Naima stepped out of the way, so the targets were once again clear for the archers. In unison that was slightly eerie, they nocked their arrows, raised their bows and drew the string. Trista held her breath as each and every one of them closed their eyes until Naima said,

"Loose!"

As one, ten arrows released and soared through the air and landed in the centre of the target. Naima smiled,

"Well done, continue."

She left them then to approach Trista with a slight smile which she returned. Naima bowed but Trista fanned her off,

"You know I hate that,"

"Get used to it, it's going to happen a lot more frequently."

"I know…you sounded great." Naima sighed and shrugged, "I saw them struggling while I was passing so offered some words of wisdom."

"Maybe so, but it was amazing." Naima nodded gratefully.

"Everything my father said was amazing."

Trista heard the love and nostalgia in her voice and her heart broke for her. She may not have known Theon Antos, but she knew what it felt like to lose a father. She could only imagine how that felt having actually known him.

"Why did you storm out?" Trista added quietly, unsure of how her cousin would react to her prying. Naima laughed,

"You mean why did I storm out after Nyron mentioned Justin," guiltily Trista nodded,

"I'm sorry…I was curious."

"It's fine, I've never been able to hide my feelings towards him." Trista's eyes widened making Naima laugh again,

"Yes, Justin and I were a couple…until he left."

"What happened?"

Naima sighed but even as she did, there was a simmer of a smile on her face as she begun to speak,

"Justin is from HighTower, another of the highborn children we grew up with. He was a year or so older than me and I was infatuated with him from the moment I laid eyes on him."

"Is he handsome?"

"Gorgeous, Trista he's so beautiful it's unfair!" Trista laughed aloud, never seeing Naima like this before and loving it. She loved seeing her cousin carefree and dare she say, happy.

"We started seeing each other and when I was fifteen, I gave him my maidenhead." Naima said gently, "It was one of the most special nights of my life, one of many after that. We were inseparable and very much in love…or so I thought."

"What happened?"

Naima's face turned sour and regrettable,

"The war happened, well, the consequences of the war happened. Justin escaped with us to Priya; lived there for four years with his family who hadn't been killed when he decided to leave."

Trista's shocked face was question enough making Naima sigh again,

"Justin and his father and sisters are from a noble house, a proud house and they refused to remain in Mortania not in the station befitting them. When his father decided, they would take their remaining wealth and go to Cotai, he didn't decline."

"Could he have done?" Trista asked quietly.

"What?" Naima's brows furrowed and Trista swallowed, unsure if she could continue.

"I just mean, if his father ordered him to leave, at what, twenty years old and he was his only son…did he have a choice but to go?"

From the way, her lips pursed together, Trista realised that this was exactly what Justin must have said to her, or at least someone else.

"He should have stayed…he never should have left me."

"I know that…"

"Twelve years I haven't heard from him Trista,"

"I'm just saying…"

"Well *don't* just say!" Naima snapped, shutting Trista up instantly. She'd never seen Naima angry before and especially not at her. "What do you know about love anyway? You can't even tell tha—" Naima cut herself and shook her head.

"Forget it, I have *your* army to deal with."

Naima stormed away, leaving Trista feeling incredibly guilty before making her way back to the Academy.

FRIEND OR FOE

Later that evening, just before the sun began to set over the looming mountains; Trista watched as another band of young people arrived through the main gates of the inner building. Seemingly heading towards the training grounds; the small group consisted of men and women, all apparently excited about what was to come.

As Trista passed by, one of them spotted her and tapped her friends frantically as she pointed her out.

How people knew who she was, she would never get used to but the group of people all turned in her direction and bowed. Respectfully, she inclined her head and smiled brightly at them. They past her then with beaming smiles and an air of excitement, that was difficult to ignore.

As Trista walked back toward to the main building, ready to wash and get rid of the day on her skin. She went over the decisions, she'd made with Oren after her wreck of a conversation with Naima. He'd explained an exit plan, and so they were leaving the Academy in three days' time.

They would leave behind a few trusted captains who Oren had introduced her to, to train the newest recruits and hopefully meet Captain Theronos before heading out to The Wide. He was on his way from Cotai, sailing above Mortania to meet them, rather than below towards Thea's Point. It was a lengthier journey but necessary to avoid detection from anyone in the capital.

They would be leaving Thelm with eight thousand arms, many of whom she would formally meet before their departure. Oren had said it was important to be seen by the people who would be fighting for her, to show that she was in this with them as many would not return.

That notion had sat with her as she'd channelled her powers and her energy into being as prepared as she could be for the impending battle.

She found Nyron sometime later, in the immense foyer talking with a young scribe. He was scribbling something into a large book he held in his hands that the scribe looked desperate to get a hold of.

Trista stopped, curious to what was going on,

"Name, family name, age, gender, area and skill. In that order," he was saying. "No information can be missing. Many of these people will not return to their families and we need to know where they come from so those families can be informed."

"Yes Lord," the scribe said guiltily before taking back the book and scurrying off to do Nyron's bidding.

"There are people who will do that for you Ny," Nyron looked up at her with a surprised smile before pulling her into a sideways hug and walking with her towards the Main Hall.

"They could, but I like helping at all levels. That's something you should learn when you become queen: no task is above you Trista."

"That's profound,"

"Everything my father said was profound."

The same wistful tone was in his voice and Trista's heart swelled with love for him.

"I'll remember that. I just thought you would want to be doing more…stuff."

"Stuff as you call it little lady, will come soon enough!" Nyron laughed ruffling her hair and Trista shrugged him off even though she loved it. Nyron always made her feel as though she were part of a real family. He didn't treat her like she was this special thing that could never be damaged. He was real and honest with her and she loved him for it.

"Oren told you about leaving in a few days?"

"Of course, I received a raven from Justin and he should arrive that same day so any new recruits will have time to train and space to rest." Trista nodded,

"Okay. I'll see you at dinner?"

"Sure thing Tris," he said with a parting kiss on her forehead and disappeared into the bustling hall.

Trista instead turned and made her way to the dormitories towards Thorn's room. She'd decided she needed to speak with him before they left for The Wide. She needed to understand why he'd been acting so strangely and finally let him know how she didn't feel about him.

If she was lucky, he would stay in Thelm and maybe even make his way back to Remora without getting seriously hurt.

After a meandering walk, she found herself outside Thorn's door and firmly, she knocked. He opened the door moments later, dressed in his usual finery, looking as pristine as ever. It seemed the weeks on the road from Remora hadn't hardened him the way it had her. Gone were her cotton dresses and soft shoes and were replaced with trousers and leather boots. She was constantly on the alert, not knowing when she would have to train, or someone may try to attack her.

Her powers hummed though her body and while she hadn't had to use them in combat since their time on the road, she found she wanted to. She craved the feeling of unleashing all that bubbled quietly inside her.

"Can I come in?"

Thorn stepped aside, gesturing with his arm that she should enter and so she walked timidly into the room. She turned to him, composed and ready to get this over with.

"How are you?"

He shut the door and they were completely alone. He took a moment before nodding incredibly slowly,

"I'm fine." Trista waited for more but Thorn was silent.

"Is that it?"

"What more do you want?"

He said in that way he now spoke, void of life or any emotion to speak of. Frustrated, Trista cleared her throat,

"Look Thorn, we haven't spoken properly and I think there are things I need to explain...about us."

"What do you wish to say?"

Suddenly more worried then she would like to admit, Trista took a seat in a nearby chair and sighed as she looked down at her hands.

"Surely it's not just me...I thought you would have things to say too?"

"I didn't come to your room and declare that I did."

Trista looked up at him and Thorn was staring down at her, his blue eyes mischievous and she hated to admit that he was right.

"Okay, well, there's no easy way to say this and I don't want to hurt you but...but...I can't marry you."

He was quiet, infuriatingly so as he stood there continuing to stare down at her. Suddenly he nodded his head and said,

"I see,"

"What I said, before," she tried to add so maybe he would give her more than that. "About not having time for us; I meant it. I don't have time for what we were anymore...things have changed...my feelings have changed."

"As they must," his calm was angering her and she didn't know why. Trista stood from her seat to approach him head on,

"Before we got here, you were badgering me to talk and now you don't even seem to care!"

"What do you want me to say Trista?"

"I want you to give a damn!!" she snapped before turning away from him. She knew she shouldn't have admitted that, knowing how it made her sound.

"I care, but why fight this when there is someone else who holds your affections."

Why was he talking so formally? Thorn had always been well spoken but something about how he spoke to her now was so stilted.

She suddenly felt his hands on her shoulders, squeezing gently. They travelled slowly up the sides of her neck, caressing the veins there so unnaturally that she sprang away from him. She caught his hands still raised where they'd been around her neck and he slowly flexed his fingers before lowering his hands to his sides.

"What are you doing?"

"Is there someone else Trista?"

For her yes, but whether he wanted her back was not so clear. It didn't matter any way, Thorn had no right to ask her.

"That's none of your business." Thorn chuckled to himself,

"Come on Trista, it's not like it's a secret," he stalked up to her again, so their faces were inches apart.

"What's not a secret?"

"Your feelings for High Lord Antos." Trista's face heated with embarrassment as Trista looked up at him. "He's what, the second man you've ever met?"

Thorn smirked down at her,

"What do you think a virgin like you could offer a man of his stature?"

Tears welled in Trista's eyes at the cruelty of his words. She clenched her fists and they ignited into intense blue flame. Thorn laughed as he stepped back from the fire,

"You bastard,"

"Maybe," Thorn shrugged before walking past her and over to his bed. Astonished at his treatment of her and her reaction to it, Trista snuffed out her flames and marched towards the door with nothing else to say to him.

"We leave for The Wide in three days and will arrive with a final host of twelve thousand men. You don't have to be a part of that if you don't want to…I won't care either way."

The last part was a lie at least but she had to find a way to hurt him the way his remarks at hurt her. She had genuinely thought she loved Thorn, they had grown up together but his disregard for her just now was so unfair and unlike him. She had never known he could be so vicious. She closed the door firmly behind her and made her way to her room.

Later that night, after a small battle, Trista finally fell asleep. She had been labouring over Thorn's odd behaviour, but when she had finally fallen, she'd still tossed and turned. It was out of this chopped sleep that, she darted up in her bed, an odd feeling surrounding her. Her power hummed within her blood, her family ring glowing incessantly on her finger. There was a tingle over her skin, making the tiny hairs on her arms stand to attention and faster than she knew to comprehend, her chamber door flew open and Oren barged in, sword in his hand but bare chested. His eyes scanned her, upright in the bed,

"You felt it too."

It wasn't a question and even if it was, she didn't have time to answer as his eyes darted to the far corner of the room. He threw out his arm and something, crashed against the wall in corner.

A groan, a choking of sorts erupted from there and Trista reached out with her power to ignite all the candles in the room. As the room erupted with light, Trista laid eyes on the cloaked figure held against the walls of her chamber, the *armed* cloaked figure.

Trista rushed from her bed and stood beside Oren staring at the chocking figure,

"Who are you?"

The figure tried to speak from behind their cloaked face but gargles came out,

"Oren," Oren immediately released the person who dropped to the ground, clawing at their throat and gasping for breath.

"Who are you?" Trista repeated. "Don't make me ask again."

The person raised up from the floor and dusted themselves off,

"Easy," they chuckled at Oren's warning, and Trista heard it was distinctly feminine.

"I always did hate magic," the woman said. "Calm down young lord, I mean you and the would be queen no harm."

"My queen asked you a question."

Trista pushed it deep down inside how that phrase made her feel coming from Oren's lips.

The stranger stood up right and peeled her hooded cloak from her head and face to reveal an exquisitely beautiful brown skinned face with large golden eyes.

"You will bow before the princess," again the woman chuckled.

"I am Princess Saicha Voltaire of Agmantia young lord. It is you who should bow to me."

OLD FRIENDS & NEW

Oren watched her intently, his eyes scanning every possible part of the beautiful woman in front of them. Trista remained by his side, not afraid but feeling considerably safer with him close to her.

"How do I know you're the Princess of Agmantia?" Oren demanded, in no hurry to back down from the cloaked stranger who claimed to be royalty. The woman merely smirked and stepped forward; Oren raised his sword in answer even when she held her palms up in surrender.

"Why would I claim to be someone I'm not? Someone so regal at that?"

"Don't move another step," Trista said. "Until we can determine who you are, you're our prisoner."

"Not only am I not your prisoner, but you could not hold me for long if I were."

This woman's arrogance was beginning to get on Trista's nerves, but she refused to let her get a rise out of her. It was only as she felt Oren relax beside her, that she knew something had changed.

"You're an assassin."

It wasn't a question and the woman bowed low, dramatically before raising up again. She moved the opening of her cloak aside, revealing a cropped top and loose-fitting trousers. They were held tight to her ankles by what looked like bandages. The material was the darkest black Trista had ever seen and what looked to be great quality.

"At your service."

"You're here to fight with us?" Oren asked,

"In a fashion," the woman said. "Do you believe me or not?"

Trista felt Oren lower his guard and the hum she usually felt when he was around, his power, seemed to simmer.

"I have heard of the Agmantian princess who gave up any claim to the throne when she took the Assassin's code…I believe you."

"Good," the woman – Princess Saicha – smiled. "Now may I know who you are?"

Oren cleared his throat and the voice Trista had learned he used in serious situations, rang out.

"I am High Lord Oren Antos of HighTower, General of the Antonides army."

The princess bowed her head, impressed it seemed,

"Well met High Lord; and to you your Highness."

Saicha turned her intense look onto Trista who nodded her greeting but offered nothing else. She was beautiful, that much was obvious, but Oren had said she was an assassin which meant she was extremely dangerous.

Oren stepped forward and stretched out his arm which the foreign princess took and they clasped arms.

"While I accept who you say you are, I must know why you're here. Your point of entry hasn't filled me with much confidence about your intentions."

Saicha smiled but laughed good naturedly,

"I apologise lord but it could not be helped. My brother and I arrived earlier today and were turned away at the gate."

"We didn't know to expect you,"

"This I understand but we could not declare who we were without some possibility of that information falling into the wrong hands. Why would Agmantian royalty be on these shores with no declaration to do so."

"And why is that exactly?" Trista finally asked, stepping forward so she was side by side with Oren again. His large arm was so close; she could feel his warmth radiating from it.

"You need not be afraid of me princess; I mean you no harm. Not that your lover here would allow anything to happen to you."

Trista almost chocked on her own breath as her eyes widened in disbelief,

"General Antos is *not* my lover." She said firmly, angrily but Saicha only shrugged,

"I see, my apologies your Highness." Trista, saw she wasn't the least bit sorry but Oren thankfully, said nothing.

"Why are you here Princess?" as she said it, she realised why Oren must say it to her all the time; to use the title sarcastically was oddly satisfying. Saicha straightened and all sense of humour was gone as she said,

"King Curian sent word for aid to Agmantia. He requested that my mother, Queen Nucea send an Agmantian Assassin to take his daughter's life."

"What?"

Oren said it before she could, but she was no less shocked. *What on earth could this mean if Curian wanted his own daughter dead?*

"My mother would not make a decision purely on hearsay and so my brother and I, Prince Aslan; were sent to determine who was worthy of our forces. We have determined that to be you."

Trista was stunned, not only from the revelation about Curian and Briseis but that Agmantia wanted to help them.

"Why would you help us, help me?"

"I have seen both the princess and her father; spoken with the latter. It is our feeling that Princess Briseis is indeed the monster he claimed her to be and we will not aid in her advance to the throne."

Oren was nodding even as Trista remained stunned,

"I have not been able to discuss this with her but I also believe my mother has her own reasons for taking part in this war. Maybe now we have decided who to fight with; she will explain further."

Oren turned to Trista,

"The Council, everyone must hear this."

"Also…" Saicha started. "It is my understanding that they have a host of thirteen thousand men."

"Thirteen thousand?"

Trista's heart raced as even though it wasn't a great deal more than their own, it was a force already formed and they were still waiting for forces from Cotai. Their numbers may well be depleted before those additional forces arrived.

"You do not have the appropriate numbers I see,"

"Something like that," Trista replied quietly,

"Tri-your Highness," Oren said as his eyes shot a look at Saicha. Trista turned her panicked eyes to him, "We will discuss this with the Council. If what the princess says is true, we have a lot to plan." Trista nodded, still shocked from the news Saicha had brought.

"She has magic," Saicha said again. "Wields it both through herself and a group of teenagers."

"The Six," Trista said quietly.

"What?" her mind raced back to a time in her room in Priya.

"I heard voices, back in Priya. I told your father about it, but it never happened again."

"So…" Oren questioned.

"So, I heard the princess and her general talking about something she called her Six. I didn't know what it meant then…now I do."

"A conversation between those two is likely to be full of truths, as they are what one would call a couple."

"Gods above," Oren said under his breath before rubbing his hand over his face.

"You will come with us to the Council and tell us all you know. If you are truly on our side, then this should not be an issue."

"It is not. I have told my brother and our aids to meet me here tomorrow morning, I trust this will not be a problem?"

"Of course not, we'll find somewhere for you to sleep until we leave for The Wide in a few days."

Saicha bowed her head in gratitude at Trista as Oren turned and held his arm out towards the door he had barged through,

"After you," with a mischievous smile, Saicha stepped toward the opening and with a lasting look at each other, Oren and Trista followed

Trista sent Oren to gather everyone for a meeting in the Council Chamber. She knocked on the door of Chief Justice Yeng herself and let her know of Princess Saicha's arrival.

Only Chief Justice Yeng, Rowan, Nyron and Naima in addition to Trista, Oren and Saicha had been invited and everyone else would be informed in the morning.

"Nothing's changed," Nyron said confidently after Trista had spoken and told them how she wanted to proceed. "Sure, our numbers are less but not by much and with our magic and the Agmantian forces; we can continue as normal."

Everyone seemed to agree;

"How soon can your forces arrive here and how many?" Trista asked Saicha who was looking intensely at Nyron. Without moving her eyes from the tall man, Saicha replied;

"It has long been an Agmantian custom not to include more than five thousand men in any foreign war."

"Only five?"

"I'm sure I could be persuaded to give you more, Lord Antos," Saicha purred at Nyron. Naima rolled her eyes while Trista looked at Oren who tried to hide a smirk on his face and Nyron merely grinned,

"I'm sure I could princess but that will have to wait."

Saicha chuckled to herself,

"Aslan and I have requested the five thousand, they should be here in a week, maybe a little more."

Everyone nodded, their gratitude evident in their smiles. Rowan looked over at Saicha thankfully as she said,

"My daughter and I owe your mother a great debt Saicha. She was a very dear friend of mine."

Saicha turned to the queen and smiled knowingly,

"One friend slain and another lost…Mother was talking about you."

"Excuse me?"

"Before my brother and I left Agmantia," Saicha began. "Mother said that she lost her belief in peace when one friend was slain and another lost…she was talking about you your Majesty."

Rowan smiled warmly, her face fresh having just been woken from sleep and in her nightclothes.

"I do hope to see her again; I have missed her friendship."

"Well, with that said;" Chief Justice chimed in. "I think we all need a good night's rest."

"Yes, we leave for The Wide in three days as planned. Everybody get their affairs together before then." Oren ordered and they all inclined their heads before rising from the table.

"Naima?"

Naima turned at the sound of her name and Trista stepped up to her, gingerly. Everyone began to file out of the room, leaving them alone.

"I just wanted to say sorry…about earlier. I shouldn't have pried into your affairs." Naima smiled and pulled her little cousin into a hug.

"I'm sorry, I shouldn't have snapped at you. Justin just brings something out of me…I'm sure you understand."

Embarrassed, Trista didn't say anything, and Naima looked at her with a reassuring smile,

"When you're ready to talk about it, I'll be around." Naima hugged her again and they turned to leave the room.

As they stepped out of the Council Chamber and into the hall, they bumped into Nyron and Saicha.

They were looking into each other's eyes, their chest touching, practically breathing each other's air. When Naima and Trista approached, Nyron looked up with a mischievous look on his face and Saicha merely cleared her throat and stepped aside to let them pass.

"There isn't a word for how disgusting you are Nyron," Naima said brushing past them. Trista held back her laughter at how unimpressed Naima was.

"Love you too sis!" he called down the steps after her as Trista followed.

"Your Highness," Saicha said with a cheeky smile of her own.

Trista made her way to her bedroom and when she arrived, she was surprised to see Oren standing outside her door. He hadn't seen her approach and she watched him slouched against the wall, looking down at his hands.

When he finally noticed her approach, he straightened almost nervously and looked over at her.

"Is everything okay?" she asked worriedly.

"Yes, may I come in for a second?"

"Of course," she turned to the door and opened it to let them in.

Trista always felt strange being alone with Oren in small spaces because she was always so aware of him. His body, his power, his scent; all of it drove her senses insane. The pulsing in her body began to beat and, in an attempt to hide it, she remained turned away from him to arrange the covers on her bed.

"Is there something wrong?"

When she turned from her unnecessary fixing, Oren was inches from her, looking down at her. She swallowed down her nerves but said nothing,

"No, nothing's wrong I just…" he went silent, but she didn't push, unsure of what she would be pushing if she did.

"You were great today," he finally said gently, looking into her eyes. Trista gave him a nervous smile,

"T-thank you but I don't know what I did…"

"You made decisions, you spoke true, you acted like a true leader today and I just wanted to say…I'm proud of you. I know my father would be too."

Trista's heart swelled,

"Thank you…that means a lot to me."

She didn't know what else she was meant to say but Oren didn't move or say anything else and so she didn't either. She delighted in his closeness, felt dizzy with his scent and warmth floating around her like a cloud of intoxication.

"Thorn and I are no longer together."

She didn't know why she said it, but she felt she needed to; that he needed to know she was attached to no one. Even if he didn't care, she needed him to know it so maybe he could decide what she couldn't even bring herself to admit.

"I see."

"I spoke with him. He understands that things are different now…that I'm different."

"Yes…you are."

The tension was thick between them in a way she couldn't explain. She wanted to be close to him, she wanted to kiss him if she was honest, but he gave no indication of wanting to kiss her. Oren continued to stare down at her before he took a small step closer to her and reached out to push a stray strand of hair behind her ear. Trista's heartbeat quickened and her face flushed as her lips parted.

"I promise" he said quietly. "When this is all over, I will explain everything."

"Everything about what?" she pleaded, so confused and flustered from his fingers lingering delicately on her face.

Slowly, Oren lowered his head and ever so softly, kissed her cheek where his fingers had been. Trista closed her eyes, losing herself in the feel of his soft lips on her face. She felt faint with the feeling, leaning into him slightly before he lifted his head, so his lips were inches from her face and murmured,

"Goodnight Princess."

He stepped back then, out of her personal space and Trista watched as he flexed his fingers and clenched them into fists before turning and leaving her room completely.

REVELATIONS

Baron Lyon Dreston was tied to a damp stone wall in the middle of Gods knew where and he couldn't tell how long he had been there.

Whether it was minutes, hours or days, all he knew was that the pain was never ending as sharp as it had been the very first time Duncan had sliced into him.

Endlessly he bled until he passed out and even the relief of unconsciousness was short lived as he was revived almost instantly.

More pain.

More screams.

All he was, was pain.

"You have nothing to say?" Duncan was saying now but Lyon could not find his words to either deny or confess. He had lost his ability to do anything but bleed.

"It is simple Baron, tell us your ill-conceived plans for the crown and our beloved princess and we'll end this."

Lies.

If he confessed what he had done, what he had planned; they would kill him for sure.

Isn't death better than this?

He couldn't help the thought creeping into his head. Surely, anything was better than this…

"Very well, I am bored of this, we'l—"

"That's enough."

At the sound of her voice, Dreston knew that if he could convince her of his innocence, then Duncan would have no choice but to let him go.

"P-please…please," his mouth was drier than he had ever felt it, his lips cracked and bleeding from the beatings, his right eye swollen shut. He couldn't see her among the darkness, but her voice carried.

"Baron, I have little time for your pleas. Tell me what I wish to know, or you will not live to see another day."

She was serious, that he knew.

"T-the king…w-wants you d-dead."

He stammered, eager to give her what she wanted, to free himself from this torture.

"Of this I am aware," she sounded bored and any hope he had of leaving this place alive dissipated from his body. "Tell me what you know of his plans."

Desperate to find something to save his own skin, Lyon exposed all he knew of Curian's plans however little it may seem. He confessed he didn't know the intricate details of her father's plans with Agmantia but confessed what information he had provided the king; about her relationship with General Beardmore and her proposition to him. His words tasted like acid in her mouth as he lost himself. He tried to rationalise that he was doing this to save his own life but it didn't stop the burn of shame.

"I have recently learned that the Samaian Redeemer will have a final host of twelve thousand men. Your addition to me and my father's army have been welcome and for that, I thank you."

Lyon let out a jagged breath as his relief left his body.

He thanked the Gods for the part he played in securing the numbers for the Greybold army.

He raised his head as far as it would go and looked through the shadows for the princess. As though she knew his need to see her, Lyon watched as she stepped forward into the light that Duncan had created.

Briseis was dressed entirely in black leather and fur. Her white hair was piled high on top of her head in an elaborate arrangement of braids. She had on dark make up, dark like her stare as she slowly began to peel her leather gloves away from her delicate fingers.

"I do not tolerate disloyalty Lyon but more so, I do not tolerate cowardice."

She stepped towards him and everyone else in the room took one step back. Briseis stretched out her hand and Lyon began to raise from his slumped position until he was completely upright looking out into the darkened room.

In an instant, his bounds were removed, and he remained hanging in the middle of the room by Briseis' will alone.

"You are a pathetic excuse for a human being who deserves all that will befall you."

Lyon's heart began to beat incessantly in his chest, terrified at what the princess had in store for him.

Unexpectedly, she smiled, genuinely smiled as she said,

"You'll be happy to know that your friends were helpful in incriminating you," she made a gesture with her hand and from somewhere behind her, the sound of a heavy door opened and closed and in moments, Lyon watched as Lord Weilyn, Lord Priya, Baron Thelm and Aml walked into the room.

"W-what is this?"

"This is your comeuppance Baron Dreston, this…is your end."

Aml stepped forward and placed three thick rolls of parchment on a small wooden table that Lyon hadn't even noticed was between them. He watched in confusion as one of the scrolls unrolled itself and a feathered quill suddenly appeared beside it.

"Your companion Aml here was more than happy to bring these along, considering what you did to his lady love and no doubt countless others."

Lyon was confused, what had Aml done to him...

"I don't understand," he breathed, bewildered.

"You are going to sign these papers Baron Dreston and all your holdings, possessions and armies will belong to me."

"I have done all you asked!" he tried to shout but his face and body ached from his beatings.

Briseis' face suddenly switched, and the most tremendous slap echoed across his face with an invisible hand, splitting his cheek wide open. Blood leaked down his face as his choked cry resounded in the close space.

He saw Duncan smile, even as blood spluttered from his mouth.

"You thought you could bed me and take my kingdom. You thought you could out smart me and my father, fool that he is and somehow rule Mortania. You have made no friends in this world Baron and it is your undoing!"

"I have done nothing you have not done yourself!" Lyon yelled, finding the strength from the injustice that was being forced upon him.

"You are not me!" Briseis thundered at him, silencing everyone; even the air stood still.

"You, Baron are not me and never will be. You hold no power here and it's high time you understood that. Sign those papers and we can be done with this!"

Briseis turned from him then and Duncan and Aml stepped forward,

"I will not sign!"

"Oh, you will," Briseis said from the other side of the room where she'd folded her arms across her chest. "I ask you to do this for politics; I don't *need* your permission."

"No one will believe you, no one will believe I gave up my life!"

"Who will say otherwise Baron?" Briseis said with a smirk. "Who in this room will even remember your name once I am done with you?"

Briseis pretended to think about it as she gestured to each of the men who had entered the room,

"The Baron you manipulated into an illegal marriage maybe?" Baron Thelm looked away. "Perhaps the man whose wife you defiled in front of him?" Lord Priya looked on defiantly, proudly and Dreston felt sick.

"Or maybe the man who you've practically enslaved for thirty years and continued to rape the woman he loves every night!"

Aml straightened his back and glared over at Lyon and it finally clicked to him,

"Alaina," he choked out but Briseis only laughed.

"You have no friends here Dreston and in light of that…sign those papers."

He thought about fighting.

He thought about not doing it, about protesting to his last breath that he would not give up his lands or his birth right; but when he looked into the eyes of all the people looking down at him, he knew he was lost.

He had nothing, he had no one and Briseis; Briseis had a lethal magic that had only not been unleashed on him until now, because she needed him.

"I will sign," Lyon whispered and instantly fell to the floor as her power let him go.

He thought someone would drag him up toward the table but no one touched him. He realised that they wanted to embarrass him further and watch him crawl across the cold, wet ground. Lyon crawled to the small table in front of him, on his hands and knees, clawing his way to the table top and took the quill into his quivering hand.

Aml stepped forward and held the scroll down although he knew full well there was no need. When Lyon scribbled his name as best he could, the scroll was replaced with another and another until he had signed his world away…and his life.

"It is done your Highness." Aml replied as he took the papers and returned to his place in the shadows.

"Good."

As she said the words, Briseis threw her arm out and Lyon slammed back against the wall, pinning him there for all to see. His bowels loosened on impact and he soiled himself in front of all of them.

The Baron cried out in indescribable pain as Briseis took her time to draw a line in the air with her finger and the baron's neck began to slice open. She watched his life slowly ebb away from him and all Briseis could think about, was how much blood came from such a small man.

When she had slit his throat and all the blood had drained like a butchered pig, with a flick of her wrist, Briseis snapped his neck and watched Lyon Dreston's head fall from his body and slam into the floor.

"Clean that up," she said. "We have a lot to do before the Samaians get here and I have my meeting with Avriel Remora."

"Yes, your Highness," Duncan replied simply as Briseis turned to leave. She turned back to them at the last minute and said,

"General Beardmore is to know nothing of this do you understand me?"

"Yes, your Highness!" the room chorused.

Briseis left the dugout and emerged into the night sky, taking a deep breath, before heading back to her tent to see what news her Samaian informant had brought her.

VENGEANCE & REDEMPTION

Avriel Remora sat in the war tent of Crown Princess Briseis Greybold, playing with a small ball of fire in the palm of her hand. She manipulated the shape, made it larger and smaller as she saw fit, getting used to the feel of her powers again.

It felt good to be using them so freely, she thought, as she delighted in the warmth of the thing. Warmth, not just from its heat but from the power that coursed through it and therefore herself.

She had allowed her powers to remain dormant for several years, not only because of what had happened after Alexander's death but because she had no need of it.

She had been happy in Remora with her husband and son and had thought she was content to live out her days with the them. The wife of a Lord, and Lady to a large estate, was a far cry from the squalor she had grown up in.

Avriel was born Avriel Theron, eldest daughter of a large family with little to no money. Her mother had died after the birth of her youngest sibling and so at twelve, she had become a mother of five overnight.

Her father, a drunk at the best of times, had taken to Avriel's new role in the house a little too literally and by her fourteenth birthday, she had already birthed and lost two of her father's children.

It was after the death of her second child, that something in Avriel snapped and in her moment of intense grief, she Ascended into the powers that she thought would never come.

Her father had never practiced their cultural gifts, had never nurtured them the way her mother had tried to, even with her deteriorating health. Their power was something living, that could only thrive within a healthy host. Avriel had thought her powers would never come, her body too weak from hunger to withstand it; but when she held her deformed, stillborn child in her arms, something inside her broke.

She had Enflamed and in an instant, incinerated her entire family. In a matter of seconds, everything she had ever known was gone.

The residents of her small southern village were terrified of her, unwilling to help who they saw as a whore who lay with her father and others for coin.

Avriel, in her fury had obliterated her village and with the coin she stole from the now vacant homes and businesses, she travelled to Thea's Point, intent on making a new life for herself. No one would know her in Thea's Point, no one would care where she had come from and Avriel found that she could mould herself into whoever she wished to be.

She bought new clothes and was reborn into an orphan girl named Avriel Ormon, her mother's maiden name and set about creating a life she could be proud of.

Avriel Ormon was helped without being ridiculed and shamed.

Avriel Ormon was treated like a normal person and was eventually directed to the home of an elderly Samaian woman who kindly took her in.

It was during her time with Onella, that Avriel learned what it was to be Gifted; the legion of exceptionally talented Samaian sorcerers who could wield magic in magnificent ways. She idolised the idea, the grandeur of what it meant to be special and so, when she was seventeen; Avriel left Thea's Point and journeyed to Agmantia to join the House of Gifts.

Her dream, however, was not to come true as the High Gifted determined she did not have enough power to warrant a place in their school. They had said, the power she did have;

though magnificent in its potential was *unhinged*, open to corruption and they wanted no part of it.

Avriel had begged, screaming that to be Gifted was all she ever wanted and would do anything to train with them. For reasons, she didn't care to know or question, they took pity on her and gave her work at the school.

There, she worked with the High Gifted, not learning from them as she so wished, but in the ways of administration to the most high-ranking scholars. She learned languages, diplomacy and politics and within this area, her expertise was finally noticed.

Avriel was referred to the capital and when she was nineteen, was taken on by the royal household as a Cultural Ambassador. She would be paid to travel and communicate with the low born, as she had once been and expand relations with them.

During this time, she met the young King and Queen, Alexander and Rowan Antonides.

Avriel had adored Rowan from their first meeting. Queen Rowan was everything Avriel had ever hoped to be: beautiful, rich and had the love of a great man and the might of a family name. Her elder sister Rayne was Chief Gifted and while Avriel idolised Rayne for her magic, it was Rowan she wanted to become.

Avriel spent her days at Tirnum Castle in her new ambassador apartments, practicing how to emulate Rowan. How to move and speak and *be* just like her. After all, someone as perfect as Rowan wouldn't be denied entry to the House of Gifts.

Avriel adored her new role despite her want to return to the House of Gifts as a student but hoped, that one day her growth in magic and knowledge would earn her a place there. So, secretly she trained herself in the magic and spells that were available to her without training, hoping her opportunity would one day come. Her magic though powerful, was not like the Gifted and manifested in ways she could not share with others because she was forbidden from doing it. Avriel remained her own tutor and built her strength in secret.

It was during her two years in Tirnum that something else drew her to Rowan; the Queen's miscarriages.

In the two years that Avriel lived in the castle, the young and perfect queen had lost four children; one of which was still born. Avriel knew that pain more than anyone and when she found the young queen in the royal gardens one night, free of guards and crying her eyes out; Avriel comforted her. Avriel told her that things would change, that she would be a mother when the time was right. Rowan had thanked her profusely and promised her anything for being so kind.

Avriel had declined her offer of a reward but mentioned, briefly; her wish to be Gifted. Rowan had promised she would speak with her sister Rayne, had promised she would get her into the House of Gifts, but when Alexander appeared in the garden and saw his beautiful wife crying; he'd whisked her away and they'd never discussed it further.

In the following months, Avriel travelled the breadth of Mortania and wasn't able to speak with Rowan again, until her work eventually brought her to Remora. In the picturesque mountain town, Avriel met a handsome young lord named Fabias who swept her off her feet.

Avriel discovered what it meant to truly love and to be loved in return. Fabias asked her to marry him less than a year later and all thoughts of being Gifted left her completely. Fabias loved and cherished her and wanted her to be his wife and a lady and she gladly accepted.

She spent the next five years in Remora, now Lady Avriel and moulded herself into the person she had always hoped to be; all thoughts of her father and old family forgotten. She hid her hair, her heritage and snuffed her powers out, in no more need of them now that she had everything she wanted. She'd honestly believed she had it all until, after avoiding the possibility with tonics; Avriel fell pregnant.

She was terrified that history would repeat itself but soon, a healthy baby boy was born and Avriel fell in love with Thorn more than she could have ever loved anyone.

Then, Alexander had died.

The Samaian world had plunged into perpetual darkness and Avriel had immediately offered her help, offered her aid to the crown to fight with Rowan and the Gifted

They'd said no, again.

Instead, they'd asked her to take care of something, something special; something more special then she could have ever hoped to be.

Princess Trista.

Lenya Sentine, Captain of the Queen's Guard had arrived on a stormy night to The Grange and told Avriel that the little princess, Trista Antonides was now in the care of a couple named Gwendolyn and Matthias Freitz. She was told to watch over the little princess, to educate her in the Samaian way, befriend her; make her feel connected to the people she had been taken from, so that one day, she would rise and reclaim her throne.

And so, Avriel had promised.

Avriel had lied.

She would not teach Trista. She would not give this little child all the opportunities, love and connection to a magic that she had been denied for far too long.

The princess didn't deserve it, and so, Avriel watched the little girl grow. She watched the flower inside Trista bloom and wilt each time the village kids were mean to her because she was different.

She knew it would break her. She knew, having no one and feeling cut off from everyone around her would make Trista doubt herself and her abilities and she wouldn't be ready to take on the pressure of battle when the time came.

Avriel wanted the princess to fail, but then, Thorn had fallen in love with her. Avriel had watched her son fall in love with the very person she despised and had given in. She had given in to her love for her only son and began to teach Trista, knowing full well that it wouldn't be enough.

Thorn meant everything to Avriel and she would do anything for him; even if it meant helping the product of the woman and system she loathed.

It was because of her hate for Rowan and her dismissal by the crown, that Avriel was going to help Briseis take down the Samaian army and finally take her place beside the throne as Chief Gifted.

She was owed this and she would do anything, even corrupt her own son to finally achieve her dreams.

Briseis entered the war tent moments later and Lady Avriel Remora rose from where she was sat on a low seat playing with a ball of fire. When she saw Briseis' eyes fall to the flame, she outed it and placed her hands into the large sleeves of her gown, clasping them in front of her.

"It feels good to use the power again. It has been a long time." She said by way of explanation.

Briseis nodded and walked further into the tent to stand across from the older woman, still dressed in her leathers; the blood of Baron Dreston still on her.

"Not so long ago as I understand it. You've been possessing your son for weeks now."

Briseis watched as guilt flittered across the woman's face and she turned away. She had not bothered to question why this woman had contacted her; why she was willing to use her son to betray her own people but now it seemed appropriate to ask.

"You regret your decision." It wasn't a question but Avriel answered anyway,

"I do not regret helping you Briseis, I regret using my son to do it."

"Briseis?" Avriel shook her head with an amused smile,

"Let's not forget who is Samaian by birth in this room. I've used my powers for longer then you've been alive."

"And that gives you the right to disrespect me?"

"No, it gives me the right to speak to you as an equal. I will not be talked down to, by you or anyone."

For the first time, Briseis had nothing to say. She had killed people for less, but the way Avriel had spoken to her; she almost admired.

Briseis finally turned toward her drinks cabinet and poured herself and her guest a drink. She handed the small glass to Avriel as she took a sip herself and the other woman did the same.

"What have you learned?"

"Straight to the point I see,"

"We are at war Lady Avriel, would you have me linger with pleasantries?"

"I would have you offer me assurances that me and my family will be safe. That you will deliver on your promises."

"What more assurances do you need? I have given my word that you, your son and husband will come to no harm. Along with your position as, Chief Gifted was it, what more do you want?"

"If Rowan finds out about my involvement in this…" the older women trailed off and for the first time, Briseis could see that she was scared.

"Rowan is alive?" Avriel looked at her with bewilderment, "Of course, she's alive. She's with Trista in Thelm."

Interesting.

The great Samaian queen had finally reared her beautiful head.

"Well," Briseis sipped her wine again. "We'll get to our disappearing queen in a moment, but what can you tell me about where the little princess will strike."

"If at all," Avriel scoffed dismissively. "She has a host of only eight thousand men, with four more to join and they leave for The Wide in three days."

Three days.

With the current climate in the North and the terrain between Thelm and The Wide, with eight thousand men it would take them at least another two to get everyone across, if they all made it. The additional four thousand were of no interest to her at the moment, the forces in Thelm could take care of them.

Thea's Reach was notorious for its treacherous terrain and if Trista's pitiful army was to even make it across, they wouldn't be a force to contend with any way.

"What do you know of their power?"

"Not much," Avriel admitted as she sipped her own wine. "They are working with the Lithanian Council so could have any manner of aid from the Empaths but I have heard no specific numbers. She also has the help of the Antos family."

"Why does that name sound familiar?" Avriel laughed as she downed her glass and proceeded to pour herself another. Briseis watched the other woman's casual movements and admired her confidence.

"Because my dear," she motioned to Briseis' glass but she declined. "General Gorn Antos was the previous occupier of that large manor you pass in the Imperial Lands. He led the army against your father's rebellion. The Antos men, Briseis, are warriors, the greatest warriors to ever exist in this world."

"What makes them so great? I seem to remember the Samaians losing the last war."

Avriel only shook her head as she continued to drink her wine, contemplative before she began to speak again.

"There is a story Samaians learn in childhood about noteworthy Samaian families. Growing up, everyone wishes to be one, to descend from one even when you know that it could never be true."

Avriel drank again and stared into the small brazier that was lit to keep the war tent warm. She stood there for a moment, staring into the flames

"You dream as a child, in your cold, straw bed about a better life, a life where you're really a long-lost princess descended from a line of Gods."

"Forgive my intrusion into your reverie but what does this have to do with the Antos family?"

Avriel turned to the princess, annoyed with the interruption.

"The Goddess Thea had five children, five children from which all the great Samaian families descend. The Antos family descend from Kriston Antonides, the God of War."

"Which means what?"

"Which means Briseis that, while the Antonides family have a long line of Makers and are highly proficient in natural magic; the Antos speciality is war. Antos men have warfare, battle tactics, skill in their blood. It's written in their make-up to be better at everything related to combat."

"Magic like that," Avriel said quietly, turning away again. "Can't be beaten…and Trista is in love with one of them."

Briseis immediately piped up, interested at this tad bit of information,

"Explain,"

"His name is Oren Antos and Trista has broken off her engagement with Thorn because she is in love with him."

"I assume we can use this information for something?" Avriel nodded,

"If you can kill Oren Antos, not only will you have rid yourself of the threat of an Antos warrior but you will break Trista; and that…will win your war."

***

Curian had erected a temporary Gods House among the camp and knelt within the warmed tent, in silent prayer.

He knew in times of need, that one's faith was the best remedy and he was no exception. He needed to find peace and he had run out of ideas on how to achieve it.

Hours passed before he left the God's House under a tight armed guard and marched to his own tent. When he entered, he was more than surprised to see Briseis lounging on one of his couches.

"What are you doing here?"

She was dressed in combative leathers and he could distinctly see blood splattered over them. What this was meant to show him, he had no idea, but it was apparent that Briseis was in the mood to play.

She lounged there, looking over at him as she reclined, and he noticed the tiny flames alight in her eyes. He powered up in response and as he did, she laughed and in seconds was standing behind him.

Curian jumped back, unsheathing his sword and igniting his left hand,

"Relax Father, if I wanted you dead, you would be."

"Then why am I still alive?" he dared to ask even as he kept his fist ablaze, ready to strike at whatever she gave out.

"Unfortunately, I still have need of you."

"What might I ask for?"

Briseis stepped toward him and Curian stepped back. Slowly, they began to circle one another.

"Despite my perfectly obvious capabilities to win this war, it seems your army don't wish to follow me into battle."

"That was in any way unclear before?"

"No, but I've been shown that it would be easier to have your men follow you into battle. There, you'll die seemingly heroically and they will continue to fight for you and consequently for me."

"Gardan told you this, you take counsel from him now?" Briseis' face went very still as her emotions were completely masked.

"From the general of my army, of course."

"He is more than that though, isn't he Briseis? I for one never took you for a whimsical whore!"

"Oh, words of poison," she mocked him as they continued to circle. "That reminds me, I wanted to thank you."

"Thank me, for what?"

"Your request to Nucea."

The blood rushed from Curian's face but even as he swallowed away his fear, he said nothing. "Agmantian Assassins, I'm flatted you sought their expertise to get rid of me. Baron Dreston was also very forthcoming in telling me what you all had planned for me. Not that it did him any good."

"Bri—"

"Uh uh uh," she said wagging her finger at him with a smile, seconds before her face turned into a hideous scowl.

"No more words, no more lies; you are dead, do you hear me…dead."

"Then why not just kill me now and be done with it!" he barked at her,

"And give you what you want, never!" her look was feral as in the blink of an eye, she was behind him with a blade at his neck.

"Ahh!"

"I know what ails you Curian Greybold, and I will crumble mountains to dust, before I let you get what you want."

"And what is it I want?" Curian choked out through clenched teeth, knowing he could repel her with her power but not sure what good it would do.

"Rowan Antonides."

Curian's eyes widened as Briseis removed the blade from his throat and walked around him to face him once more. She smirked up at him,

"You know where she is."

"I know where she is." Briseis confirmed with a sinister grin, Curian's heart swelled with anticipation and excitement before it plummeted to the ground.

Somehow Briseis had discovered his love for Rowan and would never tell him where she was.

He would never see Rowan again.

He would never be able to save his soul for all the pain he had caused.

"I must admit, you had me for a moment when I just couldn't understand what was making you so weak." Briseis looked her father up and down. "I should have known it was something as trivial as the love of a woman."

She sounded disgusted,

"It wasn't until I looked into your previously un-royal past that I realised what it is you truly seek."

She was mocking him and Curian could do nothing about it,

"Find whatever redemption you seek elsewhere old man, because you will never set eyes on Rowan again."

Briseis swiftly exited the tent, leaving Curian to crumble onto the floor and weep with despair.

PREPARATION

Prince Aslan of Mortania joined Trista and her friends and family the following morning, along with the two aids they'd brought with them from Agmantia. Trista liked him immediately although it was obvious he was taken with Dana from the start. The prince was straightforward, brazen even but there was an endearing quality about him that no one took offence by it.

Despite their petty bickering, all could see Saicha and Aslan had a genuine respect and care for one another and it was a delight to watch.

Rowan welcomed both the siblings with open arms, as she explained that Nucea had been her dear friend.

"Your mother was there when I went through a hard time conceiving. I knew her before she was."

"How is it that she never spoke of you?" Aslan asked plainly and everyone in the Main Hall where they ate breakfast, looked away uncomfortably.

"Watch yourself Prince," Nyron said simply, not in the least bit deterred by Aslan's status. Aslan raised his hands in surrender,

"I mean no disrespect warrior," he said smiling. "I just wish to know why my mother never mentioned such a dear friend and I can't very well ask her."

Rowan smiled over at Nyron,

"Thank you for your concern nephew but Aslan has a right to be a little suspicious." Nyron shrugged and continued to tuck into the mountain of eggs and bacon he had in front of him.

Rowan turned to Aslan again, Saicha was sat beside him, everyone else including Thorn and Lamya looked on,

"After the war, after my husband was killed and I had to give up my daughter, I fled to Agmantia."

Trista perked up at the new information.

"You and your siblings were very young, Aslan only a year or so old. I arrived in Noth, desperate to find my way to the palace but of course no one is permitted unless officially invited."

"To cut a long story short, I used what little remained of my magic to contact Nucea and thankfully she had someone come and find me, I would be dead if she hadn't."

Saicha seemed to concur with her story as the older lady continued,

"I spent a few months with you all at the palace, but it was deemed too risky for me to stay any longer lest someone determine who and where I was."

"There were men all over the world looking for me for at least three or four years after the war ended and I couldn't hide my power indefinitely; neither could your mother's Shamans."

Rowan looked on regrettably before continuing,

"It was then I got in contact with the Council and they said I could stay here, they had the power to cloak me, as they have done for the past sixteen years. I assumed your mother didn't talk about me because it was just too dangerous to do so Aslan. We didn't want her or her family to become accountable if people thought she was hiding me."

Saicha nodded,

"That much I can understand, at the Guild, we are constantly bombarded for information on individuals we have in our custody."

"The Assassins hold prisoners?" Dana asked innocently,

"In some extreme cases, yes."

"I wouldn't mind being your prisoner," Aslan winked over at Dana who blushed furiously but said nothing. Saicha rolled her eyes, seemingly used to his behaviour but everyone else giggled good naturedly. Trista squeezed her friend's knee teasingly under the table before smiling over at everyone,

"It's so lovely having you with us now Aslan, however short your stay will be. Your sister told you of our departure?"

"Yes, we go where you go Princess."

"Thank you, well if that's all for the morning Mother will you join me for a moment please?"

Rowan couldn't hide the beam on her face as she nodded demurely and followed suit.

"Naima, Nyron, Dana please bring our guests up to speed; Lamya and Oren, you'll be with the Council?"

"Yes, of course Princess." Lamya responded,

Trista turned to leave when a voice called out,

"What about me?"

Trista turned to look at Thorn, completely unimpressed with him since last night,

"You may do as you wish. If you'll excuse me."

Trista left the table and her mother followed close behind.

Trista led Rowan to a large library that the Justices had said they could use to discuss their plans outside of the Council Chamber.

The two women, mirror images of each other with only years between them; took their seats at the small table in the middle of the room. They were surrounded by walls filled with books and other writing materials all dating back to before either of them was born. The Council was home to a world of knowledge that people travelled the world to covet and they were privileged to be among the tomes.

"You didn't tell me about being in Agmantia," Trista said thoughtfully. She settled into the chair she usually used and began to finger through the papers she'd left there previously.

"This upset you," Rowan stated and Trista shrugged.

"Not really, I just don't understand why you couldn't have taken me with you?" Rowan sighed and reached across the table to take her daughter's hand into her own. She squeezed it gently,

"Trista, I thought I explained this."

"You did, I understand that being together creates a signal to others; that we're trackable the closer we are to each other but surely, being in Agmantia would have kept it at bay?"

Rowan looked distress making Trista worried,

"Mama what's wrong?"

"You truly have no idea how powerful we are." Trista was confused. "It's not your fault of course, Avriel was meant to educate you but she clearly hasn't. I'm just sad that you haven't had the education you would have, had things been different."

"Me too," they both sighed.

Lamya had already discussed with Rowan, Avriel's neglect of her education and Trista had stopped to wonder why but could no sooner get the answer then kill herself with worry.

"Trista I know it's hard to understand but whether I was in Agmantia or Cotai or even Yitesh; it wouldn't matter. The Everlasting is the creator of all things; it's power is present everywhere and I didn't have enough power to shield us both for as long as was needed. Not even the Agmantian Shamans or the Council collected could have enough to mask your strength."

Trista nodded her understanding. She understood what her mother was saying but it didn't make it any easier to accept. Unless...

"Could a Maker have enough?"

"What do you know of Makers?" Trista shrugged,

"Not much, Lamya told us to enquire once we got here but we haven't really had time. She said I could ask you or even my grandmother."

"Freilyn would indeed have more information than me but we can't possibly get to her until after this war is over. Why do you ask of Makers?"

Trista blushed, but she didn't know why as she confessed what Naima had said about her abilities.

"Do you think it's true, am I a Maker?"

"Trista, there's no question of whether or not it's true. If you created that sword from magic and it glowed as you say, then yes, you are a Maker. Have you been able to do it again?"

"No, just that one time."

"Then we'll not think about it too much. When this war is over, we'll focus on nurturing your abilities. Rayne may even be with us by then, she can help you."

Trista nodded, thankful for the reassurance but there was something playing on her mind,

"Everything is when the war is over…what if it's never over, what if we lose?"

"Don't think that way Trista…just don't. Everything will work out, it always does…we're together, now aren't we?"

"Yes," Trista smiled adoringly at her mother and Rowan smiled back,

"See…everything will be as it should be."

Trista hoped that her mother was right.

Trista spent the rest of the morning with her mother, going over what else was needed for their departure before bringing their list to Lamya and Dana. They had taken charge of the administration of the war effort while Naima, Oren and Nyron took charge of the soldiers.

Wars were expensive and required so many things, she had never thought of before coming here. Weapons, armour, wood, grain, bandages, medicines and everything else in between. She had been so focused on being physically ready, she wasn't sure if she was mentally ready for everything else.

She would be forever grateful to the Council and her mother of course, for starting something she only had to finish and oversee. Without the financial aid from the Council, who knew where they would be.

Trista travelled the length of the grounds later that day on her way to train with Oren. She decided to go through the kitchens so she could find something to eat, too hungry to wait until dinner in the evening.

It was as she was leaving the kitchens, chewing on some buttered bread rolls, that she bumped into Nyron and Saicha.

There was a narrow and dimly lit hallway that lead from the kitchen and food halls to the barracks and it was here she found her cousin and her new ally, plastered against the wall in a passionate embrace.

Nyron's face was buried in Saicha's neck as her head was thrown back with her eyes closed. Saicha had changed out of her assassin's robes and stood in just a cropped top and a long flowing skirt. She had taken out the braids Trista had seen and now her large afro was on display, as Nyron played in the tight curls.

Trista couldn't stop staring as her eyes followed to wear Nyron's hand disappeared under the folds of her skirt that was lifted to expose her creamy brown leg and thigh,

"Uh hmm!" she cleared her throat.

She looked away as they both looked up at the intrusion, Nyron a picture of mischievousness.

"Are you decent?" Trista said, her face hot with embarrassment.

"Never," came Nyron's amused reply.

Trista rolled her eyes and looked back at them. They were thankfully back to a more appropriate position and while Saicha looked on unapologetically, Nyron couldn't hide his delight.

"I'm sorry I disturbed you," Trista said quietly, unable to look them in the eye.

"Not as sorry as me, I was nearly done." Saicha moaned,

Nyron almost choked on his snort as he looked away. Trista got annoyed and straightened her back,

"I don't care what you do with your time here Princess Saicha but you will have more respect for yourself and others when choosing to do it in public!"

Nyron stopped laughing instantly and then the look of shame arrived. Saicha's eyebrows rose but she didn't immediately say anything,

"While I appreciate your assistance in these trying times, you are here to perform a duty and will do so without embarrassment."

"I'm sorry Tris," Trista turned her gaze to her cousin and steeled her eyes against him. Nyron cleared his throat,

"My sincerest apologies your Highness…it won't happen again."

Trista walked toward them to head toward the barracks and for a split second, Saicha remained in her way.

Trista said nothing as did the other princess before she stepped aside and inclined her head respectfully. Trista kept her head held high as she walked past them, embarrassed and shaking.

Oren was waiting for her when she finally arrived, as battle ready as ever in his leathers and armed to the hilt.

"Everything okay?" he asked as she went over to the weapons rack to pick a sword. She weighed it up in her hands before turning to him,

"I'm fine, I just caught Nyron and Saicha…together." Oren laughed,

"From your blush I can see it's the first time you've seen anyone…together?" Oren smiled, letting out something she assumed was a laugh but she didn't find it funny.

"I don't think that's any of your business General!" she snapped at him and his smile disappeared.

"Sorry…it's not. I'm sorry."

Trista felt bad. Her sexual history wasn't any of his business, but she knew she'd only snapped because it was Oren asking.

"It's fine, let's just get to work."

With that, she charged at him sending a ball of energy to try and knock him to the ground.

Half an hour later, Trista ducked and rolled forward, sword still outstretched as she dodged the fireball that Oren aimed at her head. They looked like fireballs but were actually energy balls that would disintegrate on impact but they hurt like a punch. They were special balls Oren used to train her that made the danger very real even if it wasn't fatal.

Back on her feet, she threw a fireball ball back at him just as he threw up an energy shield and her ball dusted into nothing. Quickly, she Shifted herself, so she was inches from him, and crashed her blade down above his head. Oren caught her strike just in time and their swords met with a deafening screech.

She twisted her sword, so she was now in the dominant position and struck him again. Oren met her blow for blow until the two of them were a blur of strikes and near misses in the middle of the training yard.

Oren lunged at her, slicing through the air with the power of his longsword before reaching to pull her towards him with his power. She resisted, her power defiant and unwilling to bend to his even as she felt him trying to choke it out of her.

Deep down she pushed even as she continued to physically fight him and repelled against the pull. She felt the tug snap from around her and quickly blasted him with a ball of energy that had him bowling over onto the ground. He lost the hold of his sword and it skittered across the ground. Trista motioned towards it and his sword disappeared.

Oren growled as another sword appeared instantly in his hand, he Shifted and was in front of her once again. They continued their dance of swords, Trista's eyes on him, anticipating his next moves, until he lunged at her and knocked her own sword out of her hand.

It skittered across the ground, but Trista didn't waste time worrying about it as she reached behind herself and retrieved the dagger she had there, then lunging it at Oren. He grabbed her wrist and spun her around until he had her held against him, her own dagger at her throat.

She felt the moment his power wrapped around her as well as his arms and try as she might, she couldn't break free.

"Yield?" he breathed from above her head.

"Yield," she panted as he slowly let her go. As he did so, she turned and punched him in the face.

"Oww!" he said looking at her in shock as he placed his hand to his face. "That actually hurt!"

"It was meant to," she giggled at his scowl until he began to laugh,

"You little bi—" Oren lunged after her and Trista ran off screaming.

"Aah!" she laughed as she ran from him but as she turned to see if he was still chasing her, Oren was gone. When she looked back around, she crashed into the solid wall that was his chest.

"Oren!" she giggled as he tackled her to the ground and began to tickle her.

"Stop please, stop!" she squealed in delight.

Eventually, he stopped, leaning over her as she lay on the ground looking up at him and he down at her; both panting from their ordeal.

"You did great today," he said quietly as he looked into her eyes.

"Thank you," she said with a giggle.

"No really, you've done well…I'm proud of you."

He had said it that night in her room but they hadn't had a chance to really discuss what had happened. While she was delighted, that Oren had a new-found respect for her and her abilities, he had promised he would explain everything but she didn't know exactly what needed explaining.

He'd kissed her, albeit on the cheek but he had kissed her and that was the most intimate he had ever been with her.

She was still worried that he couldn't have romantic feelings for her, but surely a kiss meant something.

"T-thank you." Was all she could think to say, even as she lay panting beneath him, close to him in a way she wanted to be for so long.

They lay looking at each other for a long time until,

"Now look who's indecent!"

Oren turned and Trista lifted her head to see Nyron walking towards them looking really pleased with himself, arms folded across his chest.

Oren rolled his eyes and got up before reaching out to help Trista do the same. They both dusted themselves off,

"Grow up Nyron," Oren said sharply but their cousin just laughed.

"Considering I'm older than both of you, maybe you're the ones that need to do the growing up."

Trista said nothing before turning to the weapons rack behind them. She materialised Oren's sword she'd discarded and began to peel off her body guards.

"As fun as this awkward situation is, Oren, Aunt Rowan asked to see you."

"Sure, I'll be inside in a moment."

"Okay, she's in the Council Chamber." Oren nodded as Nyron disappeared inside.

As Nyron exited, Oren turned to Trista who had finished putting their weapons away and stood in her regular fighting leathers.

"Trista?"

She turned to him but said nothing,

"Don't let Nyron upset you, he's an idiot."

"I know that," she said quietly before beginning to head inside, but he reached out and held her arm.

"Then why won't you look at me?"

Still, she said nothing. She couldn't admit to him all that was bubbling inside her. About how she felt about him, about the moments they kept sharing that she didn't know if they meant anything. It was driving her insane, but she wouldn't admit to something that could all be in her head. She'd die of embarrassment if she confessed how she felt, and he rejected her, even with their kiss.

"You'll understand soon," he finally said, and Trista looked at him in surprise.

"Understand what?" Oren went to speak then looked at her regrettably with a deep sigh.

"Trista, please…just wait." He whispered to her,
"Wait for what?"

Oren looked up as though he were listening out for something and shook his head, disappointed.

"Just wait…please."

Oren lowered his head and kissed her cheek again before turning and marching inside, leaving her more confused than ever.

Oren entered the Academy through the kitchens and as he made his way toward the Main Hall, he saw Rowan and Nyron. He rolled his eyes and stopped in front of them.

"Don't worry, she doesn't know anything."

"Good," Rowan replied firmly. "She can't know just yet; it will only make things more complicated for her."

"I know that Aunt Rowan, its why I chose not to tell her in the first place!"

"I realise that Oren but we both know you want to go back on that choice."

"What if I do!" he snapped at both of them, making Nyron look away guiltily. "I can't stand lying to her anymore!"

"You have to!" Rowan hissed. "Trista is too vulnerable not to let this information cloud her judgement. You say, nothing."

Oren went to protest,

"That's an order General."

Oren narrowed his eyes at her then scowled at Nyron,

"As you wish, your Majesty," he barged between the two of them but called over his shoulder. "Stay out of my head!"

ESPIONAGE

When Trista returned to her room after dinner, she took a much-needed bath and soaked herself from head to toe. She usually had to wash quickly for training or meals but she took the time to truly indulge in being safe and warm.

She let the hot water seep into her skin, rejuvenating her as she tried to make sense of her feelings for Oren and his possible feelings for her. He had asked her to wait for an explanation, surely she could do what he asked even if she was confused by it?

She hated being so unsure about things when she was finally beginning to feel confident in all other aspects of her life. She was a better fighter, she had a relationship with her mother and she finally had friends.

All that was left to the wind, was this. She had to know and she had to know now. Trista couldn't continue feeling so unsure, especially if it meant he might return her affections. Determined, Trista washed herself and her hair before stepping out of the marble tub and drying off. She wrapped the thick towel around herself but as she walked from the washroom into her adjoining bedroom, she was slammed viciously against the wall by an unseen force. Her back slammed into the wall making her arms and legs splay out in all directions as a figure stepped out of the shadows toward her. Trista dropped to the floor after the initial hit and instinctively, she tried to scream but the person reached down and grabbed her by her throat.

Trista clawed at the hand, struggling for breath as the person – the hooded person – choked her against the wall.

No, you will not be afraid again!

Trista pushed at her attacker with her power and they immediately let go and went flying across the room, crashing into the adjacent wall. Trista fell collapsed to the floor, landing hard on her bare knees again as she struggled to catch her breath. She didn't have much time as her attacker was almost immediately on their feet and marched back toward her.

Trista put up a shield against their attack as she tried desperately to draw in some air, but they walked right through it. The air of her shield rippled, as the hooded figure passed through it and reached out toward her again.

Her attacker's power clutched at her waist, throwing her across the room again, this time crashing into a nearby dresser. As she collided with the dresser, her towel unravelled and she lay there naked and exposed.

Mortified, Trista flicked her wrist and the dagger she kept under her pillow flew in her hand. She threw it at her attacker, desperate to get some distance between them but right before her eyes, a smoky essence engulfed the dagger and it disintegrated into dust.

"Try again Princess," the voice was odd; flat as though there were no life in it. The way she'd heard in the last few days from…

"Thorn?" she wheezed as the hooded figure advanced on her and reached for her again. Trista shielded but this time, around herself,

"Clever girl," the voice said as Trista struggled to her feet. "That won't save you,"

"It doesn't have to," she spat at the figure as she Shifted, still inside her protective bubble into her closet.

Trista rushed on the first robe she found almost as soon as the door swung open and she was dragged out by her hair. Trista rolled into the throw and landed on bent knee, before charging at the person and landing a solid punch right in their face.

The punch loosened the hood around their head and Trista's eyes widened at Thorn looking back at her.

"You shouldn't have done that." He said menacingly.

What followed next was a brawl. A melee of punches and kicks that had Trista howling in pain from a solid punch to her gut that knocked her to the ground. Thorn was strong, too strong and even with her training and the energy blasts she sent at him, he wouldn't quit. Everything she threw at him disintegrated into nothing, fireballs, energy balls; nothing seemed to be working and she couldn't do him enough physical damage to stop him.

"Oren!" she finally screamed. She couldn't do this on her own, she needed him.

"Your lover can't save you now Princess," Thorn mocked her,

"No?"

Both Thorn and Trista looked towards the door they hadn't noticed swing open and Dana was standing there,

"But I can."

Dana threw something into the room and a cloud of black smoke exploded into the room around them. Instinctively, both Thorn and Trista shielded their face from it and Dana took the opportunity to charge into the room and smack Thorn over the head with her staff.

He was knocked to the ground and quickly, Dana slammed the end of her staff into the side of his head, knocking him unconscious. Dana looked down, watching as blood seeped from the side of his head.

Trista rushed quickly to her feet and reached out to bind Thorn with her magic,

"Quickly, get Oren, get everyone!" Trista ordered and with a quick nod, Dana rushed out of the room.

Trista looked down at Thorn, confused as to what had just happened. She didn't have the strength to figure any of it out, so concentrated on keeping him bound and hoping he didn't wake up and be able to get out of it.

He had shown phenomenal strength and power just now and she had no idea where it came from.

Soon there was commotion coming from the door behind her and Nyron, Aslan and Saicha were suddenly by her side.

"Is he dead?"

"I don't think so," Trista responded to Nyron's question. "I don't know if this will hold him if he wakes up."

"A cage will," Nyron said angrily as he hoisted Thorn's unconscious body into his arms. "We'll put him in the dungeons until we can figure this out."

Trista nodded her agreement as she let go of the hold she had on Thorn and finally turned to the door. Her eyes immediately clashed with Oren's who had arrived and stood in the door way beside Dana looking on in obvious distress.

Nyron, Aslan and Saicha exited with Thorn while Dana stepped into the room and wrapped her arms around Trista who was visibly shaking.

"Are you okay?" she asked and Trista nodded.

"I will be, I just don't understand how he could do this!" Trista was angry, angry and afraid at what Thorn had become.

"I'm lucky you came when you did." Dana shrugged,

"I came by just to talk to you when I opened the door and saw you fighting. Trista, I heard nothing of what was going on outside your door."

That was impossible. How could Dana have not heard them fighting, the furniture around them was almost unsalvageable.

Oren stood there for a long time watching them, before he said,

"Dana?"

Dana looked up to him,

"Could you gather everyone in the dungeons to question Thorn? I'd like to speak to Trista…alone."

"Sure," Dana nodded before turning to Trista. "Get these cuts cleaned up before you do anything else okay?" Dana lightly touched marks on Trista's exposed knees and arms. Trista nodded as Dana placed her forehead to her best friend and sighed heavily.

When Dana walked away, Trista realised how far they had both come. What Dana had done to Thorn, neither of them could have imagined and Trista would be eternally grateful for the newest warrior by her side

"Thank you," Trista called out to her best friend. Dana turned back with a loving smile.

"You're welcome, your Highness."

Dana had never addressed her as such and the feeling was unsettling but also fitting.

They were both so different now, Dana a novice fighter and healer and Trista a queen in training. They had both come so far since their days in Remora and they knew it in those little words.

Dana turned to the door but stopped by Oren and placed a hand on his shoulder, leaning in on her tip toes to kiss his cheek and left; closing the door behind her.

Oren walked into the room towards her and dropped to his knees,

"Please forgive me," he said. "Please." Trista was confused,

"Forgive you for what?"

"For not being here to protect you!"

Oren looked up at her from his bowed position, his eyes tortured. He thought he had failed her and that couldn't have been further from the truth.

"Why would you think that?"

"Trista, Thorn could have killed you and I wasn't here to protect you! If my father had been here, he would never forgive me for not doing my duty!"

"Well your father isn't here and I don't blame you, so why blame yourself?" Oren looked conflicted,

"It's my duty, it always has been, to protect you and I wasn't here. I failed as your General, as an Antos and as your friend."

Trista's heart went out to him, he was distraught at what he considered dishonour. Trista reached out and placed her hands either side of his face and looked into his eyes,

"Oren, you have not failed me. I forgive you and I order you to accept that, do you hear me?" Oren smiled, really smiled and shook his head with a low chuckle.

"Yes, your Highness."

They stood looking at one another and once again, Oren reached out and stroked the side of Trista's face. She winced, not realising there must have been a bruise there. Oren held his palm to her face and it suddenly felt warm. Oren took his hand away moments later and the warmth dissipated,

"What did you do?"

"The Infirmary will only have to heal the rest of you." He murmured. Before she could respond, the door knocked and Oren turned to open it. It was Naima who smiled apologetically,

"Dana sent me to take you to the Infirmary and tell Oren that they're ready in the dungeon."

"We'll be right there." Trista replied from inside the room.

Oren smiled apologetically at Trista before bowing to her and leaving. When he closed the door, Naima turned to her cousin.

"Did I interrupt something?" Trista shook her head,

"You know something Naima…I don't know." Naima shrugged. "Let's see what my ex fiancé has to say for himself shall we?"

It was a while before Trista found herself in the dungeons of the Academy. She had gone to the Infirmary with Naima and after washing and dressing her cuts and bruises, she was fit to leave. They returned to her bedroom where she re dressed in warm boots, trousers and a thick wool jumper that gathered in thick rolls around her neck. Oren had apparently healed her face, so there was no bruising there, but she didn't want Thorn to see what he had done to the rest of her body. She didn't want him to know how much pain he had put her through.

She had to be strong in front of him when she questioned him.

She had to be a Queen.

The dungeons were of course in the farthest depths of the building and the only light, once they'd descended the flights of winding steps were from the torches lined along the stone walls.

It was silent but for their footsteps but soon, they emerged into the warm glow of the dungeon floor and Trista saw her family and friends waiting for her.

Nyron and Saicha were in deep conversation, while Dana and Aslan were speaking in hushed tones. Oren stood by the barred door of what could only be Thorn's cell, and her mother, Lamya and Chief Justice Yeng stood in a huddled group.

Everyone looked up when she and Naima entered and bowed their heads. Trista stepped forward and Lamya fell into step by her side,

"Your Highness, are you sure you want to do this? I can interrogate him if you want me to."

"I'm not afraid of him," Trista replied calmly. "I want him to explain to my face why he's done this." Lamya registered her understand as they finally approached where Oren stood, and he bowed his head to her.

She could see past his head that Thorn was still unconscious, but they had chained him to a chair in the middle of the cell.

"Open the door," Oren raised his eyebrow at her, but she didn't respond.

With a disapproving sigh, Oren turned to open the door and let her into the cell. He followed immediately after, closing the door but not locking it.

Nyron, Naima, Dana, Saicha and Aslan stood in an impenetrable line behind the bars, looking in. Rowan and Chief Justice Yeng stood further back.

Thorn was slumped forward in the chair, the chains around his wrists that were placed in his lap. His ankles were chained to the floor and his body to the chair, that was in turn bolted to the floor.

"How do I wake him?"

Dana stepped forward and handed her a small bag of what looked like herbs through the bars.

"Under his nose," Dana instructed but not wanting to get too close to him, Trista used her powers instead and sent the bag to hover under his nose until sure, enough, he shook himself awake.

Thorn was wide eyed and terrified as he came to his senses and took in his surroundings. His eyes seemed to scan everything but the two people in the cell with him until Trista called his name.

"Thorn?"

His eyes darted to hers and recognition followed by confusion appeared on face.

"Trista?"

"Thorn, I need to know why you attacked me."

Trista got straight to the point, there was no use in drawing it out. Thorn looked down at his chained wrists and ankles and began to resist against the restraints.

"What's going on, w-why am I chained up? Trista let me out of here!"

"Thorn, please."

"Let me out of here!" he screamed out again, shaking his chains and looking frantic as tears pooled in his eyes.

"Thorn don't you know what you've done?"

"Does it look like he does?" Saicha commented sarcastically from behind her but Aslan elbowed her in the ribs.

"Look at him," Saicha continued even as she rubbed her side. "The boy is clearly confused. Why don't you ask him something helpful!"

"Enough Saicha!" Nyron snapped, his deep voice echoing in the small damp space. Thorn's chains and cries were deafening but Nyron's voice carried above the racket.

Trista took a step toward Thorn, looking at his terrified face as she did so. He looked as if he didn't even know her.

"Thorn…when was the last time you saw me?"

He looked stressed by the question,

"I don't know, I…I don't—"

"Please try to remember, its important."

Thorn sighed deeply as he tried to stop his tears and thought about his answer.

"You spent the night at The Grange," he finally said. "It was raining, so you stayed with us but..."

"But what Thorn?" he shook his head like he couldn't understand something.

"You fell ill and my mother wouldn't let me see you. I tried to see you, but she forbade it and then...then you left."

Trista crouched down in front of him and took his chained hands into her own as he looked up at his blood shot eyes.

"You left without saying goodbye," he said softly. "Why did you do that?"

"Oh Gods," Trista's heart caved in her chest as the realisation hit her.

"Please let me out!" he cried again but Trista stood up and backed away from him, terrified at what this all meant. Scared, Trista turned from him, but Thorn called out her name,

"Trista don't leave me here! Please!" she couldn't look at him, she couldn't allow herself to see the boy she used to love in so much pain.

He continued to scream for his release as she marched from the cell and Oren exited behind her, locking the door as he did.

Trista marched to the end of the hallway, back to the stairs that would take them out of the darkness and turned to her friends.

"We can't discuss this in his presence," Thorn continued to scream her name from six cells away. "but Thorn claims not to have seen me since I left Remora months ago."

There was a collective intake of breath at the shocking revelation,

"Whoever we have been talking to for the past few weeks," tears brimmed her eyes as she looked down the hall to where

Thorn was being held. "It was not Thorn Remora, so we have to find out who it was."

"What will you do with him?" Saicha asked and Trista ordered reluctantly.

"He will remain here until I decide what is best to be done with him." Oren looked relieved. "I don't know if I can trust him and until I do, I can't have him running around the Council as a potential spy for whoever took control of his body."

They all nodded in agreement,

"Chief Justice, I want him taken care of until and after we leave. No harm is to come to him but he is not to leave the Academy." Chief Justice Yeng nodded.

"Lamya, I need you to find out how this could have been done."

"I already know how," Lamya said quietly and she immediately had everyone's attention.

"Don't leave us in suspense," Aslan said, and everyone was inclined to agree.

"When I discovered that you hadn't been given your initial training, I was confused as to why and I did some digging on Avriel Remora."

"Avriel?" Trista thought it, but it was Dana who voiced her dismissal of the idea. "How could Avriel have done this?"

"With untrained magic," Lamya replied regrettably. "It's my belief your Highness, that with the use of untrained magic, Avriel was able to possess her son to spy on you."

No one said anything for a long time, only the sounds of Thorn's weeping and rattling chains to keep them in their reality.

"The Council Chambers in ten minutes. We have much to discuss."

Trista turned away from them and walked back up the stairs without another word, desperate to get away from the sounds of chains, cries and betrayal.

The Antonides Legacy III

SALVATION

When Avriel Remora left her tent, she was replaced by General Beardmore, Lords Weilyn and Priya and Baron Thelm. Dreston's serving man Aml had not joined them, having taken the gold Briseis paid him and set about returning to his native Agmantia with his woman Alaina. The Six were in their own accommodation, situated close to her own but had already set on their mission to destroy any trace of Baron Dreston.

They had been instructed not to inform General Beardmore of what had taken place but as she looked at him now, Briseis knew he deserved to know the truth. She knew if he knew what she had done, he would hate her for it and she found she couldn't have that.

"With the newest information from Lady Avriel, we strike immediately, cut off their entry before they even get to The Wide."

Gardan was now saying as he consulted the map of Mortania on Briseis' large war table. A few of the lesser captains who would oversee varying divisions were also in attendance, but they remained relatively silent, awaiting their orders

"A strong tactic but surely we wish to engage in some battle?" Lord Weilyn replied.

"Of course," inserted Briseis before Gardan had the chance to reply. "I haven't put this army together, not to use it."

"Why not cut off the enemy before having to fight unnecessarily?" Gardan asked reasonably.

"What of the thousands of men who have been waiting in the cold and snow for a battle that you wish to tell them, will never come?"

Briseis scoffed, looking back at the map where she had now placed the markers for her army and that of the Samai.

The information Avriel had given her had proved invaluable and she would stop at nothing to make sure she killed Oren Antos and thereby destroy the Samaian threat from the very root from which it grew.

"General Beardmore, I am inclined to agree with the princess. It will not ignite moral in the soldiers if they feel they have been made to waste their time."

"I care not for how the soldiers feel," Briseis replied to Baron Thelm's contribution. "They should only do as I say."

The two captains shifted their eyes to one another and Gardan saw the exchange. General Beardmore surveyed the room before turning his eyes to Briseis,

"You are so thirsty for blood that you would risk countless lives for nothing?"

Slowly, Briseis turned her eyes to him and shock and confusion registered there before an intense anger that Gardan was all too familiar with. She stood staring at him until there was an uncomfortable silence in the room that grew thicker by the second,

"Leave." Her one word had everyone scurrying towards the exit until only Briseis and Gardan were left.

"I have grown fond of you Gardan. It would be a shame to have to kill you." He didn't even flinch as he said,

"Kill me for what, telling the truth?"

"Watch yourself," she warned him.

"I do watch myself and I watch you. Where is Baron Dreston Briseis?"

She said nothing. She didn't have to answer to this man or any other. Gardan looked disappointed,

"I'm watching you send thousands of men into battle where there is no need for more bloodshed!"

"You forget yourself Gardan. Your position does not allow you to question me!"

"What position is that? Your lover or the General of your army because I am both and one of them gives me the right to tell you that this is wrong!"

"I DO NOT CARE WHAT YOU THINK!"

Briseis thundered at him and the tent shook, displacing many of the objects in it but Gardan did not move.

Briseis moved from around the table to stand in front of him, staring him down in the way he had become accustomed to.

"You think I will not kill you because we have sex!"

"I think no such thing! I think I'm doing my job by advising you against rash decisions. Princess, please, think about what you're doing!"

"I do think Gardan! Every day I think about the threat that advances on us and I want to be ready so I can defeat them!"

"I understand that but if you cut them off at Thea's Reach, they have less ground. We can funnel them out, pick them off piece by piece instead of an all-out battle!"

"I WANT AN ALL-OUT BATTLE!" she screamed at him. "I want to crush that little bitch with my bare hands and watch as the life leaves her eyes. I want to seize this victory the way my father could not!"

Gardan looked at her as though he had never seen her before, as though he were disappointed in her.

"Your father defeated the Samaian king and now rots away in a prison of his own making, trying to save his soul. Is that what you want for yourself!"

Briseis stopped for a moment and looked at this man that she had become so close to and wondered what in the hell she was doing arguing with him. He might not be defying her but the fact they were even having this conversation was testament to how much their relationship had changed.

"I have no soul."

She meant it; believed it even but when she turned to walk away from him and Gardan reached out to take her hand in his, she felt that soul flutter. Gardan seemed to feel it too because he took her other hand and pulled her to him, so they were chest to chest,

"That's not true," he said gently. "I feel it…in here."

He let go of one of her hands to place his large hand against her chest. Damn him, damn him for making her feel so out of control.

"You have a soul, and a heart and I don't want to see it destroyed." He said quietly, looking down into her steel grey eyes. Briseis shook her head, trying to dislodge the traitorous thoughts that plagued her of wanting to take him to bed right then.

Instead, despite everything telling her not to say it…

"What would you have me do?"

"We use Avriel's information, we weaken the entrance to Thea's Reach, get rid of their small forces. If any get through after that, then we fight. You'll get your war Briseis Greybold and I will be by your side."

She knew he would be, until the bitter end and she didn't know if that made her happy or not. She would have a loyal soldier by her side of course, but that meant that his life would be in danger and she found that she cared about that. She cared about that a lot.

"I killed the Baron,"

"I know," was all he said before pulling her into a hug.

Briseis hugged him back and they both stood, saying nothing, holding each other tightly.

***

Rowan was alive.

Rowan Illiya was out there and he had no way of finding her; of explaining that he had been so wrong about everything.

Since Briseis had left him with her revelation, Curian had drunk himself into a stupor. He had nothing left to live for if not the hope of finally clearing his conscience with Rowan and letting her know that he was wrong and that he loved her desperately. He would gladly die there in his own self-pity and so he tried his hardest to make that happen.

He took another drink from the glass decanter he held of the best Yiteshi wine and let the alcohol take effect.

He lay there, on the floor in his tent, weeping for his last chance at redemption when the entrance to his tent flew open and Rarno stormed in.

"Curian!" he said in alarm as he rushed to the floor to get Curian upright. "My king, talk to me!"

"Ro…Rooo…" the king slurred as Rarno looked frantically around for something non-alcoholic to give him.

"Guards!" two guards rushed in and surveyed the scene in front of them.

"Get me water and clean cold towels, quickly damn you!" the guards rushed out and when they returned, both continued to stare until Rarno barked at them.

"Speak of this to anyone and I will have your limbs torn from your body, do you understand me!"

"Yes General!"

The two men hurried out as Rarno helped get his friend undressed and into his feather bed. The dead weight was heightened by his armour and so Rarno had a time of it before he got Curian in his bed and bundled within the sheets.

"Drink this, slowly." Rarno held the flagon of water to the king's lips and helped him drink it down to clear his head.

Countless sips later, his mind was clearer and Rarno looked down at him; Curian's hair plastered to his forehead with sweat.

"What troubles you friend?"

"Ro-Rowan…she is alive."

"The Samaian queen?"

Curian could barely nod even as he realised that Rarno would only see one significance of this.

"Who else knows of this? We'll have to keep the Samaian Royalists away!"

"No," Curian said barely above a whisper'. Rarno gave him some more water as he nursed him by his bed side.

"It's not about the royalists."

"Then what is it about?" Rarno urged, still worried Curian could tell, about a possible new uprising.

"Salvation,"

"What are you talking about?"

"I need Rowan Rarno…I need to find her."

"Why, how?"

Something stirred in Curian just then, something he had read or heard a long time ago that he hadn't understood at the time. It came to him now, as a possible way out, a way to find Rowan and save himself.

"Lore," he struggled out that Rarno could barely hear him, "What?"

"Lore, w-we need to know the Samaian prophecy."

"What on earth for?"

"P-please," he stuttered, looking up at his oldest friend. "It could be our only hope."

THE QUEEN

The day had finally arrived for the Antonides Army to leave Thelm and Trista Antonides had never been more afraid.

She had survived an ambush, a stint in a Dreston dungeon; fought bandits and soldiers all intent on killing her; but this moment was the scariest thing she had ever had to do. Even leaving Remora and all she had known to follow a calling, hadn't been as terrifying as leading thousands of men and women into battle.

With their departure, the war would officially begin, and she would be one step closer to her destiny.

She stood now, in her room staring at herself in the mirror at the finery she had now draped over her body and felt like a fraud.

Even as she studied the priceless Phyn leather under armour and protective body shields that her mother had made for her, Trista didn't feel like a warrior or a princess; she felt like a child playing dress up.

At any moment, someone would come to tell her that this was just a dream; that she would go to Selection as always. That her marriage to Thorn Remora was the most exciting thing that had and would ever happen to her and that this world of magic and sword play and gorgeous Samaian warriors was another world away.

This was her life now; the life that she had wholeheartedly accepted when she had imprisoned her ex fiancé and condemned his mother to death.

It had been almost too easy to say the words, as she and her would be court, contemplated the fate of who had once been her closest friends.

Once they'd left the Academy dungeons, they'd all reconvened in the Council Chamber to determine whether what Lamya had said about Lady Avriel was true.

"You think Avriel did this?"

"I don't think Dana, I know."

Lamya had explained that there were some Samai who worked with untrained, even unsolicited magic and that this magic could be used in more sinister ways than that of the Everlasting magic. It came from the same source as all other Samaian power but was disturbing in nature and only used when other magic was forbidden or unqualified.

Lamya unearthed Avriel's failed admission to the House of Gifts and confirmed Oren's description of what he thought was Thorn's magic, as that of untrained power. Combined with the only person with magic who would have access to Thorn, it was clear Avriel was guilty.

Dana however was not convinced. She had a determination on her face that was heightened by her words,

"How Trista? Avriel was always nice to you growing up,"

"I know that, but we also know she held back from teaching me about my heritage and my powers."

"Trista come on, is that all you're basing this on!"

"What more do I need?" Trista countered. "Dana, look, I'm not happy about this either but Avriel knew where I would be heading in order to have Thorn follow me. She neglected to train me for reasons as yet unknown, and Thorn has no recollection of me since leaving Remora. She's been controlling him since he met us in Drem."

"I know you don't want to think this of your friend Dana," Lamya added, sensing the heat building in the conversation. "I've researched the power Oren described and Avriel is the only one with a connection to Thorn in order to achieve it."

Dana sighed,

"I just don't understand why. Why would Avriel want to hurt us?"

Everyone heard the hurt in her voice and Naima stepped forward to pull Dana into a sideways hug.

"I think I know," the response from Rowan was quiet but everyone turned to her; questioningly.

"Avriel would want to hurt you or Trista…to hurt *me*."

The room went still as Trista, Dana, Oren, the twins, the Agmantians and Lithanians held their breaths,

"Avriel was an ambassador for the crown; I forget of what but I…confided in her once about my inability to conceive."

"It seemed like nothing at the time, but I remember telling her that I would speak to my sister about getting her into the House of Gifts…I never did."

Everyone looked sceptical until Nyron hesitantly said,

"Aunty…I don't understand why that would make her want to betray you, the crown, her people!"

"I don't know that it would, but if Avriel thought I slighted her and has the use of untrained magic, then it is possible."

There were still sceptical looks around the room, Rowan shrugged.

"I know it doesn't seem like much, but when the war broke out, we received word from Remora; from Avriel asking to help magically and we declined. We asked her to look after you instead."

Rowan turned her eyes to her daughter and Trista saw the regret in her eyes,

"I don't know a lot about Avriel Trista, but maybe rejection is her motive."

"What happens to Thorn?" Saicha asked when the silence went on for a moment too long. "Surely you won't let him live?"

"Why would I kill him?" Trista was startled at Saicha's extreme nature.

"Because he betrayed you! People have been killed for less!"

"So, I must continue a barbaric tradition on an Assassin's say so? I will not kill Thorn; I will *not* be a tyrant like the Greybolds and I don't wish anyone in my court to be either!"

"It's a good thing I am not in your court."

Trista stepped forward, her fist flaming instantly just as Saicha did the same, a *sai* blade suddenly in her hand.

"Ladies!" Rowan called out, stepping between the two women.

Trista and Saicha stared each other out defiantly until Saicha turned her attention to Trista's hand, where the flame was slowly creeping up her arm.

Saicha concealed her weapon back within her robes and the fire instantly went out. Oren looked toward Saicha, his eyes unmoving but his body alert.

"It will not help anything to fight amongst ourselves!"

"No one is fighting," Trista said firmly. "I have given my order, and everyone will follow it…even you assassin."

"I am a princess of Agmantia!"

"I am the Queen of Mortania!"

No one said anything, no one moved as Trista stared Saicha down with eyes as strong as steel.

"Thorn remains here, under the eye of the Council and if we find Avriel we'll question her. If we find out she was responsible for this…she dies."

"Tri—" Dana started to say but Trista looked at her sternly. The twins and Oren nodded in agreement but Lamya, her grandmother and her mother said nothing.

"For the part she has possibly played in sabotaging my upbringing, in betraying the Samaian race, for using her powers to possess and coerce her son into being an accomplice to treason…I, Trista Antonides of Mortania, sentence Avriel Remora…to death."

She knew everyone was not happy with her decision, but Trista also knew that it wouldn't be the last time that people would disagree with her ruling.

It didn't matter now; her choice was made, and she stood by it; whatever the consequences.

As Trista continued to look into the full-length mirror in her bedroom, her door knocked and with a last look, she turned to open it.

Her mother was standing there, dressed in some of her best clothes, her make up perfect and hair styled. She wore a crown on her head and for the first time, Trista truly understood what everyone else saw in Rowan.

Her dignity, her beauty, her strength was all on glorious display as she stood in front of her daughter as a true queen.

"Mama, is everything okay? I was just leaving."

"Everything's fine sweetie, I just wanted to give you something."

Trista noted the box in her mother's hand and widened the door to let her in,

"What is it?" Rowan handed it to her,

"Open it and see."

The smile on her mother's face was confusing. She looked happy but there was an air of sadness about it. Trista opened the box and inside was a very large crown.

"Oh…Mama,"

"It belonged originally to your ancestor Thea the Fourth. She went to war with Coz when she was only a little older than you and was the first Samaian Queen to fight on the front lines. I thought you might want to wear it when you meet your army."

"Thank you…thank you so much."

Trista was overwhelmed as she forced herself not to cry. The crown even though she'd never seen or held one, she knew was crafted specially for war. It framed the sides of the face for one thing and moulded into three sharp peaks with a sapphire moulded into the centre. It was made of silver as far as she could tell and all along, in the finest engravings were names.

"Those are the names of all the queens who have worn this in battle. Your name will be added when you eventually pass on…hopefully *not* on the battlefield!" Rowan added with a little chuckle although Trista saw that it was probably her worst fear.

If Rowan were to lose her only daughter the same way she had lost her husband, it would be an unexplainable devastation. Trista placed the box on the table beside them and reached out to pull her mother into a hug,

"I've come too far to find you, just to leave you now."

She heard Rowan choke out a cry and squeezed her tighter, as her own tears flowed.

When they composed themselves, Rowan wiped Trista's tears and said,

"When you address the army, I have a final gift for you."

"What is it?" Rowan winked,

"When you make your address, turn to me…I will do the rest."

When the crown was placed securely on her head, and her armour fastened, Trista left her room with Rowan and headed out to the front grounds of The Academy where she was told her army would be waiting.

She had foregone attendants this morning, wanting to get ready on her own, but when she stepped out of the large front doors, Trista couldn't contain the excitement and fear she felt.

As far as she could see, there were people looking at her. Thousands of them, armed and ready, some on horses; most on foot and the pride that swelled inside of her was indescribable.

She stepped into the crisp morning air in her own armour and her crown and as she did so, Oren stepped into her view.

He looked incredible.

His hair was tied up and while she saw he had his black iridescent under leathers below, his metal armour gleamed like the sun. He had his usual dual swords across his back and another at his side and when he saw her, he smiled.

He smiled in a way she had never seen him smile before and she knew in that moment that she was in love with him.

It wasn't a crush or sexual attraction; she cared about Oren more then she cared about anyone in this entire world and never wanted to be apart from him. Having him with her, on this journey of discovery; she knew she would be okay; that he would protect her always and she him.

She loved him, and when the war was over, she would tell him even if he didn't love her back.

"General," she said, honouring his title as she now always would.

"My queen," he bowed low.

He didn't take his eyes from her as he did it and that feeling inside of her beat like an incessant drum. She tore her eyes away to look behind him. There, she saw the twins and the Agmantians with Dana and Lamya nestled in the row behind.

Oren reached out to her when he rose from his bow and she placed her hand in his. He led her, with her head held high towards the front line of horses, banner men and drummer boys then towards the new horse that had been dressed for her.

Oren helped her into the saddle then proceeded to do the same on Titan that was beside her own.

With a deep breath, Trista broke the line and trotted her horse until she was facing her army, the Academy at her back. She saw that her mother was now at the front door looking on and she smiled up at her daughter reassuringly.

Oren followed on Titan and sat by her side once more. She held her finger to her throat and willed her voice to project as Oren had once taught her so she could be heard.

"I was not raised your princess," Trista began. "I was not raised among your laws and power and I was not raised in the art of war. Despite my shortcomings in your ways…I was born an Antonides."

"I was born to fight for my people, to protect them from any who would do them harm and the day has come, for me to fulfil that purpose."

Trista looked at the faces of her family and friends who had stuck with her for so long and found courage in their smiles.

"I call on you now, to defend your country, to defend your homes and families and take back what was so unjustly stolen from you. Avenge your fallen king, my father Alexander and avenge your fallen brothers and sisters and husbands and wives and sons and daughters…and do so with the might of the Everlasting."

Trista turned to her mother, unsure of what Rowan would do but trusting that this was the time.

Demurely, Rowan stepped forward and held her arms towards the sky, palms up and held her head back, eyes closed.

A subtle wind began to billow around her as Trista saw her lips move but could not hear what she was saying. She stood there for a moment, her hair blowing more aggressively now until she unexpectedly exploded into blue flame. Rowan Enflamed and slowly opened her eyes to look out at the Antonides army.

In one smooth action, she made the motion of throwing something over the army and a wave of energy engulfed them all. The moment the energy touched them, Rowan still flaming in the middle of the Academy grounds, the armour on every soldier began to glow with an intense white light. When the light faded, all stood in gleaming armour with an Agmantian steel longsword at their side.

The Antonides crest hung from the flags of their banners: a silver broadsword with a crown around the hilt, surrounded in blue flame against a white field, could be seen for miles.

The archers had newly crafted bows, the wood from the forests of Yitesh, the strings strung tight. With amazement and a new surge of confidence, Trista called out to her army.

"Will you follow me Samaians?"

"YES! YES! YES!" came a thunderous response.

"Will you follow an Antonides to victory!"

"YES! YES! YES!"

Trista took a deep breath as she shouted at the top of her lungs,

"Will you follow me as your Queen!"

The roar that exploded from them was deafening until actual words made their way to her ear,

"LONG LIVE QUEEN TRISTA! LONG LIVE QUEEN TRISTA! LONG LIVE QUEEN TRISTA!"

Trista turned to where her mother was looking up at her with tears in her eyes and blew her a loving kiss.

The soldiers slowly departed out of the Academy but Trista, Oren, the twins and Dana stayed behind to meet with Captain Justin Theronos who it had been informed had arrived in Thelm. The Agmantians had gone with the army to make sure they entered the Thea's Reach safely and the others would follow.

Trista watched her forces and the provisions file out of feeling proud. Knowing her people were truly behind her and accepted her as their Queen was something, she never knew she needed or wanted so badly until now. Being accepted into her birth right was something she had only dared to wish and now it was reality.

"Your Highness, Captain Theronos and his men have arrived!"

A young Samaian messenger approached where Trista now stood, down from her horse with her mother. Rowan was exhausted from releasing the power she had stored for the last sixteen years and would need to rest before setting out to The Wide with the army.

Rowan explained that she'd buried it, deep within herself, to one day give Trista the army that she knew her daughter deserved.

As were the rules with the Everlasting magic, Rowan had recreated the armour from the army she had observed all those years ago. She'd manipulated it to cater to her own needs but the look, the weapons and colours were all the same as the host that Alexander had rallied eighteen years ago.

"Bring Captain Theronos to me," Trista replied to the messenger with a quick smile as he suddenly noticed her mother sway where she stood.

"Mama…are you okay?" An Academy attendant was also by her side along with Chief Justice Yeng who had come along with the other Justices to bid them farewell.

"I will be, as soon as I get some rest."

"You'll meet us in a few days though, won't you?"

"Of course, I will darling,"

Rowan reached out and cupped her daughter's face.

"Nothing could keep me away from you again."

"Come now Trista, your mother must rest. She used a lot of power today."

Chief Justice said sweetly, and Trista knew she had to quickly say goodbye.

"Thank you for everything…I love you."

Tears pooled in Rowan's eyes as she pulled her daughter into a hug and squeezed her as best she could with her armour on,

"I love you more than anything in this world Trista. You, have been my greatest gift…your father would be proud of you."

Trista stepped back to look at her mother,

"You really think so?"

"I know so, sweet girl,"

"Your Majesty," the attendant interjected and Rowan nodded reluctantly.

"I will see you in a few days…send word when it's okay."

"I will."

Rowan kissed her again and turned with the attendant to walk slowly back into the Academy.

Trista didn't have time to worry too much about her mother because as soon as she turned, a young man was approaching them with the earlier messenger by his side.

He walked with confidence, arrogantly one might think but there was no mistaking that he was gorgeous.

He was dressed in much the same armour as the men who had left and Trista belated realised that it must have belonged to his father.

Trista stole a look at Naima who had gone as rigid as stone as she stared over at the Captain. Oren was expressionless as always but Nyron had that look of mischief in his eye.

Captain Justin Theronos approached Trista finally and bowed perfectly, before rising and looking her in her eyes,

"Captain Theronos I presume?" she said, and he smiled, his face igniting into a dream.

"At your service, your Highness. It is my most sincere and humblest pleasure to meet you."

"However brief," Trista said regrettably. "Thank you so much for your aid in our efforts."

"It is an honour to fight for you, as my father did for yours, there was no question of my being here. Nothing could have kept me away."

There was movement behind her, but Trista ignored it as she said,

"Be that as it may, you have my thanks. You know the General of my army, High Lord Antos and my Lieutenants Lord and Lady Antos?"

Trista stepped aside so Justin and Oren could clasp hands, then he and Nyron who pulled him into a sideways hug and slapped him hard on the back,

"Long time brother,"

"So it is," Justin replied, his voice suddenly smoother and solemn then it had been a moment ago. He approached Naima and bowed low before reaching out, taking her hand and kissing the top of it. He straightened, looked her in the eye and said,

"My lady."

The silence was deafening as Naima said nothing and no one else knew what to do. She went to open her mouth then seemingly decided against it and turned to Trista,

"Your Highness." Trista nodded and Naima walked away to her horse, mounted and took off.

Justin let out the breath he'd clearly been holding, and Trista smiled to herself; perhaps not so arrogant after all.

"Well," Nyron slapped Justin on the back again. "At least she didn't stab you this time."

Oren shook his head with an amused smirk before turning to Trista,

"Are you ready?"

Trista looked to where her squire held her horse ready for her and nodded,

"As I'll ever be."

They left Justin at the Academy with his instructions and headed out into Thelm.

It was obvious as soon as they arrived into the city, that Trista was not as ready as she thought. There was fighting everywhere, her colours meshed with that of the opposing colours of House Thelm and Dreston.

They entered chaos, the chaos of battle.

THE RESISTANCE

Trista's current host of eight thousand Samai, engaged in battle with forces that erupted from Thelm seemingly from nowhere.

When she raced from the hill side where the Academy lay nestled and emerged to the sound of hooves and clashing metal, it all felt surreal. Surely the war hadn't already begun, they hadn't even made it to The Wide.

"...is the only way we can end this."

Trista didn't hear what Oren had said to her, too engrossed in the carnage that lay before her.

"Your Highness!" Trista turned to him and his look of distress and snapped out of her daze.

"Send word to Captain Theronos, he is not to leave the Academy until all our forces are clear. If we need their reinforcements, I want them ready and able to be exactly that."

"Go, now!" Oren called out to the soldier closest to them, who took off back to the Academy.

"Get to Thea's Reach," Trista said again. "We fight to get out, not to win."

She saw it in his eyes, in the way that flame flashed within his pupils that he was proud of her decision.

"Onward!" Oren called out and they set off once again into the fray.

Trista had never seen real fighting, not like this.

She had trained with Oren, Nyron and Naima and sparred with Dana. Even while fighting bandits in a forgotten stretch of town, she hadn't seen fighting of this calibre. Even as she used her powers to move the Thelmian soldiers viciously out of her way, the way they fought against her own men was something to behold. It was clear they were not under the same orders as her troops, and that they were out to kill, to deplete their numbers she realised.

Where she could avoid it, Trista did not kill. She had left her horse long ago to get involved in the fighting on the ground, and where she could bind, or apprehend, she did, instead of wounding. In this way, Trista and her army fought through the Thelmian resistance.

She saw Oren most as he never strayed too far from her side but she saw her friends among the ruckus as she blasted her way through a wall of soldiers. With a swipe of her hand, Trista sent men flying in this way and that, winding them and knocking them unconscious.

Only she, Oren, Nyron and Naima had power that could truly cause any harm and so the other Samai relied on their skill to get through to Thea's Reach.

"TO THE REACH!"

She heard Oren call above the din as he sliced a man's head off. Trista didn't have the time to be shocked by his barbarism and instead, collected an intense ball of energy into her hand and sent it flying into the crowd of soldiers.

Everyone scattered, Samai included, some thankful for the reprieve from what fighter they were engaged with.

With her war crown, spiking high above her head, her hair behind it in a tight braid, Trista continued to blast through the streets of Thelm, intent on getting to Thea's Reach.

"Trista!" Oren called her name and she turned to see him running towards her, with her horse.

"Get on, get to the Reach opening and wait for me there."

"Why?"

"Only us and the twins can really get thi—"

Oren shot a ball of energy behind her head and Trista turned to see a man drop dead behind her. "Make sure everyone is through, then we can end this."

She nodded, not sure what his plan was but trusting it anyway.

Trista mounted her horse once more and raced through the streets of Thelm, blasting any resistance away as swiftly as she could.

With the crowds of exiting soldiers and horses and screaming citizens, to get to the opening of The Reach was no easy feat, but minutes later, Trista eyed the peaks of the mountain gorge that lead to southern Mortania.

There were large wooden doors fixed to each side of the mountain corridor, where visitors would enter from the capital but by the time she arrived, they were open.

Here the traffic was moving faster and Trista saw to her relief that her people were funnelling through.

Trista rode through the people, all parting when they saw their queen, to the front of the procession where Dana and Lamya were also at the gates.

"Trista!" Dana's cry of relief was wonderful to hear as Trista rode up beside her friend.

"Are you okay?" Trista asked and Dana nodded,

"You?"

"I'm fine, Oren has some kind of plan and told me to wait here for him."

"Nyron told me the same thing."

They looked at each other with confusion but didn't question it as they continued to usher their people through, either on horseback or on foot.

"The Agmantians have gone ahead, so everyone knows where to stop once we pass the gates."

Trista was grateful that she had people on her side who were able to take initiative, the thought would never have occurred to her.

Soon enough, the numbers thinned and the last of their troops funnelled through the gates of Thelm.

As they did, Trista finally spotted Oren in the crowd with their cousins on either side of him.

There was a mixture of Thelmian and Samaian soldiers coming up behind them as well but when Oren finally made it to her, he jumped from his horse and faced the oncoming soldiers. Trista and the twins followed suit,

"Dana, Lamya, stay behind us." Nyron called out and the woman nodded as they looked on at the soldiers hurtling towards them.

"On three," Oren turned to look at Trista and Naima on his left and Nyron on his right. "We push."

"Push, push what?"

"Them," was all he said as he turned back to the screaming soldiers,

"One!" Oren called out making Trista frantic. "Two!" Push, she could do that. How hard could it be to push at a crowd of soldiers hurtling your way. "Three!"

Trista pushed a wave of energy at the oncoming soldiers so intense, it almost made her dizzy.

In that moment, the oncoming soldiers were bowled over, almost fifty feet away. The power emulated from the four Samaians was so intense, that the street in front of them and the surrounding buildings crumbled from the velocity.

The soldiers went tearing through the air, smashing against the surrounding rock and into the floor metres behind them. They crashed into one another, breaking bones and cracking skulls as they scatted in all directions.

What was left was a heap of crumpled bodies, gathered like a wall between the start of Thelm's streets and the entrance to Thea's Reach.

The ground in front of them was void of all people as well as debris as they pushed everything so violently away. The ground was barren, the chaos they had ensured, piled up at the end in a heap of despair.

Trista had never used her powers with others before, she didn't know she could. She looked at her cousins and Oren in amazement and they smiled at her.

"That was amazing!" she cried but the twins said nothing as they turned back to their horses. Oren rubbed her shoulder,

"Let's get you out of here."

***

The war had finally begun.

Avriel confirmed that she no longer had control of her son and as such, it meant that the Samaians knew he had not been entirely himself.

She hadn't questioned what method of magic Avriel had used to possess her son, she hadn't cared, but now that Avriel had been compromised, Briseis wondered if it might be better to know how it was done. Perhaps, she could perform the magic herself, without the need for Avriel's help.

She took pleasure in the fact that Avriel truly believed that Briseis would allow her to advise her once she took the throne. Briseis had no idea what Gifted were, or why Avriel thought she would allow her to be one and have uninhibited power at her court. The thought was ludicrous but none the less, she needed Avriel for her expertise at gaining intelligence and her knowledge of other worldly magic.

Until she no longer had use for her, she would keep Avriel in her good graces but now she had the Samaian princess to deal with.

According to Avriel they would leave for Thea's Reach the following morning and so she had sent word to Thelm to stop any forces that tried to leave the city. She had received word back from Thelm only twenty minutes before that while they had counted a handful of Samaian losses, their own had been greater.

Her spies had reported that with a display of magic, four Samaians had brought the entrance to Thelm to a crumpled wasteland of bodies and armour. They'd also told her, that only eight thousand had actually left the city and not the twelve she had assumed.

Outraged at being bested at the first hurdle, Briseis called Gardan, Avriel and the lords and barons to her tent to discuss their next move.

She'd gone over her plans with Gardan and he seemed to approve. She was worried that she even wanted his approval but she ignored the sentiment almost instantly and continued to arrange her men in their sections.

"With that many men, they should be at The Wide within a few days, three at the most." Briseis was now saying. "I'll be going with the front line."

"Why?" Avriel asked.

She had been in attendance at a lot of their meetings recently and Briseis found that she liked having another woman around who was not a servant and actually had something significant to contribute to the conversation. Her knowledge, however small of Samaian warfare was invaluable along with her understanding of their customs, that could become useful.

"I want to be there to see our first manoeuvre up close. I want to see first-hand, what you say your contribution can do."

"Very well," Avriel shrugged. "If you have no more need of me, I'll be in my tent."

"You may leave."

Avriel left and Briseis turned to Gardan,

"Is the entrance ready?"

"As instructed," Gardan said. "There are men waiting there as we speak."

"Forgive me princess," Lord Weilyn interjected. "Are we sure this will work. We are in fact relying on the words of our enemy."

His questioning was justified but Briseis couldn't allow anyone to undermine her and so she barked at him,

"Do you think me a fool?"

"N-no, your Highness, I merely ask—"

"Don't merely ask." She warned him. "Lady Avriel has her uses and when I am done with them, she will burn like the rest of her race."

The room went silent as they looked over at her, shocked by her declaration but Briseis didn't care.

She would have the Samai right where she wanted them soon enough, and there was nothing Avriel Remora knew, that could stop her.

THE LEGEND OF MORTAN

Although he had been reluctant to attend the meeting, an old Samaian man sat before Curian after the promise of a small fortune in gold. Even now, in the relative privacy of Curian's war tent, the old man was wary and guarded about being in the presence of the rebel king.

He eyed Curian with suspicion and the king knew he had every reason to be distrustful.

"You know why you are here?" he asked the man quietly who had travelled through the night to get to The Wide and into his tent undetected by prying eyes.

"You wish to know our history…our legends." Curian nodded,

"What is your name?" the old man shrugged,

"You may call me Ornis if you wish."

"Well, Ornis. I need to know about the Everlasting and what it truly is."

Ornis laughed as though Curian were crazy and had asked him to fly to the sun.

"No one knows what it truly is," came his simple reply.

"Fine, then what do you know; what can you tell me?"

"Why should I tell you anything?" Curian was taken back and stared back at the old man.

"I agreed to pay you for your knowledge,"

"Our history is not for sale. You knew that when you stole it from our king."

Curian was silent for a moment, his guilt a physical weight in his gut. He looked into the old man's bright green eyes, into the wisdom that was held there,

"Why accept the gold if you will not do as I wish?"

"I wished to see the king you have chosen to be," Ornis expressed. "I wished to look into the eyes of the man who has doomed us all."

Curian cleared his throat, uncomfortable with the path of conversation and looked away from the old man's eyes.

"I ask for your wisdom so I can make amends, to right all the wrongs I have done." Ornis laughed again,

"Why should I help you clear your conscience pretender king? Why should I save your soul from the depths of Caia's realm?"

Caia was the Goddess of Death who came for all men when they died and took them to Gys, the Realm of Eternal Darkness. Where Curian would surely go unless he repaired his tortured soul and paid his dues to Thea herself. If he did, maybe Alexander, the God of Life would allow him to enter Goia, the Realm of Eternal Light.

"Surely if I do what is right, then we can all be saved?" the old man said nothing. "I want to give it back, the power. I need to know if this can be done."

"This cannot be done." Ornis turned his head, trying to determine if Curian were serious.

"There must be a way!"

"Why, because you wish it so! It does not work that way and you are no exception!"

"I don't wish to be the exception; I wish to pay my dues and rid myself of this evil!"

"*You* are the evil old king. You are the plague on this earth that destroys everything it touches!"

The old man seemed to grow as he bore down into Curian, looking directly into his eyes as though he could see his damned soul. He had asked his people to find him someone proficient in Samaian lore but who this man was, was questionable.

"What can I do, I cannot bare this guilt and taint on my soul any longer…please."

The old man calmed down visibly before staring at Curian and saying,

"The power cannot be returned…only transferred."

"How is that different?"

"Only with great sacrifice can the power leave you." Ornis ignored his question but he only asked another.

"What kind of sacrifice?"

Ornis said nothing, looking directly into Curian's eyes and with that stare it dawned on the king what he meant,

"There must be some other way."

"There is not."

Curian scoffed, disbelieving as he tried to stare the man down,

"How do I know this isn't some ploy to get rid of me? You hate me, hate what I've done, this is the best way to be rid of me."

"It is," the old man said simply, unemotionally until he finally looked away from Curian.

With a voice that wavered only slightly,

"Although what we get in return is worse than you or your daughter."

Curian was confused, even more so by the look of terror that slowly crept onto the old man's face,

"What do you mean old man?"

He took several moments before he raised his eyes again and replied firmly,

"Dragons."

Dragons?

"Are you insane? All the dragons are dead, they have been for years, even before Thea."

"Yes, but what do you really know of them?"

"Nothing, because they do not exist!"

"Not anymore!" Ornis snapped and stood up out of his chair in defiance.

"Dragons, usurper; are born from chaos, corruption…fire." Curian audibly swallowed. "Thea was chosen after a previous Keeper had given their life to rid the world of dragons; dragons who burnt the earth to ash and everyone along with it!"

"Stories!"

"History!"

Curian was silenced and so the old man continued, his eyes weary, staring out from his wrinkled skin.

"Thea's people were the second, maybe third generation since the death of dragons; and the world needed to be reborn. It needed to be nursed back to health and she did that, her line did that and you and yours stopped it!"

Curian bellowed at him now, confused and angry about what all this would mean for him,

"I know that, and I am trying to make it right!"

"Do not for one minute pretend that this is about Mortania! You want a solution to save your soul Curian and nothing more! What you have done cannot be made right, this treachery cannot be undone!"

Curian was distraught,

"What of the sacrifice, what of the transference of power you just said?"

The old man rolled his eyes and said as plainly as he could,

"The power you wield will transfer to Briseis if you make the ultimate sacrifice." Curian's heart raced, "You must decide pretender king, whether to take your own life to save your soul, even if it means bringing a greater evil into this world."

"If sacrificing myself brings evil anyway, what's the point in the sacrifice?"

"Your soul will be free, and your daughter will be no more, is that not what you want? Should it matter what takes her place?"

"Of course it matters! I want to do this to get rid of Briseis, not to bring something worse than her!"

"Then I cannot help you."

Curian was hysterical. He had been positive that the Samai would have the answer; that he could return the power from whence it came and everything he had given to Briseis would disappear.

"You have two choices," Ornis said matter of factually. "Remain as you are and watch your daughter destroy these lands or…take your own life and watch dragons be reborn into this world."

***

Scouts counted the numbers and it was determined that they'd only lost a small number of their force. While it was disappointing to lose anyone, Trista was grateful that it hadn't been worse.

There was a sadness among the troops but as she rode ahead of them, where she had moved once everyone was through the gate, she knew it was because the reality of war was so close. They had only left the Academy hours ago and some of them had already lost friends or family. Nyron would compile the list and Trista saw now, why things of that nature were so important.

The Antonides Army walked cautiously through the mountain pass leading towards Thea's Reach until they came to a colossal statue cut into the rocks either side of them.

"Kriston Antonides, your ancestor...and yours." Lamya supplied softly, gesturing to Oren as the Antonides army approached the entrance to Thea's Reach. They rode out of rank now, just casually as they observed the Mortania around them.

Trista had never seen anything so large or so terrifying in her entire life.

The twin statues of Kriston stood, guarding the entrance with a staff and arm outstretched to bid them entry.

"What do you mean?" Trista asked, still staring up at the two statues; terrified to enter. Something hummed between them, something powerful that she couldn't quite place but knew was important.

"You are descended from Thea of course, but Lord Antos is a direct descendant of Kriston's line; the God of War."

Trista laughed, her fear forgotten momentarily and turned to Oren who was mounted by her side,

"So, does that mean you're a God now." Oren smirked playfully and Trista found she liked it, this playful side of him that was so rarely seen.

"Women have been known to call out such affirmations." Trista's face heated up but she just looked away,

"You're disgusting," Oren laughed good naturedly.

They passed under the arms into the chilled path leading to Thea's Reach. While the south she was told, was covered in snow and ice, making their battleground a lot more treacherous then what was normal, the north was still relatively warm.

As they rode into the ravine, they felt an instant chill from the southern winds and Trista called for an attendant to bring her a fur. When it was securely wrapped around her, they continued into the ravine.

The trees aligning the path were clustered together in an abundance of growth that had only slightly begun to see the effects of the oncoming frost.

The Forest was to their right and while it rose up a good few yards away, it still felt ominous because of its history.

"Lamya?"

"Yes, your Highness?" Trista fanned off the title with a smile,

"Why is The Forest feared so. What happened there?" Lamya smiled at having a reason to share history with them.

"The Forest was once habitable, just like the rest of Mortania, but it is said that a free magic user was corrupted and damned the land. Free magic is power not governed by the Everlasting…much like Avriel was using."

"How did he get corrupted?"

"No one knows, only that he damned himself and scorched the earth with the birth of dragons."

"Dragons?" Trista was shocked. "Dragons exist?"

"Not anymore of course, not since a young man named Mortan Ranger sacrificed himself and his own magic to kill the dragons."

"Mortan?"

"Yes, Mortania's name sake. After he saved Mortania from the dragons, the earth was slowly reborn, and eventually, Thea was chosen to oversee that change. No one has ventured into The Forest since Mortan's sacrifice. It's seen as unlucky and I guess that developed into the stories we hear today."

Trista was thoughtful, how there was so much history and legend buried within her family and the world she inhabited yet knew nothing about. Oren was supposedly descended from Gods and dragons used to walk the earth.

"Could dragons ever come back?" Lamya looked scared,

"No one would want them to. Dragons are bad news Trista, they are only born from corruption of magic, they are beings of pure evil."

"There have never been good dragons?" Lamya was thoughtful before she replied,

"Once…a very long time ago."

"What happened to them?"

"*It*, there was only one…t was slain by its own kind. For a good dragon to walk the earth again, someone must be powerful enough to create that amount of power, and no one ever has…no one ever could."

They were around an hour into their journey when Dana approached Trista with an unsure smile,

"How are you?"

"Tired," Trista admitted with a shrug. She had gotten used to riding of course after their journey across Mortania but it was still very uncomfortable.

"Me too," Dana offered before looking behind her then back ahead.

"Is something wrong?"

"Do you think that umm, Nyron and Saicha…do you think they're serious?"

"I think they seriously make me sick," Trista said rolling her eyes. "You know I saw Nyron doing some weird tongue thing between his fingers at her earlier; they need to get a room."

"Oh," Dana looked deflated,

"Why what's…" Trista looked over at her friend. "No!"

"Is everything okay?" Oren called out to them just as Dana's eyes widened and she subtly shook her head.

"Uh, yeah, I mean yes General, I'm fine!"

Trista inclined her head and kicked her horse into a trot and Dana followed. They were a little ahead of the others when she turned to her best friend and squealed,

"You like Nyron!"

"Okay, tell the whole world why don't you!" Trista was amazed to say the least.

"This is incredible, this is so…unexpected! Why didn't you tell me?" Dana shrugged,

"I am telling you."

"Dana come on, this can't have happened over night. Why am I just hearing about this now?" she shrugged again.

"You've had a lot going on and there just wasn't a good time. It doesn't matter any way," Dana looked behind her and Trista was inclined to follow as they caught sight of Nyron and Saicha talking.

"That's who he's attracted to; cultured and exotic assassin princesses…not plain little town girls like me."

Trista felt bad for Dana. While her friend was nothing but plain, even she could see that Saicha was a lot to live up to.

"Dana, you have a lot to offer a man. You're smart and funny and amazing with your staff. You've grown so much since we left Remora, any man would be lucky to have you!"

"Just not Nyron," she said disappointedly. Trista had to think fast,

"Aslan likes you and he's a prince!"

It was clear that Dana hadn't even thought about Aslan in that way.

"I don't like him like that, I don't think about him the way I do about Nyron. I don't get excited to be near him, or get excited just because he touched me…it's not the same."

Trista looked back at Oren who was talking with Naima and sighed,

"I know how that feels," she turned back to Dana. "You might not like Aslan back but the point I'm making is that Aslan is just as good looking as Nyron, he's royalty; he's rich and he likes you. Surely that makes you feel good even if you don't want him. You're worth anyone you want to be worth it for, don't let Nyron and Saicha make you feel you're not good enough."

Dana nodded and Trista could see her making herself believe it, even though it was the truth. It wouldn't matter if Dana didn't believe it herself,

"You're right…you're right."

"Talk to Nyron, find out how he feels about Saicha and go from there." Dana smirked,

"I will if you talk to Oren," Trista immediately looked away as she blushed.

"Talk to Oren about what?"

"Come on Trista, don't be silly it doesn't suit you. Are you going to tell him you care about him?"

"No, because I don't!" she said defiantly but Dana just continued to look at her until she cracked under the visual scrutiny.

"I love him."

"Oh my Gods!"

"Shut up!"

"Is everything okay up there?" Oren called up to them.

"Ev-everything's fine Oren!" she called back to him as she flapped her hand at Dana.

"Will you shut up!" Dana giggled,

"I'm sorry but, you *love* him? Trista this is huge!"

"No, it's not; it doesn't mean anything because he doesn't love me and he never will so that's that."

"Did he tell you that?" Dana cried in horror.

"No…not exactly."

"Then how do you know?"

Trista had nothing, so she said nothing and Dana smiled knowingly,

"I'll talk to Nyron if you talk to Oren, deal?"

Trista smiled but shook her head,

"I'll think about it."

Dana rolled her eyes before winking and heading back into the fold. Oren was by her side a few moments later,

"What was all that about?"

She looked over at him, his hair tied up; his beard trimmed and his teal eyes practically shining out at her.

"Just girl stuff."

Oren rolled his eyes and Trista giggled making him smile.

Saicha Voltaire and Nyron Antos rode side by side just in front of the Antonides army cavalry, while Aslan struck up a conversation with Lamya.

It was interesting the types of people one spoke to on a journey into battle, Saicha thought to herself. In her line of work, she only ever spoke to her brothers and sisters at the Guild and since arriving back at the palace, she'd had even less to say to her parents and siblings. Being away so long made it difficult to make friends or sustain relationships, so the friends she did have were scarce.

Aslan had been a surprisingly interesting companion on their journey across the sea but even more so, was the incredibly sexy warrior she had discovered once they'd arrived.

Nyron Antos was simply magnificent. Everything about him was what she had ever looked for in a man and she had only ever met men like him at The Guild. While men at the Guild were incredibly good looking or amazing fighters, they were her brothers essentially and she could never be with them in the way she could with a stranger.

He was a warrior; he was incredibly inappropriate and ridiculously gorgeous. She had never been with a Mortanian before him, but she was very happy with the experience he had given her.

They had slept together just after she'd arrived at The Academy and while a little rushed, she couldn't say it was disappointing. They had tried many times after, but he had always been called away to do his princess's bidding. Time was of the essence once the numbers had begun to form and battle was truly on the horizon. They'd had a few hurried moments together, one of which Trista had unfortunately walked in on but she wanted to be with him again. Nyron was an incredible man and she wondered how she would approach their newfound relationship, once the battle was over.

"What's it like being an assassin?" he asked her suddenly, taking her from her seductive thoughts of what she would do to him once they were alone.

"Dangerous," her smirk displayed her teasing and he chuckled. She loved when he laughed, which was often. "Lonely, I would say."

"I'm sure you have men fighting to share your bed."

"Not everything is about sex. Loneliness comes in many forms."

"Would you ever give it up?" Saicha thought about it for a moment.

She had given up her life as a royal to pursue her yearning to join the Guild; could she really give that up too?

"What would I give it up for?" Nyron shrugged,

"A family maybe, a husband and children. Surely you don't wish to fight the rest of your life?"

She'd never thought of it that way, that she would be fighting until her dying day. Saicha had seen becoming an Agmantian Assassin as a great honour, something she could learn and become all on her own and not because she'd been born into it.

"Is that what you want?" she asked instead and once again he shrugged.

"Eventually, I owe it to my father to continue our family name. Why not return to HighTower and fill the manor with little terrors like me." Saicha smiled,

"HighTower is your home?"

The concept of home had been dead to her for a very long time,

"It might be, I'll have to find my way once this war is over; the second son of a second son doesn't have much prospects." Saicha nodded in understanding,

"Your sister will inherit the estates,"

"Yep and have her own litter of brats with Justin," Nyron laughed at some inside joke.

"Captain Theronos, they are an item?" Nyron burst into hysterical laughter,

"They will be if Naima can let go of her pride long enough."

"I see," she took a moment before continuing. "What about you?" he turned to look at her, his green eyes mischievous yet deep in an unexplainable way.

"What about me?"

"Is there anyone you care for, someone to return to?"

For the first time since she'd met him, Saicha saw Nyron look concerned if not outright sad,

"I don't think you got the memo, respectable girls don't marry men like me." Saicha snorted,

"Horseshit, what's wrong with you? I am a princess and I have bedded you." Nyron winked at her,

"Don't worry assassin, I won't stop at just one session between your thighs."

Saicha couldn't help the devious grin that spread across her face. He was completely and utterly delicious,

"You say that as though you have a choice warrior. We'll be together again soon enough."

"I look forward to it." Nyron winked at her again and trotted off to his sister and cousin.

Seeing that she was no longer occupied, Aslan made his way to her and laughed,

"What do you want?"

"Not a virgin after all I see." She rolled her eyes but wasn't altogether mad; proving Aslan wrong was always a fun pass time.

"Still none of your business Aslan,"

"Still making it my business Saicha!" he mocked her, and she gave him a rude gesture.

"What is the deal with you two anyway; nothing can come of it."

Saicha looked sombre, annoyed that Aslan had brought up the one rule of the Guild: don't fall in love.

"Nothing comes of your filthy tavern whores, but you still bed them." Aslan went to say something then chuckled. Aslan looked thoughtfully at Nyron ahead of them.

"Would you leave the Guild for him?"

That was the second time today Saicha had been asked to question her loyalty to the Guild. Despite what some believed, one was free to leave the fold whenever they wished; it was not a station for life.

"For him…" Saicha looked over at Nyron laughing with his sister, teasing her most likely and sighed. "Perhaps."

WHAT LIES BENEATH

The Antonides Army made it to the halfway point of Thea's Reach when they finally stopped to rest. While they hadn't ridden fast or hard, they had ridden for much of the day and only the failing light had been able to stop them. They also needed to recuperate from the fight out of Thelm and take a real count of their men and supplies.

The royal tent was raised for Trista while her small but growing court occupied reduced tents beside and around her own.

Saicha watched the young queen protest at having such a large tent to herself for so short a time and smiled to herself. She may have had a few run ins with the young woman, but even Saicha could see that Trista had heart, courage and a truly good spirit. It was obvious that the grandeur of her station was still very much lost on her and it made for a decent queen in the making.

The moon appeared bright in the sky and the Antonides Army found places to rest as comfortably as they could beneath it. Once all were as settled as could be in such situations; Saicha found her way into Nyron's tent and crawled into the sheets, between his legs.

He was warm to the touch, his muscles large and firm against her lips as she kissed her way up his sculpted torso. When she dug her finger nails into his biceps as she travelled up his body, he groaned. Saicha finally reached his mouth and hungrily placed hers onto his to be lost in a deep and passionate kiss.

Nyron grabbed hold of her buttocks and ground her up and down his still covered shaft as they kissed. She raised her knees so she was straddling him and swiftly removed her long robe over her head to expose her naked body to him. As he lifted his arms to take hold of her breasts, they heard a rustling at the tent opening and a sweet little voice called inside,

"Nyron…Nyron are you awake?"

Nyron sat up instantly, covering Saicha's chest with his; as they both turned to see Dana awkwardly pulling the tent flap aside. She had a small lantern in her hand and as she tried to navigate it around the tent material, she finally looked into the tent and saw them in their embrace.

"Oh Gods, I…I'm so sorry!" she scampered out as quickly as she could, her little light indicative of where she had run off to. Nyron cursed as he removed Saicha from around him and put a shirt on.

"Where are you going?" Saicha demanded.

"I need to speak to her."

"What on earth for?" Saicha asked in shock. He was leaving her naked to comfort some little girl?

"Come on Saicha, she's just a kid, let me explain."

"I'm sure she knows what we're doing."

"Don't be such a bitch okay," Nyron said gently and headed out of the tent. Saicha rolled her eyes and flopped down onto his bedrolls to wait for him to return.

Nyron rushed through the camp to find where Dana had disappeared to, calling out her name. He saw her little light almost disappear into her own tent but he caught up to her just before she entered it.

"Dana!" he hissed, not wanting to wake anyone up. From the way she stopped her stride momentarily, he knew she'd heard him, but she went to open the tent flap anyway.

"Dana wait, please. Let me explain!"

Dana abruptly spun around to face him with tears clouding her eyes.

"There's nothing to explain, I saw what I saw!" she hissed. Nyron looked ashamed,

"I didn't mean for you to see that, but please…keep your voice down." He looked around frantically,

"Don't worry," she sneered at him. "I wouldn't want people to find out that you kissed me and went on to bed someone else!"

Nyron said nothing, embarrassed as he lifted his hand to his head and scratched his neck.

"Dana, I thought I explained…" Dana nodded,

"I heard you. I just thought…" Dana took a deep breath and shook her head before dabbing at her eyes with her free hand. "It doesn't matter what I thought, I got my answer. Goodnight Nyron."

Dana turned to walk away but Nyron reached out and took her arm into his large hand,

"Dana, I didn't mean to upset you but you have to understand that nothing could have ever happened between us. I'm thirty-one years old, you're eighteen…"

"Saicha's only twenty-one, what's the difference!"

"The difference is Saicha is a hardened assassin and farm girls from the farthest reaches of the world shouldn't lose their virginities to philandering warriors! It's not fair to you, don't you see that!"

Dana's face crumbled in front of him and Nyron had never felt worse in his life. This was exactly why he shouldn't have kissed her, but she had looked so vulnerable after saving Trista from Thorn the other night.

She had done what was right and everyone was proud of her, but at the end of the day, Dana was as innocent as anyone could be and she had hurt one of her oldest friends. When she'd left Trista's room, Nyron had comforted her as any friend should; one thing had led to another and he'd kissed her.

He hadn't expected to be so taken with her but it was no secret that Dana was beautiful. She was kind and smart and loyal to Trista. She was also an inexperienced virgin, and he wouldn't be the worldly warrior to defile her when he had nothing to offer her.

He didn't regret it, but he knew it hadn't been right for him to take advantage of her pain, no matter how attractive and courageous he found her. Saicha he understood, women like Saicha he could deal with and they could deal with him.

"I'm sorry I kissed you, I shouldn't have let it happen but understand that this is better for you…I promise."

Dana looked at him with pure venom and said,

"Keep your promises."

She stormed off into her tent and when he saw her lantern light go out, he knew the conversation was over.

Nyron slowly made his way back to his own tent and when he entered, Saicha sat up and looked at him; her curly brown hair tousled from earlier,

"Is everything okay?"

He didn't answer her, instead, he got back into the bedrolls and finished what they'd started.

BOOM!

The earth shook uncontrollably, sending the Antonides camp into disarray the following morning. Stewards rushed to attend spooked horses as Saicha immerged from Nyron's tent with him rushing to put on his shirt by her side.

"Are we being attacked?" he asked Oren as they both approached the High Lord's side. Oren was haphazardly dressed but still had a sword by his side. The rest of the inner circle appeared from inside their tents, all looking half asleep and confused.

"No, this is from beneath us." Oren observed. Trista finally immerged from her own tent with the young Samaian girl who had been hired to attend to her, rushing to tie Trista's hair back. Trista fanned her off, not unkindly but proceeded to tie her hair herself.

BOOM!

She failed as the ground shook again; sending everyone into an instant panic as the tremors ran through their bones.

"What's going on?" Trista exclaimed as by now, her whole team stood in a make shift circle around her. Saicha admired that no matter what, she had a strong team to protect her.

"Earthquake?" Dana speculated,

"Out of nowhere like this?" Naima was sceptical,

"That is the nature of, well…nature." Aslan said with a shrug. Saicha rolled her eyes at him.

"It must be the terrain, it can't hold us," Lamya stated. "This ravine has been threatening to crack for years."

"So of course, it chooses now!" Trista exclaimed with annoyance.

BOOM!

The ground quaked again, sending the horses crazy and everyone tried to keep them steady as the tremors rippled out from under them. Naima placed her hand to the ground.

As the Everlasting was connected to all things; a Samaian could be connected to all things if they so wished. This connection couldn't do anything; just get a sense of presence of what lie inside or beneath something. You could tell if an animal were close to death but not what was killing it or whether a tree was healthy to the root.

"I know this pass is fragile at the best of times, but this is something else; feel."

Oren and Nyron lowered to the ground and placed their hands there, closing their eyes as she did so.

"Naima is right," Nyron said with concern. "There are no movements post the quake and tremors; there is no continuous collapse."

"It doesn't matter what's causing it, we have to get out of here. If Thea's Reach is falling into the sea, I can't lose my army before this war has even begun!"

Trista was frantic,

"General, we need to get everyone out of here immediately. Send the order."

"Yes your Highness," Oren bowed and left to inform the troops.

"Everyone, get your things together and get to the end of this ravine as quickly as possible!"

BOOM!

The ground shuddered once more, sending everyone buckling to their knees.

"How do we get across with this happening?" Dana queried as she struggled to get to her feet. The screams from the horses and shouts from the camp were deafening as everyone attempted to pack up.

"Single file?" Aslan suggested. "When Saicha and I crossed, we raced across single file."

"There were four of us little brother!" Saicha rolled her eyes again but Aslan gave her a dirty look. Nyron however was nodding,

"There may be more of us, but the premise is still the same, we race across."

"Lord Antos that is not a plan!" Lamya exclaimed

BOOM!

They all looked around at each other concerned,

"It's not, but it's the only one we have," Trista said regrettably. "Naima, Nyron get to the other side of the ravine as far as you can; we need to know where we can stop."

The twins nodded and left to get properly dressed to leave.

"I'll stay behind until everyone is through. Everyone else, get across this ravine as fast as your horses will carry you."

The ground shook again, and the horses screeched as Lamya and the Agmantians dispersed into the crowd and Dana stayed behind,

"I'm staying with you, until everyone is across."

"No Dana, it's too dangerous." Dana shook her head defiantly.

"I know, that's why you only revealed you were going to stay after Oren left. You knew he wouldn't let you do this alone!"

"No," Trista said sharply. She would not have Dana guilt trip her into letting her stay even if she was right about Oren. "Get across with the others, that's an order Dana."

Startled, Dana was suddenly humbled and nodded,

"I'll have two guards with me and I would never forgive myself if anything happened to you…please go."

Dana bowed low with a loving smile before giving her best friend a hug and turned to get her things together.

The exodus was pandemonium, but it had to be done. Where she could be helpful, she was, and Trista watched on with a heavy heart as her army quickly dispersed into the south of the kingdom.

She hoped they would not have to go too far before finding a safe place to re camp. She didn't like the idea of her army occupying The Wide and giving the Greybolds the opportunity to see what they were up against. It was abundantly clear that there weren't enough Antonides fighters, but she didn't want Briseis or her father to know that just yet.

People rushed by her this way and that, her guards behind her until the numbers finally started to thin. Trista sat on top her horse, looking down at the people rushing past her when she heard the most tremendous crack. It sounded like a branch being snapped in two, a branch so thick that it echoed through the sky like thunder.

There was a shudder through the crowds as out of nowhere, the ground began to cave beneath them.

It happened quicker than she could comprehend but one moment Trista was watching a group of young men, making sure they were filing out quickly enough and the next they disappeared, falling through the floor.

"No!" Trista screamed but it was too late, all around them the ground began to crumble into the ocean.

"Get away from the cliffs!" she screamed to no one and everyone as she panicked. Trista kicked her horse into motion and raced towards the left side of her army that were being lost to the watery depths of Crescent Bay.

The remaining soldiers and provision carts were now heading in the direction of the Forest to get away from the crumbling floor, but their weight was too much.

Right before her eyes, Trista watched members of her army and her people fall into the sea. Trista raced toward the cliffs before dismounting her horse mid gallop, landed and held her hands towards the sea.

Everything slowed down instantly and the air was void of all sound and movement as Trista held time in place. People were still running and screaming, desperate to save themselves and Trista had the means to help them. With a swipe of her hand, she re animated the people but kept the collapsing ground, still.

"KEEP GOING!" Trista called out to them as they stopped in sudden confusion.

Trista could feel the strength ebbing away from her as she both stopped and willed time to continue. Her stomach cramped at the intense use of her magic but she had to persevere.

Her people, realising what she was doing continued frantically away from the cliffs and onto safer ground at the other end of the ravine. Trista held on as best she could, her strength faltering ever so slightly but she fought against it. Still her people continued to run and ride and pull carts away from the cliff edge while she held back their demise.

A piercing pain cut through Trista's head but she closed her eyes against it as she fought to hold on. Her nose began to bleed unexpectedly, and she knew she couldn't hold on for too much longer. The crowd was thinning thankfully, but as she opened her eyes to observe who was left, she lost control completely and time resumed itself.

The ground she was standing on, crumbled beneath her feet and Trista fell through the floor towards the Agmantian Sea below.

***

The twins arrived at the southern mouth of Thea's Reach at the abandoned outpost and were struck dumb at what they saw. The outpost had always been desolated but the rubble that it had been reduced to was shocking.

The gargantuan gates that used to guard it had broken and stone now littered the ground where they once stood. The stone was piled high, blocking their path toward The Wide but they knew they had to get it clear before the rest of the army arrived.

During their ride, they felt the constant booming beneath them and it had almost derailed them from their saddles more than once, but they had to continue.

Nyron and Naima approached the rubble as close as they could with their horses, then continued on foot. They were shocked to find a group of men on the other side and also along the edge of the debris.

Naima was the first to strike, her sword clashing with that of her much taller opponent who was surprised to even see her. Blow for blow they met each other, Naima channelling strength into her sword arm so not to buckle too quickly under his attacks. When she found a clean opening to drive into his stomach, she did so; withdrawing her weapon and moving onto the next Greybold soldier who charged at her.

Nyron was in the much the same predicament as he wielded his broadsword against the beast of a man who had approached him. It was not often Nyron found a man that was physically his equal but this one had obviously not missed any meals.

Nyron cut at the large man but missed before quickly throwing up an air shield when the man swiped after his head. Not missing his footing, he swiped at the man again and this time, caught him in his exposed throat sending blood everywhere.

On they went, cutting through the men who, while trying to fight them off, continued to huddle around something at the furthest end of Thea's Reach.

"NYRON! SHIELD!" Naima called out and her brother instantly ducked, bringing a protective force field around himself as Naima sent out a shockwave of power that knocked every remaining man to the ground.

"RELEASE!" Naima called again and Nyron was instantly on his feet. He rushed to stab each disarmed man, straight through their chest. No one was left alive and when the last man was down, Nyron rushed over to where his sister was looking down at what the men had been protecting.

Her armour was splattered with blood as was his own, but she seemed otherwise okay.

"Are you alright? I felt my arm ache back there." Naima fanned him off even as she lifted her left arm to show where her armour had been dented.

"It'll just be a bruise, look at this Ny."

Nyron looked down at the small barrels of dark powder that sat comfortably in tightened crates.

"Fuck!"

"What is it?"

Nyron reached in, took a pinch of the dark powder and placed it on the floor away from he and his sister. He quickly shot a line of flame at the powder and his sister watched as the tiny speck exploded into a blinding light that they both backed away from, shielding their eyes from the glare.

"That's what it is," Nyron replied sombrely.

Nyron stepped around the now scorched earth towards the open expanse of The Wide, far off into the distance and could just make out a dark jagged line on the horizon. Naima was suddenly by his side,

"Thea's Reach is unstable yes, but this was deliberate," Nyron said, clenching his fist together in pure rage.

"Help me gather all of this together. It can't be near us in case they have some way of using it from afar." Naima agreed, "Trista can decide what to do when she gets here."

WHAT THE HEART WANTS

The explosion on the Southern entrance of Thea's Reach, sent such a thrill through Briseis, she couldn't begin to describe it. The hairs on her arms tingled with the excitement of destruction and as she watched the clouds of smoke erupt in the distance, her thirst to begin this war was finally sated.

There was no telling how many of the Samaian army had been taken out by her machinations, but it could not be all of them, no matter how much she would have wished it so.

Still, those that hadn't been killed in the collapse would be severely injured. Saving that, the debris created from the blasts would make it near impossible for what remained of the army to get through.

"You have done well Lady Remora, this powder you brought us is ingenious."

Avriel bowed her head demurely but the small smile on her face was triumphant.

This woman had a cold heart Briseis could see. Whatever motivated Avriel Remora was a force she didn't need to know about to appreciate was powerful.

The woman had told them about a powder with destructive properties when connected with fire. She had brought the substance with her from Remora and as such the supply was limited. Still, when she had demonstrated what it could do; Briseis and Gardan had been shocked and amazed. They had deployed men to the entrance as quickly as possible and now she watched the aftermath of that decision.

"It was created many years ago but was outlawed for the destruction it causes. Only a few even know how to make it."

Briseis turned to the woman from where she sat on Axus. She was in her fighting leathers and furs to keep out the cold;

her hair braided back from her face. The air was chill making her cheeks flushed and Briseis looked fresh and energised.

"Thankfully I am one of these people, although it takes time." Briseis nodded her understanding,

"We wait for the scouts to return," she said finally. "Get the full account of what is over there and then we move out."

Gardan motioned to his second to spread the word amongst the troops. Briseis turned Axus back towards base camp and Gardan obediently followed,

"Lady Remora, make sure we have a sufficient supply of your black powder."

"Of course," it wasn't lost on Briseis that Avriel never used her titles; that she avoided being submissive to her despite doing everything she was told. She ignored it for the moment and called over to Gardan,

"General, follow me."

She rode a few minutes towards the camp before changing direction completely and galloping into some nearby trees. Gardan kept with her pace until they were further enough away from camp that only the smokes of various fires could be seen above the bare branches.

Briseis pulled Axus to a sharp stop before dismounting and tearing her furs from around her shoulders and laying it out on the floor. Gardan came up behind her and when she turned to him, she dragged him towards her by his own cloak and kissed him.

It was passion and excitement and the thrill of the hunt that had her clawing at his hair and pushing her tongue into his mouth. She reached down to untie his trousers when his hands, stayed hers.

"Here?" She gave him a mischievous grin,

"Why not?" Gardan laughed,

"It's freezing for one," he pointed out but Briseis only took the corner of her lip into her mouth and with a wave of her hand, sounds dimmed, and it was warm.

"A cocoon, just around us."

He didn't waste any time questioning it further and drew her back to him to kiss her again. This time he went to untie her trousers and within minutes, both were naked from the waist down.

Gardan spun her around so her back was to him and pushed her down onto her hands and knees so he could grab her hips. Seconds later, she had arched her back and Gardan entered her with a firm thrust that had them both sending expletives out into the air. He held her hips firm as he pounded into her from behind, Briseis panting and calling his name as he pleasured her.

For countless moments, they enjoyed the feel of one another until their coupling came to its fever pitch and with a mighty thrust, Gardan climaxed. Briseis followed soon after as he continued to pump into her.

When they'd both caught their breath, he released himself from within her and pulled up his trousers but didn't re tie them. Briseis turned to face him,

"I am pleased with today's events."

"I can tell," he said smiling down at her as she spread her legs and pulled her top leathers overhead. She lay there moments later, naked before him, leaning back on her elbows. With a salacious look, he removed his own clothes and nestled himself between her thighs, the horses their only audience.

He delayed entering her as he looked down at her,

"What is it?"

Gardan reached up and stroked the side of her face,

"You are so beautiful."

His voice rumbled in his throat as he lowered his head to kiss her before raising his hips and pushing himself into her. She gasped against his mouth as he began to move, grinding into her as they kissed. Her breasts were pressed deliciously against his chest as he moved within her and moved his mouth to kiss along her neck. He thickened as she tensed around him and wrapped her legs tighter,

"I would die for you." Gardan whispered into her ear and Briseis knew it to be true. Briseis shifted so they were eye to eye as he moved within her, stretching her so deliciously.

"You are so beautiful."

The confession fell from her without her consent, but she didn't regret it. He was beautiful, inside and out and she was thankful that he was in her life. Briseis had never felt this connected to anyone but somehow, Gardan had penetrated more than her body and somehow her heart. No, she wouldn't think like that. Gently, Briseis raised her head to kiss him once more and made love to him in the snow.

When they returned to camp a few hours later, the scouts were waiting for an audience with her along with her father and Rarno.

"Where have you been?" Her father demanded but Briseis ignored him as she stood at the top end of the war table and Gardan took his place by her side.

"That is not your concern. Bring in the scouts!"

Curian said nothing but his anger was evident on his face. Two young soldiers entered the tent and bowed accordingly,

"The powder was used effectively your Highness; the southern entrance is now destroyed with minimal passage for an army."

"That is good news,"

"There were not however any casualties, other than our own."

"What?" Rarno questioned and the scout swallowed as he looked around the tent.

"The southern entrance was destroyed before anyone was actually there. Once the men were readying to leave with the remaining powder two people appeared and slaughtered them"

"People?" Briseis this time.

"A man and a woman, Samaian. They killed everyone there."

"All twenty of them?" Curian asked in disbelief and the scouts nodded.

"They were packing the powder and moving some of the wreckage with their magic when we left them."

"Leave us," Briseis finally said and the scouts rushed to exit.

So, no fatalities but who were those two people? Could one of them be Oren Antos?

"We leave for the Wide immediately," she said. "We show them that the Greybold Army is much more than twenty men and will not be defeated so easily."

***

Oren arrived with the first escapees of the army and made his way to where Nyron and Naima stood talking. He had left one of the captains in charge of getting everyone settled for the arrival of the remaining troops and dismounted Titan to stand beside the twins. He noticed the pile of bodies first and as he hugged his cousins, he asked about them.

"They were packaging this," Nyron explained. "Not the strongest members of a garrison by any means but they had to be sufficient to deal with igniting this correctly."

Oren agreed,

"My father talked about this, he said it was outlawed years ago. Trista's Great Great Grandfather decreed, after his wife was killed in a building collapse."

"It could still be valuable to us Oren; we can't ignore that fact." Naima said.

"You're right and we won't but we have to tell Trista first."

"I understand that, but if she rejects the idea will you try to enforce it." Oren's face went rigid,

"I'll not go against my queen's decisions Lady Antos."

Naima squared up to him and Nyron stepped back with a cheeky grin on his face, arms folded across his chest.

"Using titles doesn't make what you're saying any less stupid. She might be our queen Oren but she's *your* Intended. When are you going to admit that you love her and start making decisions based on your military expertise and *not* your heart?"

Oren said nothing for a long time before looking away from Naima.

"Fine," he finally said. "I love her."

"Thank the Gods!" Nyron said with a cheery laugh but Naima was still on the war path.

"No offence Oren but we already know that, when are you going to tell Trista?"

"I can't tell her, not yet."

Naima rolled her eyes but before she could go into one, Nyron put an arm on her shoulder and she went quiet.

"Why not cousin?" Oren finally looked back at them.

"It's just not the right time. She's young and confused and....it's not the right time Nyron." Nyron looked on at Oren with concern,

"Oren...maybe she wouldn't be confused if you let her in on things. You can't keep her wrapped up like this forever."

"I swore to protect her with my life Nyron, that doesn't go away because I love her!"

"I get that Oren but you're not protecting her with your sword; you're protecting her with your heart and that can get you both hurt or worse." Oren sighed,

"Look, I'm not talking about this with you two. I'm not telling her until she's ready and I don't think she's ready."

"When will she be ready?" Naima chimed in, seemingly annoyed. "According to you oh wise one, when will the helpless woman be ready?"

"Give it a rest Naima, not everyone's a hardened love hater like you."

Naima's eyes narrowed and Nyron's widened as his mouth turned it an 'O'. Naima stepped up to Oren, her hands clenched into fists and Oren simply sighed heavily before looking down his nose at her.

"Listen you little shit, do what needs to be done without getting the rest of us caught in the middle. Tell her, don't tell her, I don't care; just stop being a little bitch about it because no one ever lost a war by being fully prepared."

Naima barged past him, nudging his shoulder hard. Nyron let out a low whistle as he stepped back to his cousin again,

"You're a braver man then me taking on Naima."

"I shouldn't have said that," Nyron shrugged,

"You shouldn't have...doesn't make it any less true."

Oren looked out towards the army that continued to arrive and get themselves settled. Men and women littered the now destroyed building and surrounding land, making as much room as they could for themselves and the weapons and provisions that they hadn't lost on the way.

"I don't want her to think her feelings are because we're Intended." Oren confessed suddenly. "I don't want her to think that something magical made her feel the way she does about me and how I feel about her."

Oren turned to look at his cousin,

"I've felt what's in her heart Nyron and if she realises that I know, she'll be embarrassed and if she thinks my feelings are because of the Everlasting she won't think they're real." Nyron looked thoughtful,

"I know I'm not very smart, but shouldn't you explain to her that they *are* real, that you love her *despite* the Intent; not because of it?"

"I will," Oren said quietly into the wind. "When she's ready."

Night fell and Trista still hadn't returned. Oren, the twins, Dana and the Agmantians nestled around their large campfire and noticed the same fires from the opposing camp. They were all wrapped in their furs, trying to keep out the bitter southern winds but Oren was getting agitated.

"She should be here by now."

Lamya was the last of their immediate crew to return and she'd said, she hadn't seen Trista since she'd given the order for them to leave. People were still funnelling into camp, but Trista and her guards should have been among them.

"I'm going to get her." Oren turned to mount Titan,

"I'm coming with you!" Dana called out and rushed to find her own horse. Oren didn't prevent her and so she took that as his agreement.

"As will I," Aslan offered.

"Nyron, you're in charge!" Oren called out.

Once again Oren turned to mount Titan and within moments, he, Dana, and Aslan took off back down Thea's Reach.

After an official count, the numbers were brought to the twins, Saicha and Lamya who stood around the map table of the tent Trista would occupy when she returned.

"Including the injured from Thelm and the explosions on the Reach, we've lost about two hundred and thirty soldiers and countless supplies." Naima was saying as they went through the inventory. She, her brother and the assassin were going over their options and everyone let out a deep sigh.

"In the grand scheme of things, it could be worse." Naima rolled her eyes, snapping at her brother.

"How could it be worse Nyron? We've lost arms before the war has even begun; arms we barely had in the first place. We've lost provisions into the ocean and our queen is missing. Tell me; how could this be worse?"

"We could all be dead for one thing!" he snapped right back. "You saw what we found, what that powder was capable of. We're lucky to have got this far with our lives!"

Naima was silenced but the look in her eyes was defiant as always. Saicha looked between the two of them thoughtfully,

"I have seen worse odds in battle, this is not the end of the world Naima."

Naima turned to her, questioningly,

"You have seen battle?"

"Assassins do not always work in the shadows. We are sometimes commissioned to work alongside others, as I am doing now." Naima nodded and inclined her head respectfully,

"Then what do we do now?" Nyron asked, exhaustedly.

"You start fresh Lord Antos."

Saicha leant on the large table that lay between them, resting her weight on it,

"You lead this army to their base at The Wide so that when Trista returns, her army is ready for her."

"We can't make a move without Oren's say so."

"It's not a move," Saicha stated simply. "It's a smart decision to better position your forces. When the princess and the general arrive, they'll want to begin the war properly anyway, so why not help them do so?"

Nyron looked over at Naima and shrugged,

"We wouldn't be making decisions about the war Nai,"

"So the princess says one thing, and you leap to it like a puppy?" Nyron's face suddenly switched and he looked at his sister with utter distain.

"Don't push it Naima," Saicha threw up her hands in mock surrender.

"I'm not trying to cause an argument, but it seems the smart thing to do." Nyron looked thoughtful before saying,

"If Trista had been with us, we wouldn't have been here anyway."

"What are you saying Nyron?"

"I'm saying I'll suffer any consequences when Oren returns but we move the troops out to The Wide and get this war started. He left me in charge, didn't he?"

"Only because he was mad at me," Naima said insolently but Nyron just poked his tongue out at her.

"I'll tell the men to ready for departure." Saicha offered and exited the tent. Nyron turned to do the same when Naima called out,

"Brother," Nyron stopped in his stride but didn't turn around.

"I'm sorry," she said quietly. "It's just…I'm scared."

Her voice cracked and Nyron turned to her; his older sister who looked at him pleadingly as she shrugged,

"We've prepared for this war most of our lives, we've grown up around fighting but this is truly *our* fight and it's failing before it's even begun!"

Nyron didn't say anything as he watched a single tear escape his sister's eye.

"We lost mother and we lost father and Uncle Gorn and I'm terrified that we're going to lose everyone else too and it just makes me…just…" Nyron went up to her and wrapped his sister in his arms, hugging her tight.

"I'm scared too," he murmured into her hair and held her as his big sister wept in his arms.

"Promise me you won't leave me too," Naima mumbled into his chest before looking up at him. "Promise me Nyron. I couldn't bear to lose you, not ever!" Nyron stared back at his sister before leaning forward to kiss the middle of her forehead,

"I promise."

Nyron was back in his tent, laying on his back staring up at the ceiling some time later when the folds of the tent opening pulled back and Saicha was suddenly there. They had moved everyone to The Wide and set up base and Oren, Dana and Aslan still hadn't returned.

Without any words, Saicha climbed into his bed rolls and proceeded to grind herself onto him until he was firm enough to mount. She lifted her night clothes and when he entered her, they both let out a breath of relief and satisfaction. He massaged her breasts as she rode them both to completion before she collapsed on top of his bare chest, both their hearts pounding from the adrenaline.

As they both lay there, his body still inside hers and stroked her soft curly hair, Dana's face popped into his head. He dismissed it immediately and kissed the top of Saicha's head absentmindedly,

"You have lost many people during these tumultuous times it seems."

"Yes," it wasn't a question, but he answered anyway.

"I have lost no one but myself," she said against his chest, her breath tickling the hairs on it. Saicha raised her head and bore her hazel eyes into his,

"I do not care for my position as a princess and even less now, my position as an assassin."

"What do you care for?"

Saicha looked up at him from under eyelashes, intensely before her cheeks flushed and she looked away and placed her cheek on his warm chest.

"Saicha?"

"It does not matter," she kissed his bare chest before readjusting herself to lay comfortably on him.

"Nyron?"

"Yes," he stared into the darkness of the tent with a million thoughts running through his head. The war, his sister, his parents and of course, his little cousin, missing in the dark.

"Do you think Trista is okay?"

Nyron swallowed audibly, his own fears voiced by the woman laying with him.

"She has to be," he pulled her closer to him and continued to stare into the night.

CLARITY

Oren was terrified.

As he, Dana and Aslan navigated the unsteady path beneath them, he was worried that he wouldn't find Trista and even more so that he would and that she would be dead.

No, he knew she wasn't dead, he would have felt it if she was. They were connected in a way she didn't understand yet, but he did.

Now that Oren had truly admitted his feelings for Trista, it felt as though everything was heightened in that regard but he knew it wasn't the only reason why. He felt her on a normal day, her energy; their link to each other but this was something else.

It felt like admitting it to Naima had let his love for Trista loose in his blood and his ears thundered with the intensity of it.

He knew how to make it go away but that wouldn't be a for a long time yet, if ever so until then; he would have to deal with the pounding in his blood.

He'd rode Titan hard, pushing his beloved mount to his limit as they raced as far down Thea's Reach as they could go with limited light. When the night began to turn it's darkest, Oren slowed his steed and created a large ball of light to shine over them and follow them along the volatile path. They passed cracked earth and fallen trees and forestry but it wasn't until they came upon a gaping hole in the ground, did they realise what had truly happened.

Oren's heart was filled with dread as he looked out across the expanse of air, to where the other side was barely visible.

Crescent Bay, already a chunk bitten out of the side of Mortania's coast, now had an extra missing piece that made the path from Thelm to the south even more hazardous. For their remaining army to get through, they would have to march through the Forest and no one had ventured there for years. What they would find in there was unknown and more time and effort than they had.

"TRISTA!"

Oren jumped from Titan's back and Dana and Aslan followed suit as they surveyed the destruction around them. With the help of Oren's light, they saw discarded armour and weapons, and splintered wagons that had been left behind in the panic.

The three of them caught sight of bodies; arms and legs peeping out from thick branches and piles of rock that lay scattered around.

"Gods no," Oren heard Dana murmur but refused to acknowledge it.

"TRISTA!"

"How can we expect to find her in this?"

Aslan was confused but Oren ignored him as he concentrated hard, closing his eyes slowly and taking a deep breath. Dana came up beside him, watching his face intently and waited patiently until his eyes shot open and he looked down into the gaping cliff side.

"She's down there," he said with astonishment.

"Wait, what? How do you know that?" Dana questioned,

"I just do, I have to get to her!"

"How Oren?" Dana demanded. "I want to find her as much as you but we can't see two feet in front of us and that drop is steep!"

Oren ignored her and marched to the end of the chasm and peered down into the darkness. Oren began to peel away his armour,

"Oren what are you doing?" Dana panicked,

"I'm going down there of course,"

"We don't know what's down there!"

"I know Trista's down there!" Dana was silenced as she saw the intensity and fear in his eyes.

"Let me," Aslan offered. "You're the only one here with powers General, we need you up here."

"He's right Oren," Dana added quickly, "Send Aslan down with your powers, then he can assess the situation down there."

They watched him think about it for two seconds before nodding reluctantly. He made a gesture with his hand and suddenly, length of rope materialised in his hand.

"Take this with you," he said firmly. "I can't see what's down there to manipulate it so you'll have to tug on the rope so I can bring it back up. I'll lower you down and when you get to her, tug and I'll stop. Tug twice when your attached, understood?"

Aslan nodded as he took the rope and wrapped it securely around his hand.

"Understood General."

Dana had never seen Aslan so accommodating but even he could tell this was a serious situation. Oren was certain Trista was down there but there was no way of knowing what state she would be if she was.

Aslan was suddenly lifted into the air and a look of surprise went across his face,

"Well this is new," he laughed nervously as Oren descended him slowly down the side of the cliff, the light going along with it.

It felt like a lifetime before they heard anything and Dana watched the fear creep onto Oren's face until there was a distinct tug on the rope.

"Aslan, do you have her?" Oren called down but they heard nothing back, Aslan too far down to have heard them.

Moments later, there were two tugs and Oren began to reel the rope in. It was an eternity before the top of Aslan's head protruded over the top of the cliff, and when his body came into view, he had Trista cradled in his arms.

"She's unconscious," Aslan reported "There's a nasty wound on the back of her head but she's alive."

Oren landed the prince on his feet and Aslan handed Trista to him, slumping to the floor once he'd done so.

Oren sat on the floor with Trista in his arms stroking her hair away from her face before checking the rest of her body for any other injuries. Dana rushed over to hug Aslan when his hands were free.

"Thanks the Gods, you're safe. What was down there?"

"Just rock for metres down of course but she'd landed on some type of ledge. Any further down, she would have been in the sea."

Oren said nothing, still checking Trista over.

"I couldn't get to her at first, there was some kind of barrier around her, it shocked me. I tried again and it seemed to allow me in."

Oren didn't reply as he continued to stroke her hair and look into her dirt smudged face until he finally declared,

"We need to get her back to camp. I don't know how bad this wound is and I can't seal it while she's unconscious."

"You can't ride back with her like that, we need a wagon or something." Dana agreed before Oren finally loosened his hold on Trista and signalled to Dana to take his place. She did so gladly while Oren looked around at one of the splintered wagons and got to work.

With his powers, Oren fashioned a wagon that could carry Trista back to camp. Dana had bandaged her head wound as best she could but she really needed the help of the physicians at camp. So, as the night drew on and they made their wagon with minimal sleep, they made their way back to the others.

Aslan walked ahead with his horse with Dana beside him while Oren walked beside the wagon that Titan was pulling.

After moments of tense silence, Dana turned to Aslan and asked,

"What is Agmantia like?"

"You have never been?" Aslan was shocked and a little amused but Dana only shook her head.

"Before I left my home, I'd never left Remora. My father promised to take me to the capital one day to learn about the materials he used so often, but we never got around to it." Aslan nodded his understanding though she realised he felt sorry for her.

"I love Remora, my home, my friends but…" she looked out toward the sea that they could hear but not see and sighed. "There are whole worlds out there, whole other people that I've never met."

"Like me?" he had a cheeky smile on his face and Dana blushed,

"Don't worry about it, where I am from there is no one as pale as you; even the Mortanians."

"What do you mean?" Aslan smiled as he thought of his home,

"The sun shines in Agmantia nearly all year around making everyone gorgeously tan. Our summers are long and our winters mild; we have rainy seasons of course for the crops to grow but there are some places, deep in the countryside where the air is moist; we call them rainforests."

"We have large animals called tigers and little friendly human like creatures called monkeys."

Dana looked over at him in awe then deep regret,

"I've never seen anything like that."

"You would…if you were to come to Agmantia with me." Dana almost choked on her shock and mirth, her face blushing furiously.

"Me, go to Agmantia? I could never do that!" Aslan smiled with a shrug,

"It seems to me that a few months ago, you could have never been a trainee physician or wielded a staff the way you do. The future is what you make it Dana Black."

Dana blushed again because he was right. There were a great many things she was doing now that she had never thought possible in a thousand years.

"Would you…come to Agmantia with me, see my home?"

The idea was completely inconceivable as she replied,

"Your home is a castle, mine is, was a small cottage. I don't think it would be my place."

"Your place would be wherever I wish it to be and besides, I live in a palace," he winked at her and Dana giggled.

"A glorious palace nestled within the rainforest with cascading waterfalls in the place of some walls. Bright coloured birds soar in the air and there are attendants to satisfy your every whim."

"That sounds wonderful but…"

Aslan studied her as he waited for her to finish,

"Why do you hesitate?"

Why was she hesitating?

There was nothing stopping her from being the guest of a foreign prince in his beautiful palace and living out dreams, she never knew she had. Still, the one dream she did have was Nyron Antos and he was, well…she didn't know what he was. He had said he was no good for her, that there kiss never should have happened. Did he know that that kiss had meant everything to her, that she wanted to be everything to him? It didn't matter if he did. Nyron had made his choice and he'd chosen Saicha Voltaire. Dana turned to Aslan,

"If we survive this war…I will go to Agmantia with you your Highness," Aslan beamed at her, appreciatively.

"I'll anticipate the end of this war more than anyone here."

Dana giggled again and playfully nudged him in the side as they continued along the path.

Trista had regained consciousness a few moments ago but she was not ready to face whatever she would find when she opened her eyes.

They were moving, that much was obvious as she felt the movement and slow bumps in the road. Where they were, or how long she had been unconscious wasn't as easy to tell, but once she realised she felt relatively okay, the first thing that came to mind, was Oren.

She hoped he was okay, wherever he was and that she would be able to see him soon. When she'd fallen, and passed out, she thought she would never see him again. No matter how she felt now, she knew she still had this war to fight and she couldn't very well do it without him.

Slowly, Trista began to open her eyes and as if she had summoned him from her very mind, Oren was there. He was walking alongside her, his torso obstructed by the walls of the cart she lay in and almost as soon as she opened her eyes, he turned and looked down at her. A smile appeared on his face, a warm and comforting smile that she returned without thinking when suddenly…

Are you alright?

It was Oren's voice but she could distinctly see he hadn't spoken.

The only time anything like this had remotely happened to her was in Remora and even then, she hadn't known why or how. Still, how did she reply? Not wanting to exhaust herself any further she nodded, and he smiled,

Good, you should rest until we get back to camp.

Her eyebrows furrowed and Oren seemed to chuckle,

I'll explain everything later but we'll be back soon so just rest.

She nodded again and tried to convey her gratitude,

You're welcome, Princess

She didn't know how he'd understood her, but she smiled any way and closed her eyes to try and rest her body and regain her strength, both physically and magically.

She didn't realise she'd fallen asleep until she woke up and there was the distinct glow of candle light above her. She was in a bed, her bed in her tent with the tip of the roof rising high above her. She was warm and the bed was draped in furs but she heard commotion in the adjoining compartment.

Gingerly, she got out of bed and found some clothes. She found her trousers, boots and a woollen over shirt and quickly dressed to make her way into the meeting area.

When she entered, everyone in the room rose from their seated positions and where Oren, Naima, Lamya and Nyron bowed, Dana rushed towards her and hugged her tight.

Trista hugged her back, squeezing her dearest friend tightly to her chest.

"Don't ever scare me like that again," Dana whispered into her ear as they held one another.

"I'll try," she whispered back as Dana loosened her hold on her and lead her to a now vacant chair. Trista took the seat gladly, conscious of how weak she still felt but smiled at them,

"How are you feeling?" Naima asked quietly,

"Tired, weak but alive so, there's that."

Chuckles went around the space. Trista looked around the room at all of them.

"Thank you all so much for being the strength I constantly need," she looked down, almost ashamed. "I wouldn't have made it this far without all of you and I want you to know that I appreciate it with all my heart."

She looked up at them again, each in their eyes as she said,

"Forget about the title and the grandeur…you five are my family and I love you all more than anything in this world…I hope you know that."

"We know Tris," Nyron smiled at her.

"So," Trista let out a pent-up breath. "What happened?"

Nyron and Naima explained about the explosive powder they'd found and the men they'd had to apprehend it from. They explained their move to The Wide and that on her say so, the war could truly begin.

"Tomorrow then, we move out tomorrow morning. Naima will oversee the trebuchets construction and position the archers. Nyron will head the vanguard and cavalry until Captain Theronos arrives. Once we see the might of Briseis' forces, we can better determine how to attack." Agreement went around the room. A message had been sent with Aurora to Captain Theronos about the collapse of The Reach and that they would have to travel through The Forest. They could only hope that their reinforcement arrived in time and without any battles of their own to report.

"We use the powder first," Trista agreed quietly and Nyron looked up at Naima who looked over to Oren. Oren continued to look at Trista,

"I don't want too much close to us to be used against us. We launch it, ignite it and get rid of as much of their forces as we can before anyone engages in any fighting. I didn't come all this way to lose any of you now. Dana," she turned to her best friend.

"I want you to stay with the Agmantians. They're seasoned fighters and you'll be safe with them if your own skills fail you."

"Where will you be?" Trista straightened her back,

"I will be wherever I am needed…with the General by my side."

"We need you to kill Briseis," Naima said sharply. "You can't do that gallivanting around the troops."

Trista looked at her cousin sternly and Naima straightened her own back,

"When Briseis shows herself, I will go where I am required but until then Lady Antos, I will be where I am needed and that is amongst my people."

Although the words resonated with all of them, Trista aimed them at Naima.

"I will be among the men and women who may lose their lives to save my crown. If they need me gallivanting among them before my true fight begins, then so be it."

Naima bowed her head respectfully and Nyron smiled to himself,

"If you'll excuse me, we have a big day tomorrow."

Trista turned and entered her bedroom as everyone exited in respectful silence.

THE FRONT LINE

Briseis looked around her war tent at her father, General Rarno, Gardan, Lords Weilyn and Thelm, Lady Remora and her Six.

"The time has come ladies and gentlemen for this war to finally begin. We have waited months, years even to determine the might of the Samaian army and what we are truly be up against and from what I see, we have nothing to fear."

Briseis walked among them in her layers of bear fur, her beautiful face shining out of the shag of the covering,

"We are many and we are mighty, and our power will be displayed on this battlefield in ways that none of us could have ever imagined."

"When this war is done, we would have brought Mortania into a new age; an age of prosperity, growth and power...the Age of Men."

Pride simmered around the room as Briseis looked over at her father and he nodded, seemingly in approval. Curian rose from his chair and approached his daughter,

"It is no secret that we have had our differences but today...today we come together to claim our victory once and for all. I commend you Briseis, my daughter...my heir; for being and doing all that I could not."

Everyone in the room looked over at the princess who had gone silent.

She studied her father for a moment before they all saw her swallow before nodding her head with a demure and appreciative smile.

"Thank you, Father," Curian bowed his head before reclaiming his seat.

"We attack at first light," Briseis called out, turning from her father to the others. "This ends now."

***

The camp was alive with the exhilaration of war.

While there were only mere hours until the sun broke across the sky, the Antonides camp was buzzing with activity and considering many of them may not return, everyone was in particularly high spirits.

Trista had retired to her bed once she'd spoken to her court, eager to rejuvenate her magic and her strength. The others had gone on to perform their various duties and the fighters among them, completed their pre-war rituals.

Men and women were drinking by open fires and eating heartily as for some if not many; it would be their last proper meal. The finality of it all brought a weird sense of calm, that had them singing and laughing well into the night until the General made his rounds,

"Get the rest while you can!" Oren barked out to them, "We have a war to win tomorrow!"

Everyone raised their mugs and cups and pitchers in salute, cheering as they did so making Oren laugh, a little.

"Get to bed, all of you!" he called out again and the good-natured mumbles echoed through the camp. Soldiers nestled down into their bedrolls as well as they could, closest to all fires, some using their powers to warm themselves where possible.

The other, higher ranking officers made their way to their tents including Dana and Aslan who walked side by side laughing,

"You do not!" Dana laughed into the early hours of the morning,

"I promise you, we do!"

"You do not have birds that can speak!" Aslan laughed along with her, equally as drunk as Dana as they walked among the troops.

"Well, they don't speak but they repeat words you teach them,"

"You'll have to show me then, Prince Aslan. I will not believe it until I see it," Dana giggled to herself as she teasingly punched his shoulder.

They stopped walking as they approached her tent and Aslan looked down at her, his eyes suddenly hooded. He reached out and placed a strand of hair behind her ear and Dana blushed,

"I think the General said we should get some rest, that includes the both of you."

Both Dana and Aslan turned at the sound of Nyron's voice and Dana, angry; scowled at him but said nothing. Aslan however, wasn't as accommodating,

"But it does not seem to include you Lord?"

"No, it doesn't." Nyron stepped up to Aslan who followed suit.

"I don't take orders from you Lord Antos…remember that." The two men squared up to each other, both urging the other to make the first move.

"You're not the prince of this land…remember that."

"You're not the prince of any land, second son."

Dana watched as Nyron's fist clenched by his side, turning his knuckles white,

"Nyron can I talk to you, please."

Aslan shrugged before turning back to Dana and kissing the side of her face briefly,

"Goodnight Dana Black, we will share many kills tomorrow."

Dana smiled sweetly, as Aslan departed to his own tent. As Aslan disappeared into the dark, Dana turned to march into her tent and Nyron followed,

"What was that about?"

"What?"

"That pissing contest!" Dana snapped at him but Nyron ignored her, asking instead.

"Have you kissed him?"

"What? That's none of your business!"

"I think it is!"

"Well it's not! It stopped being your business when you told me you wanted nothing to do with me!"

"I never said that," Nyron ground out, raising his arms in frustration. Dana folded her arms across her chest, infuriated.

"Who I choose to spend my time with is none of your business Nyron." Dana swallowed and looked away from him before saying, "The same way who you sleep with is none of mine."

Nyron looked hurt but he knew he had no response,

"You told me I was too young, that nothing could come of this so what gives you the right to come between Aslan and me?"

"So there is something going on with you?"

"You couldn't stop me if there was!" she hissed at him. "I don't belong to you and you made that choice…not me."

Nyron marched up to her so he was towering over her and even though she wasn't scared of him, he did intimidate her.

What would she do if he tried to kiss her again, the way she desperately wanted him to?

"I said those things to protect you Dana, don't you understand that?"

"Protecting me doesn't mean keeping me in your pocket until you're ready to play with me." Nyron looked horrified,

"I know it doesn't, I don't mean that at all!"

"Then leave me alone!" she screamed at him.

"I can't!" he shouted back as he stepped forward, lifted her into his arms and kissed her.

Dana wrapped her arms around Nyron's neck and melted into him because she didn't have the power not to. His lips were powerful and demanding and the sweetest thing she'd ever tasted as he used his tongue to set her entire body on fire. She wanted him, to be with him completely but as she threaded her fingers through his hair, she felt his hold on her go lax. Nyron stopped kissing her and gently, lowered her to the ground.

His breathing was ragged, his large chest heaving in and out as the adrenaline coursed through him.

"Dan—"

"No."

She didn't need to shout or scream for him to know that she was serious.

"I won't let you do this to me again," she whispered before looking up at him, her eyes shiny with tears. "I wanted to try at whatever this could have been, but *you* said no and now it's my turn…please leave."

Nyron looked pained,

"Dana, please don't waste your…" he looked down at her body and groaned. "Please don't throw yourself away on some philandering foreign prince." Dana scoffed at him, more hurt then she could ever remember being.

"It's an upgrade from a philandering native noble, wouldn't you agree? Please leave Nyron…I have nothing left to say to you."

Nyron sighed heavily as he looked down at the petite brunette in front of him,

"I care about you…more than I should. Please don't do something stupid just because I did."

He turned and left the tent, disappearing into the night.

Saicha watched Nyron march out of Dana's tent and back to his own, clearly angry and wondered what on earth he was so mad about.

The following morning, General Oren Antos, sat atop of Titan, looking over at the Greybold army.

As if universally understood that this was the morning to begin, the front line of each army stood with miles of land between them. They had used their powers to build four trebuchets through the night and he waited beside them and their operators now, with Trista beside him.

The vanguard, the archers, the cavalry were all in position with their commanding officers among them, ready to give their orders.

The sun was still rising as the horses whinnied and the thousands of souls on The Wide, held their breath for the first attack.

The sun continued to rise beautifully and as the colours of the sky melted into the land and brought its light, Oren felt it unfair that there would be so much death and annihilation beneath such beauty.

He turned to look at Trista, the beauty beside him, who was staring at the same scene intensely.

He had been wrong to shield her the way he had, he realised now, but there was no way to take it back. He had made his bed and he would have to lie in it until this war was over; whatever the outcome. Either he would win this war for her and she would become Queen and he would belong to her forever, or they would lose and it wouldn't matter that he never told her. Victorious was the only way he was coming off this battlefield and so he had a lot to think about when that time came.

"Your Highness," he murmured so only she could hear and she turned her crowned head towards him with a tender smile.

"Yes General?"

"When the war is won, I wish to speak with you about something…something important."

"You can't say it now?"

"No, not yet. Promise me…" he said. "Promise me that after the fighting we'll talk…just me and you."

Trista looked over at him and something in her face was questioning but she nodded,

"You and me."

He nodded his thanks,

"When you're ready your Highness."

Trista turned from him and took a deep breath before inclining her head slightly. Oren took that as his signal and almost instantly, a tiny bead of light ignited in his ear as well as Trista's beside him.

"Lady Antos?"

"Here," came Naima's voice into their ears and even Trista was a little impressed, Naima was yards away on a hill behind them.

"Lord Antos?"

"Here,"

"Captains?"

"Here!"

The powerful voices echoed within their ears and with their confirmation, Trista nodded again.

"Archers," Oren called out,

"Received," Naima's voice echoed once more, and the archers got into position. Naima was impressed with Trista's response to using the powder and so, with a nervous excitement that could only come from a fight, she readied her team.

"NOCK!" she bellowed out and the archers nocked their arrows. Naima's hand ignited into flame as they did so,

"DRAW!"

The archers aimed their arrows and in doing so, exposed the tiny packets attached just above the arrow head,

"LOOSE!"

The arrows flew from their bows and out across the field into…nothing. They were too far back to have actually hit the opposing army and so the arrows landed in a line on the empty wasteland.

The archers who had just shot, stepped back and another line of archers took their place. These had larger bows with the same packets attached just above the arrow head,

"NOCK!" Naima called again, "DRAW…LOOSE!"

Once again, they fired into the wasteland a little further in front of the first arrows.

"Archers complete General," Naima called down their connection.

"Lord Antos," Oren responded in turn and Nyron stood to attention.

***

Gardan was worried.

The Samaian army had fired their arrows but hit no one and did not seem intent on advancing on them. He had the might of the Greybold army at his back and of course Briseis and her Six by his side but he knew there was something wrong.

"This is going to be easier than I thought," Briseis commented beside him. Her father and General Rarno were on their horses on the other side of her and while they looked confused, Gardan could see they were also concerned.

"We advance now, General."

"Princess, I don't think…" Briseis turned her cold eyes to him and he knew that now was not the time she would listen to his concerns or reasoning. Gardan turned from her without response,

"FORWARD!"

The cavalry line of the Greybold army set off into The Wide as Briseis looked on with pure excitement. She was armoured in the best Agmantian steel with her hair braided tightly so it hung down her back and out of her way. Her sword was down her side along with daggers in her sword belt.

The horses galloped into The Wide, toward the Samaian army who remained still even while the soldiers on horseback screamed in their attack. As the horses edged closer to the enemy, Gardan watched the Samaian archers intently until a movement caught his eye. The one mounted Samaian, he couldn't tell if it were a man or a woman, swiped their hand in the direction of charging cavalry.

The powder!

"SHIELD YOURSELVES!"

Gardan screamed into the early morning sky, his shout immediately lost in the explosions that erupted from The Wide in front of them, where the Samaian army had ignited the black powder into their front line.

THE WAR

Trista and her most trusted, looked on as the front line of Briseis' army was obliterated. The powder rigged arrows had ignited all at once with the help of Naima's magic and sent horse and soldiers, flying into the air in all directions.

Admittedly, she was surprised it had worked, she hadn't expected Briseis to allow her men to walk into the fight without even questioning it. Briseis had clearly underestimated her and it added to her confidence.

Trista gave the signal and Oren ordered the release of the trebuchets. They had been rigged with the remaining barrels of powder which were now launched into the air.

Naima and the archers ignited their hands and sent shots of fire into the air, igniting the powder as it rained down on the Greybold army below. Trista watched in amazement as fire fell from the sky and burned Briseis' cavalry. She knew she shouldn't be excited by the deaths of innocent people, but she rather it the Greybold soldiers than her own.

With a flick of his wrist, Oren ordered their own cavalry to move in to finish whatever destruction the powder had created. Thick black smoke, rose high into the sky, obstructing their view and moments later, their own men were lost to it.

"General, the smoke."

Oren worked quickly to clear the smoke from the air and Trista watched the thick clouds shrink before her very eyes. Where they went, she didn't have time to question, but soon enough, the skies were clear for her to see once more. Trista saw the myriad of people now fighting in the lands beyond and she signalled once again to Oren,

"Lord Antos!" he called down to Nyron

"FORWARD!" Nyron's voice echoed in their heads as he led the vanguard toward the fighting and truly launched the Battle of the Heirs.

Dana had been instructed to remain with the Agmantians for her safety but until they entered the fighting, she remained at camp with Lamya and the physicians. While she was not yet in the initial fighting, Nyron and Aslan were and she was terrified that they would not return.

She knew it was silly to think that something could happen to them so soon in the war, but anything could happen and she may not see either one of them again.

She knew Saicha had gone with him, anxious as she said for some real fighting and Dana hated herself for even being jealous of that simple concept. Yes, she could now hold her own with a staff and sword if necessary, but she knew she would never be as dangerous as Saicha the Assassin. She hated that she could be so petty in the light of so much destruction but at least they were winning…so far.

It was quiet for the moment; no real casualties having arrived and Dana had the chance to speak with Lamya about all they had seen and would do once the fighting was over.

"It still hasn't sunk in that my best friend will be Queen and is out there right now, fighting a war." Lamya smiled sweetly as she arranged rows of bandages and bowls of clean water and salves within easy reach.

"Well, at the moment, she's orchestrating a war not fighting one…and I for one hope it will stay that way."

"She's been training months for this, why wouldn't you want her to fight?"

Lamya sat on one of the many vacant beds and looked Dana squarely in the face,

"War changes you Dana. You felt it yourself when you came to me after killing one of those bandits. It's a change that can never go back and I don't wish that for our queen." Dana nodded her understanding,

"I don't think any of us can avoid that change now," she looked out of the small medical tent they were sat in towards where the fighting was taking place. They couldn't hear anything so far away but something made her think she caught the distinct clash of sword on sword.

"I don't think any of us would want to…we've gained too much."

"That is true," Lamya agreed. "Now you have something to lose."

Saicha and Aslan Voltaire remained with the reserve forces of the Antonides army while Nyron's vanguard and Naima's archers handled the initial attack. With their limited numbers, they didn't want to attack with their whole force, at least until they knew how long it would take for Captain Theronos' men to arrive.

"I want to be out there!" Saicha cursed. "I don't want to be babysitting!" Aslan looked around as he sat on a rock, resting his weight on his scabbard sword.

"You call heading a division…babysitting?"

"It is when I could be tearing limbs from bodies with my bare hands" Aslan scoffed,

"Don't flatter yourself, you just want to be near Nyron Antos."

Saicha snarled at him and Aslan threw his hands up in mock surrender,

"What you see in that savage, I'll never know."

"It's a good thing its none of your business then," Aslan was unable to respond as a horse came galloping up to them, the rider practically falling off as he held the reins so loosely.

By the time, he reached the siblings and the thousand or so men behind them, he had fallen to the ground and they were able to see the extent of his wound. He had been run through his shoulder and the cut was gushing with blood,

"Get this man to the physicians!" Aslan yelled out as he grabbed the man's legs while another two men grabbed his arms as best they could and carried him to get medical attention.

Dana was washing her hands when Aslan brought the first man in and after that, it felt like they wouldn't stop coming. Broken legs, punctured lungs, missing limbs came at her hard as fast.

She remembered all that Rayne and Lamya had shown her, had entrusted her with and got to work trying to save the lives, of her best friend's people.

***

The fighting raged on for a day before it was too dark to continue. The Antonides and Greybold armies fell back so each side could collect their dead but Briseis was enraged.

"Get those men out there!" she shouted at Gardan in her tent that evening, while the cries of dying men echoed all around them.

"The men are tired and are of no use to anyone like this!"

"They're soldiers, they're meant to fight; there are no breaks in war!"

"When was the last war you fought?"

Briseis reached out with her power and grabbed Gardan by the neck. She held him high above the ground as she choked him, looking directly into his eyes as his face turned blue.

He wouldn't try to stop her, he didn't even claw at his throat but stared back at her as she attempted to kill him. She let go and he fell to the floor in a heap, gasping for breath. He spluttered uncontrollably as she paced her tent,

"First light!" she said without an apology and marched into her bedroom, leaving him to regain his composure.

***

Another day and night went by and the conflict thundered on. The Antonides army had taken out a good number of the Greybold forces with the black powder but there was still a formidable host of men up against them.

They all knew however, that despite their weary bodies and depleted powers, they were lucky to be alive. Despite their magical advantage, the Greybold army were still impressive fighters and were not backing down so easily.

They also had the protection of the Six.

The teenagers had been present on the battlefield, shielding all Greybold soldiers from truly fatal attacks. They worked as a single impenetrable unit, a force against any of the Samaians who were weaker in power. They were the secret weapon that Briseis had said they would be and it would be difficult to win the war, with them still alive.

They all knew however, that no matter the turnout of soldier against soldier, the war would never be over until one princess killed the other.

The evening before the third day, Trista, Oren, Naima, Nyron, Saicha and Aslan stood around the war table of Trista's tent. Aslan, Saicha and the twins were covered in blood, dirt and grime and as she laid eyes on them, Trista felt incredibly guilty.

She knew this was her place, to oversee the battle before her true fight with Briseis but she couldn't help feeling that they were doing all the work while she just stood around ordering them to do it.

She had to focus on the task at hand, and turned wearily to her cousin,

"What's going on down there?" Nyron shook his head,

"They are many and they are strong. I took down many soldiers due to my own strength and training, but this is not going to be an easy fight. The powder did any amazing job at the beginning but if we have any chance of holding them off, we'd need more. If we continue like this, we'll exhaust the men before we've even begun."

"We don't have anymore!" Naima hissed at him but Nyron banged his fists on the table.

"Don't you think I realise that Naima!"

No one said anything, unsure of how to respond to the change in Nyron's character. He rarely shouted and even then, it was never at Naima.

"What about the rejuvenating powers?" Dana asked quietly. "Aren't you getting stronger while you're together?" Nyron shook his head again,

"Unless the Everlasting is under our control, the rejuvenation doesn't work the same. We're using it quicker than it can fill up."

There was a stretch of silence until Saicha chimed in,

"We need to take out the Six."

"How do we do that? None of us are strong enough to get past their magical defences."

"That's because they can see you coming." Saicha said smugly, taking down her hood, revealing her stunning face. How someone could be so beautiful but so deadly was beyond Trista's understanding.

"Leave the children to me," she said. "Hopefully it will buy the reprieve we need." Trista had seen Saicha on the battlefield, how she cut through men like they were made of silk. She had watched her slit a man's throat after having already stabbed him the chest and was terrified for the Six, even if they were her enemy.

As the assassin finished speaking, a guard entered the tent and bowed,

"General, Captain Theronos has arrived."

There was a collective gasp around the room,

"Now that is the reprieve we need!" Nyron said joyfully but Naima's face was a scowl. Eager to hear what news the captain had brought, the group held their conversation until he arrived.

Captain Justin Theronos stood before them moments later, looking battered but beautiful. There was no denying his good looks, but Trista saw the terror on his face, she just didn't know the reason why.

"Captain," she called out to him and obediently, Justin stepped toward her, his blue cape billowing behind his armour as he bowed in front of her.

"Your Highness. I came as quickly as I could but The Forest…" he trailed off before looking around the room and stopping whatever he was going to say.

"All that matters, is that we are here. All thirty-five hundred of us…"

"What happened to the other five hundred!" Nyron demanded as Oren simply looked at the captain intently.

"The Forest is as they claim" Justin said, his voice quivering. "It is not a place for mortal men."

No one knew what to say. They had heard stories of things people had seen when venturing into The Forest, if they ever came out alive.

Trista touched the captain's shoulder,

"I'm happy you made it here at all. My mother is with you, and safe?" Justin nodded,

"She is being housed along with the rest of my men. Justice Rubio is with her."

"Good," she replied. "General."

It was only then that Justin seemed to look around the rest of the room and when he laid his eyes on Naima, they all saw the relief and admiration on his face. Oren dismissed it and brought Justin up to speed on all that had taken place in the last three days of battle.

"Has the Greybold princess shown herself?" Justin asked when Oren was done.

"Not yet," Trista said angrily. "Until then, let's all get some rest before tomorrow."

Everyone began to file out and for a fleeting moment, Naima had to walk past Justin.

"Lady Antos," he murmured humbly. She looked at him with eyes of cold steel, said nothing and took off after her brother.

It wasn't until she was half way to her own tent, that she heard her name being called again.

"Lady Antos!"

Naima turned even as men were being rushed past her towards the physicians with severe injuries. Better injuries than fatalities, she thought to herself although she had already seen many men fall.

Captain Justin Theronos practically jogged up to her and she looked at him with complete and utter disdain.

Why did he have to still be so gorgeous after all this time when all she wanted to do was claw his eyes out? His moss green eyes and hair so black, it was almost blue. His lips were another matter altogether and she almost shivered with the thoughts of all those moments she had stolen kisses with him.

No, she wouldn't think that way.

She wanted to hurt him, to make him suffer the way she had suffered all these years without him. She knew it was young love, she knew he had no choice but to leave with his family but that didn't matter. He should have stayed…he should have loved her enough to stay.

"May I speak with you?" Naima looked at him from the tip of his boots to the top of his head,

"I have nothing to say to you,"

"Nothing at all?"

Naima was taken back before composing herself and smirking at him,

"Actually, I do have something to say." He piped up as Naima sauntered over to him.

"Stay away from me," she said coldly. "Don't speak to me, don't address me, don't even think about me. You're dead to me Captain and I wish I had the power to erase that I ever knew or loved you."

"Loved?"

Shit!

Even during their time together, they had never discussed how they felt about one another; it was just something they felt and knew…or so she had thought.

Maybe Justin hadn't known how she felt about him, maybe if he had, he would have chosen to stay with her?

Naima pursed her lips together, refusing to go down that road of thought and narrowed her eyes him,

"Stay away from me Justin…forever this time."

When everyone had finally left the tent and it was just Oren, Trista and her attendants, Oren turned to her and quietly asked,

"Your Highness, may I speak with you?"

Unsure of why he was being so formal with her, Trista looked over at Oren nervously and nodded.

"Ladies, please leave us for the moment."

Her attendants left into her bedroom and she and Oren were left alone. She took a seat on one of the low chairs in the room, expecting him to follow suit but Oren remained standing, looking down at her.

"General, what is it?"

Oren sighed and looked directly into her eyes,

"I have to get out there."

Trista's heart dropped because she knew what he meant and why he was saying it, she felt it too.

"I can't stand around giving orders, it's not who I am!" he was getting heated, not angry just passionate.

"Please," he said stepping closer to her and getting down on one knee so their eyes were level. "Please let me go to the front and I promise…I will return to you."

Trista swallowed all the objections she wanted to give him. Oren was a warrior, from a long line of warriors. He was literally born to fight and she wouldn't be the one to deny him.

"Yes," she said quietly, looking down into her lap where her hands were folded. No sooner had she done it, Trista felt his fingers under her chin, lifting her face back to his.

"Trista look at me," she looked. She looked into his teal green eyes and got lost in all the emotions she was keeping from him. "I will never leave you…ever."

"I know,"

I'll always be with you

Her eyebrows rose to her hairline,

"H-how are you doing that?"

"It's something we can do, you and I…together."

"How?"

"Just…feel it."

She didn't know how but she knew exactly what he meant. She reached down inside her to that feeling, that weird sensation she always felt around him and felt it flutter to life. She'd learned to ignore it, to push it to the back of her mind but suddenly there it was and the first thing she felt was…

Woah!

Take your time…don't exert yourself too much

You can hear me?!

Yes

He smiled at her and Trista beamed at him, teeth gleaming.

This is amazing!

It is…you can speak to me whenever you need to

Even when we're not together?

Especially when we're not together

He chuckled and Trista laughed too until they both stopped and looked into one another's eyes.

I'll never leave you Trista, I will always protect you.

I know, she smiled shyly. *Because your honour demands it*

She chuckled but Oren didn't say anything, only getting to his feet and stepping back to look down at her.

"I'll be back when your war is won."

Trista nodded as he bowed to her and swiftly exited the tent.

As she composed herself and tried to get her heartbeat to slow down, she suddenly heard,

Not only because my honour demands it

Trista rushed out of the tent, only catching Oren's back disappearing into the crowd.

TRANSFORMATION

On the morning of the third day, Dana watched when Trista exited her tent with her maids hurrying behind her. She was in her armour again and took off to the battlefield on horseback moments later.

The General and Captain Theronos had left long before their princess, Trista had left to join Naima, Saicha had left with Nyron and Dana was joining Aslan to finally march into the battle. She had remained with Lamya and the physicians to help with the wounded, but she couldn't avoid the fighting any longer.

She'd watched Nyron leave too of course and hated that Saicha was by his side. While she had, no issue being partners with Aslan, she couldn't stop worrying about Nyron. They hadn't spoken since she'd asked him to leave her tent, and Dana found she regretted it. She'd wanted to hurt him for hurting her, not alienate him forever.

Still, it didn't matter. Dana knew she had to get on with her life because no matter how she felt about Nyron, he didn't feel the same way about her.

She and Aslan, once they were ready mounted their horses and headed back into the destruction that took place through The Wide.

Dana had of course, never seen war. Dana had never left Remora before this and despite all the places and people she had seen since then, nothing could have ever prepared her for what lay in front of her.

The air was dark, both from the early morning and the tragedy that lay around it. There was shouting and screaming from men, women and horses and there was blood…there was blood everywhere.

She and Aslan dismounted when they approached the battlefield and as the prince loosened his sword, he looked to her,
"You're still coming to Agmantia with me, aren't you?"
Bewildered, Dana nodded, and Aslan winked her,
"Then you won't be dying today will you?"
The confidence that surged through her at that moment was indescribable, as she tightened her hold on her staff, loosened her wrist and barrelled into the fight.

That felt like hours ago now, but there was no way of telling how long she had been out there, killing and surviving. Dana fought now, with her staff in a crowd of screaming and dying people and focused on the task at end: *don't get killed*.

She broke jaws, she cracked spines and knees, her thick staff a perfect match for her size and growing skill against swords and axes of all kinds. Yes, a sword could run her through, but Dana didn't worry about that, she concentrated on bettering her opponent and disarming him before his axe or sword could slice through her.

As another man fell to his knees before her, Dana slammed the end of her thick staff into his head, cracking his skull. The blood sprayed so high; it coated her face, but she no longer cared. The blood of men she had never met and would never see again had been over her and it would be there for a long time after she'd washed it off, she knew.

Another one went down and another until a sudden blow to the head sent her ears ringing and Dana was suddenly face down on the floor. The once dry and hard ground had now been disturbed by boots and hooves and was now a series of mounds and grooves of dirt.

Her hands opened up, sending her staff rolling away, her hands scrapping along the ground. She tried to roll over, terrified suddenly of being stabbed in back. Just as she rolled, an axe landed in the space where she had been. Shocked that he had missed, the man on the other end of the weapon hesitated, and, in that moment, Dana reached down her exposed leg to the dagger that was strapped there. She went to plunge it into his thigh just as blood spurted out of his mouth and Dana saw the sword that now protruded through his neck.

She scampered backwards as the man dropped to the floor and Aslan stood behind him, covered in his own kills. He quickly pulled her to her feet,

"Are you okay?" she nodded, still shocked from the kill. Aslan nodded and set off into the fight again,

My staff, where is my staff?

Dana crouched, scanning the chaos for her staff, conscious of wayward arrows, daggers and swords that could catch her unexpectedly. Finally, she saw it, laying a few feet away from her and she charged towards it.

Just as she bent to retrieve it, an arrow flew over her head. Her heart pounding, Dana gripped her staff, the familiarity of it giving her immediate strength. She gathered herself once more and saw a man charging after an Antonides warrior who was engaging in their own fight.

Dana ran for them and using her staff as a vault, she lifted herself into the air and kicked out at the man's head. He felt instantly and Dana slammed her staff into his chest, winding him before smashing it into his head, killing him.

Dana swung her staff around her head before ramming it into the torso of another soldier. One on the left, one on the right before she spun with her staff, crouched low and swiped the legs out from underneath the two men she had hit.

They fell back, their heads hitting the ground where Dana struck her staff into each of their groins. They cried out in agony before Dana dragged her dagger once again from her leg and stabbed one of them in the eye and the other in his suddenly exposed neck. The blood sprayed over her face once again before she raised her head and Aslan was in her view.

"ASLAN!" Dana screamed across the battlefield. The prince turned in record time and drove his sword into the belly of the man coming for him. Aslan sought her face out in the crowd and saluted her before taking off again.

I can do this!

Dana felt triumphant as she took off toward another enemy.

Saicha had seen the havoc that Briseis' little group of helpers were able to inflict on the other fighters and so she had taken it upon herself to remove them as a threat. She watched them even as she fought men twice her size and weight, learning the moves they favoured over others. They worked as a unit, that much was clear but what was also obvious was the way they rallied around what seemed to be their leader.

She had seen how the children could move when they had come across them in the Greybold war camp and despite her reservations about their power and strength, she knew she had to try and get rid of them.

Saicha cut through another man, his longsword a formidable weapon even as she cut into his neck and let them fall to the floor in a heap of gargling blood and metal.

Swiftly, she moved on, silent as the grave even among the clamour of the fighting, her eyes trained to be able to survey one thing but to do another. She set her sights on the leader of the young group and while slicing into more soldiers of the enemy side, she made her way to their leader.

He was good but he was sloppy and Saicha knew it would be easy enough to take out the Six leader as long as she caught him off guard. She watched as the Six worked together, cloaking their best fighters and deflecting incoming arrows or surprise attacks that others may not have seen coming. It was a tactical manoeuvre, one she almost admired but this was not the time for admiration.

Until she found her opening, Saicha was fighting with Nyron at her back and she found she liked it. He was more than an incredible lover, but an even better warrior and she admired him. Even as she kept her attention on the Six leader, feet away and her own opponents in front of her, she saw Nyron's manoeuvres and kills and saw that he was sensational. Just as she disarmed someone with her *sai*, from the corner of her eye she saw someone charging for Nyron. Quickly, she discarded her opponent's weapon, before reaching out and piercing their exposed throat with her fingers. It was a move she didn't use often, ripping a man's throat out, wasn't particularly nice work.

She threw his innards onto the floor as he fell and turned to throw a dagger clear across the field and straight into the would-be attacker's head. He collapsed just behind Nyron, who once he'd killed his own opponent spun around at the sound. Saicha approached him to retrieve her dagger and he nodded his thanks before in a rush, she lowered her mask and kissed him before running off back into the fight.

Nyron didn't have the time to recover from Saicha's kiss before he saw Dana looking over at them just before Saicha took off. When she smashed a fallen man in the face with the end of her staff, he knew it was his face she had seen.

***

Briseis was not happy.

She had lost a considerable number of men in the first two days of fighting, and now, on the third day it was only getting worse. Despite her Six doing much to take many Samaian lives and protect countless Greybold ones, it just wasn't enough and still she had not seen the Redeemer. This would not do.

Briseis ha thought she would have overwhelmed the Samaian army with her numbers, but they just seemed to respawn. It was time for more drastic measures and so Briseis turned from where she stood looking down onto the battlefield and marched back to her war tent.

"Lady Avriel!" she called out to the woman who followed her. When she got to her tent, Briseis turned in all her armoured glory to where Avriel now stood looking at her.

"You can do what we discussed?"

"Yes."

"How does it work?"

"The less questions the better," Avriel replied, expressionless. "Do you wish to proceed?"

Briseis stared back at the woman, defiantly. She was scared of nothing and no one and wouldn't be intimidated by this pathetic woman who believed herself superior.

"Do it now."

When she stepped out of her tent moments later, Briseis stood in the most incredible new armour.

She stood in black from head to toe, a black so dark it gleamed like a moonlit ocean surface. The sword she held by her side was large blackened steel that she held expertly by her side. It had ridged edges, a blade that would cause incredible damage to the flesh it would undoubtedly pierce through.

She had let her white hair loose and it blew now in the icy winds shining as brightly against the armour she wore.

"Your Highness?"

Gardan approached her, confused and questioning.

"If she will not show herself, then I will draw her out." Briseis stared across to the fighting where her destiny awaited. "I will end this."

Briseis walked toward Axus and mounted her horse,

"Princess, please think about this."

Briseis looked down at him,

"You do your thinking here General," she laughed mockingly at him. "I'm going to take back what is mine."

She kicked her horse into gear and raced towards the fighting.

Briseis charged into the thicket of battle, her vision focused solely on getting to the brunt of the fighting; everyone and everything around her was secondary. She barely saw the men, enemy and ally alike fall around her. The screams and grunts of soldiers echoed all around as the now dimming colours of Samaian magic followed.

Axus raced on and when Briseis saw that it would be too dangerous to race him further into the fighting, she raised herself in the stirrups before launching herself out of the saddle and flipping forward to land directly in the midst of the fighting.

The ground cracked where she landed as she shook her hair from her face and looked around. Briseis drew her sword and Enflamed, grey flame billowing around her as she charged forward and slaughtered her enemies.

On and on she cut down, men and women alike; blocking incoming attacks with her magic and sending bursts of fire to incinerate her rivals. One man she noticed as she sent a fireball toward him, made a gesture and the ball disintegrated before it connected; simply fizzling out. Enraged, Briseis focused her energy towards him and threw out fireball after fireball until he wasn't quick enough to extinguish them. She threw three consecutively and the man, seemingly exhausted wasn't quick enough and the third slammed into his side, setting him ablaze. Satisfied, Briseis continued her way through the fighting, cutting down any and all who were not Greybold coloured.

It was as she was fighting that she felt the most tremendous burst of energy come from somewhere behind her. She turned, intrigued by the magic she felt there and laid her eyes on a mountain of a man. The energy coming from him was unmistakably powerful, but she did not know who else in the Samai camp, who could wield the Everlasting so well.

From the corner of her eye, Briseis saw a soldier rush at her with his sword. She reached out, throwing up a solid wall of air that he crushed into, shattering his sword and forearm in the process. She clenched her fist and threw the man clear across the battlefield, where he landed; she couldn't have cared less.

Briseis set off into a run, away from the large man and tearing through any who got in her way until she crashed into something and fell backwards onto the ground.

"Aaaah!" Briseis screamed out from the unexpected hit but quickly covered herself with a protective shield; giving her time to get to her feet. It was the smart move as she was rocked again. She watched the fireball bounce off her shield, but she quickly got to her feet.

Briseis stood to face her attacker and when she laid eyes on the Enflamed Samaian man in front of her, she knew she was about to have the fight of her life.

The man charged at her, tremendous rage on his face and when his sword crashed down to her and connected with her own, lightning seemed to spark from the two blades. Briseis' sword armed ached with the connection, but she blocked again and set into a melee with the man who was clearly intent on killing her.

Naima's heart pounded in her chest as she watched her brother take on Briseis Greybold.

"NYRON!"

Naima, fighting back to back with Trista pointed a few yards across the fighting to where her brother had engaged in a fight with the Greybold princess. Trista's eyes narrowed determinedly as she set eyes on them.

The Agmantians were scatted around along with Dana, Justin and Oren who was currently fighting a Greybold soldier one on one.

"She's here!" Trista was surprised she hadn't felt her presence around them but none of that mattered now, Briseis was finally here and she looked terrifying. She was holding her own against Nyron Antos dressed in truly impressive armour.

Trista raced towards Nyron and Naima followed, sprinting as fast as they could over dead and injured bodies and the continued fighting around them.

I'm going after Briseis

Trista called out to Oren and hearing his voice in her head was more comforting then she ever wanted to admit.

You can do this…I believe in you, he said softly making her smile to herself.

Within seconds the girls had arrived, and Trista shot out a wave of energy, making Briseis fall to her knees.

"Nyron get out of here!" she screamed at him just as Naima began to drag him away. The rage in his eyes was subdued as he realised it was Trista who had spoken but reluctantly stepped back.

Briseis got to her feet, her lip split, blood seeping from it and turned to Trista with a smirk,

"There she is…the lost princess."

She hissed the words at her, and it made Trista feel sick as she looked into the cold grey eyes of the woman who had caused her so much pain.

Trista drew her sword but Briseis only laughed,

"Oh no Trista… you won't be needing that."

Trista looked at her in confusion, her eyes squinting just as what felt like a punch to the gut rocked her, making her stagger backwards. She fell to the ground, her stomach aching from the surge of pain.

Trista forced herself to look up to Briseis whose face began to change. Her features altered right before her eyes and in seconds, where Briseis once stood, Avriel Remora was now in her place. Trista and the twins looked down in horror at the older woman, smiling cruelly up at them.

Sorry, but you're not who I'm after right now

A voice seeped into her head, Briseis' voice she realised.

The words pierced into her mind, cold as ice. Trista was still reeling from the blow to her gut and the confusion at Avriel's appearance. Thunder rolled overhead,

Poor little princess.

The words slithered through the air into her brain making her feel sick.

Avenge him, Briseis hissed in their minds. *If you can.*

Oren!

The realisation was instant as Trista turned to where Oren had been and her vision centred on him, clear across the battlefield fighting someone.

Trista watched as the soldier Oren believed he was fighting, transformed into Briseis Greybold.

He'd raised both his arms above his head to strike his sword into his opponent, but the shock of the transformation was evident on his face.

In that moment of confusion, Briseis with an Enflamed hand, punched into Oren's exposed stomach; right through his armour and out the other side.

"OREEEEN!"

Before she'd even finished screaming his name, Trista Shifted behind Oren, reaching out for him, before he hit the ground. She crumbled to the floor under the weight of him and when she looked toward Briseis, nothing was there but a shadow and echoing laughter, where a woman once stood.

In the second that Trista Shifted across the battlefield, Naima turned and punched Avriel Remora dead in the face, splitting her lip and knocking a tooth out.

"What did you do!" Naima screamed at her. Avriel spat the blood from her mouth onto the floor and looked up at Naima with vengeful eyes.

"I helped," she hissed, no sign of regret on her face. "You should be thanking me!"

"Here's some thanks!" Naima crouched down and punched her again. She went to do so a third time, her other fist grabbed at the older woman's neck but Nyron stopped her.

"Naima, stop!"

Nyron dragged his sister from the other woman as Aslan, Saicha, Justin and Dana approached them.

In the split second that the six of them looked over to where Trista had Shifted, they watched in amazement as Briseis disappeared like dust on the wind.

The fighting seemed to stop as everyone stood in amazement at what had just happened.

"We have to get over there." Dana said quietly.

"I'll take her," Saicha said referring to Avriel and took hold of the woman from Nyron's grip and dragged her to her feet.

"Let's have a little chat, shall we?" Saicha hissed at her before slowly, Avriel shook her head,

"No…I don't think we will."

Avriel closed her eyes, murmured a few words and before their very eyes, she also dusted away into nothing.

"Where did she go?" Naima was furious as they all looked around in confusion.

"My guess would be to Briseis," Aslan offered, and they were all inclined to agree.

"Go the princess and the general, we have business to attend to."

Saicha didn't offer any further information before lifting her assassins hood and leaving them, with Aslan following behind her.

Nyron took hold of Dana's hand and just as she was about to object, she felt a tug in her gut and when her eyes focused, she realised they had Shifted a short distance from where Trista lay on the ground with Oren in her arms and it didn't look good.

***

Briseis launched out of her bed and threw up all over the floor. Heaving, trying to catch her breath; her head spun with delirium as she tried to get her thoughts together.

Oren Antos was dead.

At least he would be in a matter of minutes and then the Samaian princess would be after her; she had to be ready.

The magic Avriel had performed had worked perfectly but it had been an understatement when the older woman said it would take a lot out of her.

They had discussed the procedure many times, knowing there was no way she would have been able to get to Oren without someone, namely the Samaian princess intervening.

"It is done then?"

Briseis looked up to where Avriel stood in the doorway, her face slowly bruising, from what she didn't know. It was then she looked down at herself and realised that Oren's blood was on her.

It seemed her manifestation returned with all the evidence of what it had done out of her body.

"It is."

Avriel smiled then, a triumphant smile that had Briseis' already clouded mind thinking cautiously,

"Then she will be coming for you."

"Of course she'll be co…" Briseis looked over at the older woman who was edging herself slowly into the room.

"What did you do?" Avriel smiled again, a sinister curl of her lips this time.

"I took care of myself…as always."

In an instant, Avriel threw out a fire ball that if not for her reflexes would have burnt Briseis to dust. Briseis threw up a shield instantly, the fireball disintegrating against it but Avriel wasted no time in sending another.

Briseis, caught off guard and weak from the body switching spell, stumbled back and over the bed. The blast barely missed her stomach and grazed her side, making the skin blister and bleed. Briseis landed hard on her back and without thinking, shot out a blast of her own fire in front of her. It hit something and she heard a crash, but whether it was Avriel she wouldn't know until she got up.

Get up Briseis!

She would not go out like this, unaware and against some bitch of a woman who never respected her from the beginning.

Briseis got agonisingly to her feet, scanning the now blasted room where remnants of flame etched around the material that draped the thin walls. She continued to scan the room until she caught movement at the corner of her eye. She threw her power towards it but in the second she did so, her throat constricted and Briseis was suddenly choking.

She fell to the floor, clutching at her throat, trying desperately to repel the magic but she realised with dread that she just couldn't. She had only ever been challenged by her father magically but this, this was something else entirely.

"All my life I have had to fight," Avriel's voice echoed through the tent and despite her struggle for air, Briseis tried to look so she could face the woman who was killing her. "I refuse to fight you too."

Avriel was finally in view and she looked down at Briseis as though she were the scum of the very earth.

"If you think I was going to take orders from some nobody who stole the power from my people then you were sadly mistaken. I will kill you and your father and take control of your armies and I…I will be Queen of Mortania."

"Tri-ta!"

Avriel chuckled,

"There are many things you don't know about my people Briseis but I will tell you before you leave us."

Briseis was turning blue as the air struggled to get through. Her mind was clouded with the desperate need for air.

Where were her guards?

Where was Gardan?

She had left him to command the troops while she performed the spell with Avriel but surely he would see she was missing?

"Trista had to fully Ascend into her powers, *all* of her powers before I could defeat and then take them from her. If you were to kill her, well, we need not worry about that now. However, if a fellow Samaian were to take it, a new chapter begins. A new world order of *my* making, a world that was denied me for far too long."

Avriel looked down at her with pity,

"It's a shame you will not live to see it."

Briseis' rage at the audacity of this woman, shot through her like nothing she had ever experienced. It was a mania of such magnitude that she simply stopped trying to breath in; closed her eyes and locked into her power.

When she opened her eyes, Briseis released a wave of such cataclysmic energy that before her eyes, proceeded to scorch Avriel into nothing. The woman screamed as she burnt alive but Briseis kept streaming fire at her until she felt so drained, she collapsed to the floor in the midst of fire and ash.

"THE PRINCESS IS IN TROUBLE! GET THE PHYSICIANS!"

The whole camp was alive with commotion as the news spread that Princess Briseis had been injured. Curian ran out of his tent, having distanced himself from the fighting and demanded the first person he saw to tell him where she was.

"Her war tent your Majesty; she seems to have been lost in the fire."

"*Fire*, what fire?"

Curian rushed away from the soldier before he could answer, towards Briseis' war tent and what he saw confused him to no end.

The exterior of the tent was in relatively normal condition, but fire and smoke clearly blazed from inside. Men were rushing in and out to douse the flames, but it did not seem that they had found the princess.

Could this, really be it?

Could Briseis really be dead?

Curian ripped off his cape and crown and marched towards the entrance to the tent with only his armour and sword.

"Your Majesty, you can't go in there!"

"Do you propose to stop me?" the frantic soldier did not reply as Curian barged past him and into the thick smoke that clouded within.

"Briseis!" he called out, "Briseis can you hear me!"

With a wave of his hand, Curian parted the smoke from in front of him; and doused the flames. What he saw confused him further, as the inside of the tent looked like a war zone.

Everything was burnt and blackened, furniture and materials burned to ash, wooden beams and fixtures splintered and broken. It looked like a fire had blazed for hours rather than minutes.

"Briseis!"

A groan from somewhere underneath the rubble and with his power, Curian moved some debris aside and there she was, wounded and blackened with soot and ash.

"F-father," her voice was broken and husky and, in that moment, everything he had ever felt for her as a father came flooding into the forefront of his mind.

She was his daughter, he loved her. He loved her too much to do this…didn't he?

Still, it could be his only chance.

He knew what she was capable of, what she planned to do to the world and the power it would give her.

He *couldn't* let that happen. He couldn't continue to make Mortania suffer because of his mistakes.

Curian drew his sword and he saw her eyes widen in shock. Curian raised his sword above his head,

"I love you Briseis."

Firmly he brought his sword down to pierce into her body.

"NO!"

The body his sword connected with, was not Briseis' but General Beardmore's.

Blood splattered from his mouth as Curian's sword sunk into his back, and he fell forward beside Briseis, protecting her even in his imminent death.

Curian stumbled back from his sword, still stuck in General Beardmore's back, horrified at both what he had done and what he had been prepared to do. He shook his head in disbelief, looking at his hands, not sure who they belonged to. He looked over at where General Beardmore had fallen and somehow Briseis had gotten free of the debris on top of her. She leaned over General Beardmore now, stroking his face,

"No, don't you dare die!" she cried. "Please don't, please don't die."

"I…l-love you Briseis." He choked out as he lay on his side, looking up at her with a sword sticking out of his back.

Tears fell from Briseis' eyes as she nodded,

"I love you too."

What had he done?

Briseis fell onto Gardan's chest as his eyes fluttered closed and he took his final breath.

Briseis cried out as she wept over her general's dead body and Curian almost lost it. Briseis couldn't cry, she didn't love or feel as others did. This was not right.

Briseis turned to her father and with her eyes blazing she said hoarsely,

"You…killed him."

"I-I…"

"You tried to kill *me*," it wasn't the first time but it didn't make it any less wrong.

Briseis reached out and with no flare or effort of any kind, simply snapped her father's neck and he fell to the floor in a heap of armour.

The moment it happened, Briseis screamed out as the most debilitating pain ripped through her body and a blackened orb exited the centre of her father's chest. It floated above his chest plate before sailing across the room and slammed straight into Briseis' heart.

"Aaargh!" Briseis screamed in excruciating agony, her chest heaving as she fell to the floor beside Gardan.

Suddenly, her fingers began shaking and she screamed out again as her fingernails began to extend into claw like nails.

"What's happening to me!" she screamed into the tent, but no one answered, no one came as her body began to distort, her bones cracking as they transformed into something, something no one had seen for a thousand years.

REBIRTH

Blood was everywhere.

Oozing endlessly from his wound where Briseis had used her power to burn through the metal of Oren's armour and straight through his body.

"Oren," she didn't know what else to say. She knew there was no time to get the help he needed, and she didn't have the skill to do anything faster.

"Y-you threw the b-bread roll at me," he choked out.

Trista stroked his face as she looked down at him,

"What?" Trista was confused. He coughed and blood escaped his mouth. Trista's heart jolted as she continued to hold him, there on the ground and gently stroked his face.

"T-that's when…when I knew…"

"Knew what Oren, *what?*" his breathing was laboured, and she saw the energy it took to speak but still, she didn't understand.

"T-that I lo…" his words failed him,

"Oren, no! Please stay with me!"

Trista shook him, desperate to keep him alive just a little bit longer but Oren's eyes rolled back into his head as his final words faded into the wind.

"Oren…Oren…?"

Nothing.

"Oren?"

Still nothing.

As she registered what had happened, Trista's blood boiled and her skin began to heat. It heated until she glowed like the fires in a forge before letting out the most tremendous scream,

"NOOOOO!"

Thunder boomed overhead, and lightning flashed with an ear shattering crack that ripped across the sky, as Trista screamed into the darkening night and burst into flames.

In the second it took her to do so, Nyron who was a few feet away immediately dove for Dana, throwing his body over hers as he threw a shield up around them.

Naima, and Justin made their own shields, but Naima was a touch too late, as the edge of Trista's power caught her, knocking her clear across the tattered earth and into a nearby rock mound, cracking her head. Naima lay unconscious as Trista blazed, scorching the earth around where she knelt with Oren in her arms.

When she finally stopped screaming, and the flames slowly died away there was nothing but charred earth in a perfect circle, a mile wide. Piles of ash where people once stood, littered the battlefield like ant hills.

Nyron slowly eased himself off Dana, checking her over even as his shield still pulsed around them. He brought her chin to his face with his index finger,

"Are you alright?" Dana held her hand to her head, a headache slowly growing there but she nodded, looking into his eyes.

"I think so," she turned her head, cutting their almost hypnotic connection. "Where's Naima?"

Nyron turned to where his sister had been, his eyes frantic until he saw her a few yards away with Justin over her just as he was with Dana. Nyron closed his eyes for a moment and smiled with relief,

"She's fine, Justin is with her."

Nyron got to his feet and gently helped Dana up onto hers, keeping her close to him as they gradually made their way back towards Trista; their hearts heavy with what they knew they would find.

A few yards away, Justin cradled Naima in his arms, desperate for her to open her eyes as ash floated in the air around them.

"Nai? Wake up Nai please," he tapped the side of her face, shaking her as he did so until slowly, she opened her eyes and Justin crushed her to his chest.

"Thank the Gods!"

He sat her up so he could look at where her head was bleeding and held his hand over it to seal the wound with magic.

"That will hold until we get back to camp."

Naima nodded, until fear flittered across her face,

"Where's my brother, where's Nyron!" Justin looked around himself until Naima pointed him out.

"There, with Dana but…what in the…" Naima looked at the destruction around them and tears welled in her eyes as she struggled to get to her feet and walked towards her family.

Nyron and Dana stood staring down at where Trista sat with Oren still cradled in her arms. Even as they watched her, they couldn't believe what they were looking at because Trista wasn't exactly herself.

She looked like Trista, the young woman they knew and loved but she was made of pure energy…of power. She sat there glowing, pulsating with blue power; every detail of her face, hair and armour all intricate, just not *real*.

Her head was hung low, crying they could see as they all were. Tears streamed down Dana's face and Naima's once she and Justin joined them. Everything was so still, no one knew what to do or say as Trista silently cried over Oren's body.

They looked on as all of a sudden, Trista lowered her head to kiss Oren's forehead and as her lips connected with his skin, he disappeared into tiny white balls of light just as Gorn had done all those weeks ago.

The others watched in amazement as Trista stayed there, unmoving. They weren't even sure, if she knew they were there. Swallowing down her tears, Dana stepped forward and reached out to her friend. Nyron grabbed hold of her wrist to stop her but she shook him off as he continued to approach her best friend.

"Trista?" her voice was soft but determined as she reached out and placed her hand on Trista's glowing shoulder. As Dana's hand connected, the power faded, and Trista turned her head to look Dana in the face. She looked human again but the pain in her face was even more devastating this way. Her eyes were puffy, and the tip of her nose was swollen and red.

"He's gone," were her first words.

"Trista I…"

Trista stood, so fast none of them saw her do it; she was just suddenly upright, and her face was removed of any emotion. Her face was perfect, no puffiness, no tears as though she'd never been crying.

She turned away from Dana and simply walked in the direction of the Greybold forces.

Dana, Justin, Nyron and Naima looked at each, confused but it wasn't until Dana went to run after her that they saw where Trista had stepped were footprints of energy that faded as she took the next step.

"Trista wait, where are you going!" Dana caught up to her, stopping in front of her but too afraid to touch her again. This Trista was different somehow. Different in a way that was dangerous.

"Get out of my way Dana."

"Where are you going?"

"I'm going to kill Briseis Greybold." Trista thundered at her and Dana visibly recoiled. Her eyes flashed to Nyron who was immediately by her side,

"Trista…Oren is gone. We need to calm down before we do anything irrational and get someone else killed."

Trista turned her eyes to him and bore into his face. Nyron swallowed, intimidated by her state.

"My very purpose is to kill her, is it not?"

"Yes, bu—"

"Then get out of my way."

"We need to be smart about this," he reasoned.

"OREN IS DEAD!"

The ground shook from the power in her voice as lightning flashed overhead and thunder rolled but no one dared say anything.

"She killed him, and I am going to rip her heart from her chest. Now…step aside."

Dana and Nyron regrettably moved aside but Naima was not to be deterred, calling out to her cousin.

"What about the army, what about your people!" Trista didn't turn around to reply,

"I know what I must do…your choices are up to you."

"Trista stop!"

Trista raised her hand and the four of them were thrown back clear across The Wide, crashing through piles of ash.

Trista lowered her arm and continued walking towards the remaining Greybold Army when an ear-deafening roar echoed across the sky.

The Wide was now free of all soldiers for a mile in any direction because of Trista's power burst, so where was this sound coming from?

Trista looked ahead, toward the Greybold camp and Tirnum miles behind that. From there, Trista watched as a nightmare was born before her eyes.

The roar came again, shaking the ground with the force of it as a monster leapt into the sky.

It was white, white like the snow in the Remoran Mountains. It had two monstrous horns protruding from its head, a head that roared again and the earth trembled. Two colossal wings spread out from either side of it and beat down so hard, she saw people scatter in all directions even from so far away.

The beast lifted into the air and with another roar, let out a stream of grey flame. Watching the fire blaze into the earth, Trista's eyes narrowed in calculation.

This couldn't be what she thought it was, but even as the incredible thought took root, a sharp pain hit her, and she collapsed to the floor.

Come find me little princess, the voice said; Briseis' voice said. *Come find me to end this once and fall.*

What have you done Briseis!

The beast roared again and Briseis' voice echoed once more,

I will burn your beloved city to the ground. Tirnum, your history and all your ancestors and their works will be turned to ash and smoke.

The beast circled in the air and took off south towards Tirnum

Find me and fight me little princess. If you can

Trista stared after the beast as she flew into a speck in the darkening sky.

"It's a dragon."

Naima's voice behind her, she didn't bother to turn around knowing that the rest of them would be there.

"It's Briseis,"

"What?"

"I don't know how; I just know I have to kill her…and I can't do it alone." She finally turned to her family. "Briseis is going to wipe out Tirnum City and we can't let that happen or all of this would have been for nothing."

They all agreed,

"Nyron, you're with me. We'll head to Tirnum together and try to stop Briseis somehow. Naima and Justin get the remaining troops and my mother to meet us as fast as you possibly can. Dana, I need you to find the Agmantians and pray that they have plans for reinforcements to combat whatever we'll find in the city."

Trista finished her orders and with a small wave of her hand, three horses appeared beside them: Trista's own and two others,

"I've never been to Tirnum so I can't Shift there, and Nyron can't Shift me and the horses. We'll ride, Dana will take the other and Naima and Justin will Shift back to camp."

They all nodded their understanding. The riders mounted their steeds and took off across The Wide.

Naima looked over at Justin and with a shrug from both, they both Shifted and disappeared from the plateau.

***

When Saicha grabbed the Six leader from behind, he never saw it coming. He was so invested in the torture of a soldier he had in his grip of power, that his mind wasn't taking in the hooded figure who stalked him from across the battlefield, slowly making her way towards him.

Saicha grabbed him by the neck and with a swift motion, she broke it; dropping him to the floor.

As swift as the wind, Saicha raced through the remaining members and with her *sai* in her loose but sure grip; she took them all out.

Without their leader, they had a weak offence, seemingly focused on defending others and themselves rather than doing damage as their leader had done.

"Please no!" the remaining female Six member begged for her life and something in that plea, called out to Saicha for a small moment.

In that split second it took to think about taking her out, the young woman shot out at her, sending Saicha flying across the ground. Disorientated, Saicha quickly composed herself and flipped forward onto her feet.

The girl shot out at her again, but this time the assassin was ready for it. Saicha dodged the oncoming blast, once, twice; three times; all the way advancing on the young woman with her *sai* still in her hands.

"You underestimate me young one," Saicha warned her before charging at the girl. When the girl shot another energy blast at her, Saicha dropped to the ground, sliding across the ground and behind the girl before jumping up and landing her *sai* into the girl's armpits and tearing all the way down her sides.

The girl howled with pain as she fell to the floor, bleeding out among her kinsman.

As Saicha looked down at her kill, the most horrific screech echoed into the air. It sounded like a woman in severe pain but moments later, the screech was replaced by a thunderous roar that had her turn towards where it had come from. She turned in time to see a monstrous white head with a mouth full of sharp white teeth, claw its way into view.

The beast roared and Saicha fell to the ground in awe even as she couldn't take her eyes off it. It stretched its wings, two white wings with the membrane almost translucent, the dimming light still shining through highlighting the veins running through it. The beast beat down its wings, sending everything in its proximity, including Saicha flying in all directions as it lifted into the air.

It rose into the sky and with another roar, let out a stream of grey fire, torching the earth beneath it. Saicha watched on in horror once she was face up, lying on her back, watching terror of the likes she had never seen.

The beast hovered there for a moment before it took further off into the skies and turned in the opposite direction of Thea's Reach, back towards Tirnum.

"Saicha!"

She heard her name and knew it was her brother calling her, but she couldn't take her eyes away from the monster that was slowly becoming a dot in the distance.

"Saicha are you hurt?" Aslan demanded as he scrambled across the ground towards her and checked her over frantically. Belatedly she fanned him off,

"I'm unhurt…what was that?"

"I don't know, and I don't want to find out!" he replied dramatically. "We have to get back to the princess and the army," Saicha was inclined to agree but she couldn't find the means to get up off the floor.

What was that thing?

"Saicha come on! We can fight our way out of here, but I don't particularly want to!" Aslan dragged her to her feet.

She'd forgotten they were in the midst of the Greybold camp and at any moment, soldiers would come out of their daze and continue fighting.

"We need horses," Aslan scanned frantically for any horses that had not been felled or injured by the beat of the monster's wings. Soldiers lay scattered everywhere, some injured, some dead but many just dazed by what they had seen. It was a tragedy to watch as men no longer knew what or who to fight,

"There!" a few horses stood a few yards away and Aslan expeditiously made his way towards them, his sister in tow. They got to horses with minimal resistance and when they finally mounted, they both turned to race back to the Samaian camp. Both had taken to picking up additional weapons and as they approached the centre of The Wide, they both drew their swords to defend against a lone rider who was coming towards them.

"ASLAN!"

"Dana?" Aslan questioned even as he kept his sword drawn,

"ASLAN!" the rider called again and within moments, he could see it was in fact Dana.

The three of them brought their horses to a sharp stop, all three out of breath,

"You're safe, thank the Gods!"

"As are you! Where is the princess?" Aslan asked,

"She's on her way to Tirnum with Nyron…Oren is dead."

"God above!" Aslan's shock was echoed on his sister's face. "There was nothing she could do, no magic…nothing?" Dana shook her head,

"Trista has…changed. She's gone to fight the dragon…she's gone to fight Briseis."

"I'm confused, how is she to fight both? We saw that thing; it will be a miracle to even get near it!"

"Briseis *is* the dragon." Aslan looked at his sister and laughed but when he turned to Dana who didn't find it funny, his laughter ceased.

"You can't be serious!"

"Trista sent me to find you. We must meet her in Tirnum with any Agmantian reinforcements. You do have reinforcements, don't you?"

Aslan smiled at Dana's worry,

"That my dear, we do."

THE MAKER

Trista and Nyron raced as fast as their steeds would carry across The Wide, through the scattered forces of the Greybold army and into Tirnum City. They city was gigantic, a monster of a thing that Trista had never experienced before, even in Dreston.

Tirnum was arranged like layers of an onion, with Tirnum Castle at the centre, where to the south, it overlooked the ocean. Open land as well as some large homes and establishments lay in the surrounding circle and beyond that was the inner city. All of this was encased inside a wall that separated the rest of the city from the high-ranking nobles. There were Greybold troops just outside these city walls, and the dragon circled both there and the inner city, spewing flames into the innocent people below.

Thousands of them stretched through the Imperial Lands all the way to the walls of the city. It seemed they had been waiting for something to come out of The Wide but now had a bigger problem, in the dragon that flew overhead.

The soldiers were frantic and now unorganized as they tried to run from the flying beast. If what was left of the Antonides army made it to the city in time, it wasn't clear what they would find once they did.

Trista and Nyron dismounted their horses undetected as people rushed to get away from the fire. They used their powers to get through the crowds relatively quickly until they reached the wide-open gates of the city.

Buildings burned and people screamed as their houses and businesses fell apart, melting around them. Chaos reigned as no one knew what to do or where to run to get away from the thick smoke and blistering flames.

"Why is she doing this to her own city!" Nyron yelled into the anarchy as they watched hundreds of people try to make it out of the crumbling city.

"It's not her city," Trista replied thinking to what Briseis had said to her. "It's our legacy and she wants all trace of it gone."

"How can we stop this!" Nyron called back, distressed at the blazing city in front of him.

Even with their powers this was a lot for just the two of them to maintain. Their forces were still back at The Wide, they had been weakened from their own fighting and whoever Naima and Justin brought back with them, might not have the power to be of any help.

Their thoughts were interrupted as Briseis soared overhead, letting out another roar before raining fire on the city. It was getting dark now and the fire, though destructive was beginning to light the sky with its flame.

"We get high," Trista finally answered,

"What?"

"We have to get as close to her as possible," she repeated as she watched the beast soar overhead and spray a solid stream of fire onto buildings in the distance.

"We have to take her out the sky."

"But *how* Trista!"

Trista reached out and with an Enflamed hand, she traced around Nyron's body in the air.

"I've placed a shield around you, it should protect you from Briseis' fire."

"*Should!*" he said looking down at himself but there was nothing there. Their usual shields or protective barriers would hum with power, but he remained as he was.

"Add your own shield if it makes you feel better," this Trista was a lot less patient. "We have to get to the top of the castle."

"Where's your shield?" Nyron asked unsheathing his sword.

"I don't need one."

Trista and Nyron ran. They ran persistently thorough the blazing streets of Tirnum towards the castle, using their powers to assist them. Their feet barely touched the ground as they sped through the narrow streets, avoiding roaring flames and buildings collapsing around them. Trista ran through flames like it was nothing but air and came out the other side unscathed. Her black hair streamed behind her like a cloak of ink as she jumped and vaulted over any obstacles in her way.

She checked Nyron was keeping up with her before turning back to jump off a recently collapsed building. Trista launched into the air and landed on the other side, one knee down and her hands on the floor to steady herself. The ground cracked where her knee had connected with it, but she paid it no mind and set off again until she finally approached the gates of the castle itself.

Nyron came up behind her, slightly out of breath but otherwise fine and looked at his cousin,

"Now what?"

Trista looked up to the highest point of the castle and leapt into the air with Nyron close behind. She grabbed hold of the castle walls that were thankfully still intact even as Briseis continued to terrorise the rest of the city only a few metres away. Why she hadn't attached the castle yet was anyone's guess.

The smoke and ash had travelled though, and slowly built in and around the castle, choking the few people who remained inside the gates.

Trista landed on the other side of the castle walls and found guards littered in the courtyard,

"Over there!" one of them yelled and in seconds, they were rushing towards her.

Nyron drew his sword but as he did so, the blue flames around Trista's eyes ignited and with a wave of her arm the twenty or so soldiers rushing towards them dissipated into dust. What used to be their bodies floated into the ash that slowly filtered into the air. Nyron's eyes widened,

"How did yo—"

"We have to get inside," Trista ignored him and headed into the castle.

On they raced, until they came upon the Great Hall and at the far end stood a large throne with smaller one, though not by much beside it. That large throne was hers, Trista thought absentmindedly. That smaller one for maybe a consort, a consort she would never have…ever.

Trista knew she would have gladly spent the rest of her life with Oren. She had never known love, but she knew what she had felt for him had to be it. However short their time together had been, Trista knew her heart belonged to him and always would.

"Thea's Tower would be this way," Nyron offered as she continued to stare at the two thrones. "It's traditionally the Queen's Apartments, it's quicker if we go this way."

Trista had forgotten that Nyron had lived within these walls, that he would know the layout. She followed him without question through the deserted halls of the castle even as fire and blood raged outside the walls.

They were happy not to meet any resistance, but it bothered Trista that no one had been left behind to man the stronghold. They progressed through the castle until they entered what looked to be a training ground and it was here, they met their resistance.

A group of soldiers were patrolling around the courtyard, although it was unclear what they were doing there.

"Who goes there?" a guard bellowed, challenging when he laid eyes on them. Trista stopped this time, looking at each of the men in turn before saying,

"Let us pass and you will not be harmed."

"Who are you?"

Without hesitation, she stepped forward and called out strongly,

"I am Queen Trista Antonides of Mortania and you…are in my way."

"You are the Redeemer?"

Mumbles as her identity filtered through the crowd of fifty, maybe sixty men.

"I am."

The guard who had spoken scanned her from head to toe while his comrades came up around him, creating a barrier.

"We serve the rightful King and heir, not you."

"Move from this place or die. The choice is yours."

The guard visibly gulped but took a stand and unsheathed his sword; Trista sighed.

"You will never get to it!" the guard shouted before charging at her and his kinsmen followed.

Trista did not so much as blink before snapping her fingers and breaking the necks of the entire first row of men who ran toward them.

The men behind them were either too stunned, too stupid or too slow to stop their charge and when Trista drew her sword, they instantly regretted it.

The weapon glowed within her hands and when she placed her hand against her sword, then pulled one hand away, she had two swords in each one. Trista proceeded to slice her way through the men who came at her with the speed and precision that Oren had instilled in her all those months ago. With one sword, she blocked, with the other she cut, slicing through men like silk, leaving their blood splattered on the floor like a canvas of death and ruin.

Nyron and Trista fought through the soldiers, taking them on one by one and dropping them to the ground like flies. Nyron was twice the size of some of them and so they posed no real threat to him. Combined with their powers, speed and agility, the two of them were no match for the small hoard.

Trista ran one of her swords through the gut of one of the soldiers so far that her clenched fist touched his insides. She twisted the blade as she looked down into his face and watched the light extinguish from his eyes. She kicked him off her blade with her foot before spinning to swing her sword behind her and decapitate the man who had appeared at her back. His head bounced and rolled to land on the floor beside Nyron's foot who was covered in his own kills but looked at his cousin's handy work.

"Let's go," Trista made to continue towards Thea's Tower when Nyron stopped her,

"Trista?" she turned to look at him. "Don't become Briseis." Trista's eyes furrowed together in confusion.

"Excuse me?" Nyron walked up to her, stepping over the head and the other lifeless bodies that lay on the ground around them.

"Do not become the monster you're trying to rid this world of. I mean, was this necessary?" Nyron gestured to Trista's kills and the difference was obvious.

Where Nyron's men had been cleanly run through whether their stomach or neck etc. Trista's opponents had been butchered. Their insides lay splattered on the ground where their heads had not been taken from their necks or their limbs from their bodies.

"I know you're hurti—"

"They took him from me," Trista replied quietly and very simply, looked up into Nyron's eyes as she said,

"I will take everything from them."

"Trista, these people were innocent except for being on the wrong side. They didn't kill Oren!"

"THAT DOES NOT MATTER!"

Nyron stumbled back at the velocity of her words, the venom in them. She truly had no thought for the lives she was taking now that Oren was gone.

"I will not allow his death to go unpunished."

"I don't want that either but you're not an animal. He wouldn't have wanted this!" Trista stared back at Nyron with a steadiness and certainty he'd never seen from her.

"I have this power because of him and I'm going to use it, to murder any person who gets between me and avenging him. If you have a problem with that, it's best, you stay here."

Trista turned then and ran towards the tower with Nyron calling out after her, before rushing forward so not to get left behind.

***

King Curian was dead.

His body lay as proof on the ground in front of him and his daughter, Princess Briseis was nowhere in sight.

General Ignatius Rarno looked down at his best friends twisted and trampled body and ordered the remaining men to have him properly prepared for burial. He didn't know how or when he would perform the military rights for his friend, but it wouldn't be for now.

He just had to get Curian off the floor. He was a king, not a peasant and he deserved more than this behaviour. His body had been trampled by that monster that had escaped this tent. He was virtually unrecognisable, and it made Rarno sick to his stomach.

He hadn't wanted to believe what the Samaian man had told Curian, but it seemed now that he had been right, Briseis had turned into that thing. Magic, dragons and all the things that allowed those things to exist in his world, he didn't understand but war, he knew.

"Ready the men and prepare to depart for Tirnum."

"General?" the young captain beside him asked in confusion.

"We're taking back the city."

"But…h-how General?"

In truth, Rarno didn't know how just yet but his men had to know the fight wasn't over.

"Ready the men," he repeated, and the captain had no choice but to obey. The other men in the room, carried Curian's body out for preparation and Rarno turned his attention to the other distorted body on the floor.

Captain Beardmore was no king.

He could rot where he lay.

General Rarno and the remaining Greybold forces from The Wide, advanced on Tirnum City when the sky was darkening and set about trying to infiltrate the castle and take the throne of Mortania.

***

Dana, Aslan and Saicha had arrived in Tirnum City a little before the Greybold troops arrived, marching towards the castle, but on whose orders, they didn't know. None of them had seen King Curian since the battle or since Briseis' transformation. It wasn't likely that he was still alive but they had yet to see Briseis's General and so it was unclear who was leading the opposition.

The trio continued towards the city however, and when they finally arrived in the previously stark and barren Imperial Lands it was heaving with soldiers and escapees from inside the city. They knew that Greybold forces were still behind them, but this was a whole other army onto itself. Briseis had been prepared for the Samaian forces to get this far south.

Aslan, Dana and Saicha tried to get through the crowds and remain on their horses but it was becoming increasingly difficult. Where the Greybold forces remained unmoving but vast, common people rushed around them trying to escape the flames. The only positive in all this was that the heat of the dragon's flames was heating the city. The cold and snow that blistered around them was held back by the intense heat of the dragon's fire. It was uncomfortable but at least they wouldn't freeze to death.

"We have to get to the other side of the city; to Thea's Point!" Aslan called out as they looked over the frantic citizens and soldiers trying to save themselves.

They could all see that within the walls was burning, fire everywhere with smoke to match rising into the air. Amongst the devastation, the dragon was clearly visible; soaring over the city and burning any and all that wasn't already on fire.

"*She's* heading to Thea's Point" Saicha pointed out and sure enough, they watched as the monstrous beast banked right and headed away from the castle towards the coast.

"Where the hell is Trista!" Aslan called out. "If that thing gets to Thea's Point, we could lose the *Agmantian* Army, we could lose our brother!"

"I know that Aslan!" Saicha screamed back at him as he stared into the sky as Briseis got smaller and smaller in the distance.

As they stared at her, helpless to stop her tirade; a piercing roar escaped her, and the creature began to turn.

"Sh-she's coming back!"

"Why?" Dana said it to herself more than anyone else but even as she voiced it; Saicha turned her head back towards the castle.

"Trista."

Suddenly, there was thunderous rumble and the three of them turned within the crowd atop their mounts to see the soldiers all go incredibly still. Almost immediately, all the soldiers drew their swords and began hacking into the crowd and the fleeing citizens.

"What in the wo—"

"She's doing this," Saicha concurred as their horses reared into the air with fear. "Briseis is controlling them!"

"We have to get to Thea's Point, to Rian!" Aslan screamed back. "If we don't get our army here, she's going to kill her own people!"

"She's killing *Trista's* people!" Dana realised in horror. The three of them turned their mounts and took off into the crowd to get to the Agmantian Army and Tirnum City's salvation.

***

Thea's Tower was the tallest point of Tirnum Castle. A spiralling maze of rooms on each ascending level, it overlooked the sea towards the distant Agmantia. There was a balcony that went around the perimeter of the tower so one could see all across the city and beyond.

The long line of Samaian queens had traditionally resided in this tower; where they housed their ladies; held their dinners and parties and when required to leave society in the last stages of their pregnancies; it was here they lived.

Rowan had mentioned it briefly to Trista and said that after her first and second miscarriages; she hadn't stayed in Thea's Tower.

She and Alexander had gone against tradition and she'd stayed in his bed throughout. He was there in the bed with her when she woke up with blood between her legs and again when she returned from the adjoining wash chamber to tell them their child had died…again. It was in this tower that life was meant to begin for the following Antonides dynasty, and it was here; that Trista would do so once again.

She and Nyron reached the highest room of the tower and looked for a way onto the roof; finding none.

"What do we do? The roof covers the balcony."

Without a response, Trista reached towards the roof and blew a hole straight through it with a burst of energy.

"You could at least warn me!" Nyron called out making her smile before it disappeared.

"Stay here,"

"Wait, what? I'm coming with you!" Trista turned just as her cousin stepped towards her; holding out her hand that connected with his chest.

Nyron looked down at her hand and tried to step forward but couldn't,

"Why bring me if you were going to do this alone!" he snapped at her but once again, she smiled lovingly.

"I won't let anything happen to you or my family ever again. You have to stay here, protect the castle."

"From whom, we killed everyone outside."

"Not everyone," Trista replied softly. Nyron looked at her quizzically.

"I have gained something," she said without looking at him. "I can feel her army, the soldiers marching here this very second, I can see them all."

Trista looked up at him then and Nyron could see the tears in her eyes,

"I must do this as you must protect our family and my people from what would come if I do not destroy her." Nyron nodded, suddenly overwhelmed by the certainty in her eyes. Trista stepped forward and hugged her cousin so tight and he hugged her back.

"I love you Nyron Antos."

"And I love you Tris but…" he stepped back to look down into her face. "Why are you talking as if you'll never see me again?"

Trista stepped back from him but said nothing. She looked up into the hole she had created in the roof and with a sudden jump; she leapt through and onto the roof. Nyron heard her up there then, there was silence.

Trista let her presence out onto the wind, letting Briseis know she was there.

I am here. Face me if you will

Trista stood two hundred feet in the air atop Thea's Tower and looked out onto the horizon towards the lights of Thea's Point.

There was nothing but smoke and flames beneath her but there, a small way in the distance was Briseis.

Seemingly done with the city, she was heading towards Thea's Point and there was no way Trista could allow her to destroy there as well. Many more innocents would die if she did and she had to bring it to a stop now.

FACE ME BRISEIS!

Trista screamed into the dragon's mind, willing her to take the bait.

You made it! Briseis replied with amusement, still heading in the direction of the coast. *I am done with you princess. I have more of your people to destroy.*

And when they are all gone? Will you rule a kingdom of ash? How long do dragons live anyway?

There was no reply for a long while as the beast continued to fly. Despite these new powers she had received, Trista still didn't know what Briseis being a dragon even meant and she was betting on the fact that Briseis didn't either.

You don't want to stay this way, forever do you? Fight me. Fight me and end this.

You are the key Briseis seemed to realise something.

I am the key

Trista didn't know she was the key to anything but if it got Briseis away from Thea's Point…

The dragon banked suddenly and headed back towards the city, towards Trista,

"NYRON GET OUT OF THIS TOWER NOW! GET AWAY FROM HERE!"

Trista called down to him and felt his presence get faint as he left the tower.

With a deep breath, Trista braced her legs apart and gradually a large bow appeared in her hands with a full quiver of arrows strapped across her back.

She'd been given the weapons when they left for The Wide, but she didn't think she would need them, trusting Naima's archers completely.

It appeared in her hands now, from where she had left it in her war tent. Trista nocked her first arrow; aiming it directly at Briseis who was coming in fast.

A spell formed on her lips; a spell she didn't know she knew, and the arrow glowed for a split second as it was released and went directly through Briseis' wing membrane.

Briseis howled in pain, twisting herself with rage in the air but not stopping her flight path. Trista nocked another arrow, spelled it and released it almost instantly; this time connecting with Briseis' chest.

Briseis howled again, this time mere metres away but with determined wings and an arrow sticking out of her chest, she continued towards Trista.

The spell had guided the arrow to strike true but Trista knew she needed more, to get the beast out of the sky.

In a moment of clarity, Trista didn't reach for another arrow.

Silly princess. Today…you die.

Briseis taunted as her wings stretched out to bring her to a sharp near stop, the arrows still in her wing and chest. She hovered there; wings flapping back and forth to keep her airborne and opened her jaws, preparing to burn Trista alive.

No princess, Trista said. *Today,* you *die.*

Trista took a deep breath and drew her bow but as she pulled the string back, a thick arrow of pure energy appeared. The arrow glowed with an infusion of clear energy and blue flame just as Trista had been when she was laying over Oren's dead body. Trista aimed as she watched the flames grow inside

Briseis' mouth and just as the dragon let out it's fire; Trista let her arrow fly.

The arrow grew as it soared through the air, the arrowhead getting longer and thicker as it closed on its target and struck straight through Briseis' throat and out the back of her head.

Briseis roared as she fell rapidly from the sky, in a mass of flame and wings. Her body imploded from its own fire as she crashed into the opened lands between the castle and Thea's Point.

The fire that escaped her before she fell, exploded onto Thea's Tower, sending Trista and any who remained inside, crumbling to the city floor.

FAMILY, FRIENDS & FATE

The two Agmantian royals and Dana Black; the young girl from a small town in the farthest reaches of Mortania; fought their way through a stampede of people and soldiers desperate to kill or avoid being killed.

The three of them rode away from any fight they didn't have to engage in, but when Dana was thrown from her horse and nearly crushed beneath the hurrying feet of escapees; it was Saicha who helped her up and then onto her own horse to continue on their path to Thea's Point.

With the added weight, their mount moved slower but by the time they were out of the throng of people; it was easier to push through.

The ride to Thea's Point was a long one but the three of them kept their pace even as they watched the beast overhead.

It was flying back to Tirnum Castle as they had already seen but even, they could see that there was somehow more determination in its flight path. It was making a direct line for what they could now see from this side of the walls, was a very tall tower amongst the other turrets of the castle.

Aslan had ridden on ahead when Saicha stopped for Dana and so he wasn't with them when something hit the dragon and it faltered in the sky.

"Trista!" Dana shouted behind Saicha's ear. "Trista must have hit her!"

Saicha didn't reply although she was inclined to agree but the question still remained; how had she done it and where was she? Saicha pushed their horse faster, much faster than it was ready to go but she pushed anyway. She had to get to her brothers; she had to make sure her brothers and their army was safe.

There was a howl from above; a deafening roar of pain and Dana saw that Briseis had been hit again. She didn't fall; however, not directly and continued to head directly for the tower. The path they'd taken stopped Saicha being able to see the dragon, but Dana could.

"Trista's up there!" Dana shouted. Saicha was desperate to see but she couldn't turn properly; she had to keep the horse going.

"Oh Gods!" barely a breath from Dana as a terrible screech echoed across the sky.

"What, what is it?" Saicha couldn't hide her indifference any longer. Dana was saved from answering as a thunderous boom resounded overhead.

"OH GODS! FASTER SAICHA, FASTER!"

Saicha didn't know when or how they were thrown from the horse. All she knew was that she was soaring through the air and when she landed on the hard, cold ground, she blacked out.

***

Aslan had never ridden faster than he was as that very moment. He had gone hunting and racing in the jungles of Agmantia since he was a child. He'd raced from bullies at the academy who teased him for being the youngest most insignificant royal. He'd run from the palace guards when he should have been where they could always protect him, but never had he been as afraid when running, then he was right now.

He had never been so afraid to hear such chaos behind him; knowing his sister might be in it and not being able to do anything about it. Dana was with her too and it had killed him to leave her but both he and Saicha knew, without saying that one of them had to get to Rian and he had been further ahead.

He continued to go on ahead even as the ground rumbled beneath him, almost felling him. He couldn't look back; even as remnants of dust and debris seemed to come up in the air behind him. It almost choked him, stumbling his horse so much he was almost thrown from it.

He couldn't stop his mission to warn Rian and the rest of their forces and so he ignored it and just kept going.

He continued now, towards Thea's Point but as his horse pushed as far as it could, he saw something ahead…people; lots of people.

It didn't take long before banners appeared; the glorious display of purple and gold that represented House Voltaire.

The royal purple field with a golden jaguar in the centre and the four stars representing the four core values that all Agmantians lived by: Strength. Honour. Duty. Family. Aslan slowed his horse steadily as the crowned jaguar banner, trimmed with gold came into view and just behind it; he could just make out his older brother; Rian.

A guard raced out to meet him, even as he continued towards them.

"Who goes there!" the guard called out but as Aslan was finally close enough to be seen; the guards face humbled and he bowed his head.

"My sincere apologies my prince. Please forgive me!"

"Don't worry about it," he replied as he came up beside the guard and he turned so they could ride back to Rian together.

Rian was a king in all but name, Aslan thought as his older brother came into full view. He sat atop his white stallion, dressed in all the Agmantian steel armour he could possibly wear without falling over. His hazel eyes shone out from his tanned brown face; eyes serious and calculating until he finally realised it was Aslan and a smile instantly appeared.

Despite his jealousy of his brother's position and the insecurities that brought with it; Aslan knew that his brother loved him, and he loved Rian in return. It had just been the two of them growing up once Saicha left and it had given them a bond that no one else could understand.

"Brother!" Rian called out as Aslan approached him and put his horse by his brother's own. He reached out and they clasped hands,

"It is good to see you," Rian said, his deep voice ringing true and powerful.

"It is good to see you too brother, although we must not waste time. You are needed in the city."

Rian was instantly serious once again and nodded,

"We met much resistance at Thea's Point where you said to alight but we got through them easily."

"How many men were there?"

"A few thousand at most, they weren't too much trouble." Aslan observed his brother's practically clean armour and realised it must have gone extremely well if Rian hadn't had to engage in battle yet.

"What can you tell me? We saw…something in the skies but we were not able to tell what it truly was."

"It's a dragon," Rian snorted as he turned to look at his two generals beside him but when he realised his brother wasn't laughing; he cleared his throat.

"What?"

"It's a dragon, more specifically it's the daughter of King Curian. Trista believes she turned into that, thing."

"…how?"

"We don't know how or why. What we do know is that Briseis burned Tirnum City and it's still burning. Her armies are in the lands between here and the city and Trista's forces are on the other side. We need your help to save the people and end the Greybold army."

Rian took a deep breath and looked to the sky,

"We saw it fall out the sky just now, but it seems our fight isn't over just yet." Aslan shook his head.

"Head to the back, rest up; change your horse and find something…Agmantian to wear."

Aslan laughed at his brother and realised that it felt good to laugh despite the chaos around them.

"Where is Saicha?"

"She was behind me; she'll be here soon." Aslan said gently but clasped his brother's arms again before continuing to the back of the hoard. He heard Rian give the order to continue their march towards the city.

***

Naima lay in the back of a covered wagon with the Queen Mother as they travelled with the remaining Antonides army towards Tirnum City. Once she had Shifted to the Antonides base camp, Naima had felt dizzy and knew she wouldn't be a good enough fighter to go back onto the field. Justin had walked with her then, back to Rowan where she was helping the physicians and trying to heal all who could be healed with salves or powers. Lamya remained with the wounded and would do until the war was truly over, one way or another.

They both lay now in a padded wagon, Rowan nursing her niece as she best she could even as they worried about their loved ones outside.

"Your mother always wanted a daughter."

Naima lay down with a cool wet cloth on her forehead, looking up at her aunt but said nothing.

"Even as a little girl, she knew she wanted to be a mother, we both did. We both wanted to have little girls that would play together and grow together just like we did."

Rowan looked sad as she nursed her niece.

"When she got sick and it was clear that there was nothing, we could do to save her, she called for me and asked me to do something for her. Do you know what she asked?" Naima shook her head,

"She asked me to protect you and your brother. She asked me to be the mother you would no longer have, to love you and raise you and become the mother I always wanted to be."

"You see, I'd lost a few of my babies by then and Renya…Renya knew that I wanted children to love so badly, that she gave her children to me."

Rowan laughed ironically,

"My big sister trusted me with her children, and I left you both behind because I was too powerless to do anything else!" Naima shook her head as she tried to sit up.

"Aunt Rowan you can't blame yourself for mother dying or doing what you had to do to keep your own child safe."

"I should have done more for you and your brother and maybe you wouldn't be here, and Nyron wouldn't be out there!" Rowan snapped. "If I had done more, *been* more for Renya; for you and your brother, for Trista and Alexander…" Rowan couldn't stop the tears that streamed down her face.

"If I had been the queen, I was supposed to be, our children could have grown together like we wanted all those years ago. Our children would be safe but they're not…and that's my fault."

Rowan broke down beside her niece and Naima could do nothing but comfort her with a hug and gently strokes.

"You were the best mother to us Aunt Rowan," Naima said quietly. "We spent some of our best days and years at the palace with you and Uncle Alex. Nyron and I, we treasured those visits. We fought with papa to let us stay with you because you loved us so much that he had to put a stop to it!" Naima laughed at the memory.

"I won't have you flittering off pretending you're royalty all the time. You are Antos, *not* Antonides." Naima mimicked her father's voice and remembered how much she missed him. The pain of it, hit her in the chest but she didn't mention it. it was clear Rowan was dealing with her own emotions right now.

"Where papa was strict, you were the loving mother we needed, and we appreciated that. You couldn't have done anything more then you did, for us, for Trista or Mortania."

Rowan nodded wanting desperately to believe in her niece's words, but something stopped her from truly forgiving herself.

"I know there are so many things that were out of my control but there were so many that weren't. Being nicer to Avriel, paying more attention to Curi—"

"What?" Rowan looked at her niece guiltily before taking a deep breath, knowing she had to confess.

"Curian Greybold grew up on my father's estate. I've known him since I was a child."

"Why didn't we know about this?"

"Alexander didn't want anyone to blame me for Curian's attacks, thinking I could have done something to stop my childhood friend and maybe, they would have been right."

"Have you tried speaking to Curian now, about his daughter?"

"Naima, I've been on the run from him for over sixteen years. I didn't know if he'd sooner kill me than speak to me!" Naima nodded, understanding the predicament but still shocked by the revelation.

"Curian was lost and it seems his daughter is too. I just hope Briseis finds her way before it's too la—"

Rowan's serine face suddenly contorted in agony. She fell forward onto the bed, across Naima's legs, clutching at her head.

"Aunt Rowan? Aunt Rowan!" Naima panicked as she struggled with her own pain to hold Rowan against her.

"Aunt Rowan what's wrong?" Naima felt helpless, she didn't know what to do,

"Tris...ta...hurt," Rowan squeezed out as her eyes rolled back into her head and she passed out.

"LAMYA! LAMYA HELP!" Naima screamed out, shaking Rowan desperately.

***

When Princess Saicha Voltaire regained consciousness, the first thing she saw was the purple and gold of her House. It was dark but the fire from the city and of the torches the army marched with, created a haze of light. She felt like she was dreaming, the colours hazy as they went past her in the distance.

No, she thought to herself while pain unexpectedly ripped through her body from an unknown source. Her brother *was* coming; this couldn't be a dream. Rian was here.

The colours continued to go by, blowing in the wind above thousands of feet of Agmantian soldiers, and Saicha knew she had to get their attention. She was laying on her stomach, looking over at the Agmantian army but she found she couldn't move. She tried moving her legs and thankfully they responded, but it didn't seem to get her anywhere as the pain shattered up her calf.

Painfully, Saicha rolled onto her side to look down at her legs and to her horror, her right leg was broken. The bone was protruding through her skin, the flesh underneath exposed. Tears of pain welled in Saicha's eyes, but she blinked them away and took a deep steadying breath.

She had to remain calm, she had to get to her brother before he disappeared and never found her. Saicha looked to either side of her, through the dust, ash and smoke still billowing in the air and laid eyes on a large rock protruding from the ground. Determinedly, she crawled towards it as best she could before she grabbed hold and used it to pull herself along the ground.

"Aaargh!" she screamed as it took all the energy, she had to drag herself forward. When she was close enough to it, she used her waning strength to turn onto her back and lean against the rock. Breathing exhaustedly, she looked own at her leg again. She had suffered breaks before and so was grateful it was not anything more serious for the moment.

It was only once she finished assessing herself, that she thought of Dana.

Where was she?

Panicked, Saicha looked around the open land, desperate for some sign of Dana Black. Her eyes scanned the expanse of plains, until she registered a small mound in the distance. It could have been a boulder like the one she rested on; it could have been a horse but she knew in her heart it wasn't.

Saicha fell onto her stomach again and with defiant determination, she dragged herself across the hard ground toward the dark pile.

Her leg screamed at her, her arms ached but when she finally reached the pile, all her physical pain was forgotten.

Dana was laying on her back, her body twisted in an unnatural way and there was an obvious hole in the side of her head.

"No…no," Saicha could barely get the word out as tears streamed down her face.

This wasn't right. This wasn't supposed to happen. Dana was the nicest, sweetest and most caring person that Saicha had ever had the privilege of meeting; even if she had been sure that Nyron had feelings for her. None of that mattered as she looked at the face of the sweet young woman who had lost her life so unfairly.

If not for the blood and exposed wound, she looked as though she were sleeping. Her eyes were closed, her face calm as though in a peaceful and dreamless sleep.

Saicha fell onto Dana's body and cried harder than she had ever cried. There weren't words for the despair that coursed through her at the loss of such a wonderful human being.

Little town girls were not supposed to die this way. She was the assassin; she was the killer. She deserved to be on the ground…not Dana.

Her brother's army continued to march toward Tirnum in the distance and she couldn't even call out to them. There was nothing between here and Thea's Point in one direction and Tirnum in the other. Where it hadn't been scorched by Briseis' fire, it was just a thoroughfare between the two cities.

She had to get someone's attention, or she and Dana would be left there for who knew how long.

Saicha lay crying over Dana's body, exhausted and helpless when the ground began to tremble beneath them. The rocks, stones and debris all around began to shake as the dust once again became unsettled. Saicha looked up and around anxiously, knowing she wouldn't be able to survive anything else. She scanned the thick clouded air for some sign of what was happening until, she saw a distinct blue light in the distance.

No, she realised as she continued to stare. It was blue fire.

Trista.

She couldn't see her clearly but there was no one else it could be. Saicha screamed out to her,

"TRISTA! TRISTA WE'RE HERE!"

Almost instantly, the blue fire was by her side and as it dissipated, Trista stood in its place.

She was dressed in her Agmantia armour but there was barely a scratch on her. She looked at Saicha, confused until she turned her head and took in Dana's body.

All confusion and pretence were gone, as pain registered across her face, followed by an incapacitating rage. Trista dropped to her knees by Dana's side,

"I-I don't know what happened," Saicha wailed, so unlike her it was terrifying. "We were riding, and we got thrown from the horse and I woke up a-and I found her…like this."

Saicha couldn't contain her sadness but Trista just stared down at her best friend.

Where anger and pain had been, Saicha watched as guilt replaced it and tears pooled in Trista's eyes.

"I did this."

"What?"

"I shot Briseis out of the sky," Trista explained and for the first time, Saicha registered the large crater sized hole in the ground some metres from them. "I didn't think anyone would be down here."

Trista fell onto her friend's chest where Saicha had been only moments before and sobbed. The grief that echoed from those tears was indescribable as Trista's body shook with the force of her pain and tears.

The three of them remained there until Trista finally composed herself and straightened up. Trista held her hand over Dana's chest as she had done with Oren, and gradually Dana's body dissolved into little white lights.

She turned to Saicha and held her hand over her broken leg. White light shone over her leg and when Trista took her hand away, her leg was healed.

"How did you do that?"

"The Gods have given me many gifts," Trista replied quietly. "Get out of here Saicha."

"What, I can't leave you."

"You must, my fight isn't over."

Trista stood and looked out to where she had just come from.

"I must finish what I started." Trista turned back to Saicha with determined eyes that didn't bode questioning. "Get back to the others, tell them to protect my people and apprehend the castle."

"Trista, where are you going, I can't leave you here alone!"

"YOU MUST!"

Trista's voice boomed so that it resonated all around them, straight into Saicha's soul. She nodded vigorously,

"Get as far away from here as you can…don't look back."

Saicha nodded again and after testing her leg, which felt normal; she took off towards her brother's army.

Trista turned back toward the crater, and slowly walked towards it.

AMONG GODS

The dragon was gone and in its place, was the princess who it had once been.

Briseis lay naked in the centre of the crater that her previous form had made, and from where she stood on the edge of it looking down at her, Trista could feel she was still alive.

The now familiar humming of the Everlasting power that they both shared, reached a fever pitch now they were finally together.

Trista had used her ancestral Maker magic to take down a beast of ancient magic. It was almost poetic but now the power wanted out. It pulsed within Trista, but it was split within Briseis and needed to connect and be complete.

Trista felt the urgency in her blood, she had since Oren had died in her arms and now as she looked down at the woman who had taken him from her, she needed that connection that could only come from taking Briseis' life.

She had no issues with doing so.

She was going to tear her spine out, and there was no one around to try and stop her.

The strength of the Everlasting that exuded from Briseis was too strong for one person, and Trista deduced that Briseis must have killed her father. There was no way she could have this much power without having received it from another source. Her own powers, the new ones at least had come from another place, another time even.

The only way to take another person's powers was to kill them and even then; it was dependent on who was being killed and who did the killing. Curian had done it to Trista's father and Briseis had done it to her own, corrupting the power so mercilessly that it had broken out the only way it knew how; evil.

She knew next to nothing of the dragon legends and wasn't entirely sure whether Briseis could change at will, so she approached the matter with caution.

Get up Briseis

Trista spoke into her mind, not advancing toward her just yet.

Get up Briseis…now

She was playing dead it seemed and so, igniting her hand; Trista shot out a stream of fire at Briseis.

Briseis Shifted from her space on the ground just as the fire hit, burning a hole into the earth.

Briseis now stood on the other side of the crater and as Trista watched her, armour magically appeared on her body with a great sword in her hand. In response, Trista Made a sword right then and there.

Much like the one she had made while training with Nyron, it was made of pure energy, glowing with the power that coursed through it.

You have truly Ascended I see

Briseis spoke into her mind but Trista said nothing,

You may have stopped my dragon form, but it won't last long. Once I kill you, I will have all the power of the Everlasting and dragons will be reborn once more to purge the world of Samai

Trista looked over at her enemy, a young girl much like herself who had risen to the lure of darkness.

The Samai are who make this land what it needs to be, destroying them will only destroy you.

Briseis laughed, the sound creeping into Trista's mind and making her feel dirty.

Let us finish this once and for all, she hissed.

Gladly

Briseis leapt into the air, sword outstretched, and Trista did the same, meeting her in the middle. When their swords clashed, a blinding light flashed on connection and a burst of power blasted them apart from each other.

They were thrown back so violently, their legs dug deep groves into the earth but neither were deterred as they looked up to face one another and charged again across the flattened earth.

Trista ran with the tip of her energy sword brushing lightly over the ground, while Briseis held hers in both hands. The women raced towards each other, into the depth of the crater and as Trista swiped her sword up, Briseis brought hers down.

The sound it created was akin to an explosion as Trista's energy sword disintegrated Briseis' weapon. The steel shattered into a million pieces causing Briseis to protect her face from the spray of the shards. Trista moved to run the sword straight through Briseis with no hesitation, but she spun out of her position and Trista missed her by a hairsbreadth. Briseis elbowed Trista in the back of the head, sending her careening forward from the force of it and she lost control of her energy sword. Trista quickly recovered just as Briseis materialised another sword in her hand and Trista did the same just in time.

This time, the connect of steel was a painful screech as their weapons scrapped against each other. Green eyes bore into grey for the very first time and within both, tiny flames ignited.

Both of the girls were incredibly strong, the power surging through both of them was potent and visceral but Trista felt her control slipping.

…the physical power it takes to maintain that strength, is not worth it if you can get out of it instead.

Oren's words came flooding back to her and Trista loosened her hold so that both swords dropped to the ground before elbowing Briseis in the face once she was close enough. Briseis stumbled back with bewilderment and touched her nose to see the blood that spilled from there.

"You bitch!"

"Powers aren't everything" Trista smirked as she stood up straight and spun her sword in her hand before placing her feet in her fighting stance. Briseis turned and did the same, the two women face to face with longswords in their hands and determination in their eyes.

Briseis struck first with her power, but Trista was unmoved as the power bounced of a shield, she had put around herself. Briseis growled at her and when she charged at Trista again, she didn't miss.

The two princesses met each other blow for blow as Agmantians and Samai continued to fight against Man in the surrounding lands, miles around them.

A mixture of magic and strength exploded from the girls as they shook the earth. The speed was phenomenal as blurs of blue and grey fire danced in the dust trying to end the other's life.

Trista fell onto her back from a particularly strong energy blast from Briseis, hitting her head on the ground where her shield faltered from the impact. She felt slightly dizzy and as her vision slowly cleared, Briseis was suddenly bearing down on her. Her face was obscured by the flame that raged from around her, but Trista knew instantly what was happening; this was her dream.

The dream she'd had most of her life had finally come true but what did it mean? Was this the moment of her death?

Trista felt Briseis' excitement emulating from her like something living.

"This must be what my father felt like…when he killed your father."

Trista hated that Briseis' words hit home, that she still hurt for a father that she never knew, and never would. Briseis raised her sword to strike down into Trista's chest,

"Goodbye, Princess," Briseis crooned triumphantly.

Briseis brought her sword down to strike into Trista's chest but instinctively, Trista raised her arm and blocked the blow. On connection, a blinding white light exploded from them, sending Briseis flying away from Trista and crashing into the ground.

Trista looked at where her hand still hovered in the air and saw that she was once again made entirely of power. She hadn't quite mastered this element of her new powers and had no idea how she was doing it.

She stood up though, unquestioningly and walked steadily over to where Briseis had crashed. She found her, laying on the ground twisted in an unnatural way but still very much alive. Blood dripped from the corner of her mouth and seeped from her nose but Briseis was smiling,

"W-what are y-you?" she spluttered her, blood bubbling from her mouth as he spoke. Trista looked down at herself, radiating power and feeling stronger than she ever had.

"I am the Keeper of the Everlasting," Trista replied knowingly. "Its power flows through me."

She *was* the Everlasting, right now, in this moment; she was the power that made all things. When she became that power, as she was now, she was undefeatable.

"All m-my life," Briseis choked out. "I w-wished to b-be you."

Trista stood confused, looking down at her mortal enemy, the woman who'd had her on the run for months, the woman who had killed Oren.

"Y-you were l-loved and p-protected…even from afar."

Briseis choked on the blood that unexpectedly gushed from her mouth.

Trista tried not to empathise with the girl who had seemingly grown up feeling just as alone as she had.

"You could have had love Briseis, as I could have but…" Trista really looked into the face of the broken woman in front of her and her heart went cold. "You took him from me."

Purposefully, Trista bent to one knee and reached out towards Briseis with a clenched fist. Her body still radiating with power, Trista pushed her fist slowly through Briseis' chest. Trista's hand burned through armour and flesh as Briseis screamed out in unbearable agony.

Looking her straight in the eyes, Trista continued to push until her knuckles grazed the bones of Briseis' spine. Trista opened her hand, took hold of it, and pulled, snapping it completely.

The light died from Briseis' eyes and her screaming ceased, as Trista pulled her hand out and dropped the fractured bones on the floor in front of her. She looked down at the blood, coating her powered arm and got to her feet once more.

She continued looking down at her, the woman who had murdered Oren and, in some way, Dana too and felt complete.

All of a sudden, a black orb floated out of Briseis' chest as her lifeless eyes stared out towards nothing and hovered above her. Trista watched as the orb began to change and slowly all the darkness drained from it and the orb was a brilliant white that she had to shield her eyes against.

The orb descended towards Briseis once again and when it touched her, Briseis' body disintegrated into little grey lights – much as Oren and Dana had done – but something was left behind when her body finally disappeared.

Trista, with a deep accepting breath, returned to her normal form and all traces of Briseis' blood had gone. She reached out curiously to touch…

"Eggs?"

There were two of them, one blue and one white with layers of thick scaling. *Dragon* eggs, she realised. Her fingers trembled as she reached out and touched the blue one but before she could register the feel of it, she blinked, and the eggs were gone.

Confused and a little afraid, Trista looked around her and saw blinding white all around. There was an endless sea of nothing but white; no Briseis, no eggs, just…nothing.

Trista turned sharply, looking in all directions but having no real point of reference when there was suddenly a woman standing in front of her

She was beautiful, more beautiful than anyone could ever imagine to be, and Trista knew instantly who she was.

Thea's hair was long, so long it trailed on the floor behind her in thick black waves. It shone brilliantly, a stark contrast against her white gown that blended into everything else around her. An intricate silver diadem lay on top of her head and a ring, much like Trista's own was on her left hand.

The Great House will deliver a child,
To remake the world once more.
Lines of magic chosen,
For the truest power to be born.
To Make the strength needed,
To balance the world of Men.

Beasts of fire will soar the skies,
Purely once again.

The words seeped into her head just as Briseis had done, but this time it was soothing and welcomed; like a hug from a loved one. Trista knew it was Thea who had spoken although her lips hadn't moved.

"You were born," her lips moved this time. "Not only to save your family and Mortania, but to birth true magic back into this world. For fulfilling your destiny Trista, you will receive a gift."

This was it; this was what her mother had warned her would happen.

"What kind of gift?" Thea smiled, a sad smile that she seemed unable to hide,

"A choice," she said and everything went black.

VICTORY

The Agmantians led by Rian Voltaire, arrived in the Imperial Lands just outside the city gates and lay waste to the Greybold army that fought against the Antonides forces, who had finally arrived from the other side.

They boxed in the Greybold men so they had nowhere to go and it turned into a bloodbath of epic proportions as the war raged on with no news whether the princesses of either side had won.

Justin Theronos, in the throes of fighting could see Tirnum Castle, looming over head and knew he needed to get the remainder of his men inside, in order to take it over as their strong hold.

From where he fought, he could not see the Agmantian forces, but had given his orders that they were to get into the city and take the castle whenever they were able. Nyron had sent him a mind message, weak as it was but he'd heard it and had to execute Trista's plans.

Fires still ravaged the city and if anyone was trying to put it out, he had no idea. All he knew, was that he had to get rid of the enemy, so they could truly take control of the city and its people. They didn't have the manpower or time to do a clean-up mission until after the war was won.

The dragon had not returned and so they were thankful for small mercies but where Trista was, they were yet to discover.

Justin fought now, cutting through hordes of men who stood between him and the city walls. Despite having to defeat the Greybolds for obvious reasons, they also had to clear a path for Queen Rowan, Naima and the other injured that needed help.

The Dowager Queen remained in the covered wagon with Naima and Lamya, the former of which was still recovering from hitting her head; but his men had given him a message that Rowan was in pain. Something had happened to her that the Empath Lamya had had to sedate her with her own version of magic.

Even in her catatonic state, Rowan shook while constantly calling Trista's name. She was connected to Trista in ways, they had yet to understand but they knew something must have happened to the princess. It pushed them even more, to get into the city so they could devise a plan to find her.

As Justin continued to fight through the crowds, he felt a sudden pulse of familiar power and his eyes frantically scanned the battlefield for the source. He cut down men that came at him from all angles until suddenly, he spotted him: Nyron.

Relieved, Justin tried to get to him but when he finally did; his relief was short lived.

"Nyron!" the older man held his side even as he continued to swipe with his sword arm,

"Brother!" when Nyron saw him, without any preamble, he collapsed onto Justin's shoulder, trying to keep himself upright.

Nyron had been weakened from his wound but he was surprisingly covered in dust and soot. Nyron smiled with obvious relief at Justin, who returned the gesture just as he sent an energy blast out to a soldier who began to charge at them.

Quickly, he sealed Nyron's wound only briefly wondering why he hadn't done it himself.

"Where's the princess?" Justin demanded as he struggled with Nyron, trying to get clear of the oncoming enemies; blasting through them even as his own power weakened with the effort.

"The tower...crumbled...lost her," Nyron hissed through the pain. Justin's eyes widened,

"She'd dead!" Nyron shook his head,

"No!" then he looked away as he winced from his wounds. "I don't know Justin. I left her on the roof of Thea's Tower and before I could get clear of it...the tower fell."

"It's a miracle you got out al—"

Justin was cut off as the sound of a war horn echoed through the air. They'd sent no orders and Oren was no longer with them. Amidst the chaos, Nyron and Justin looked around with confusion until a haze of purple and gold came into view.

The thunder of a thousand hooves rose up around them until the colours engulfed them and Justin realised, they were being surrounded.

"The Agmantians...they made it," Nyron breathed out just as a shudder went through the ground and a bright light shot up into the sky; above the flags of the Agmantian army.

"Trista," Nyron knew without question and in the back of his mind, Justin did too. He shot out another blast as a soldier came for them but even, he knew there was not enough power behind it. The soldier barely stumbled as he continued towards them and Justin tried to decipher how he was going to protect Nyron and himself. As he readied his sword to take on the man one handed, an arrow went through the soldier's eye and an Agmantian soldier stood behind him.

Many Agmantians remained on horseback but foot soldiers entered the fray in glorious steel armour that glistened in the moonlight. The ground continued to tremble, and Justin knew, it wasn't only due to the new forces. Trista was somewhere fighting and if she was, he had to as well.

He realised then amongst all that chaos, as he tried to save one of his oldest friends; that he had to get back to Naima. He couldn't die without telling her how much he still loved her. It was true, they had never said the words to each other before; believing foolishly that they would have forever. He had left her behind, and he knew she hated him for it. Even so, he had to try and make her see that he had to leave so that he could return to her. That he thought about her every day; that he had a mountain of unsent letters because he had never known the right words to say.

He shook Naima momentarily from his mind and focused on getting her brother, her only family to some help. He readjusted Nyron who was getting heavier by the minute as his wound hindered him. Justin pushed toward the soldier who had saved them,

"I am Captain Theronos and this is Lord Antos, cousin of her Highness Princess Trista of Mortania. He needs help!"

"At once Captain!" the soldier shouldered his bow and threw Nyron's other arm around his shoulders so they could carry him out of the fighting.

"Cover!" the soldier called out and instantly, groups of Agmantian soldiers they hadn't taken in, were protecting them from any on coming attacks.

Nyron cried out suddenly and Justin looked down to where his wound had opened up again, despite being sealed with magic.

"Hold on brother!" Justin urged him as they finally made it out of the fighting to the legion of Agmantian captains, giving orders.

Seemingly from nowhere, two more soldiers came out with a stretch bed and helped get Nyron onto it. While the Agmantians had seemingly rolled in immediately to the fighting, their physicians and learned men had obviously stayed behind to create a base. It was here they brought Nyron and set him down on a cot. When Justin saw that Nyron was truly safe, he bid him farewell and hurried back into the fighting. He was weak, but he wasn't injured so he had to keep going. Even with the Agmantians arrival, the Greybold army were still fighting back and they would until every last one was dead.

Justin barrelled into the chaos, cutting down all he could, and saving the few remaining citizens who hadn't been able to make it out. It was during the pandemonium that he saw Naima fighting.

Shocked, Justin quickly made his way to her, watching in confusion as she cut another soldier down.

"What are you doing here?" he shouted at her. When she saw him, her eyes were wild,

"Where's Nyron, where's my brother?"

"H-he's with the Agmantians, he's safe," relief blossomed on her face.

"He's hurt though, isn't he?" Justin nodded before pulling her towards him and cutting at the soldier who had come up behind her. He fell to the ground, dead and Naima looked at him thankfully.

"I have to get to him!" she shouted again, "I have to know he's okay!"

"I'll take you to him," Justin offered and ran off towards where he had left the Agmantians.

Justin ran, dodged and cut down any in his way, checking intermittently that Naima was keeping up with him. When he turned to do so, to his horror, he saw a soldier aiming a bow at her. Instinctively, he sent an energy blast towards the man, intending to knock him down, but his power sizzled on the air, completely empty.

In the split second it took to realise that he had no way to stop the arrow, Justin raced towards Naima, calling out her name,

"NAIMA!"

She wasn't even that far from him but she was far enough. Confused, she stopped, looking at him with her head tilted to the side, just as he crashed into her, intent on knocking her out of the way, but the arrow pierced straight through their chests. She didn't have all her armour, having taken it off when she was with Queen Rowan, and in her panic to find her brother, had rushed into the field.

As a consequence, the arrow punctured straight through her back and into Justin who was holding her. He felt it within his chest but knew instinctively that he would survive this and she wouldn't.

Naima choked out, blood splattering onto his chin,

"I love you," she said and collapsed into his arms.

"Aaargg—" Justin's scream was cut off, as the archer returned and shot him again through the head.

Feet away, in the relative safety of the Agmantian medical tent, Nyron bolted upright in his cot and screamed out his sister's name,

"Naima!" one of the physicians rushed to him, trying to calm him down but Nyron pushed them out the way to get out of the bed.

"Get away from me, I need to get to my sister!" Prince Aslan, hearing the commotion, rushed into the tent and saw as Nyron fell to the floor from the pain of his injuries. Tears streamed from his eyes as he struggled against his pain to stand up as well as fight off the physicians.

"Captain!" Aslan called out confused, but Nyron ignored him as he continued to struggle. "Nyron!" he finally called out and the large man looked up at him, eyes red with tears.

"My sister's dead!" he shouted. "Naima's dead!"

Aslan rushed to him, pushing the physicians aside,

"How can you know this?" he held the big man's shoulders as he sobbed uncontrollably. Aslan didn't bother to repeat the question, it didn't matter how he knew, it was just very obvious that he did.

"Get someone to scan the field for a Samaian wom—"

"My prince!"

Nyron, the physicians and Prince Aslan looked up to where an Agmantian soldier rushed in, cutting off his sentence.

"What is it?"

"Captain Theronos has been killed my prince, they're bringing him in."

Aslan was shocked, Justin had been with them only a few minutes before.

"There is a woman with him…also killed."

The groan that exploded from Nyron was ungodly. It erupted from the depths of his despair, a place so deep and dark, Aslan felt it vibrate his bones.

"Bring them both in…they are friends of the Samaian queen."

The soldier nodded and exited as quickly as he had come. Aslan turned to where Nyron sat on the floor, crying, with no care to who saw him.

Aslan didn't know what to do. This type of emotion was beyond him and he had no idea how to comfort Nyron, a man who he'd never truly got along with. He tried to think how he would feel if Saicha had been killed and found her couldn't begin to fathom it. They had a complicated relationship, one that had to be refined once she'd returned from the Guild but he could never imagine losing her.

"We need to find Trista," Aslan said quietly as the physician slowly helped Nyron back onto his cot to finish tending his wound.

"She's fighting Briseis."

Saicha's voice appeared from nowhere and Aslan turned to look at her standing in the opening of the tent.

Saicha looked forlorn and even as a physician who had appeared only moments before poured some substance on Nyron's wound that sizzled, he didn't even blink.

Aslan rushed to his sister and uncharacteristically pulled her into a hug. In light of what they had learned, he was overjoyed to see her.

"Thank God!"

Aslan hugged his sister, but she so obviously didn't hug him back. When Aslan stepped back to look at her, his hands on the sides of her arms; he looked into her eyes.

"Saicha…what happened?" he patted her body, looking for wounds but finding none. "Saicha, where is Dana?"

The single tear that fell from Saicha's eye as she turned to Nyron was answer enough and Aslan shook his head in disbelief.

"Where is she Saicha?" Nyron's voice was void of anything but the answer was obvious as tears now streamed heavily from Saicha's eyes.

"Trista took her," she replied, her voice cracking. "Trista took her and healed me before going after Briseis."

"You left her?"

"She ordered me to!"

"When since do you take orders from anyone!" Nyron was blaming her, Aslan realised, but still, Saicha didn't know Nyron was hurting over his sister.

Saicha looked away from Nyron and turned back to the direction she had walked from,

"Trista is no longer as she was," Saicha turned back to them briefly. "A Queen gave an order and I obeyed…no matter how much I wished not to."

The three of them remained in contemplative silence when there was suddenly an uproar of cheering and hollering. The reason spread through the camp like wildfire and soon it was clear that the war was won.

They had pushed back the Greybold army and the Agmantians and Antonides forces were now intent on taking the castle.

No one said anything, no one knew what to say as a war ceased around them, but Oren, Dana, Naima and Justin were dead, and somewhere in the distance, a young queen was fighting the most important battle of all.

***

Lamya raced along in the wagon that held Queen Rowan, holding her hand tightly. She had sedated her with a mind manipulation that was meant to keep her unconscious of her pain, but it didn't seem to be working. If nothing else, it just kept her from screaming out, but the mumbles remained.

Something had happened to Trista and it was affecting Rowan in ways that was completely beyond her expertise.

She raced along now, back towards Tirnum City in the hope that they would find Trista and she would be able to save her mother. Lamya felt every bump in the ground as she raced past and through a war that she had yet to see.

Lamya could defend herself when needed but she was no warrior. She had never seen battle the way Naima or her brother or any of the other Samaians had. The twins had had to fight for a long time after Alexander's death, just to stay alive. They'd had to defend themselves against people who would want to do them harm just because of their heritage when they were only teenagers.

Lamya cursed herself now for letting Naima leave the wagon in her weakened state, but there had been no stopping her. She's said she felt her brother's pain, something they'd always been able to do and that she had to be with him. Naima was determined and strong, they all knew that and there had been no keeping her there, once she thought her brother was in danger.

Lamya also cursed herself for not staying in Mortania; for not doing more during the years of Curian's reign to prepare herself and even Trista for all that would take place in the years to come. If she had been able to determine what Avriel was truly about, then maybe she could have helped Trista.

All of that was speculation now as they raced towards the fighting when they should have really been trying to avoid it.

Rowan moaned in her sedative state and Lamya fanned her to try and keep her cool, when suddenly Rowan's eyes darted open and she stared at Lamya wide eyed,

"Lamya?" Lamya nodded. "Trista was hurt, trapped but now she's…she's beyond my reach."

"What does that mean?" Lamya asked as she got increasingly worried,

"I must get to her before she makes her choice."

"What choice?"

"Her choice that will change everything…for all of us."

Battle thundered around the two women in the wagon but only when they heard a thunderous cheer rumble around them, did they know that the battle had finally been won.

The wagon came to a sharp stop eventually and a guard came to the opening, telling her it was safe to exit. Lamya helped Rowan out of the wagon, her footing unsteady and looked around at the carnage around them. There dead bodies and wounded men littered everywhere. Some wore Greybold colours, some wore Antonides and Agmantian but they were everywhere.

Tirnum City still burned in the distance, how destroyed it was they had yet to find out, but all around them was death.

Tears pooled in the women's eyes as they turned to look down a path that had seemingly opened up in the crowd out of nowhere.

Down this path, came Prince Aslan, Princess Saicha and Nyron on a crutch. They were accompanied by another Agmantian, dressed in the royal colours who could only be Prince Rian.

None of them looked happy despite the rejoicing that went on around them and even as she watched, Rowan could feel her daughter; somewhere…out there.

Lamya bowed to the royals and asked,

"Where are the others?"

No one said anything and Lamya's heart plunged to the centre of the earth.

"Dana, Naima and Captain Theronos were lost to us Lamya," Aslan said quietly. "Trista took Dana…Justin and Naima are being cleaned."

"No…no," Lamya clutched at her chest as she fell to her knees and wept. Saicha stepped forward; her eyes red, from her own tears.

"We were thrown from our horse and Dana...I..."

Lamya broke down, a wail of the likes few of them had witnessed and Rowan rushed to cradle her in her arms. The men looked on, unsure of what to do to comfort them.

"Why was this allowed to happen!" Lamya cried out angrily. Rowan watched as Saicha looked away, her guilt so potent it was almost a living thing.

"No one knows why the Gods do the things they do," Rowan replied as she held her. "How were you thrown Saicha?"

Saicha shook her head,

"The dragon...Briseis fell from the sky and crashed into the land between Tirnum and Thea's Point. Dana and I were trying to get to my brother, to safety and...we were thrown from the horse."

Saicha's voice broke as she spoke, the words thick and sharp in her throat. "Dana screamed for me to go faster...but it wasn't fast enough." Saicha choked on her last words but Rowan nodded her head, seemingly with understanding.

"Where is Trista?" Rowan asked quietly.

"She healed me and sent me back. She stayed to fight Briseis."

"Where?" Saicha shook her head,

"I can't go back there,"

"I'm not asking you to," Rowan replied sharply. "Something has happened to Trista and I have to know where she is."

"The injured remain behind," Rian suddenly said. "There is much to do here, before we can get to the castle and take completely control of it as the princess wants."

Everyone agreed,

"My general will remain here, clear the bodies and take any prisoners. Miss?" he gestured to Lamya who looked up at him, "Can you remain here with Lord Antos?" she nodded.

"Saicha, we'll head into the city and see if we can get into the castle through the fire. See what is left of it."

Saicha agreed silently,

"What about me?" Aslan asked, almost offended until Rian said.

"Take her majesty Queen Rowan to find her daughter."

Aslan nodded and Rowan looked up at him thankfully,

With the help of a sturdy and healthy Agmantian steed, Prince Aslan and Queen Rowan made it to the bare land where Saicha said she and Dana had fallen.

The ground was scorched beyond recognition with the patterns of power and energy blasts. Blackened earth and overturned rocks littered everywhere around a huge crater with something small in the centre.

It took her a while but with Aslan's help, Rowan finally made it into the centre of the hole, and looked over at her daughter laying in the ground in the middle of a broken world.

The earth was shattered with the aftermath of a battle none of them would ever witness but Rowan could only concentrate on the immense power that now began to engulf her only child.

She watched her daughter rise into the air in a kaleidoscope of colour and magic then slowly descend before a blinding white light shown out and disappeared leaving something very special behind and Rowan knew instantly, the choice that Trista had made.

THE CHOICE

She was in a bed.

She was in a big, soft bed, which was obvious without even opening her eyes.

How did I get here and where...where is Thea?

Slowly, Trista opened her eyes and confirmed she was lying in a very large bed; with plush white sheets and pillows she had somehow become tangled in, apparently during the sleep she didn't remember having.

Where am I?

Sluggishly, she untangled herself and sat up to find herself amid unmistakable opulence.

The stone walls all around her were adorned with luxurious draping and intricately woven tapestries. The sizable bedroom had shelves of books, two big intricately carved wooden cupboards and a chest of drawers with all manner of beauty products and other things she didn't recognise on top of it.

The bed was canopied, with delicate white gossamer hanging gracefully on either side but artfully gathered at the far end so she could see out into the rest of the room. There was a vanity table opposite; white wood like the other furnishings from what she could see but with gold finishing. Gold on the handles and skirting of the drawers and painted on the carved design on the legs.

She could see a small portion of her head in the vanity mirror and placed her hands to her head where her curls, much longer then she remembered, draped over her breasts, covering then entirely if the blush pink satin nightgown she was wore wasn't already doing so.

Where in Gys, am I?

Curious, Trista climbed out of the bed and her bare feet sunk into the fluffiest dark blue rug she had ever felt. She noticed then that the entire room was an array of white, gold and blue decor against the stone walls. The room was much bigger than she'd first realised too; with three white wooden doors leading to who knew where.

Needing to explore, she looked down at herself and wondered where she could get something to cover up. Before the thought had finished, light grey slippers and a fitted bell sleeved robe appeared on her feet and body, fastening itself just under her breasts with a large silver button.

So, her powers worked here but…how?

Perplexed but rather amused, Trista approached the closest door to her and opened it to reveal a room filled with clothes. Gowns, shirts, dresses; trousers, riding and fighting leathers, shoes and…tiaras.

Wait…

"Trista!" Trista spun at the sound of her name, dropping the tiara she had picked up and it clattered to the ground. A door, somewhere outside of the room opened and moments later, a woman appeared in the closet doorway.

"Oh darling, there you are!"

Rowan.

Rowan looked as beautiful as ever in a gown of the deepest green. Her hair was piled high on her head, a delicate diadem settled neatly amongst her own curls. She looked the same as she had left her just less…weathered.

Wait…the same as what…as when?

"Mama?"

"Have you just woken up?"

"Y-yes," came her feeble and confused reply. Rowan rolled her eyes mockingly but not unkindly before grabbing her daughter's arm.

"Come on young lady, it's not every day my eldest daughter turns eighteen. If you thought your Ascension party was something; this is going to blow your mind!"

Rowan giggled as she pulled Trista from the closet, back into the bedroom and through one of the other doors to a large bathing room.

Trista saw the other door, now open led to some sort of living room and deduced her mother must have entered through there.

So, it was her birthday; or at least her party but...

"*Eldest* daughter?"

"Don't tell me you've forgotten Freya already!" Rowan laughed as she made a gesture with her hand and the faucets in the sunken bathtub turned on. Water gushed out and the tub filled with steaming water, bubbles flowing as Rowan made a stirring motion with her hand.

Trista was shocked stupid; she had a *sister!*

"Come on Trista, we can't possibly start the party without you. Your father can't wait to see your birthday dress!" Rowan said excitedly and Trista's heart stopped once again.

"Father?" Rowan nodded as she fussed around with some bath oils. "W-where is he?"

"In his chambers with your Uncle Gorn, something about rebels at the Northern border." She fanned off the idea flippantly, "He'll handle it as always, he wouldn't miss your party for the world!" Rowan reassured her as she ushered Trista out of her robe and into the bathtub.

She bathed thoroughly, feeling somehow that she hadn't been able to do so in a very long time but when she looked at her fingers and toes; all were perfectly manicured and her skin was smooth to the touch. Dismissing it, Trista finally stepped out of the tub where two young women had now arrived, seemingly to attend her because she was of course, a princess.

Wasn't she?

Trista felt this was right, her mother, her royalty…everything was as it should be, but her heart was telling her otherwise.

The young women proceeded to do her hair and makeup and within an hour or so, she looked at herself in the bedroom mirror and didn't recognise who she saw.

Trista stood in a satin silver gown with embroidered detailing on the hem, sleeves and bodice. Her hair had been straightened and hung all the way to her buttocks and a silver crown with diamonds encrusted all over it, had been securely fitted onto her head. It gleamed in the candlelight of the room; diamonds glittering as she turned her head this way and that. Her makeup was kept light, with emphasis on her eyes making the green sparkle from behind the ink black of her lashes.

Rowan appeared beside her, having left earlier to get ready herself and stood now in her own gorgeous dress. It was an elegant navy blue gown with gold stitching that clinched in her waist with an embroidered corseted bodice. She was wearing her Queen's crown now and in her hands, she held a large velvet box.

"Mama?"

Rowan smiled lovingly at her, tears of joy evident in her eyes.

"You look beautiful Trista." Trista blushed her thanks as her mother stepped forward holding the box out to her. "You had something from Grandma Freilyn on your Ascension Day but this…this is from my mother. She would have wanted you to wear it."

Rowan opened the box to reveal an exquisite chandelier diamond necklace that when Rowan put it on her, fit perfectly on Trista's neck; nestled neatly atop her cleavage.

"It's beautiful…thank you Mama."

Rowan hugged her tightly,

"I love you, my miracle girl" her mother whispered softly, and Trista's heart swelled with emotion. This moment with her mother was something she had always dreamed of. The closeness that could only come from a mother's love was something she had craved, even from Gwendolyn.

Wait…who is Gwendolyn?

The queen and princess stood hugging when a door opened behind them in the outer chamber and they heard footsteps approaching. A voice carried with the footsteps and Trista's heart stopped in her chest as she realised who was coming.

"Where is she, where is my darling girl?" a deep voice boomed before revealing the face of the man it belonged to.

Alexander Antonides, King of Mortania, her father was standing in front of her, beaming with pride and love.

"Papa," it wasn't even a sound, it was barely a breath as Rowan stepped aside and Alexander held out his arms to his daughter.

Trista ran into her father's arms and crushed herself against him as she burst into a fit of sobbing.

"Hey, hey! Trista what's wrong!"

Alexander held her back to look down at her as she cried and gently wiped her tears away with his thumbs as he held her head in his large hands.

His face was strong but kind, beautiful in a refined and handsome way that she couldn't explain. She had his eyes, she saw immediately, the same large, doting eyes that looked back at her every day in the mirror. His hair was long and currently braided, his eyebrows thick but perfectly arched and currently knotted together as he looked down questioningly at his daughter.

"Trista, sweetie what is wrong?" He looked so worried it was comical, but Trista could barely speak. Here he was, looking at her, talking to her, as if he were real and not…

Not what…dead?

"I've missed you so much!" Trista slammed herself back into his chest,

"Missed me? Trista, I've only been in the North a week."

Something was going on here and Trista simply couldn't figure out what it was. What did it matter anyway, her father was here with her; as he should be. As he always had been, but something in the back of her mind, told her, that simply wasn't true...

"I just love you so much," she said trying to control her tears as she breathed him in and squeezed him tight.

"I love you too, you know that." Trista nodded but refused to let him go,

"I do now," she whispered and she tightened her grip on him, never wanting to let go.

Trista held onto her father a little longer before she felt Rowan take hold of her shoulders and turn her to face her again,

"Let me fix this," she said and waved her hand over Trista's face. "You can't have a puffy nose and red eyes at your birthday party, now can you?"

Trista smiled, happier than she had ever remembered being and shook her head in agreement. She turned to her father, dressed similarly to Rowan in navy blue robes and trousers, the Antonides crown on his head and beamed up at him.

"Thank you both, for doing this for me."

"Nonsense," her father said pulling her back into his embrace and kissing her forehead. "Nothing but the best for my eldest miracle daughter."

What followed was a whirlwind of an evening and celebration for the eighteenth birthday of Crown Princess Trista Antonides of Mortania.

Trista's parents walked with her from what she knew now was her bedroom, through the castle to the Great Hall where at the closed doors, Princess Freya; her little sister met them in her own beautiful party dress.

Freya was eleven or twelve years old and looked like a miniature version of Trista. She ran into Trista's arms and hugged her,

"Happy birthday Trista!" Trista laughed as she looked down at the beautiful little girl and held her face lovingly in her hands.

"Thank you Freya," as she hugged her little sister, a large white wolf came bounding down the hall and sat by Freya's side.

"Phoebe says happy birthday too!" Freya laughed while rubbing the huge animal behind the ears. Stunned, Trista could only smile,

"Thank you Phoebe!" Phoebe stood again and licked Trista's hand affectionately. This wolf must be Freya's pet, and if no one else was alarmed by a wolf in the castle, then she wouldn't be either.

The royal family stood outside the entrance to the Great Hall, and after a large fanfare and announcement, they entered the room. Trista was blown away by the multitude of people in the room, all of which she didn't recognise. She walked behind her mother and father towards the thrones at the other end of the room, conscious of the smiles and nods and bows from all the people around them. Phoebe walked beside Freya and Trista marvelled at how normal this was.

Once she and her family took their places on their thrones at the far end of the hall, the party began, and people approached Trista with presents and good wishes. One by one, strangers approached her until a familiar face came up the dais;

"Rayne!"

"When did we lose our manners young lady?"

Rayne Illiya, dressed in a long white robe with gold ribbon on the hem and large belled sleeves approached with a haughty air about her that Trista found she missed.

Why would you miss it?

"Aunt Rayne?"

"Has that title changed since I saw you yesterday?" She replied, clearly annoyed and Trista couldn't help but laugh, shaking her head as she stood to hug her aunt.

"No, no it hasn't"

"Good, you've been avoiding your magic lessons but since it's your birthday I won't go into it!" Although it was clear she really wanted to, Trista laughed again.

"Thank you, Aunt Rayne."

"You're welcome, not getting a scolding is your gift by the way."

With a flick of her wrist, Trista felt her own wrist tickle and looked down to see a diamond bracelet appear there.

"And that," Rayne said before winking and leaving the dais completely, disappearing into the crowd.

Trista couldn't help but laugh as she admired her gift, lost in the perfection of it all. Her parents, her sister; her entire family were all alive and well and she was the princess of this realm as she was born to be. She turned to look at her father who smiled back at her.

The gifts continued until everyone had been presented to her, then the music began. Musicians played songs she recognised and ones she didn't and Trista danced until her feet ached. There was music, dancing and food in abundance and Trista could not remember having ever been so happy. She laughed and danced with people she had known her entire life, who praised her and made her feel loved. Her Godfather Gorn asked for a dance and she obliged him happily, even while having the strange feeling that he shouldn't have been there either.

She breathed him in, remembering the warmth of him, as Gorn swung her around in his arms and she giggled incessantly at the jokes he made.

"Trista,"

"Yes Mama?" Trista turned to her mother when her dance with Gorn had come to an end in the middle of the dancefloor,

"Your father wishes to speak with you." Trista nodded her head and left to where her mother had indicated.

Trista made her way to a small meeting room adjacent to the Great Hall where she found her father leant over a table with a map on top of it,

"You wished to see me Papa?"

Alexander looked up then and beamed at her before holding out his hand for her to take. She took it and stood by his side, as close as she could be to him and looked down at the map in front of them.

"Mortania?"

"Our kingdom...our legacy."

Alexander continued to look down at the map until he spoke, quietly but clearly.

"Now you are of age, suitors have been calling; demanding to know who you are Intended to. I've put them off for now, but I have known for some time who you must marry."

She had known that this was coming but she was still surprised none the less.

"Oh," her father looked apologetic.

"While there's no timescale on your wedding, I didn't want you to feel obligated to your duty; pressured by the identity of your betrothed."

"Isn't the very nature of my duty, is that it is an obligation?" Alexander looked up and smiled at her proudly,

"That is why you will make an amazing queen someday." Alexander held her cheek lovingly,

"Who is it?" She said quietly and Alexander removed his hand,

"Thantos of House Thelm, he'll be arriving in two days to formally announce the engagement."

Thantos Thelm! She hated Thantos!

He teased her mercilessly as a child and always thought he was better than everyone else.

"Papa, he's five years older than me, he's…mean!" Alexander smiled although she could tell he wasn't happy,

"I'm sorry it is not someone you like. I have seen his…questionable and entitled behaviour and I can only imagine it will get worse once he becomes your Consort."

Trista's heart ached but something told her it wasn't just because she had to marry Thantos. Alexander pulled his daughter into a hug,

"It is not easy being a ruler, or the Keeper and you will have to do many things you don't want to do Trista. The key, is in being true to your heart and the power that lives inside you."

Trista leant back from her father to look up into his face,

"What if my heart and the power want two different things Papa?"

Alexander smiled his sad smile again,

"That is when your choice is the hardest."

Trista returned to her birthday party with her father, a few moments later and danced with her friends from around the kingdom and across the seas. Prince Aslan had come from Agmantia for the occasion but his older brother Rian was fighting barbarians in the Agmantian rainforest. Their sister, Saicha was an Agmantian Assassin so Trista had never met the rogue princess. Her cousins, Naima and Nyron were there, Nyron drinking way too much and Naima never leaving her husband Justin's side. They'd just had a son, little Ardus and her Uncle Theon was delighted to finally be a Grandfather.

Trista danced for hours and forgot about her impending engagement as she drank the finest Yiteshi wines and ate the most sublime meats. She danced with her mother and of course her father and her father's brothers, Uncle Brennan and Justin. It was while she was dancing with Freya, twirling the little girl in the middle of the dancefloor, that Freya suddenly let go of Trista's hands and took off into the crowd,

"Oren, you're back!"

Trista's heart began to thump rapidly in her chest as Oren Antos approached them through the crowd.

He was dressed in the most fetching trousers, shirt and long coat; a level of formal attire she had never seen him wear. His hair was brushed and tied away from his face in a neat bun, his beard trimmed to perfection. His teal eyes twinkled mischievously as he crouched down for Freya to jump into his arms for a hug,

"Hey little princess!" He said kissing Freya's cheek. "Hello to you too Phoebe!" He chuckled as he ruffled the wolf's fur who had come to fuss around his legs.

Oren lowered Freya to the ground before walking up to Trista and bowing perfectly at the waist. He raised his eyes to look at her, still bowed and said,

"Hello, Princess."

Trista leapt into his arms and the tears came like a waterfall, tears of happiness and joy that he was here, alive.

Why wouldn't he be alive?

Trista dismissed the thought as easily as it had come and squeezed him so tight, she thought she might break him.

"Hey, what's wrong Princess?" he said with shock and a little worry.

Trista didn't reply, her arms still wrapped around him and silently, Oren led her away from the staring eyes on the dancefloor and into the corridor until he came to the open door of an empty chamber.

Trista continued to cry as Oren held her, revelling in the warmth and feel and even smell of him once again.

"You're weird at the best of times but this is just odd! Are you sure you're okay?" Oren laughed good naturedly. She'd never heard him laugh like this. So, happy and carefree.

"Oren, you di—"

She knew if she finished her sentence he would think she was crazy but she knew it to be true: Oren had died. He had died in her arms and now he was here like nothing had happened.

"I've missed you so much," was all she could think to say but he just chuckled.

"Missed me? Tris, I only went to the North with your father a week ago."

"It feels like forever," she mumbled, unsure what to make of what she knew to be true and what was standing in front of her, very much alive. "Anything could have happened to you."

"Well it didn't. I even made it back before the end of your party!"

He looked pleased with himself, happy and it was so different to how she knew him it threw her. Maybe he hadn't died, maybe she was crazy…

"Listen Tris, now we're alone; I guess now is as good a time as any to tell you."

"Tell me what?" Trista used her magic to fix her makeup, she knew she must look a fright from all the blubbering she'd done. He smiled when she'd done it and shrugged with a cheeky grin on his face,

"You're not the only one off the market."

Trista's eyes narrowed into his face and all other sound seemed to disappear,

"What are you talking about?"

"Ella, I asked her to marry me…she said yes."

Time slowed down and her head ached; this could not be happening. Oren couldn't be getting married…

"I don't understand," Trista collapsed into a nearby chair, holding her head where a headache had begun to form. "I just don't understand…"

"I got back to the manor this afternoon but I asked her at dinner. Tris, can you believe it; you'll marry Thantos and I'll finally be with Ella…we'll be family."

Ariella Thelm was Thantos' younger sister so if they indeed married a sibling, they would be family even though they technically already were.

"No!" Trista flared up as she shot up from her seated position. "No, it's not perfect Oren it's not. You can't marry Ella!"

Oren looked truly perplexed,

"Why not? You told me to go out with her!"

"I would never say that Oren, *ever*!" He looked confused and then was suddenly very angry,

"Is this about us?"

"What?" Oren sighed heavily,

"Trista, you're my best friend. I thought you understood when I told you, I don't feel that way about you!"

At first she had no clue what he was talking about, then an echo of a memory flashed through her mind of the two of them in the castle gardens; fighting...

"What, no!" Oren growled,

"Come on Trista don't do this again. I thought I made myself clear?" Oren looked her square in the face. "I do not have romantic feelings for you."

Trista wanted to cry again but she was too angry to find the tears. This couldn't be happening; she couldn't have Oren back but he would belong to someone else.

She loved him, she loved him desperately and she couldn't lose him again.

"No, nooo!"

Trista closed her eyes, trying to stop the tears from falling but she couldn't. They seeped out of her closed eye lids hot and heavy,

"Trista...Trista look at me..." Oren's voice was soothing but when she opened her eyes to finally confess what she hadn't been able to before he died, Thea was once again standing in front of her.

"Where is he?" she screamed at the goddess.

Thea looked at her, unfazed by her yelling,

"Your choice is this Trista Antonides: choose Oren and he will be returned to you, just as he was. Your destiny will continue and your friends and family; any of which who are, will remain dead. Or..."

"Or what?" Trista's heart ached,

"Choose your father…and everything will be as you saw."

Trista stared at Thea Antonides, her ancestor and couldn't believe what she had heard,

"What?"

"Time will rewind, Curian will not rise and your father will not die. You will grow with a family who loves you, as the princess you were born to be."

"And my friends…Dana?"

"Dana does not exist to you in that life. You will never know her or remember that you ever did."

The choice was clear.

If she picked Oren, the pain of losing her friends and her father would remain, loneliness and pain would be all she ever knew, even with Oren by her side.

If she picked her father, she would have the family she always dreamed of, the life she had yearned for but Oren and Dana; the two most important people in her life would be gone.

"Which do you choose?" Thea echoed and before the thought had taken root, Trista's choice had been made.

INTENDED

Trista was in a bed once again. There were worst places one could wake up when they passed out from supernatural forces, but this was beginning to get ridiculous.

She realised two things instantly: that she wasn't in any pain and that she wasn't alone in the bed. She was lying on her right side and as she opened her eyes, she saw a large tattooed arm hanging loosely over her from behind, on top of the covers.

She drew in a subtle breath and as she knew it would be, the distinct manly scent of wood and leather and that hint of metal tickled her senses.

A single tear escaped her eye and sunk into the pillow she lay on, as she lifted her hand from on top of the covers and traced her fingers delicately over the lines of his tattoo.

This close to it, she could see now that the lines were the smallest of letters, letters in what she knew was the ancient language. Her fingers traced the lines, back and forth on the top of his hand, terrified that he would disappear.

His hand jerked suddenly, and she felt him take in a deep breath, before tightening his arm around her.

A sob choked inside her throat as slowly, so very slowly; Trista turned in the bed, even under the weight of his large arm on top of her and came to face, with Oren.

He was sleeping, breathing softly; his hair loose around his face; the right side of his face buried in pillow.

Her fingers trembled as she reached out again and touched the stubble that was coming through on his face. He twitched and almost instantly, his eyes opened.

The teal green of the one eye she could see shone out at her as Oren smiled at her; a real genuine smile that reached his twinkling eyes.

"Hello, Princess," he said, his voice rumbling in the small space between them.

Trista looked over at him, stared into his face before sliding closer towards him; his face still cupped in her hand and kissed him. He rolled onto his back with his arm around her, so that she fell on top of him, her curly hair framing them in their own little world as they kissed.

His lips were soft, softer than anything she'd ever felt; his tongue a welcome intruder to her own mouth and she couldn't get enough of the feelings that exploded within her. Breathless, Trista eventually lifted her head and looked down at Oren Antos,

"I love you," she confessed.

"I love you too," he replied without hesitation as he threaded his fingers into her head and drew her head down, to kiss her again.

The power that always pulsed between them began to pump uncontrollably as Trista moved her leg so she could straddle him. He sat up in the bed, his arms wrapped around her as he pressed her breasts into his chest. Their fingers were in each other's hair as they kissed, his lips travelling down her neck and onto the tops of her now pulsating breasts. Oren took his hands out of her curls and reached in between them to tear at the nightshirt she was in, ripping it clean down the middle.

The power between them jolted and a moan escaped her from nowhere. One of his large hands took hold of her exposed breast and Trista gasped at the rush of sensation that went through her.

He massaged and kneaded her breasts as they kissed before grabbing hold of her to spin her onto her back. Her hair exploded around the pillow as Oren ripped down the rest of her nightdress, exposing her stomach and legs to him. Trista was unafraid and totally free, knowing she wanted this to happen with Oren more than anything in her life.

He reached down towards her underclothes and gently, peeled them down her legs so she was completely bare before him.

He looked down at her for a moment, gazing intently at every inch of her delicate body. Without taking his eyes off her, Oren lifted his shirt from the bottom and pulled it neatly over his head, revealing his amazing body.

Trista swallowed, her mouth suddenly dry as she looked her fill at his large chest and taut sculpted stomach. She ran her hands appreciatively up the ridges of his arms before he lowered himself to her again, putting his mouth delicately onto hers.

Her nipples grazed against the dusting of hair on his chest and sent an energy running through her veins that she couldn't explain. Trista moaned as they kissed, sounds she'd never known she could make, while her hands roamed over his tight back muscles and broad shoulders.

She felt him raise his hips and fumble between them and when he lowered them again, she felt something thick press against her stomach.

Her eyes shot open then fluttered shut again as he began to grind against her lower region. The feeling was indescribable; unlike anything she'd ever experienced of course but something that her body seemed to be familiar with; like it knew what it wanted before she did.

Oren kissed her once more before lifting his head to look down into her eyes. He stroked some stray curls from her face, both breathing heavily. Trista was so lost in his kisses; she didn't feel him adjust his position between her legs. The energy began to bang like a drum and after an intense pressure at her tender opening, Oren pushed into her; making her cry out.

He kissed along her jaw and into the space between her neck and shoulder as he ground his hips and member into her. All at once, the drumming sensation stopped and Trista felt an intense feeling of completion. Oren pushed into her again and a sharp pain erupted inside her, making a stray tear fall from her eye. She squinted her eyes shut against the sting but Oren kissed her eyelids lovingly until she opened them to look up at him.

"I love you," he said again as instinctively Trista raised her hips and wrapped her legs around his waist.

Trista held onto Oren, consumed by him and didn't try to wipe the tears of joy that escaped her as she made love to the man she adored.

A while later, they lay in each other's arms,

"You never told me what this meant."

Trista murmured as she lay against Oren's chest. They were laying on their side, looking at each in contemplatively and adoring silence. They were both sated after their lovemaking and Trista had never felt so close to someone before. She felt like she was a part of him, and he a part of her.

"It's the mark of an Intended," he said quietly. "When you're chosen to marry into the royal family, it appears on you. Men usually on your arm or leg; on women, usually their backs or up their sides."

Trista's eyes widened as she spun around to look at him,

"You're my Intended?" Oren nodded before she punched him in the chest,

"What was that for!" he chuckled as he cradled his chest like it had seriously hurt.

"Why didn't you tell me?" Trista demanded and his smile faded before he shrugged,

"I didn't want you to think we loved each other because of the Intent…I wanted you to love me on your own, as I love you."

Trista grabbed his face and kissed him passionately before leaning back to look him in the eye.

"I've never loved any one before loving you."

"Not even Thorn?" Trista shook her head,

"Not even Thorn."

She kissed him again before an insecure thought came into her head,

I never loved Tysha. We were close, but it was just sex.

She'd forgotten their connection and blushed furiously that he'd heard her jealous thoughts.

When you threw the bread roll at me at dinner, Oren's voice echoed sweetly into her head. *That's when I knew I loved you*

"Do you remember dying?" she asked quietly and he nodded before taking her chin with his index finger as he so liked to do.

"Now, I only want to focus on living…with you."

Oren kissed her again until everything was forgotten for just a little longer.

***

Dowager Queen Freilyn Antonides, Trista's grandmother, had sent her personal guard to determine the victors of the Battle of the Heirs, as it was being called, and when she understood that it was indeed her granddaughter who had won, they were instructed to bring her family to her seaside estate.

The Agmantian forces had finally taken control of Tirnum Castle, while the remaining soldiers and court, made their way to Freilyn's estate. Prince Rian and his generals had captured and questioned General Rarno of the Greybold army and he was currently imprisoned in the Tirnum Castle dungeons. They had apprehended many of the higher-ranking lords, including Baron Erik Thelm, his daughter and Lords Weilyn and Priya. They had seen no sign of Baron Lyon Dreston and assumed he was among the dead they had yet to discover.

There was much to do by way of rebuilding the city and the castle, but all of that would be taken care of once Trista and Oren woke up.

Rowan and Aslan had witnessed a miracle in the abandoned lands outside the city, where Trista and Oren had appeared, side by side unconscious with two dragon eggs laying either side of them. The princess, the newly resurrected General and the eggs were transported to Freilyn's home under Rowan's watchful eye.

The couple were placed in a room so they would be together when they finally awoke. Three days later, it was reported that the couple had finally awoken and would be joining them for dinner in moments. Rowan had been to visit them, to explain all that had happened and Lamya sat now with the princess' closest friends and family waiting for them to appear.

Lamya looked around the sea of faces in the dining hall and her heart still hurt that Dana, Naima and Justin were missing. Dana's death hurt her that little bit more, as she had grown so close to her. Of all the people who deserved to be here, rejoicing in their victory was the gifted young woman who had potential to be so much more.

Still, she knew her pain was nothing compared to that of Nyron Antos. The young lord had lost his sister and Dana and no one had been able to get a word out of him. The fact he was even at the dinner was a miracle in itself. He spent the days since leaving the battlefield by his sister's side, having declined to have her sent to the ancestral plains to await burial. He preserved her with his own magic and sat by her side each day.

Along with the Agmantian royals, another face that she knew would be well received once Trista woke up, was Rayne Illiya. The Gifted sorceress sat now with her little sister at the head of the table with Freilyn and one of the old queen's advisors.

There was much to discuss and Lamya had said as much to her own grandmother who had remained in Thelm. They still had Thorn Remora under guard, but once news of his mother's death had reached him, he'd demanded to be released and sent home. They saw no reason to deny his request, now that the threat of his mother's magic was gone and so, Thorn made the journey back to Remora.

Lamya sat at a table quietly, contemplating all they had lost when the large door at the far end of the room, opened and two people stood in the doorway. Lamya jumped to her feet, desperate to get a look at the young couple as they walked towards them. They were dressed similarly in grey and blue, clothes that had undoubtedly been left for them in their rooms. Trista in a long gown, her hair tied in a long braid over her shoulder and Oren in shirt and trousers. They looked refreshed and alive and dare she think it, happy. Trista was happy, the world could see that; but there was a reservation about her smile that could not be denied. She was guilty Lamya realised. Guilty that she was happy when so much had been lost.

The pair reached the head table and Trista let go of Oren's hands to walk up to the old lady in front of her, who she instantly bowed to.

"Grandmother," she said softly as Freilyn's eyes welled with tears and pulled her granddaughter into her arms to hold her. Before long, Rowan stepped in, as did Rayne and the four women held each other for a very long time with their supporters looking on.

When Trista finally stepped away from them, she took Oren's hand once again; almost drawing strength from him Lamya observed and turned to everyone on the tables below the raised platform where her family sat.

Everyone she knew was there, including Prince Rian who had returned from the capital only earlier that day. There were additional people of Freilyn's household who were permitted to attend.

"There are no words to describe my gratitude to all of you for what you have done for me and my people…for what you have done for your country."

Trista looked into their eyes, catching Lamya's gaze who smiled back at her reassuringly.

"There are many ways I will be able to show my gratitude to you in the days to come but now, I wish to focus my energies on those whose days have run out."

Trista turned to Rowan who nodded and rose from her seat,

"If you would please follow me." Rowan called out and walked toward the exit so everyone would follow.

Rowan led them from the dining hall and into an inner courtyard where four pyres had been raised. Lamya had tried to ignore their construction, but now they were not to be ignored, along with the ritual to come.

Countless pyres had already been erected in The Wide for the fallen soldiers but this was something personal.

They all stood in a line in front of the pyres when Trista, slowly raised her hands and little white lights descended from the sky, separating so that in a matter of seconds, the lights turned into Gorn and Dana. With a look from Rowan, Nyron raised his arm and Justin and Naima's bodies appeared on the other two pyres.

They all appeared to be sleeping, their bodies washed, dressed and preserved but for all those who wished they would, they would not be waking up.

Rayne paced along the pyres murmuring Samaian prayers over each of the bodies. She burned herbs for cleansing and blessing and said the ceremonial rites. When she was done, Nyron stepped in front of Naima's body and lowered his head to kiss her forehead.

"You were the best of us," he said. "The right one, the strong one…the good twin. When Mother died, even though you were hurting as much as me if not more, you looked after me Nai. You taught me to not be angry at the world for taking her away from us."

Tears fell heavily from Nyron's eyes and it was hard for the others not to follow suit.

"How can I not be angry at the world now?" he snapped, his rage evident. "I can't do this without you Naima."

Pain resonated through them all as Nyron, the strong, funny, mountain of a man cried over losing the last of his immediate family.

"But I will," he finally choked out. "I'll carry on our family name so that you, and our parents will never be forgotten. I love you, big sister…and I promise I'll never leave you."

Nyron stepped back into line and Lamya took hold of his hand, squeezing it comfortingly. Rowan stepped forward, tears in her own eyes as she approached Gorn,

"You pledged your sword and your fealty to my House; Antonides from yours; Antos. You honoured and protected us, killed any who opposed or harmed us and died to uphold that vow. From that day until your last, your sword, your shield and your life were ours and now you are released. Be free General Gorn Antos, knowing you fulfilled your duties as a true Samaian warrior…and a very dear friend."

Rowan stepped back and Oren held her hand tightly, with Trista's in the other. Lamya watched them, being strong for each other as Rayne finally stepped toward Dana.

"For one who was not born with the Everlasting coursing through her veins, I never knew someone so special. A truly beautiful, brave and bright young woman who had her entire life to make an impression on the world."

"Be free young Dana, knowing you fulfilled your purpose as a true friend and a guiding light to us all." Trista came up beside Rayne and looked down at her best friend,

"It doesn't feel right being here without you," she said softly. "Before I had a family, before I had friends or subjects or even enemies…I had you. You were by my side before I was anything because you always saw the best in people even when they didn't see it in themselves."

"I'm sorry I couldn't bring you back but I know…I hope, you would want me to be happy and I can only pray to the Gods that you're happy where you are too. I'll love you always."

Trista stepped back and once again Rayne stepped forward.

"Bless Gorn, Dana, Justin and Naima with the blessings of our ancestors and the power of the Everlasting."

Rayne raised her arms and the four pyres exploded instantly into flame, sending their loved ones, on their very last journey.

THE PRICE OF HAPPINESS

The mood was sombre, Saicha thought to herself and it was making her angry. Only two days ago they had said goodbye to family, friends and the fallen from the war, but still; there was a lot to be celebrated.

They had won, Trista had defeated Briseis and fulfilled her destiny. Now, in all but acknowledged name, she was the Queen of Mortania, yet no one was mentioning it; not to mention the two dragon eggs that no one knew what to do with.

They had been left, guarded in the basement levels of the estate until Trista told them what must be done with them.

Now, everyone sat in the dining hall, eating distractedly because no one was truly hungry.

Saicha was not unsympathetic to their pain, of course. She, more than anyone had felt the brunt of losing one of their own. She had been with Dana in her last moments and Saicha had never felt guilt like it. She hated that she had lived, and Dana had not.

Since burning the pyres, the Samaians had countless meetings, including Lamya who acted as the link with the Lithanian Council about the future of the kingdom. As foreign rulers, the Agmantians were not permitted to attend but everything still hung in the air about what was to happen. Saicha wanted to be free of this place, of her guilt about the part she played in Dana's death.

Saicha turned to look at Nyron sat beside her who appeared dead even though he was very much alive. Dana's death had hurt him, but losing his sister, had torn at him in a way that was unexplainable. She knew now, that any notion she may have had for Nyron to return to Agmantia with her was futile. How or even why, she didn't know but Nyron had loved Dana

Black, and now that she was gone, there would be no space for another woman in his heart. The fact that Mortania was the link to his family, he would never leave with her.

Saicha's own brothers were on the table opposite her, deep in conversation about God knew what. She hadn't had a chance to catch up with Rian properly since his arrival, but they all needed to decide when they would be returning home. To her right sat the Antonides women with Oren and Lamya, deep in a conversation of their own.

Unsettled, Saicha stood from her seat and made her way over to her brothers, dropping down on the chair beside Rian.

"Sister," he acknowledged with a genuine smile. Saicha hugged him, she had missed her big brother no matter how uptight he could be sometimes.

"Brother," Aslan looked up at her.

"How are you?"

Saicha sighed, the answer too complicated to even consider. She didn't know how she felt.

"Tired," she decided. "In all my years as an assassin, I've never felt such fatigue." Her brothers nodded as though they understood but, how could they?

"Seeing Dana that way…I've never felt such guilt and regret and I wish to leave it all behind in this place." Aslan nodded, she knew he had grown close to Dana as well. Rian placed his hand on her shoulder,

"Maybe you should speak to someone about it," he added conspiratorially, and Aslan smiled sweetly.

"What do you mean?"

"She didn't want to intrude during such a difficult time. She's in the Dowager Queen's apartments."

Saicha looked from one brother to another and interpreted their warm smiles. Saicha rose from her seat and rushed out of the hall, no one looking her way.

She raced down the hallways to Freilyn's apartments and when she reached the guards at the front doors, they let her in without question; knowing of course who she was and that the Dowager Queen wasn't even in attendance.

Saicha hurried into the large meeting room and there, on a chaise lounge in the middle of the room reading, sat her mother.

Queen Nucea looked up as her daughter entered and a smile erupted on her face as she put the book she was reading down and held her arms out to Saicha. She was dressed in an elegant black dress that fitted to all of her beautiful curves and her long locks were braided intricately away from her beautiful face.

Saicha rushed into her mother's arms, unsure of why she felt so emotional but knowing she needed to be close to her,

"My darling girl, are you alright?"

Saicha held her mother tightly and as if a dam had burst, she realised that she wasn't okay and began to cry. It started off as just a few tears at first, until she felt like she was drowning in sorrow,

"A young woman is dead because of me," she whimpered as her mother lifted her face to look into her eyes. "An innocent, blameless young woman died instead of me!"

"Instead of you?" Nucea asked quietly.

"She did not deserve to die Mama, not someone so pure,"

"And you did?"

"Mother, I'm an assassin!" Saicha was angry and pushed away from her mother as he finally let her feelings out. "I kill people all the time, I deserved to die, not Dana!"

Saicha was distraught but Nucea simply walked toward her and pulled her back into a hug and rubbed her back gently.

"You are no less worthy of living just because of what you do in life. You are a daughter and a sister and yes, a skilled assassin. Would you wish us to live without you?" Saicha sniffed hard,

"The world doesn't need another assassin, it needs good people," Saicha pushed. "Good people like Dana Black and for all my skill I could do nothing to save her!"

"It wasn't your responsibility to save her Saicha,"

"No," the two women looked up suddenly toward the door where Trista, Freilyn and Rowan now stood looking over at them. "It was mine."

Trista walked slowly towards them and Saicha composed herself before standing to meet her in the middle of the room. Trista's eyes were also brimming with tears, but she refused to let Saicha see them fall. Saicha could see that Trista was different now, strong and more sure of herself that she knew she had to do the right thing even if it pained her to admit it.

"I killed Dana…not you. I put her life in danger, as I did every one of you and that is something that I will have to live with for the rest of my life…that I killed my best friend."

The pain in her voice was indescribable. The words were torn from her lips that quivered with hurt and everyone in the room felt it

"Don't blame yourself for what I did Saicha. Dana wouldn't want that and neither do I."

Saicha looked over at the young woman she had grown to respect and slowly nodded her head. Trista held out her hand for Saicha to take,

"Saicha, you and your mother saved my family long before I was born and you continue to save us now with your efforts in this war and for that…I thank you; I could never blame you."

"That is why that I will have my coronation three months from now, and you all will be there." They all gasped.

"We will spend that time rebuilding the capital and trying to get back to some form of normality."

They all nodded and Freilyn beamed at her granddaughter,

"It is as though your father speaks through you," she said quietly, her voice quiet but firm. She was a sweet old woman, refined from years of wealth and privilege. She beamed at her granddaughter,

"He would have been so proud of you."

"Thank you, Grandmother,"

"I will prepare the arrangements for your coronation," Rowan added, "Everything has to be perfect." Trista smiled her appreciation,

"Let's get some rest," she said. "There is a lot of work to be done. I hope you will stay with us until then Queen Nucea, Saicha?"

Nucea looked at Rowan as she spoke,

"I will have to return to Agmantia to tie up some things, but we will return in time for your coronation."

Trista smiled again as she turned to leave, Saicha by her side.

"I'll catch up," Rowan called out. "I'll see Grandmother Freilyn to bed."

Trista and Saicha left their mothers to go to their own rooms when Saicha stopped walking,

"Trista?" Trista turned to her expectantly. Saicha looked uncomfortable but she knew she had to ask before she lost her nerve.

"Do you think Nyron will ever forgive me?" Trista sighed heavily but shrugged.

"Honestly, I don't know." Saicha looked disturbed. It was clear to all that Nyron wasn't her fan these past few days and it hurt her more than she'd like to admit. She had to make things right with him before she left. Three months was a long time to get back into someone's good graces.

"I do know," Trista continued. "That Nyron is hurting and lashing out by finding someone to blame…but that someone isn't you. When he realises that, then I'm sure things will go back to the way they were."

"How can they, knowing what I know about his feelings for her?" Trista looked apologetic.

"Only you know if you can be with him, knowing how he feels about Dana because her dying…only makes her more desirable."

Trista was right and Saicha hated that.

"Give him time," Trista said softly before heading back down the hall.

***

Trista sat up in bed, watching Oren peel off his shirt and throw it into a nearby basket with his trousers and underclothes. She had returned to their room before him and washed and changed for bed. Oren had spent some time with Nyron and was now back, changing for bed.

She watched as he tied his hair up into a top knot and walked naked into the adjoining washroom. Absentmindedly she licked her lips as she watched him before blushing furiously.

They had made love constantly in the days since Thea had brought her back to him and she couldn't get enough of him. Feeling so physically close to him was something she couldn't begin to describe, and she never wanted that feeling to go away. She loved him with everything she had, every fibre of her being; even her power called out to him in ways she was only beginning to fully understand. They were made for one another and she felt it in every breath she took.

He returned after bathing; a towel wrapped around his waist that he suddenly ripped off to dry off the rest of his body. She stared as he dried himself, completely oblivious to her gawking at him,

"Stop it," he said as he dried down his arms.

"Stop what?" he looked up at her as he threw the used towel into the same clothes basket and walked over to the bed.

"Lusting after me," he leaned onto the bed to kiss her quickly on the lips. "I can feel it."

Okay, maybe not so oblivious!

Trista giggled,

"What are you talking about?" Oren chuckled and she found it was one of her most favourite sounds in the world. He pulled the sheets back and climbed into the bed with her. As he made himself comfy and looked over at her, she felt their usual pull towards each other but it felt stronger somehow, like an incessant banging that made her feel warm and breathless, a lot like when they were making love and she was about to…

"What is that?"

"That, is what I feel for you; I just know how to turn it off or else I'd be walking around like this all day."

He lifted the sheet and showed her his hardened member. Trista screeched and giggled, slapping the sheet back down.

"Stop it!"

"It's true," he explained with a teasing smile. "When we slept together the first time, the bond between us was sated; that's why we don't feel it all the time now. However, it can escape when you're feeling…happy to see me." He winked at her and Trista blushed

"I'll try to keep it in, wouldn't want you getting a bigger ego, now would I?"

"Oh no," he said reaching out to pull her to him. "We wouldn't want that."

Oren kissed her and Trista sighed deeply as she fell into his kisses. Her whole body erupting with love for him as he let him undress her.

Sex of course, was new to Trista but she doubted there was anything better or anyone better to do it with. Oren made her body ignite from the tips of her toes to the ends of the curls on her head. When he kissed her, she felt alive and free like nothing could ever make her unhappy again. Feeling him move within her was incredible, and as he entered her, she gasped, blown away by the love she felt for him.

A while later, Trista lay with her back against Oren's chest as he ran his fingers through her hair. They both lay happier than either of them could remember being; sated when he said,

"Do you have your pendant?"

"Pendant?"

"When you received your family ring, there should have been a pendant with it."

Trista thought back and nodded,

"Yes," she held out her hand in the dimly lit room and the pendant appeared slowly in her hand. "I never knew what it was for but kept it with my things anyway."

Oren reached over to the small table that was on his side of the bed and went into the little draw underneath it. He pulled out a long piece of string that had a pendant much like her own on the end of it.

He shuffled himself so he was facing her, and she was looking up at him. He clicked his fingers and the candles in the room, brightened, lighting up his face. Trista smiled, so much in awe of him but in light of his revelation about their connection, she tried to hold it in.

Oren took each pendant in one of his hands and slowly placed them together in front of her. A faint blue light flared up between his fingers, making them both look away and when it faded away, in place of the pendants was a ring.

It was a diamond, a very large, exquisitely cut diamond from what Trista could tell. She'd only ever seen diamonds on Avriel and none of them had been like this.

It was set into a silver ring and sparkled as Oren turned it this way and that,

"I was fifteen when I was told I was meant to marry the future Queen of Mortania"

Tears welled in Trista's eyes as she looked at the ring, then at the man she loved.

"I've known my destiny for eight years, but I never imagined I would love her the way I love you. Even if we were not Intended for one another Trista, I would love you. I love your spirit, your bravery and even your fear. I love your trust in me and your faith in others and most of all, I love your heart."

A single tear fell as he looked into his eyes, looking into hers.

"When you claim your crown in three months' time, Trista Freilyn Antonides…will you marry me?"

Oren took her hand and held the ring by her finger. Trista nodded,

"Yes," Trista breathed out.

Oren slipped the ring onto her finger and as it fit into place, Oren's left arm jerked and slowly, his tattoo began to disappear.

"What's happening?" she asked, worried but he just shook his head.

"I don't know, it doesn't hurt."

They both watched as slowly, the markings faded until his arm was completely bare as though nothing had ever been there.

"I guess that makes it official," he chuckled. "I no longer need to be marked because we're finally together."

Trista launched herself into his arms with fits of giggles as she kissed him until she was breathless.

A NEW ERA

The next three months went by in blur for Trista Antonides and her friends.

Messengers were sent to the farthest reaches of the country and the world, looking for members of the families whose lands and titles had been stripped from them.

They were not to get them back without trial of course, but to return the lands to the families who had nurtured them before Curian's rebellion, was important to Trista.

The Samai were to be returned to their former glory while simultaneously, not alienating Man. They didn't want another uprising and so, the families of Men were judged just as their Samaian counterparts, and if found to be lacking in morals, their holdings were not returned.

The overseeing of these reinstatements was primarily overseen by Lamya and Queen Rowan, while the actual rebuild of the city and surrounding lands was by Oren and Nyron.

The Agmantians had returned home shortly after to give the others some space, as Freilyn's home wasn't big enough to accommodate everyone. They remained in Agmantia for the first two months, by which time Tirnum Castle was ready for habitation and Nucea returned with her husband and her children. They'd all been there for nearly a month, in preparation for the coronation and wedding.

Even before she took up residence, Trista made a multitude of changes to the castle. While she wished to stay true to the castle's history, she wanted nothing that reminded her or its new occupants of the Greybold family and their influence in the years they had ruled.

Gone were the menacing colours of their house and trophies of their kills and in their place, were the silver and blue of House Antonides. Flags and banners and sigils were stitched and embroidered on everything from the curtains to the napkins. The Antonides sigil was placed everywhere, to show their rightful leader had returned and windows were made larger to let in the glorious light that seemed to shine brighter now that Trista had returned to her birthplace.

Among the constant change, Trista felt guilty at having to use the treasury that Curian and Briseis had amassed to refurbish the castle. The Lithanian Council continued to help where they could, but they were not to be an endless supply of funds. Trista used the treasury not only to rebuild the castle and its grounds, but to recruit an entirely new household of staff.

Groundsmen, cooks, stable hands, blacksmiths and many more positions were advertised, for people to join the new Antonides reign. No one was to be excluded or not given a fair shot, and within two months, the city was thriving almost as it once was. They rebuilt Thea's Tower and the city walls along with Gorn's residence in the Imperial Lands and Thea's Point was bursting with new arrivals from all over the world who wished to see what the Samaian Queen would do next.

In almost three months, with the help of a tremendous amount of Samaian magic, that generated rapidly as Samaians returned to the capital with Trista as the new Keeper; Tirnum City was reborn into the melting pot of life that it was truly meant to be. Mortania by extension; was returning to its height of magnificence, a force to be reckoned with among the other world leaders.

The rains came, thick and fruitful that drenched the previously dried lands around the capital and far beyond. Farmers rejoiced as their livelihoods were slowly but surely restored and they could reclaim their independence.

Alongside the country rebuilding itself, with Trista overseeing the construction with her most trusted constantly beside her; she was also planning her wedding.

Oren had asked her to be his wife almost three months ago, and they had decided to hold her coronation and their marriage on the same day.

It would be a day to be remembered for years to come and Rowan and Rayne had taken charge of the two parts of the eventful day. As the day drew closer – two days away to be exact - Trista was more than a little terrified.

Not of the wedding or getting married to Oren but the fact that she would be getting everything she had ever wanted; and surely something was bound to go wrong.

She said as much to her mother as they sat going through the seating plan for the coronation. She and Oren would be married in the Tirnum City Gods House before her coronation in the Great Hall of Tirnum Castle.

They were in the study that adjoined Trista's bedroom, the bedroom that used to belong to her parents. She would share them with Oren once they were married. He was currently in the apartments next door, at her mother's request. Now there was ample room, she didn't see the point in them sharing a bedroom.

"Nothing is going to go wrong my darling girl," Rowan reassured her.

"What if it does!" Trista exclaimed irrationally as she stood from her position at the large desk in the middle of the room. She threw the seating chart down on the table, frustrated.

"I have never been this happy before, this…safe. Something is bound to go wrong; I can feel it."

Rowan stood up alongside her and took hold of her daughter's hands, holding them steady in front of her as she looked into her eyes.

"*Nothing* is going to go wrong Trista! You have earned this, all of it and it is going to go perfectly; I'll make sure of it." Trista looked back at her mother pleadingly,

"You promise?" she felt ridiculous saying it but something about her mother's assurances, made her feel like she could accomplish anything.

"I promise, my miracle daughter."

Trista chuckled as she released herself from her mother's hands and walked across the room to a nearby window. She looked out onto the courtyard below where people were busy going this way and that; the castle already like a hive of bees going about their business. She was building her life again and absentmindedly, she thought how unfair it was that Dana wasn't there to see it.

"You said that in my vision…that's what you both called me."

"What do you mean darling?"

Trista turned to her mother and smiled, sadly;

"After I killed Briseis, Thea appeared to offer me my choice. I chose Oren obviously, but I never told you over what." Rowan waited for her to continue as Trista returned to her side,

"Thea offered me a new life…with you and papa," she confessed quietly. "A life where we were a family and I had a little sister and you called us both your miracle daughters." Trista laughed good naturedly at the memory even though it pained her.

"I wanted that," she admitted. "I almost forgot who I was the more time I spent with them, believing that was the way it had always been. I wanted that family with papa still alive so much, but in that same world…Oren didn't love me, and I didn't know Dana."

Rowan looked at her sympathetically,

"I realised that no matter how much I wish I had known my father and that I could bring him back to you…a life without Oren or Dana would never be enough."

Trista looked directly at her mother as she asked her for forgiveness,

"I'm sorry I couldn't have made us a real family again."

Rowan, with tears in her eyes reached out to her daughter again and hugged her,

"We have always been and always will be a real family Trista. Whether your father is here right now or in Goia; we are always family and we will never leave you."

Rowan brought her daughter into a tight hug and as they held one another, the door knocked and the women stepped apart, smiling sweetly at one another,

"Come in!"

A young Samaian girl stepped through the door and bowed low,

"What is it Endora?"

"Her Excellency, Rayne Illiya is here to see you your Highness."

"Please, let her in."

"Yes, your Highness," Endora replied with a beaming smile as she left the room to admit Rayne.

Endora had come to the castle during the rebuild asking to be hired into the queen's household as she had served the previous princess under duress. Endora had shown a vigour and respect for a rule that she hadn't been old enough to witness. Her want to prove herself as a true Samaian and the fact that magic had been reborn to her, made Endora the perfect candidate to be one of Trista's ladies. Her personal household would grow as she got used to the position but for now, Endora was doing a great job.

Rayne marched into the room as though she owned it and Trista ran into her arms to hug her, with a smile on her face. The woman looked regal, even without the titles and Trista marvelled at the strong line of women she had come from. She was saddened that she had never met her Aunt Renya, or her father's brothers but she would, one day.

"Is everything okay?"

"Everything's fine Aunt Rayne, I'm just so happy to see you. After everything, having my family here is just…you know." Rayne held her soft weathered hand to Trista's cheek.

"I know sweet girl, but you are not to worry about any of that now. You are to be crowned soon; are you ready?"

"Nope," Rayne flicked the tip of her nose with a playful smile.

"I am your aunt and the most powerful Gifted in this country,"

"Not to mention the humblest." Rowan added to which Rayne shot her a narrow-eyed look. Trista giggled then straightened her face as Rayne turned her attention back to her and held her face in between both hands.

"I will make sure that everything will be perfect Trista, do you hear me?" Trista nodded, her cheeks rubbing against her aunt's plans. "Your mother and I will not let anything happen to destroy this most special of days. I even hope to have a surprise for you."

"Really, what?"

"It wouldn't be a surprise if I told you, now would it?" Rayne unexpectedly tilted Trista's head to kiss the top of her forehead.

"I'm so proud of you and I…" Rayne suddenly looked very uncomfortable, which was unusual for her.

"What is it Aunt Rayne?"

"I want to apologise…for how I acted in Dreston. I want you to know it hurt me not to tell you who I was, but it was necessary for your development. I love you very much Trista, from the moment I brought you into this world."

Rayne let go of her face and Trista beamed at her and her mother who looked on lovingly,

"Rayne was the first person to hold you as you came screaming into the world Trista, you can trust her to guide you through it."

Trista looked over at her aunt and mother and felt truly blessed to have them in her life and told them as much,

"I love you both so much,"

The sisters looked at one another and for the first time, she saw how alike they truly were. The greying black curls, and oval shaped eyes with a distinct emerald green of their eyes was very fetching even in their ageing faces.

"There is still a lot to be done before the big day so I best be going,"

"Did you find who I asked you to?" Trista quickly jumped in,

"Oh yes, that's why I came. I've found her and she'll be here at dinner as you asked."

"Thank you," Trista smiled again,

"Rowan; would you help me in my chambers please?"

"Of course," Rowan replied to her sister before giving Trista a kiss. "We'll see you at dinner Trista."

Trista nodded as they left and slumped back down on her chair and thought about how lucky she was.

She had family, she would soon be married to Oren and she would finally be crowned queen.

Nothing could go wrong now, just as her mother had promised.

In another part of the castle, Oren and Nyron strode through the barracks having completed another day of recruiting to the royal army and general city forces. Even though the war was finally over, a queen and her kingdom must always have militaries and it was the Antos' job to make sure Trista had them.

"We'll have guards at every door, every window and entry point from the Gods House to the Great Hall. Shields will be around the open space in case of any aerial attacks and archers posted on every battlement for the walk you'll take from one end of the city and back to the castle." Nyron explained, looking down at the list he'd brought with him.

"We can't be too careful about who is left out there who isn't happy about Trista's coronation," Oren agreed.

"I want nothing to spoil the day. Even if the buildings are falling down around her, Trista must not know a thing…I want it to be perfect for her."

"What about you Oren?" Nyron asked gently,

"What about me?" they stopped in the courtyard just outside the barracks and Oren turned to him. They stood in their military uniforms, so pristine and sharp lined it would have made their father's proud.

"It's your wedding day too," Nyron said. "It should be perfect for you too."

"It will be. I'm marrying the woman I love; nothing could be more perfect than that."

Nyron smiled at him and without addressing it, Oren pulled him into a hug. They hadn't spoken much about how Nyron was feeling but Oren knew it was still a lot for him.

"I miss her so much Oren," Oren nodded,

"I know...me too."

The pain was obvious in Nyron's stance, and Oren realised that he wasn't only talking about missing his sister. Oren reached out to touch his cousin's shoulder gently.

"Dana would want you to be happy Nyron," he said cautiously. "She would want all of us to be happy and to live the life we were blessed to keep. Will you deny her that?"

They'd all known by this point that Nyron had feelings for Dana but the extent of them and whether Dana had even felt them back; they didn't know. Nyron wiped his nose and when he looked back up at his cousin, his eyes were red.

"I told her that she was better off without me...that I wasn't good enough for her. I keep thinking that if I had just given into my feelings, if I had given us a chance...if I kept her close to me..."

Oren didn't know what to say,

"I should have been there to protect her," he said finally as the tears brimmed in his eyes again. He wiped them away viciously,

"I should have been there to protect them both."

Oren rested his hand on Nyron's shoulder and said,

"Be the man Naima always believed you were and for Dana...be the man she loved." Nyron looked sceptical. "Be happy, live your life; fall in love again..." Oren hesitated,

"Saicha doesn't deserve the cold shoulder Nyron...it wasn't her fault."

"I know that!" he snapped making Oren jump. Nyron looked back at his family and confessed,

"If I forgive Saicha and give into my feelings for her…I'd be betraying Dana." Oren shrugged,

"If you don't admit your feelings for Saicha…you'd be betraying yourself."

It was clear the thought had never occurred to him and a sense of understanding spread across Nyron's face. Oren took hold of his shoulder and walked his cousin back into the castle.

They walked slowly back inside when Nyron thought out loud,

"What will I do after the coronation?"

"With Naima gone," Oren said quietly. "You're the heir to Illiya."

Nyron looked at his cousin again as the realisation hit along with the guilt.

"I guess I am."

Later that evening, the Great Hall of Tirnum Castle was abuzz with the excitement of the hundreds of people in attendance.

The room looked and felt the way it did during Alexander's reign, when there were no worries of war or rebellion and people were happy.

There were miles to go before Tirnum and Mortania would be fully whole again, but for the last three months, stability had been brought to the kingdom and a sense of hope for all that lived there.

For this special pre-wedding and coronation dinner, royals, high and low born, all collectively rejoiced their new soon-to-be queen. Everyone was dressed in their best clothes for the final dinner that the Great Hall would host before Trista was officially crowned.

Trista sat at the head of the hall with Oren and her mother by her side. Queen Nucea, her husband Prince Tagnan and her children joined them as the only other royals in attendance, while Trista's most trusted; Lamya and Nyron sat on the table a level below.

Chief Justice Yeng and the other members of the Lithanian Council had travelled from Thelm; carefully considering Thea's Reach was still being fortified and also joined them on a raised table of their own. Alongside them were, Gwendolyn and Matthias Freitz, Lord Fabias Remora and Thorn.

She hadn't expected him to accept her invitation, but when he did, she was glad that he didn't hate her too much, to say yes. In her letter to him, she explained all that had happened since leaving Remora and in his reply, he seemed to understand and not blame her for the end of their relationship

Trista had also invited Dana's father, but he had declined the invitation. Trista knew that he blamed her for losing his wife and daughter and she couldn't blame him. Trista explained in her letter to him, that he would be welcome in the capital and the castle whenever he felt she was worthy of his forgiveness. She had accompanied the letter with the titles to his land and home, taxes of which he would no longer have to pay. She hoped he wouldn't see it as a bribe but if Dana had lived; she would have earned much more than free taxes. It was because of Dana that Trista had survived her early days trekking through Mortania, and she would pay that debt to Dana's father, if she couldn't pay it to the woman herself.

Slowly, Trista rose from her seat and the room almost instantly went silent. She was in a dress of the deepest blue that complimented the sapphires that adorned her neck and the family ring on her finger. Her engagement ring sparkled on her left hand also as she raised her hand to place a stray curl behind her ear,

"Welcome!" she called out, magnifying her voice magically. "Welcome one and all to this wonderful evening. Thank you all for making your way across the country to attend the upcoming festivities because it is for all of you that I have done this and that this night and all the others to come are even possible."

Smiling faces beamed up at her as she continued, reaching down for Oren's hand who took hold of it, reassuring her with a firm grip.

"I will save the speeches for the coronation and of course, my wedding," she looked down at Oren who winked at her before she looked back to her audience. "But I...want you all to know that I appreciate the support and dedication you have shown me over the past months. Whether it be rallying in your towns, cities and villages or providing aid from overseas...thank you, from the bottom of my heart, for bringing me home."

Trista looked down at Oren again,

"There are so many who aren't here with us today, people dear to me and Lord Antos...but there is one person who was able to make it. Oren," she tugged on his hand making him get to his feet, confused.

"I wanted to do something to show you, even a little bit how much I love you and want to make you happy...as you make me happy."

Oren blushed as he looked around then back at her,

"Trista what are you doing?"

Trista turned without saying anything to the door of the Great Hall and raised her free hand. Guards opened the door and collectively, everyone's heads turned towards it.

"Oh my!" a happy but clearly nervous voice carried through the hall. "I didn't expect this much people!"

"I...Iona?" Oren stared down the Great Hall at Iona then back at Trista who smiled nervously at him,

"It was my fault you lost your father...I hope your surrogate mother can begin to heal that wound a little."

Oren pulled her into his arms and kissed her before resting his forehead onto hers,

"I love you,"

"I know," Trista said gently. Oren actually chuckled before he turned to run from the dais to barrel down the Great Hall towards Iona who finally saw him.

"Oren!" she squealed as she ran towards him, her large breasts bouncing uncontrollably as she went. When they reached each other, Oren lifted her into his arms and swung her around.

"Oh my!" Iona said again even as she squealed with happiness in her son's arms. Trista looked on as tears welled in her eyes.

Nothing could go wrong now, she thought to herself, nothing at all.

THE ANTONIDES LEGACY

The following morning, Trista Antonides stood in the depths of Tirnum Castle in a thick dark blue robe looking down at the two dragon eggs that lay in a cushioned chest, adorned with gold and jewels.

Her robe was hooded and trimmed with white fur as the depths of the castle were inherently cold. Even with the humming ball of power in the centre, there was a constant chill in the air.

Her long black hair was loose, and the fur framed her face as she looked down questioningly at the eggs. It had felt appropriate to place them in the same room with the Everlasting, where even after everything that had happened above ground, it still radiated its power in the chamber so far below the earth.

The pillars with the names of her ancestors towered around her, some more faded than others, depending on how old they were, and the eggs were displayed alongside them, just behind the orb.

Someone had to walk all the way into the chamber and around to see them and they were truly magnificent. Roughly the size of watermelons, the eggs glistened iridescently in the glow of the Everlasting side by side, unmoving.

In the months since they had begun the renovations, Trista had come to visit the eggs many times, but nothing had changed; nothing had *hatched* more specifically.

Briseis had become a dragon, through what Trista had learned was the murder of her father. The Everlasting's power had become so corrupted it changed the princess into the beast to wreak havoc on the world. Trista of course had stopped her and now, if Thea's words were to be believed, then these dragons would be born soon as well, but for Good:

The Great House will deliver a child,
To remake the world once more.
Lines of magic chosen,
For the truest power to be born.
To Make the strength needed,
To balance the world of Men.
Beasts of fire will soar the skies,
Purely once again.

The Great House was of course House Antonides and she was the child to remake the world. She had become a Maker, balancing the power in the world around them and as a reward, dragons would be reborn as carriers of good magic and not as creatures of destruction.

Trista, lost in her thoughts of the possibility of what these creatures could do; reached out to touch the white one and was surprised, not for the first time that it was warm. Both eggs were warm to the touch, but she felt nothing inside, nothing stirred, and she wondered guiltily whether they ever would.

"I'm getting married today," she whispered to the eggs; not entirely sure why she was speaking to them, but she felt drawn to them.

"I'm marrying Oren Antos, probably the most gorgeous man I've ever laid eyes on!" gently she stroked the scales of the blue egg,

"He loves me, I know he does but he's so…him and I'm just…me. Somehow, I don't quite believe that this is real…that he was truly meant for me, that I…that I'm allowed to be this happy."

She hadn't wanted to admit it to herself, that she was afraid that this wasn't real. That she would wake up in a bed as she had so many times and everything would be as it was. She would be lonely and alone, living in Remora waiting for her life to begin.

"I wish…"

What did she wish?

That she didn't feel so guilty about having all her dreams come true? Yes, she wanted to be free of the guilt that she had everything she wanted and that Dana, her best friend in the entire world…was dead.

Trista's hand jerked as the egg shifted beneath her touch,

"I don't blame you Trista."

Trista froze.

Her hand stayed motionless where she had jerked it away from the egg but suddenly, it began to tremble.

"I don't blame you…not even a little bit."

Fearfully Trista turned around to face the voice behind her.

"Dana?" her voice croaked out as she stared at the ethereal looking figure in front of her. She could see the rest of the chamber behind Dana's body but besides that, she looked the same.

She was in a long white dress, her hair long and braided as she had begun to wear it and she smiled at Trista with tears in her eyes.

"I'm d-dreaming," Trista whispered but Dana shook her head,

"No, you're not. Rayne did say she had a surprise for you." Trista's eyes widened,

"Rayne did this?" Dana nodded. "How?"

"I don't know but…" Dana stepped forward and her body was corporeal, as though she'd literally stepped through a door from the other side. Trista rushed into her arms and the girls hugged each other tightly as they cried with happiness. Trista squeezed Dana hard, feeling her body and her arms and the realness of her.

"I'm so sorry!" Trista bawled into Dana's arms. "I'm so, so sorry Dana!"

Dana continued to hold her and stroke her back,

"I told you, I don't blame you. There is nothing to be sorry for!"

Trista stepped back reluctantly, holding Dana's hands tightly as she looked into her eyes,

"I was reckless, I didn't think about anything else but killing Briseis! If I had been more careful and listened to my powers, I would have known you were down there!"

"Trista!" Dana shook her friend to attention, her face serious and intense. "This is *not* your fault do you hear me!"

Trista continued to weep helplessly, her body weak from the weight of her guilt.

"Things happen and people die…it was just my time." Now it was Trista's turn to be angry,

"You're eighteen years old! How could it possibly be your time!" Dana sighed with an acceptant shrug.

"Trista, I don't make the rules okay. I just know that this is the way it's meant to be. I'm happy here. I get to be with you, watch over you." Trista was momentarily intrigued,

"W-where is here?" Dana smiled, the thought of it bringing a smile to your face.

"Goia, where we all hope to go and Trista; it's beautiful…please don't be sad for me."

"I miss you Dana…I want you here with me." Dana pulled her friend back into a hug,

"I'll always be with you, just the way your father is and your whole family, who send their love by the way. We're all so proud of you." Dana raised her head and looked behind her as though someone had spoken. Trista looked too,

"What is it?"

"I have to go." Trista shook her head and held onto Dana tighter,

"No, please, don't go!"

"I have to, it's taking a lot power to have me here Trista."

"Dana please, please don't leave me!" tears came anew as Dana began to step back. Trista tried to keep a hold of her, but Dana let go and retreated until she was transparent again and there was nothing left to hold on to. Trista dropped to her knees, her head hanging in sorrow.

"Please…tell Nyron that I love him, and I want him to be happy…with whoever he chooses."

"Please don't leave me." She knew the request was futile, but she said it anyway, desperate for Dana to stay.

"I love you too Trista Antonides," Dana said as she slowly began to fade. "Be happy with Oren, be an amazing queen…and thank you." Trista's eyes shot up to look at her friend

"F-for what?" Dana smiled as she blew her a kiss,

"For showing me what an adventure life could be."

Then, she was gone.

Hours later, Trista Freilyn Antonides stood at the alter in the Tirnum City Gods House and married Oren Angelus Antos in front of her family and friends.

She stood in a magnificent ivory dress, with a long veil and train that covered the steps on which they stood. Oren stood opposite her, holding her hands in his, in his formal wear looking as handsome as she had ever seen him. His hair was in a sleek ponytail, his beard perfectly trimmed and his eyes radiating with love and happiness.

When the vows were said and they had taken their first kiss as husband and wife, they exited the Gods House in a golden carriage with Nyron at the head of the procession as their protector. They travelled the cobbled streets of Tirnum City, waving at the sea of smiling faces that looked back at them from the city streets. Samai, Agmantians and Men lined the roads, throwing flowers and confetti and shouting blessings to the happy couple.

Trista had never felt such adulation before and was overwhelmed by the love she felt from the people who only three months ago had been struggling to feed themselves. She prayed for the souls and their hearts to be as full and happy as hers, as she made her way back to Tirnum Castle, where she would finally be crowned queen.

When she and Oren finally entered the castle gates, he climbed out of the carriage and helped her down onto the red carpet that awaited her. The skirts of her wedding dress, in all its ivory, gold and embroidered glory was arranged around her as she waited to be told to enter the castle. Nyron was readying her path while Rayne arrived with Rowan and entered the castle ahead of them.

Trista watched everyone rushing around her nervously and her hands began to tremble. Oren took hold of her hand and kissed the back of it,

You're doing great, he said into her head and she smiled.

I'm terrified!

Oren leaned forward to kiss her as Endora who had come from inside the castle, fussed around Trista, arranging her dress.

Everything is going to be perfect, I promise

As Oren stepped back from kissing her, two other women approached them, holding a glorious large blue velvet robe in their hands, that they would place over her dress.

It was the Antonides blue with their sigil embroidered on the back in silver thread: a broadsword with a crown around the hilt surrounded in flame. It was trimmed with white fur and pinned at the neck by a large sapphire broach.

Oren stepped aside so the girls could dress her and arrange the large hood neatly down her back,

"It's heavy," she murmured as Oren came to stand in front of her again.

"As will be your crown," he said gently. "A burden I will share with you when you need me to." Trista stepped into her husband's arms, careful not to destroy the arrangement of her clothes and kissed him again, deeply.

"I love you Oren," Trista whispered, and he smiled, the smile that made her knees weak.

"I love you too, wife."

Trista giggled at the word and stepped back from him, trying to make her face serious. Oren laughed back,

"You have to do this part on your own, but I'll be with you as soon as it's over."

Trista nodded nervously as he finally turned to leave and entered the castle through a side door

"Are you ready your Highness?" Endora asked as Trista positioned herself in front of the large double doors with two smiling guards on either side.

"Finally…yes I am."

Lamya, along with the hundred people that were permitted to attend this historic occasion, stood and turned towards the doors of the Throne Room when the herald announced Trista's arrival.

"Princess Trista of House Antonides!"

The doors opened and Trista was revealed once again in her magnificent wedding dress that was now covered with the Antonides Royal Robe. She looked nervous but happy and Lamya smiled at how humble she remained.

Musicians began playing a soothing melody and Trista walked elegantly down the continued red carpet towards the front of the room. She passed reinstated lords and ladies, dignitaries, ambassadors and royals from other kingdoms. Empress Ailonwy of Coz had made the journey from the northern most continent with her brother-husband and even King Venelaus of the hidden and majestic Phyn had left the waters of the Dyam Islands to attend. The sea king and his wife and daughter sat on thrones placed in large glass cases of seawater; their magnificent colourful tails clear for all to see.

Trista bowed her head to the sea king as she walked past him, just as Lamya had told her to do. The glass cases because of their size had to be placed nearer the back of the room so to avoid any feelings of disrespect; Lamya told Trista to acknowledge the king and his family personally.

The young girl continued her walk towards the large throne at the far end of the room where her mother, Rayne and Oren waited for her.

A less elaborate throne was beside Trista's where Oren would sit once he was acknowledged as Prince Consort.

Trista was near the front now where Lamya could see her clearly along with the beaming face of Nyron Antos who stood on the other side of the aisle. Rayne stepped forward to face her niece, a rare smile on her face as she begun the short ceremony.

"You may be seated!" the crowd all lowered back to their seats. "We are gathered here today to crown as Queen our princess…and our saviour, Crown Princess Trista Freilyn Antonides."

Trista, as she had been told, dropped gently to her knees before Rayne on the carpeted floor. Rayne stood in the white and gold robes of the Gifted, another member of which and joined them for the occasion. They had travelled from the now semi operational House of Gifts in Agmantia and appeared with a large cushion in their hands. On the cushion lay the orb and sceptre of Mortania.

Rayne, with gloved hands – she was not permitted to touch them because she wasn't royalty – reached for them and handed them to Trista.

"Do you pledge your life, heart, body and soul to the Everlasting?"

"I do."

"Do you pledge to remain its Keeper until your last day and pass those responsibilities to the anointed and acknowledged children of your Intended union?"

"I do."

"Do you swear to uphold the rights and ideals of the Everlasting doctrines and to enforce those principles into your family and subjects where pertinent?"

"I do."

"Do you swear to protect all subjects in your care regardless of race, gender or social standing; to raise arms against any who would harm you, your family, your people or the Everlasting power?"

"I do."

Rayne stepped to her left to stand beside the other Gifted and called out,

"Receive your destiny, as it was meant to be!"

Trista raised her head but remained kneeling as she was told and looked ahead to where the room seemed to *bend*.

Lamya smiled, watching the confusion on Trista's face, not wanting to miss anything of what was sure to be a wonderful moment. Trista continued to stare where the room was changing until a shape began to appear; the shape…of a man. Slowly, the shape became clearer until the ghostly figure of King Alexander Antonides appeared before them.

There was a collectively gasp from those who had never been to a Samaian coronation and those that had, beamed with pride at seeing their former king. Only the true heir could be visited by the previous ruler and Alexander was in full view of everyone.

"I, Alexander of House Antonides pass the Crown of Mortania to…" he looked down at Trista and smiled lovingly. "My brave and beautiful daughter…Trista."

Tears fell down Trista's cheeks as she looked up at her father, smiling back down at her. Alexander raised his arms to the large crown that sat on his head and lifted it off. He took a few steps towards where Trista still knelt and bent to place it neatly on her head.

The crown seemed to move through a force field that no one could see, as on Alexander's head it was a large golden, jewelled thing. When he reached out to place it on Trista's head; it transformed into an elaborate diamond crown that glistened in the candlelight.

"Rise," her father said, his voice echoing through the Throne Room. "Trista of House Antonides, Second of Her Name, Lady of the Imperial Lands and Queen of Mortania."

Trista stood and walked the few steps to the throne. She turned with the orb and sceptre in each hand and sat down.

"All hail Queen Trista!" her father called out
"ALL HAIL QUEEN TRISTA!"

The room thundered with the cries of a hundred people, making Trista jump. She looked over at Oren who smiled, seeing her surprise even as he continued to call out her praise.

Her father's spirit remained beside her as they yelled her name until she felt a tingly on her shoulder and she turned to see her father's ghostly hand resting there,

"We will be watching over you Trista, always."

Alexander lowered his head and kissed the tip of her nose. His lips tingled on her skin, the power travelling through her,

"I love you Papa," she whispered, and Alexander smiled,

"As I love you."

Alexander straightened and turned to the crowd, to Rowan Trista realised, when she saw her mother blow a teary-eyed kiss in her father's direction. He bowed to her and stepped back until he disappeared completely.

Rayne and the Gifted appeared before her again and she placed the orb and sceptre back on the cushion. Trista stood once they had taken them away and addressed the room,

"This morning, many of you witnessed me pledge to share my life with High Lord Oren Antos of High Tower, my husband…and your prince."

Oren stepped forward, looking as handsome as ever and for the first time, nervous. She'd never thought what Oren might feel about becoming royalty.

As he'd been instructed, he walked up the steps to kneel in front of her, where Rayne appeared and handed Trista a silver and sapphire circlet on his head which she placed on Oren's head.

"Rise Prince Oren," Trista called out and Oren stood to take the throne beside her. "All hail Prince Oren!"

"ALL HAIL PRINCE OREN!"

The crowds thundered again, to which Oren humbly bowed his head. He and Trista took their seats on their thrones to deafening applause.

"No ruler is truly powerful without the minds and expertise of their betters and so, in the presence of you all," Trista called out once everyone had quietened again. "I choose now my advisors and the highest members of my court."

Trista named Nyron, Captain of the Queen's Guard as well as High Lord of Illiya. Lamya was named Chief Royal Advisor and Rayne as Chief Gifted. She reinstated Alexia Sentine as Agriculture Ambassador and Oren remained General of the Royal Army. Lastly, Trista named her adoptive father, Matthias Frietz as Royal Treasurer. She had never known anyone as economical as him and knew he would do a great job looking after the country's finances. Her mother Gwendolyn cried so uncontrollable, that Matthias gave her a stern look that Trista laughed to herself, knowing that some things would never change.

***

Once the deeds for the lands and titles, were given to those who had been found, Trista and Oren's wedding reception finally began.

The citizens rejoiced in the streets of the city and across the country, as news of the union and coronation spread far and wide. Peace was finally upon Mortania and people could sleep well at night.

A banquet like no other descended upon them where Trista and her closest friends and family, finally rejoiced in their victory. They ate and danced and drank until they were fit to burst, that even Nyron seemed to be having a good time. Trista had given him Dana's message and it seemed to have lifted a weight off his shoulders because he had spent most of the evening with Saicha Voltaire. They hadn't left each other's side and Trista hoped that they could find happiness with one another.

As the festivities wore on, a messenger approached the thrones,

"Your Majesty, there is a visitor for you!"

A green tunic wearing messenger spoke humbly as Trista was feeding Oren a strip of chicken breast off her fingers. He bit the tip of her fingers as she turned to answer and giggled,

"Visitor, who?"

"He said his name is Kemar, your Majesty. He said he knew you in Dreston, we tried to turn him awa—"

"No!" Trista cut in abruptly. "Please, no. Have him brought here immediately!"

"Yes, your Majesty!" the messenger took off.

"Trista what is it?" Oren asked but she didn't answer him as she stepped down from around the dining table and raced towards the door, still in her wedding dress. Oren looked toward his cousin, and Nyron quickly followed her out the door with Oren close behind.

Trista was running frantically when halfway down the large hall leading to the main castle doors, Kemar appeared with the messenger and two guards accompanying him. When he saw her, Kemar bowed but Trista flew into his arms and hugged him tight. The guards around them, unsure of what to do, looked on, their swords at the ready,

"Trista?" Oren and Nyron had caught up with her, "Who is this?"

Trista continued to hug the Samaian man who hugged her back and Oren was getting more than a little agitated,

"This man saved my life Oren," Trista replied still hugging him; but as Kemar could see Oren's face her, he slowly let go of her. He smiled at Trista,

"I think you should explain your Majesty," he replied in that soothing way and Trista turned to look at Oren who didn't look impressed.

"Oh," she returned to Oren's side and took his hand into hers,

"Oren, this is Kemar. He looked after me when I was imprisoned in Dreston Castle. I thought I'd lost him when I was sent to Priya with Rayne's magic but…he's here." Trista turned back to Kemar, her eyes full of thanks and humility.

"I wouldn't have made it out of that prison without you Kemar."

"I did what any true Samai would do," he replied humbly making Trista smile as she provided the delayed introduction.

"Kemar, this is my cousin Captain Nyron Antos" Nyron nodded his greeting with a smile. "And this, is my husband Prince Oren." Kemar's face was grief stricken as he bowed quickly,

"My apologies great prince, I was not aware." Oren stepped forward and lifted the man from his bow,

"The apology is mine, I was rude. Any friend of my wife, is friend of mine." The two men clasped arms and Trista smiled,

"Join us for dinner, please say you will!" Kemar shook his head at Trista's request.

"I cannot your Majesty. My wife and son are waiting for me, I just…I just wanted to know that you were okay."

"Bring them!" Trista insisted but Kemar declined once more.

"Your Majesty please, we must really be getting back home. It cost a lot for us to come here and we are a humble family…I really must get back."

She hadn't realised what she was asking of him. Things weren't as easy for others post war as they had been for her,

"Then stay here," Oren offered. "Not just for tonight but always."

"Your Highness?" Kemar looked at Oren questioningly as did Trista and Nyron.

"What is you and your wife's trade, occupation?" Trista's face lit up as she realised what Oren was doing.

"I am a baker and my wife is a seamstress."

"Well," Trista added. "I am always in need of dresses and I have had a hankering for cake these past few days."

"I eat like a horse," Nyron raised his hand with a smile. Kemar looked to all of them, unsure if they were serious.

"I couldn't possibly, I…I couldn't…"

"Have your wife become the Royal Seamstress to her Majesty the Queen and you become the Royal Baker, oh, I'm sure you can." Oren winked at Kemar and Trista giggled with excitement, clapping her hands together.

"Guards, have this man's family brought in from outside and move them into suitable quarters!" Trista called out as she grabbed Kemar's arm who smiled shyly,

"I guess that's settled,

"I guess it is."

***

Across the castle, in their temporary rooms, Aslan, Rian, Saicha and their parents Nucea and Tagnan sat in the audience chamber of their own rooms going over their plans for departure back home.

They would be staying the extra day to gather their belongings but after that, it was back to the crystal-clear waters of Agmantian shores.

"We've been away too long," Nucea was saying. "You know your father hates being away from home." Rian and Aslan played cards while Saicha sat on the couch beside her mother. Aslan laughed,

"What doesn't father hate?" Nucea went to answer then stopped herself, looking towards her husband for an answer. Tagnan raised his eyes from his book but didn't respond. "Exactly."

Aslan burst into a fit of laughter while Rian and Saicha smirked. They all knew their father was a serious and scholarly though devoted man. He spent his time reading and learning, assisting his wife when she requested his counsel but rarely interfered with the running of the kingdom.

Nucea laughed despite herself as she leaned away to kiss her husband on the temple,

"I have simple tastes Aslan," their father said. "You should try it." Rian nodded, a lot more like their father then he would readily admit. "What will you all do when we return home?" Aslan didn't miss a beat,

"I thoroughly intend to visit the brothel in Noth Bay. I found the talent in Thea's Point to be truly lacking."

Saicha and Rian's eyes widened at the crassness of Aslan's response to which Nucea just cleared her throat with irritation. Aslan seemed to remember where he was and who was talking to and smiled sheepishly at his parents.

"I was thinking I might go to Yitesh after Rian's wedding." Rian looked up, shooting daggers in Aslan's direction as he saw his brother's attempt to deflect the conversation.

"What is in Yitesh?" Nucea demanded,

"Adventure," Aslan said simply. "Until I am appointed a position that requires me to remain in Agmantia, I plan to have as many adventures as possible."

"Lucky for some," Rian mumbled,

"Says the would-be King,"

"Being King is not luck, it is my duty."

"A pretty comfy duty isn't it,"

"Do you want the responsibility of the crown or just fruitless adventures?"

"Boys! Enough!"

Aslan's retort was cut off as he threw his hand of cards onto the table they were playing on.

"If it is adventure you seek Aslan, then I'm sure you will find it in Yitesh. A suitable marriage and position will be arranged for you when you return."

Saicha and Rian smirked to themselves. Nucea had basically said that Aslan's Yiteshi adventure would be his last.

"And you Saicha…what will you do?" Saicha looked over at her mother,

"I will return to Agmantia." They all heard the unenthusiastic tone but didn't dare mention it. They'd all seen her with Lord Antos but how he felt about her in the wake of Dana's death, they weren't so sure.

"Will you return to the Guild?" her father asked but as she went to reply, the door knocked and when Nucea permitted them entry; a messenger arrived to say that Lord Antos had called to speak to Princess Saicha. Aslan made a whistling sound but the look Saicha gave him made it choke him. Saicha rose from the couch beside her mother and went out to meet him.

Nyron had changed out of his formal clothes from the festivities and was now in casual shirt and trousers with boots.

"I hope I wasn't disturbing you. It's not too, late is it?"

"No…not really."

"I could come back," he motioned behind him but Saicha shook her head. It was clear he was nervous but she wasn't sure what about just yet.

"It's fine Nyron…what is it?"

Nyron looked extremely uncomfortable as Saicha looked her big hazel eyes into his green ones.

"I had fun tonight…a lot of fun,"

"I did too," Nyron shuffled nervously.

"Saicha I…I behaved…well, I was unfair to you after Dana died. I was hurt and angry and I wanted to lash out and I…I took it out on you." Saicha didn't say anything,

"I came to apologise because…because it wasn't fair of me to treat you like that and after this evening I…"

"You wish to pick up where we left off?"

"Yes, no…well, no; not like that. It wouldn't be just about sex."

"What would it be about Nyron?"

She could see he was struggling, and she wasn't being difficult to be mean, but she had to know. She knew what she wanted him to say, she'd known it for a long while, but he had to be sure how he felt about her.

"I cared about you, I still care about you and if I'm going to find any happiness now that Dana is gone…I want it to be with you." Saicha scoffed,

"So, I'd be second pick is what you're saying?"

"Saicha please…don't."

His eyes pleaded with her and despite herself, she fell into them hook line and sinker. Saicha had been struggling with her feelings about Nyron and about returning home with her family. Would she continue to be an assassin, knowing how she felt after Dana's death? Something had changed in Saicha that made being an elite assassin a lot less appealing then it was in the beginning.

"What are you asking me Nyron, be clear."

Her heart was beating a mile a minute as she anticipated having to close the door in his face. Nyron took a deep breath and walked up to Saicha so she had to tilt her head to look back up at him,

"I'm asking you to stay in Mortania with me, to see where this could go for us. I'm asking you to give me a chance to make this up to you Saicha."

A while later, Queen Nucea looked up at the chamber doors as her daughter stepped back through them. The boys had gone to bed, but she wanted to make sure Saicha was okay before she retired herself,

"Darling…are you alright?" Saicha approached her with a shy smile and nodded,

"I won't be coming back to Agmantia with you mother." Nucea smiled and held her daughter's face in her hands.

"I didn't think you would be."

***

Queen Trista Antonides lay in bed the following morning, the entire castle still asleep around her after an evening of rejoicing. Her husband, Prince Oren lay contently beside her, when she shot up in their bed breathing heavily, waking him instantly. Panicked, Oren held her shoulders as she tried to catch her breath,

"Trista, sweetie what's wrong?"

Trista turned to look at him, her eyes wide with blue flame circling her pupils and gasped,

"The eggs!" Trista grinned widely. "They've hatched."

EPILOGUE

*Year 1037 A.E.
Imperial Mountains, Mortania*

"What if I mess up again?"
You won't.
"But what if I do?"
You won't!

The voice that spoke into her mind chuckled with amusement and Freya turned to look at her dragon with mock anger,
"It's not funny Illeria!"
It is to me

Freya rolled her eyes at how unsympathetic her dragon companion could be about matter of the heart. Prince Allaro of Coz was arriving today and the last time she'd seen him, she'd made a complete fool of herself. She'd forgotten all the new dances out of sheer nerves and when Allaro had finally asked her dance; she'd fumbled through it; stepping on his toes during the whole routine.

I don't know how to dance, Illeria continued as Freya slumped on the floor beside her large scaly body and rested her back against it. She was bundled up in her furs and leathers against the chilly winds of the mountains but Illeria's body kept her warm.

If I like a male, I bite him.

Illeria was sixteen years old, the same as Freya; having hatched when Freya was born but dragons aged a little differently. She was almost fully grown, standing, Freya did not even reach the top of Illeria's forearm.

"Well that doesn't work with humans," Freya sighed as Illeria's wing covered her from the sunrays above.

They were hundreds of feet in the air, resting on a mountain peak, far away from home so Freya could think,

Are you done hiding?

"I am not hiding" Freya sulked,

If you're not hiding, you won't mind that your father is coming.

"What, where?"

Freya scrambled to her feet to look up into the sky and sure enough, she saw the colossal underbelly of her father's dragon Pythos, descending onto the mountain top.

There was barely enough room for the large pure white dragon alongside Illeria's silver/grey scales and magnificent wings. Freya dusted some of the thin snow off of her clothes and stepped around Illeria's wings to where her father dismounted Pythos.

Prince Oren strode towards his daughter, his eyes disapproving in his barely wrinkled face. He was dressed entirely in black as usual, with his short hair cropped to a dignified length once he took his wind helmet off.

"Freya!"

"I'm sorry, I'm here! Please don't call the guards!" she replied quickly, as she waved her hands in the air in mock surrender.

Freya saw instantly that she wouldn't be getting in trouble for this. Her father's eyes were suddenly twinkling; he could never stay angry at her for long. He pulled her into a hug before kissing the top of her head. She turned her head to rest her cheek on his large chest,

"Why did you fly off…again. Your mother was worried sick." Freya slumped her shoulders and sighed before looking over her father's arm to the world below; towards the castle where her mother ruled.

"She's not worried about me." Oren released her from the hug to look down into her little face. His eyes became serious, concerned as he placed his large hand on her mass of curly black hair.

"Freya, that's not true. Your mother loves you very much." Freya looked up at him,

"I never said she didn't love me Daddy, I said she isn't worried about me. She's obsessed with Ermias and his ceremony, it's all she talks about!"

Ermias had turned eighteen and so he was officially being sworn in as Mortania's heir. He would be king in all but name when their mother was away or if she gave him something to oversee. It was a big day for her brother and her family, but Freya had never felt more isolated from them. Oren looked shocked,

"That doesn't mean that she isn't worried about you. Freya, you and your brother are the most important things to us, always."

Freya rolled her eyes; she was tired of having the same conversation with her father. It didn't change that her older brother Ermias, was the all-important heir to the throne and she was the spare that couldn't get anything right.

"Freya, look at me."

Freya looked up at her father and despite herself, tears welled up in her eyes and she didn't even really know why. His eyes were so much like her own, a teal green unlike the emerald that Ermias had inherited from their mother.

"Ermias inheriting the throne does not make him more important than you. You'll inherit High Tower just as I did. Is something wrong with that just because it's not a royal position?"

"No, of course not!"

"Then what is it...really?"

Freya looked away from her father, embarrassed for saying things she knew weren't true. She knew she would have many responsibilities once she became of age but none of them helped her fit in with Allaro and the other young royals her age.

"I just needed some time by myself,"

"For what Freya," Freya huffed, frustrated before flaring up at her father.

"I don't want to embarrass myself in front of Prince Allaro tonight. Everything I do is wrong; I can't even be a princess right and I was born this way!"

Oren chuckled to himself,

"You like him," Freya's face flushed red, but she said nothing.

"You, Freya Dana Antonides are my daughter and therefore the most clever and beautiful young woman in this world,"

"Daddy!"

"No, listen to me. You might think you're not doing so well at court, but you can change that whenever you like because you are perfect at everything else." Freya said nothing,

"You're smart, funny, talented and one of the best dragon riders I know."

"There are only nine of us,"

"And you're better than all of us, even me!" Freya chuckled as they both knew her father rode dragons better than anyone alive. Her father pulled her into a tight hug and Freya thought randomly that he was always warm. He was warm and smelt like whatever he'd bathed with mixed with metal and leather. It was a scent that was so innately him, she always felt safe around it. Oren looked up at Illeria,

"Bring her back to the castle right now Illeria," Illeria snarled,

I'll bring her back when I want to bring her back

Pythos growled at Illeria who huffed, making thin snow, blow into the air then settle. Only their riders and other dragons could hear a specific dragon and Illeria was still very much a teenager where Pythos was an adult – and also her father – who continued to scold her.

"She said of course she will," Freya lied but Oren chuckled,

"I bet she did," with another kiss on her forehead, Oren turned to climb back into Pythos' saddle. As he got ready to put his wind helmet back on, he turned to Freya who was climbing onto Illeria and said,

"Oh, Theon and Naima are at home getting ready for Ermias' party."

"Naima is here!" Freya screeched with excitement. "Everything is right with the world once again!" Her cousin Naima Antos was her best friend. She and her twin brother Theon, were born a week before her and Freya spent most, if not all of her summers in Illiya with her Uncle Nyron and Aunt Saicha.

"You better get home quickly then," Oren said with a smile as his face disappeared into the helmet. Freya snapped her fingers so her long curly black hair was instantly in a neat ponytail so she could place her own helmet on,

"Let's go Illeria!"

Good, I need to stretch my wings. It's cramped here

Illeria spread her glorious wings and with a tremendous flap down, lifted herself into the air. Soon they were in the skies, heading down the mountain back to Tirnum Castle.

Oren watched his daughter fly away into the afternoon skies and smiled contently,

Did you find her?

Oren smiled at his wife's voice in his head,

Yes, she was up in the mountains
Again? Is she okay Oren…really?
She will be. We're on our way back now.
Good, I miss you

A smile spread across his face as he thought of his gloriously beautiful wife waiting for him at home; their family and friends ready to celebrate his son's eighteenth birthday and swearing in celebration.

Everything was indeed right with the world and would only get better.

I'm on my way.

PRONUNCIATION GUIDE

ANTONIDES - An-Toe-Nee-Deez
AVRIEL - Av-Re-El
BRISEIS - Bri-Say-Uss
CURIAN - Kerr-Ry-Yun
DRESTON - Dress-Tun
ILLIYA – Ill-Ee-Yah
IONA – Ee-Oh-Nah
JARN LAKE – Yarn Lake
LAMYA - Lah-My-Ah
LIYA - Lie-Yah
LYON - Lee-On
MORTANIA - Mor-Tan-Yah
NAIMA – Nay-Eem-Ah
NUCEA – New-See-Yah
OREN - Or-un
PHYN - Fin
PRIYA - Pree-Yah
RIAN - Ry-Un
SAICHA - Say-Sha
THEA - Thay-Yah
TIRNUM - Ter-Num
YZNA-TUM - Eaze-Nar-Tomb

ACKNOWLEDGEMENTS

The Antonides Legacy is a project fifteen years in the making.

From an initial few words in the back of a notebook, to being added to a word document on a computer with a really big screen and a modem attached, it has really come a long way.

While my writing is obviously the physical work that has gone into this, there have been so many people along the way who have helped shaped my writing and the story itself.

My mum Josephine, the first to read a few chapters when it was called *Zaigon* and featured petty overseeing Gods, always made the time to ask about my writing even if she didn't actually finish it! It was this initial reception that made me want to finish and make my writing better. I thank her profusely for this!

Actually, getting people to read my work has been a trial in itself and even though it felt terrible at times, that I couldn't seem to hold an audience; it was this seeming lack of interest that pushed me to write better so that people *would* stay interested.

It was not until much later in the writing process, that I got my head around a simple truth: I needed to share my stories with people that actually cared about the content.

In so doing, I discovered *Wattpad* and the millions of online readers who were able to give me the feedback I so desperately needed, to see if my writing was even any good! With over ten thousand reads later, thank you to those readers and their comments and likes that helped me shape my story and gave me the drive to be a better writer.

Thank you to my cousin Daniel for creating wonderful images that initially brought my characters to life, you are so talented and I love you so very much.

Thank you to my good friends Malachi and Rela, who were the first to buy a copy of my book before I'd even figured out how to format the thing properly! I hope you enjoy your two new copies.

Thank you to my little mate Natalie, for taking the time to read the first two books and give me a few pointers when words all started to mesh into one.

Thank you to Zeus, for always encouraging me, believing in me and listening to my crazy plot ideas. Thank you for the money you have invested in me and my ventures to help get them off the ground. I love you so much for your strength and support.

Thank you to my family and friends who have shared or posted or liked anything to do with my stories and always supported me. Your belief in me has helped me finally put these creations out into the world and I appreciate it more than you could ever know.

Thank you lastly, to *you* reading this.

If you have got this far, you have finished reading my babies and ultimately, despite writing for the joy of it, it was written for someone to read and enjoy and I hope with my whole heart that that person is you.

Thank you for supporting my dream.

Printed in Great Britain
by Amazon